THE INDICTMENT

THE INDICTMENT

MacKenzie Canter

Carroll & Graf Publishers, Inc.
New York

First Carroll & Graf edition 1994

Carroll & Graf Publishers, Inc.
260 Fifth Avenue
New York, NY 10001

Library of Congress Cataloging-in-Publication Data

Canter, MacKenzie.
    The indictment / MacKenzie Canter.
        p.   cm.
    ISBN 0-7867-0073-4 : $21.00
    PS3553.A545I5   1994
    813'.54—dc20   94-7544
                                                                CIP

Manufactured in the United States of America

For Rhodie, Mary and Ellie.

ACKNOWLEDGMENTS

This novel would not have been possible without the sustaining encouragement of my wife, Rhoda. Special thanks and a fifth of Irish whiskey are owed to my colleague, Edgar B. May, Esq. I also want to thank my agent, Ron Goldfarb, Esq.

PROLOGUE

Sometimes I would lie to Peyton. Afterward I would lie to myself, telling myself I got carried away. But I knew better. It was a cheap trick, a little passion kicker.

It was all a game, I thought. A game called "pretend." Peyton knew that, I thought. But I never asked because if I had it would have ruined the game.

My lies would cause Peyton to quiver and hold me tighter. I tried to time my lies to evoke the maximum response, which, as if detached, I would observe.

One time I tried out I-want-you-to-have-my-baby. The intensity of her response startled me. Those words somehow were impervious to the banter with which we washed away lies told during lovemaking. They lingered, embarrassing both of us.

I suppose there's a good side to me. But it wasn't the side Peyton brought out. And I knew I brought out the bad in Peyton. The dark angels of our natures danced a pas de deux. Transfixed, I saw it happening but did not stop it.

It never should have started. And once it started it never should have gone on. Yet it was the wrongness that drove us. It bespoke a grim emptiness of soul that we were drawn to illicit passion to disentomb feelings that still thrilled but no longer were innocent.

*   *   *

The swirling motes of dust had seemed to climb the shaft of late-afternoon sunlight which, angling from the loft window, transected the meridian of the tousled damp sheets and painted Peyton in glowing pastels while leaving my half of the bed in toned shadows.

That afternoon I told Peyton young sinners could be forgiven but not old fools.

"Speak for yourself," she said, rolling onto her back and lighting a cigarette.

"You think we're not fools?"

"It's the old I was taking exception to. I'm used to being a fool. 'Course, I'm not as foolish as some people, taking up Roger's dare."

Peyton laughed and brushed her ash-blond hair from under her neck. She rolled onto her side and kissed me.

"Was that for me, darling?" she asked.

"I didn't get all the way over," I replied.

"I should say not. You landed flat on your fool back." Peyton laughed softly and kissed me again. "You're going to break your fool neck, you keep that up."

"Fucking is more dangerous than a five-meter board," I replied. "You mess up more lives than your own."

Peyton propped herself up on her elbow. She leaned toward me and whispered, "I don't have a life unless I have you. So don't tell me about other lives."

"That's not what we learned in Sunday school."

"I've got the guts to risk being happy." Peyton turned on her back, rested her head on my stomach, and blew a smoke ring.

"You better have enough for both of us," I replied, watching the smoke disappear in the shaft of light.

"You read your old books and leave the guts to me," Peyton said without looking at me.

Sometimes the murmuring ghosts decamp, allowing me to lull myself into the hope, shading into the conviction, that the last argument I advanced has proved unassailable. I allow myself to believe that if I have not acquitted myself before the bar of my conscience, I at least have debated to a draw.

Then the ghosts return with a starkness so palpable and vivid as to defy the dawn, surreality trumping reality. The sensations evoked by their visitation, far from being erased by the diurnal weave of the ordinary and the necessary, are set off by it, as if raised in bas relief. They follow me from my bed into the day, a waking dream from which there is no waking.

At night, when the whiskey has deserted its post, the ghosts come again. I wake from my stupor, stabbed by slivers of memories as disordered and jogged as the shards of the highball glass I find shattered on the floor beside me.

Descartes was wrong. It is not in thinking that we are. It is in remembering. We are memories refracted by memories crystallized from memories forgotten. Nothing more.

CHAPTER 1

June 15, 1989, started out like all the other balmy late-spring Saturday mornings I used to take for granted. I was awakened in midmorning by two heavyweight seagulls fighting over a charred remnant of chicken skin stuck to the grill. Their girl-friends, all seventy of them, perched along the railing of the deck, cheered them on. I opened the window and cursed them and their mothers, to no avail.

My head throbbed and I had a vague memory, which I knew would become sharper—for the worse—as the day wore on, of making a fool of myself Friday night at the country club bar. I decided to pretend I was sleepwalking, take a handful of aspi-rin, and try to go back to sleep. With a little luck maybe I would wake up at noon, get in a swim, have a beer, and escape my punishment. But I felt guilty about that. Hangovers are meant to be suffered. So now you're a masochist on top of all the rest of it, I chided. What's next?

Struggling to open the tamper-resistant sealing and childproof cap of the aspirin bottle ended the debate. No way a sleepwalker could get that sucker open, short of using an axe. I cursed the bottle and its inventor and debated taking it out to the driveway and backing the Dodge over it. But I finally found a paring knife which didn't have a broken tip. When I wedged the cap off, it

13

made a pop louder than a bottle of cheap champagne, which evoked an unwelcome memory.

I filled a saucepan with tap water and walked onto the deck while I waited for the water to boil. The sun had burned off the mist and the pine planks were warm to my bare feet. The contenders had fought to a draw. The fatty strip of chicken skin was scarred by pecks but remained glued to the grill. The girlfriends had left their calling cards all along the rail. I watched a pelican glide and strike, shattering the glassy surface of Pascamany Bay.

I was debating whether to clean the grill before the end of June when the phone rang. It was Peyton.

"He's dead," she said as soon as I picked up the phone in the kitchen.

"Roger," I managed to say after taking a long time to turn the range eye down to med lo. I stood over the pan, letting the steam coat my face. I dumped Southern States' no-name instant coffee into the pan.

Unsure of what I felt, I let the silence pend, afraid to break it, afraid of what it might contain. A piñata of woes. I splashed coffee into a plastic Chirkie Cougars Booster mug that made me think of Roger's glory days as a halfback.

"I'm sorry," I finally said. "Is there anything I can do?"

"Kendall," Peyton said, drawing my name into overlong syllables, the way she did when she was irked. "Do me a favor, sweetie. Don't go on automatic pilot. Not now, okay?"

"I didn't mean it like that." But I had. I was buying time with conventional phrases.

"Aren't you even going to ask?"

"All right," I said. "How did it happen?"

"Beaten to death," Peyton replied in a quiet voice that sounded precise rather than sad. But, I told myself, people reacted to grief in different ways. I splashed bitter and scalding coffee on my lip.

"Jesus Lord. Where?"

"The QT of all places."

There were a half-dozen motels, spaced between cut-rate liquor stores and crabshacks, along 201 south of Lassington that brazenly advertised "special nap rates" and "noon to five rest rates." I thought of Gail somebody, the teenaged former receptionist for Vista Mer. Someone had told me that her husband had threatened to kill Roger. I tried to think who had told me that.

"Hold on a sec." Peyton's voice broke off.

I considered, maybe hoped, Peyton was trying to find a tissue to wipe away the tears I hadn't heard in her voice.

I heard the dry clunk of Peyton's phone being placed not very gently on a hard surface. I heard her steps click across the floor. It sounded like she was wearing high heels and I wondered why, at the same moment feeling lust sweep over me at the thought of Peyton's long, fine legs, perfectly turned on the lathe of Eros, ending in her baby-blue slingbacks. I had a vision of her scarlet-lacquered toenails peeking through the open toes of the slingbacks, winking at me.

Then I heard the clicking grow sharper and the blurred but nonetheless professionally crisp vowels of a broadcaster in the background.

"It's just coming on WYFR now," Peyton said, picking up the phone. "Can you hear it?"

"Not really," I replied, but I could hear it well enough. "You want me to hang up and turn on my TV? Call you back later?"

That was what I wanted. I wanted a break from immediacy. You're like every lawyer I've ever known, Peyton had told me, just after the affair started. You don't let yourself experience anything until you've gone and labeled it. But that kills it, the holding back. You talking about lawyers or lovers? I had asked her. I'm talking about lawyers as lovers, she said, laughing her bad-girl laugh that hadn't changed since high school.

"I said, can you hear it now? You listening?" Peyton asked. Before I could answer, I heard her receiver being slapped down again. I heard a scraping sound. I could tell where Peyton was. She was in the kitchen, sitting at the counter on a bar stool. I guessed she moved the stool closer to the little TV Roger had installed when he refinished the cabinets.

"Now you can," she said. Peyton must have half turned the

receiver toward the TV. Over Peyton's slow breathing, I could hear Donnie Smith, the weekend anchor for WYFR, talking to a reporter on live remote. Donnie, a black kid from Charleston, not even thirty, already had perfected the trick of making his rich baritone voice convey urgency while still sounding cool and detached. He had a way of reading the results of livestock sales which made you want to pay attention. The word at the club was that Donnie was about to be picked up by one of the major regionals, just a notch below the networks.

"... tell us about the scene of the crime," Donnie was saying.

"All that we know right now, Donnie," an excited female voice replied, "is that the murder occurred in Room 126, in the rear of the motel. The room has been cordoned off by the Crime Scene Investigative Team. The rear of the motel is separated by a barbed-wire fence from the Southern & Atlantic Railroad right-of-way, which—I'm looking at it right now—is overgrown with brush and scrub pines."

"Is there any indication that the killer or killers—on that point, let's put the pin there for a moment. . . . Do we know if there is one or more than one killer involved?"

"We don't. Not yet. Deputy Sheriff Molly Berton, the spokesperson for Sheriff John Cane, has declined to release any details until after the CSIT has completed its work. They're in there now, in the room. The van you can see beside the fence is the CSIT van."

"What about the means of escape?" Donnie asked. "Is there any indication that the killer or killers got away on foot, perhaps by going across the right-of-way? Has the right-of-way been examined for tracks?"

"Donnie, there appears to be a break in the fence. Make that several breaks in the fence. It is rusted and some of the stakes are broken. So, yes, that cannot be ruled out. But we just don't know. Not at this point."

"Have you been able to talk to management?" Donnie's reference to "management" made me smile. The QT was owned by the Wraithes, who were regularly hauled into court for creating a public disturbance, legal shorthand for drunken brawling, at the VFW hall a quarter of a mile down the road from the motel.

"I spoke briefly to Mrs. Estelle Wraithe, the executive vice president of the corporation which owns the QuieTown Lodge. She was not able to tell us anything except that only eight rooms were rented last night. Six in the front section and two in the back."

"Marina, do you know whether Sheriff Cane has been able to nail down the time of death?"

"Donnie, the only thing we know right now is that it was sometime before nine this morning when the day maid went to clean the room and found the body of Mr. Dufault."

"One last thing. Marina, is there any indication—and I know this is early on so we can't expect anything definite. But is there any indication of any tie-in between the murder and the Vista Mer project?"

"Donnie, as you say, it is early. I raised that point with Deputy Sheriff Berton and she declined to comment, saying only that all possible motives would be investigated in due course. Back to you, Donnie."

"We'll come back to you live at News at Noon. Stay with it. And thank you, Marina."

"Thank *you,* Donnie," Marina pertly chirped. It could have been a tea party rather than a report on a murder. Kindly please pass the cucumber sandwiches and a blunt instrument.

"For those of you who tuned it late," Donnie continued, "there has been what is being investigated as a homicide at the QuieTown Lodge south of Lassington on Route 201. The body of prominent Chirkie County developer Roger W. Dufault was found early this morning. The report, unofficial as yet but confirmed by several sources, we have is that death was due to multiple blows to the head. The Crime Scene Investigative Team of the Chirkie County sheriff's office is at the QuieTown Lodge as we speak. The public has been advised to stay away from the immediate area.

"Deputy Sheriff Molly Berton, spokesperson for Sheriff John P. Cane, has declined to comment on whether any suspects have been identified or any aspects of the investigation, apart from confirming the identity of the victim and that the death has been classified preliminarily as a homicide and is being investigated as such.

"The victim, Roger W. Dufault, was well known in Chirkie County and in surrounding counties. Mr. Dufault was the president of General Development Corporation, headquartered in Lassington. Recently, General Development Corporation has been in the news as the developer of the controversial Vista Mer project opposed by environmental activists.

"We hope to have a comment from Mrs. Dufault when we come back to this story live at News at Noon. Other stories we are . . ."

I heard the hollow thunk of Peyton's receiver being laid down on the counter and the click-clack of her heels on the ceramic tiles.

I could hear Peyton breathe into the receiver before she spoke.

"What do you think?" she asked.

"I'm thinking you foxed yourself up and I'm wondering if it's a good idea."

"You mean, like wash off the makeup and answer the door in a terry-cloth robe and scuffs? Maybe pull my hair back and tie it with an old knee-high? Look like something the cat dragged in? That what I'm supposed to do?"

"I'm wondering why you would agree to talk to a minicam crew," I replied. "Write out a statement and hand it to Marina. Let her read it. Tell the world you're grief-stricken and want to thank all the people who have shown you love and support. Brought you covered-dish casseroles. Something like that. Nothing live. No pictures."

"One. Just one," Peyton said. "Lima beans baked in mushroom soup with bacon strips on top. Mrs. Thurgood, bless her soul." I heard the rasp of a match and Peyton exhale.

"The sonofabitch slapped me right in front of everybody. You forget that?" Peyton asked, but the note of irritation I had heard earlier was gone from her voice.

"Christ no, I haven't forgotten that," I replied. "Nor has anyone else."

"So you're saying I'm a suspect or something?"

"It doesn't make sense to call attention to yourself. That's *all* I'm saying."

"What difference does it make?" Peyton asked, but I could tell it was almost rhetorical.

"The difference is called proper appearances. This isn't Miami Beach where the widow can get away with throwing a party. You show up on TV looking like Vanna White and it won't go unnoticed."

"You think so?"

"I know so."

"Vanna White, huh?"

"Better," I said.

"All right," Peyton said. "I'll look like shit. Just for you." She kissed the receiver.

"Don't."

"Why not? You afraid our little affair will come out and you'll get your name in the paper? That's what's bothering you." Peyton laughed softly, kissed the receiver again, and hung up.

I poured the coffee down the drain, found a Blue Ribbon in the back of the refrigerator, and went back to the deck. It was hot now, well over ninety, I guessed.

I had managed, after several false starts, to break off the affair six months before Roger's death. For that I was grateful. The shadow of guilt gradually had lengthened until finally it angled forward to darken the prospect of desire.

I decided we don't improve morally as we get older. We just learn that Newton's law of equal and opposite reactions applies to more than physics. We figure out finally that illicit pleasures are paid for with interest on the installment plan. Morality is knowing the price and deciding it's not worth it.

CHAPTER 2

Ever since Chirkie Gold & Country Club started letting in anyone with serious money as long as he didn't blow his nose on his sleeve, the true arbiter of social distinction in Chirkie County has been the very selective graveyard adjacent to Holy Redeemer Episcopal Church, constructed in 1726 by slaves detailed by members of the vestry which included Thomas Dufault and Rodney Wilkinson. The church is briefly mentioned in several travel guides to the region under the consolation-prize category, "worth a visit." Left unsaid but clearly implied is the caveat, "if you have nothing better to do."

I always have believed the guidebooks erred in giving Holy Redeemer short shrift. Holy Redeemer is unusual for its design, which, developed by the vestry as work progressed, exemplifies the virtues and perils of committees. One guide describes the style as Byzantine Georgian Colonial but that is as much forced labeling as undeserved flattery. There is, however, a primitive vigor to the style (in contrast to the faith of the congregation) subtly underscored by the unusually large bricks which took on a peculiar orange hue when fired due to traces of copper ore in the clay.

Holy Redeemer overlooks a marsh that in the eighteenth century had been a tidal creek where hogsheads of tobacco were loaded for the voyage to the clay pipes of the mother country.

The creek is today a marsh polluted by waste glues emitted by my client, Chirkie Tire Mart, one of the largest retreaders of tractor tires in the entire Southeast.

The Wilkinson square, marked off by badly eroded granite angles and the initial "W," is not only closer to the church than the Dufault plot but also, as Mother once proved to the consternation of Grace Dufault, slightly larger than the Dufaults' share of the hallowed ground. Also, Mother said, the Bible verses on the Wilkinson memorials are legible.

The marsh sent to Roger's funeral a delegation of green flies that made the baleful, damp heat even worse. Father Vickery, his bald dome glowing wetly and rubescently, clipped through the graveside service at a record pace, skipping one page from the Prayer for the Dead contained in the 1928 edition of the Book of Common Prayer. Perhaps the humidity made the pages of his prayer book stick together.

Apart from a few old friends—I counted myself, with a twinge of guilt, Porky Bryan, and Tim Dugan in that category—and the usual, professional representatives of socially prominent families, Roger's funeral was poorly attended. The leeches who had hung out with Roger when he had the Midas touch and on whom he had lavished finder's fees, sales leads, pep talks, a "can-do" attitude, and, principally, rounds of drinks, had been too busy making their first millions to see Roger off to the Great Recreational Community in the Sky.

Paul Wilson Bryan, who for twenty years has discouraged the nickname "Porky," thereby ensuring its durability, was present, graying around the temples, portly, and looking every bit the chief executive of the principal financial institution in Chirkie County. Porky was accompanied by his wife, Caroline, whom Tim Dugan once, underestimating Caroline's sense of humor, addressed as "Porkette," which resulted in Tim being disinvited to attend the 1982 Christmas party of Chirkie Savings & Trust Company.

Tim Dugan, who somehow had managed to carry into his middle years the slack restiveness of a bored teenager, arrived tardily, accompanied improbably by his girlfriend of the month, the new day waitress at the Aimes Point Inn. Tim surprised everyone by proving he both owned a dark suit and remembered where Holy Redeemer was located. Tim's height varied with his slouch. But he was over six feet, even if not the six feet four he claimed. Mother once said Tim just missed being ruggedly handsome. As a teenager he was too chubby and by twenty too dissolute.

After the mourners retreated to the air-conditioned comfort, a foretaste of the life hereafter, someone mumbled, of Holy Redeemer, I stayed for a minute at Roger's grave. A large and ornate wreath with the state seal had caught my attention during the service. I checked the tag. It had been sent by Elliot Stevens Dean, the lieutenant governor.

When I heard the engine of the backhoe begin to idle, I turned and joined the reception in the vestry hall. Someone poured me a glass of iced tea and I made small talk with Porky and Caroline. Roger's mother, Grace Dufault, and Peyton were motionless, facing at close quarters, and watching one another's eyes. From the way their lips moved, they seemed to be biting off words in bursts.

Tom Kennelly, editor of the *Lassington Standard*, had written Roger's obituary. Kennelly charitably had referred to Vista Mer as "visionary but controversial," and hadn't mentioned the fraud charges leveled at Roger when Vista Mer went down the tube, stranding dozens of irate creditors. The obituary had taken up a quarter page below a photograph of Roger holding up one end of a stringer of sea bass. Roger, chest hair spilling from a half-buttoned, floral print shirt, was grinning beneath the visor of an Atlanta Braves baseball cap. Had the photograph not been cropped, it would have shown me holding the other end of the stringer. Staunton Yester, who had caught most of the fish, had taken the photograph, which Peyton must have selected.

I joined Peyton after Mrs. Dufault turned to receive mourners. I told her the photo was a good choice.

"She didn't think so," Peyton whispered, nudging me in the direction of Roger's mother. "I said to her, 'Grace dear, but that's the way Roger *was.*' Then Gracie gives me her cold look—the one she uses to remind me I'm a Winifree—and says 'Not, dear, what he could have been,' implying—the same old shit—it was my fault Roger didn't go to medical school and end up a stuffed shirt like his daddy.''

Staunton's photograph captured the exuberance which stayed with Roger even when bad times got worse. At his best, Roger's exuberance would shade naturally into a radiant optimism that resulted in spontaneous generosity (usually in bars). For Roger the glass was never half empty. It was always half full and a waiter was on the way with a fresh pitcher.

When it came to promising commissions and finder's fees, Roger had no peer. With a few drinks in him Roger was Mother Theresa to every ne'er-do-well lot salesman, loan originator, mortgage broker, registered rep, and land speculator in Chirkie County. There was no shortage in any of these categories owing to the boom which hit Chirkie County after the bridge over the Pascamany was completed in 1982, putting waterfront lots in Chirkie County within ninety minutes' driving time from Richleigh.

Roger trusted in the spur of the moment, which he too often mistook for inspiration. Rather than admit an impulse betrayed him, Roger would blame himself for faintheartedness, for holding back rather than plunging in full measure. Roger was one of those gifted child athletes who apply to life the first rule of batting: If you think about the ball, you can't hit it. It was an article of faith with him.

''I need you,'' Peyton whispered, giving my hand a quick squeeze. She pivoted on a three-inch spike heel and joined Mrs. Dufault at the head of the receiving line.

On the way out, I stopped for a minute in the vestibule. The sunlight ignited the stained glass, turning the flock of sheep at Jesus' feet incandescently white despite the dust on the old window. I opened the door and looked into the shadowed sanctuary. The communion rail was bathed by rays angling from stained-glass windows. Staring at the prism of streaked hues, I suddenly remembered first communion. Palm Sunday, 1961.

✯

The boys' and girls' confirmation classes had formed separate lines. On cue with ''Onward Christian Soldiers,'' the girls in white dresses marched down one aisle, as we, wearing our first dark suits, filed down the other. The columns met at the altar and fanned out along the communion rail. After the rector finished beseeching God to forgive sins—which from the perspective of thirteen-year-olds were more desired than repented—we each received a white Bible with our name printed in gold and a palm frond. Then we filed up the center aisle to take our seats in pews marked by white ribbons.

From our pews came a persistent chirping as if from a field of crickets. Girls we had known all our lives, suddenly, impossibly grown up, crossed and recrossed their legs, seemingly incapable of attaining a restful alignment of thigh and ankle. For the girls, first communion meant first high heels and stockings. No more frilly white socks and flats. Each note rising from the scrape of new nylon caused tension to build the way it does before kickoff.

Twelve inches to my left the legs of Peyton Winifree basked in a roseate glow from a stained-glass window. When she crossed her thighs and her hem slid over her knee, I stopped breathing. Peyton looked so incomprehensibly grown up, it occurred to me she had gotten permission to skip our generation the way I had skipped second grade. She was thirteen going on twenty-two, and it wouldn't be right to hold her back. She had hearts to break and tongues to scorch. Peyton didn't look at me once. I didn't blame her.

※

Roger and Peyton had relocated of necessity to Rose Cottage when their home at Aimes Cove was auctioned off. Roger had forged Peyton's name as co-guarantor of the Vista Mer note. First to go on the block when the note went into default was Roger and Peyton's custom-built home, which provided only slight gain to Chirkie Savings & Trust Co. Roger had refinanced the property only eight months before he hit bottom.

Roger had inherited Rose Cottage from Cornelia Wilkinson Dufault, the maiden, great-aunt we shared. Aunt Dufault, had lived for forty years at the two-story, clapboard house located a mile or so downriver from Regent's Glebe, the eighteenth century manor home exactingly restored by Dr. and Mrs. Dufault. When Regent's Glebe had been a plantation, Rose Cottage had been the overseer's house.

Aunt Cornelia was the granddaughter of Col. Thomas Fiske Dufault who had whipped the Yankee cavalry at the Battle of Finney's Oaks, the sole engagement in Chirkie County, a matter of no small moment when the centennial of the War between the States arrived with the fervor of a camp meeting. During the centennial years, Roger and I used to bike along the dirt path which followed the Pascamany to Rose Cottage, where Aunt Cornelia would regale us with stories of the war and its cruel aftermath. Tales of valor, unconsummated loves, and the predations of hideous creatures called Carpetbaggers.

I learned in Sunday school that the reason the North won was because Lee, being a Christian, and, in particular, an Episcopalian, wouldn't fight dirty like Sherman and Sheridan. Lee and Jesus even looked alike, with big, haunting dark eyes that called you to repent, enlist, or both.

Peyton answered the door on the second knock. Her haggard look appealingly complemented her faded blue jeans. Worn out but still hot to trot, the style of the Boomers' last stand.

Ann Claire clung to Peyton. I knelt and hugged her. She was stiff to my touch and deaf to the inanities I murmured about how it was going to be all right. She was eight, old enough to know it wasn't.

Roger, after several rounds of drinks, sometimes had launched into perorations of his love for his children which, depending on the state of his marriage, were coupled with vows that only over his dead body would Peyton ever get custody. Beside the plats thumbtacked to the smudged and peeling walls of General Development Corporation's cluttered office were crayon drawings by Ann Claire and Roger IV. The only photographs in his office, apart from those of dreams-for-sale-with-great-appreciation-potential, were of his children.

Peyton eased Ann Claire off her hip and motioned for me to enter. The sitting room was littered with balled-up quilts, board games, stuffed animals, and old newspapers. Roger IV, ten, looked up from the television without showing a trace of recognition.

"Coffee?" Peyton asked, rubberband between her lips, pulling her hair into a ponytail.

I looked at the two-burner range. Brown threads of gravy were burned onto the stovetop. Empty cans and torn plastic wrappers littered the countertop.

"Let's go out," I replied.

"Where?" Peyton asked. She tucked in her T-shirt and slipped on navy loafers with lime-green tassels.

"I don't care," I said. "Something the kids like."

"Pizza," she said with a shrug. "It's kind of cheery."

About halfway to the Pizza Hut, Peyton twisted the rearview mirror toward her and put on makeup. She rummaged in her handbag and found a pair of pearl earrings. It was not yet noon when we arrived. Chairs were still upended on tables. The kids immediately went to the video games.

"Want to hear something weird?" Peyton asked, taking a leather case of cigarettes out of her handbag, handing me the case and her lighter.

"Why not?" I said, offering Peyton a cigarette and clicking the lighter. Peyton put her hand on mine and drew the lighter toward her cigarette. She puffed quickly and exhaled slowly, keeping her hand on mine.

"I think someone was in the house," she said.

"Why?" I asked, pulling my hand away.

"Why do I think so or why was someone there?"

"Both," I replied.

"Things were moved around. Stuff in drawers was mixed up."

"When did you notice it?" I asked.

"When I got back from the funeral."

"Maybe you imagined it," I said. "You ever find the will?"

Peyton shook her head. The waitress brought a pitcher of beer.

"Rog talked on and off about a will," I said. "I did a draft for him a few years back."

"Roger told me he had a will, but it doesn't surprise me he didn't get around to it. He didn't get around to *lots* of things."

Peyton found a few quarters to give to Roger IV, who appeared at her elbow. "Including yours truly," she continued, giving me a rueful smile to which I didn't respond.

"Anyway," Peyton said, "I want you to help me pull together Roger's assets. I can't make heads or tails of his papers and I haven't dared set foot in that rat's nest he called his office." Peyton tapped her glass, watched the beer fizz, then looked away.

"I have cash for two weeks' groceries if the kids don't hide junk food in the cart," she continued. "I haven't had a job since I was twenty-two. There are no jobs here anyway. I don't want to sponge off Gracie, though I'll probably end up doing it."

"I'll get you a check to help over the hump," I said. "Least I can do."

"Won't take it," Peyton replied. "But, darling, I'll take your time."

I didn't want to work on Roger's estate. I knew George Carey would appoint Peyton as administratrix if Roger hadn't left a will. She would be lost amidst the wreckage of Roger's affairs. The estate, likely to be insolvent, would not be able to afford an accountant.

Yet there could be the odd promissory note. Maybe even a poker chit. Someone who knew what he was doing should pick through the chaos. But I didn't want to be the someone. Roger had the disdain for paperwork of someone who firmly believed he was superior to pencil-jerkoffs, as he called bookkeepers, accountants, and, probably behind my back, lawyers. The mess in Roger's office in the Trak-Auto shopping center appalled me.

Yet I knew more about Roger's various deals than anyone except Staunton Yester, who was supposed to be drinking himself to death in a trailer in the hills above Harston. I wasn't that busy and my conscience was twitching.

"If no will turns up, I'll get Carey to appoint you administratrix," I said. "I'll do the paperwork."

"If you're going to do the work, *you* might as well be administratrix."

"Administrator," I corrected her.

"Whatever, darling." Peyton reached across the red-and-white checked tablecloth and put her hand familiarly on mine.

It didn't really matter. It was the same work whether I was administrator or attorney for the estate. I said I would arrange for us to appear in court in a week or so. She could tell Judge Carey she wanted me to be administrator. I knew Carey would agree. He liked me for some reason, and even if he didn't, he would agree. Carey had about as much love for intestate estates as he did for contested divorces. He often said judges who went to hell were assigned those dockets.

When we returned to the Cottage, Peyton gave me a kiss on the cheek which slid to my mouth once she made sure the kids weren't looking. I renewed my offer to give her a check as we parted. She waved me away over her shoulder.

I checked around. As I expected, Roger hadn't kept his promise to make a will. Then I made an appointment with Judge Carey.

On Thursday afternoon I sat on the bench beneath the granite obelisk on Courthouse Square, the county's memorial to the men who had fallen for the Confederacy, and waited for Peyton.

Watching the Pascamany flow, I found myself repeating the Eagles' line: every form of refuge has its price. My middle years stretched flat and straight before me. Dreams are supposed to die hard. Mine hadn't got the message. That should bother me, I decided.

That I became a lawyer perhaps was foreordained. Even as a child I could argue persuasively both sides. It's a gift, but one with a price, Father, once the finest trial lawyer in the tidewater, had warned.

Rhetoric doesn't require conviction, Father explained. You can get so good at arguing, you stop believing. Being able to argue both sides doesn't mean you're excused from picking sides. Say what you have to say during summations but live your life as if it were your own closing argument.

Father took his advice to heart even when it ran counter to friends' well-intentioned advice and all odds. In 1958, he announced his candidacy for the gubernatorial nomination of the Democratic Party. The Democratic primary was tantamount to the general election. Since its invention in 1872, every Democratic candidate selected in the "closed" primary had gone on to win the general election.

Primaries are civil wars which engender a bare-knuckled viciousness general elections never attain. What was called the "reform wing," Father later said, consisted of himself, a handful of professors emboldened by tenure, black civil-rights leaders in Richleigh, and the Scotch-Irish Democrats of the southwest corner of the state who, ornery by nature and contrarian by philosophy, opposed as a matter of principle whoever was in power in Richleigh. During the Lincoln administrations, northern Democrats who supported their brethren in the South were called copperheads. During the Eisenhower administrations, southern Democrats who supported the civil-rights plank of "national" Democrats were called worse.

Vigor alone would have been forgiven. The South had a proud tradition of élan in a hopeless cause. The problems began when the party pros realized Father had a fighting chance. By July, his campaign had attracted the attention of the "national" press, which resulted in unsolicited contributions from north of the Mason-Dixon line. A handful of professional volunteers from Washington and points north arrived to help.

Old friends probably had hoped to remain old friends, a possibility contingent on Father being regarded as a harmless eccentric. But once his campaign could no longer be ignored they turned their backs to us, in a genteel way.

We couldn't be expelled from the country club since we were shareholders, but Father discovered his reservations for tee times frequently were misplaced by the steward. Service in the dining room grew progressively slower as the pace of the campaign accelerated.

One Sunday we waited a half-hour for service. Finally Father walked over to a waitress, took the order pad from the pocket of her apron, returned to our table, and pretended to take our orders. The crowded dining room became still as a tomb. Then Father strode through the swinging doors which led to the kitchen, pushing them open with a shove which caused them to slap the wall. Seconds later he returned with a tray laden with a pitcher of iced tea, a basket of beaten biscuits, and a bowl of mashed potatoes. We ate in unbroken silence and left.

Father, Mother later told me, had expected to lose the business of institutional clients when he defied the advice of friends and announced his candidacy. But he hadn't counted on losing the personal business of old friends. They let him find out when the clerk called the term day docket and another lawyer answered the call.

Chirkie County in the fifties was solidly in the hands of good families who valued good manners more than punishment of infidels. (Later we were to learn the two were not incompatible.) So the retribution threatened by rednecks was never allowed to exceed throwing eggs. But "horseplay" among boys was not interdicted by the sheriff's department. The chant, "niggerlover, niggerlover," greeted me when the school bus arrived at my stop. When Mrs. Grady went to the teachers' lounge to smoke a cigarette, I would be subjected to a bombardment of spitballs, rubberbands, and paper clips.

During recesses I waited in vain to be picked for teams, which was just as well because I was busy fending off the assaults of Grevey Rails, self-appointed scourge of niggerlovers, whose advance to the fifth grade was largely due to "social promotions." Grevey's academic career, which ended in the seventh grade, was marked by two distinctions: commuting to school in his own pickup truck which he parked in the teachers' lot, and diddling fat Wanda, who scraped plates in the cafeteria. (In the pickup truck, during recess.)

Thirty years later, I was appointed by Judge Carey to defend Grevey Rails, charged with a bungled B&E of Woolworth's. (Two crates of floral-print shower curtains were found in his truck.) Three decades of odd jobs and cheap whiskey had left him a wizened, deferential little man who had no memory of what I could not forget.

I hired Anita Grogan six years ago as a combination legal secretary and real-estate paralegal. Her husband, an Air Force master sergeant, had taken up with a female Spec 5 in his squadron who worked on more than Pratt & Whitney engines. Anita, about forty at the time, had come to me for advice when Sergeant Grogan found a new love in coveralls.

Statler Air Force base, ten miles southeast of Lassington, is a maintenance base, far from a prestigious post. The volume of divorce work generated by the new coed Air Force has kept the county bar busy. Noncoms seemed to graduate from servicing turboprops to each other.

After her divorce I offered Anita three thousand dollars more than she was making as a math teacher at Lassington High. She had two kids. I knew she would accept, although she was way too smart for the job. She knew that, too. Anita learned all there was to learn about billing, basic legal forms, and real-estate settlements in a few months. All I had to do was to show up at settlements in a clean suit, offer incantations, hand around a few papers, crack one-liners which Anita dutifully has smiled at for six years, and admonish every property owner to have a will. Go for the spin-offs Father told me and you won't starve.

If the market is up we average about nine hundred dollars a week in settlement fees. I have an interest in a title insurance agency, so I pick up a commission on the binder. Once in a while we get the work on a commercial tract and make good money.

I do a fair amount of criminal defense. I've had some successes defending dope raps and the word has gotten around. So I get private pay work in addition to court-appointed cases. Our "tough on crime" state legislature for the tenth year has refused to raise the rate of twenty dollars per hour for defense work. But Carey usually lets us pad within reason our invoices.

I represent Chirkie Savings & Trust, just as Father used to before his problem with the bar. I work out loans gone bad, trying to avoid conflicts of interest whenever possible.

I've managed to build a law practice that pays me well for doing again (and again) what I do well. I don't know whether to think of it as a rut or a groove.

There are about forty lawyers in the county bar. Most are locals. The rest are ex-Air Force JAG, like Bobby Vecchio, the district attorney, who stayed on after their hitches at Statler were up and those who wanted a small-town practice and happened to pick Lassington for no particular reason. No one makes serious money by the standards of lawyers in Richleigh, the state capital, but we pass the work around. We resolve most matters over a few beers at the country club. That way we don't have to beat up on each other in court and spoil good relations among the bar. We get by. We get along.

Peyton, late as usual, pulled up in Roger's Jeep. She looked prim and proper. Hair braided into a bun. Low cordovan heels and navy linen suit. Little cameo earrings. We walked across Courthouse Square without speaking. Warren Closter, Carey's ancient bailiff, ushered us into Carey's chambers.

George Carey, in his shirtsleeves, rose from behind a cluttered desk and greeted us. Carey had taught Sunday school at Redeemer for thirty years and had been on the bench for twenty. As he got older, he seemed to save his patience for his students

"Allow me first to say how sorry I am," Carey said to Peyton, enveloping her hands in his. We took seats on an overstuffed, black leather Chesterfield. Carey asked if any will had been found. I told him none had. The matter at hand was attended to with dispatch. Carey endorsed the order I had prepared appointing me administrator and waiving bond.

We emerged into bright daylight. Peyton unpinned the bun and shook her long, blonde hair loose.

"Come home for lunch," she said, slipping her hand into mine. "Kids won't be back until four."

I made up a transparently phony excuse about a commissioner's hearing.

Peyton pursed her lips and put on her sunglasses. Then she slowly pushed them down the bridge of her nose until her pale-blue eyes peeked over the frame.

"I'm getting the impression that you liked me better as a wife than a widow," she said. "That so?"

"Timing's bad," I replied. "Be patient."

"Twenty years, darling, is a lot of patience," Peyton said, watching me closely.

I didn't reply.

*   *   *

The next day, Staunton Yester called me.

When Staunton had signed on as sales manager for Vista Mer, he was in his early sixties and recently divorced from his third wife. Staunton had been devoted to Roger whom he served as coach, confidant, prospect warmer-upper, sidekick, and straight man.

"Hear from that young couple from Onniston?" Staunton asked me, then broke into a rasping cough.

"Couldn't get financing," I said. "I had to give them back their deposit."

"Bastards were playing us, trying to make a quick buck by flipping the contract."

Yester paused. I could hear him take a slow drag on one of the Pall Malls to which he was addicted. Staunton once told me he wouldn't mind his emphysema if it didn't interfere with his smoking.

"Peyton said you're administrator of Roger's estate."

"True," I agreed.

"I was too sick to make it to Rog's funeral or I'd told you then. There's things in Rog's office Peyton don't need to know about, things Carey shouldn't know about, and things you don't want to know about." Yester paused before continuing. "I'll be up and about in a few days. Give me till Wednesday."

I guessed it was flake. Roger once told me he hit a line now and then when he needed to rev up for cold calling. Goddamned hardest work on the face of God's earth, he claimed. Some days coffee just won't cut it.

"If you have a key to GDC's office, that as a matter of law is permission to enter," I replied. "If you were to remove your personal effects, you would be within your rights. By Wednesday."

"Aye, aye, Cap'n," Staunton replied, and hung up.

A week later, I summoned my courage. My work had thinned out. I couldn't think of any excuse, apart from the heat—and that didn't count—for putting off seeing how bad the mess was in Roger's office. Peyton had dropped off the key along with a grocery box filled with scraps of paper (mostly bills).

I slowed when I drove past the QuieTown Lodge. It was all but deserted. Heat waves shimmered in the parking lot, which was occupied by two cars. South of the QT, I passed liquor stores, crab shacks, pit barbecues, antique-and-curio shops, tackle-and-bait shops, gun-and-ammo shops, and free-will gospel chapels.

The Trak-Auto shopping center is three miles south of Lassington on 201. It was the oldest strip shopping center in the county and showing its age. Roger's office was above the 7-Eleven in a cinderblock office building. Stairs rusted where the gray paint had blistered and peeled led to a balcony cracked so badly the reinforcing steel, also rusted, was visible. The General Development Corporation office, at the end of the balcony, overlooked a gravel lot beyond which, half hidden by a chain-link fence entangled with honeysuckle, were a dozen trailers strung together by clotheslines. Two civil warrants in debt from the general district court and several notices of attempted delivery of registered mail, probably summonses, were taped to the door.

When I got closer, I noticed the door was ajar. I looked at the lock. The wood around the cylinder was splintered. I pushed open the door and entered.

GDC's offices consisted of a cramped reception area and two small offices, one slightly larger than the other. Newspapers had been stuffed by someone into plastic grocery bags and left in a pile on the receptionist's desk. The bottom half of a beer can was jammed with sodden butts.

I started with Roger's rolltop desk. Little yellow-and-pink squares with scribbled phone numbers covered the wall beside the phone. There were plenty of cubbyholes in the desk and a secret drawer Roger had shown to half the county. If Staunton had found Roger's stash, that was probably where he found it.

The buttons on the phone were begrimed, the numbers faded. The shoulder rest glued to the handset was stained with sweat and hair oil. Someone should have put a phone in Roger's casket. Roger was worthless when it came to paperwork but could work a phone like Menuhin caressing a Stradivarius. Roger could make the expression of the most mundane pleas-

antry seem the vouchsafing of a privileged confidence. He was
the only guy I knew who could cold call "marks," Roger's
term for potential buyers, and keep them on the phone just to
hear his voice.

A stack of bills was impaled on a miniature sword blade
which jutted from a hunk of polished quartz. In the secret
drawer I found the 1984 Yellow Pages and an unopened pint
of Jack Daniel's. Correspondence had been dumped in a tray
marked "In." There was no need for an "Out" tray. Rog didn't
believe in writing. The letters, some postmarked months ago,
had not been opened.

I shuffled through the tray. Familiar handwritten initials,
"PNN," penned above the return address of the university law
school, caught my attention. The envelope bore a postmark of
June 10, 1989. I sliced open the envelope and unfolded a letter
from my maternal uncle, Pierce Niles Nesbitt. Niles had written
to complain about Roger's delay—"a delay as inexcusable as
protracted"—in recording the one-half interest of Addio, Inc.,
in the Vista Mer project. To the right of the "cc" was a name
I recognized: Rosalyn Cubertson, Esq., Banks & Worth.

I remembered Cubertson from law school. No one could forget her. She made sure of that, thriving as she did on contro-
versy. The hotter the antagonism she engendered, the colder
became her logic, the softer her voice, and the sweeter her
smile. She wore vituperation from the left as a badge of honor.
Niles, I knew, had admired her greatly and not just because her
political views paralleled his. They both were underdogs who
had triumphed, who'd beaten the odds. But more than that, they
were underdogs who steadfastly refused to pay homage to, or
even acknowledge, their roots.

Cubertson was the perfect type to make it at Banks & Worth,
the largest law firm in the state, and by reputation (well deserved, based on my experience) the most supercilious.

I slipped the letter into the envelope and the envelope into
my pocket. Neither Roger nor Niles had mentioned they were
doing business. It was hard to imagine a more unlikely match
than Niles and Roger. The aesthete and the booster.

I knew Niles worked a few deals on the side. All law professors do. It's the next best thing to tenure. But Niles did consulting work for Wall Street firms in connection with securities issues. The idea of Niles being involved, either as a lawyer or an investor, in one of Roger's real-estate deals, was odd.

The Vista Mer files were missing. Roger had kept them in grocery boxes in the closet. I searched the cabinets and closets, gave up, took the Jack Daniel's, and left.

Driving back to the office, I decided to call Niles. But I never got around to it.

CHAPTER 3

It had been the worst summer for recaps, Waylon Rumbert said, that he could remember. There had been a rash of tread peel-offs, some resulting in blow-outs. Someone must have screwed up the bonding resins, he confided to me. That or the carcasses hadn't been scarified deep enough.

At his deposition, Waylon blamed the heat and consumer abuse for the peel-offs. He also said the state legislature was at fault for raising the speed limit on interstates to sixty-five just before the hottest summer in twenty years. Waylon asked me after the deposition if that had been a good thing to say. I told him it would have been better to blame the peel-offs on evil rubber spirits.

Chirkie Tire Mart had offered to reimburse Tidewater Tire City for the refunds it made to customers. But Charlie Gilbert wanted more. Charlie, through his lawyer, John Threll, demanded that Waylon take back all remaining retreads, even the tractor, boat trailer and implement tires—none of which had caused any problems—and refund $7,213.85, which didn't include any offset for the tires sold. I told John to read Charlie the disclaimer of warranties printed on the bill of sale and ask him whether he had sold any of the retreads as new.

Two weeks after Roger's funeral, I was indexing Charlie's deposition in preparation for cross-examination and struggling both to stay awake and make myself give a damn when Anita buzzed me to let me know that a Mrs. Tessie Coles was on the line. It took me a second before I remembered that Mrs. Coles was Niles's housekeeper. She had been with him ever since he took the position with the law school in 1958. I told Anita to put her through.

"Lawyer Wilkinson, you remember me?" Mrs. Coles said in a small, hesitant voice. "Mrs. Tessie Coles?"

" 'Course, I do, Mrs. Coles." I remembered Mrs. Coles as a small woman the color of teak. She had a formal, grave demeanor which matched the starched white pinafore she wore over her slate-gray, pleated dress.

Mrs. Coles had to be well into her seventies. I guessed Niles had told her she should have a will and directed her to me. I was a little miffed Niles hadn't called me first, but he was like that, well-meaning but thoughtless.

Anita had a simple will form on the disk drive of her computer. I reached for a legal pad, planning to jot down the essential information, give my notes to Anita, and have her fill in the form. It would take only a few minutes. Mrs. Coles couldn't need much in the way of a will. I figured to do the work *pro bono* as a favor to Niles.

I rested my clipboard on my knee and readied my pencil, waiting for her to continue.

"Now, Mrs. Coles, what can I do for you?" I finally said.

"Not for me that you'd be doing . . ." Her voice sounded far away. She let it trail off as if she were embarrassed. Oh, shit, I said to myself. Not one of these. I knew what that tone of voice meant. Some relative got busted and Mrs. Coles got the job of lawyer scouting.

"Now, Mrs. Coles, you're going to have to let me know what the matter is. A family member in trouble?" I said, prodding her. I didn't want to get involved in defending some nephew or grandchild who had gotten busted. I wanted Mrs. Coles to get on with it so I could refer her to Sammy Thornton, a black lawyer I knew in Waterson. I tossed my legal pad onto my desk and rocked back in my chair.

I began to feel peeved with Niles for referring Mrs. Coles to me. He probably figured I had nothing better to do, a presumption that grated. Niles didn't bother to hide his disdain for my jack-of-all-trades small-town practice. The only thing which excused his attitude was that he was oblivious to it.

"A family member," she said after a pause with enough of an edge in her voice to let me know she resented my patronizing manner. "I 'spect you'd better get out here to see about your family member."

"Now, Mrs. Coles, I'm sure you realize . . ."

"I found Professor Nesbitt gone to the Maker, least I hope that so, when I went out to the house this morning," she said.

"Dead?" I said, reaching for my legal pad to steady myself. "Are you sure?" I jotted "rescue squad" on my pad and drew a line beside it. Then I wrote: "stroke/heart attack?"

"Sure I'm sure," she replied, her voice resuming the quiet, shy tone.

"Have you called anybody?" I underlined "rescue squad," then I drew a box around it, waiting for her to answer.

"I thought it best to call you first," she finally replied.

"Now, Mrs. Coles, here's what I want you to do," I said, speaking slowly as if to a child. "Lift up Professor Nesbitt's feet and put them on a chair and cover him with a blanket. Keep him warm. Stay right where you are. You did the right thing to call me. Now I'm going to hang up and call the rescue squad right now, so I want you to . . ."

"I wouldn't be doing no calling if I was you," she replied. "Ain't going to bring Professor Nesbitt back."

"Now, Mrs. Coles . . ."

"Not lessen you want the rescue people to find out 'bout Mr. Nesbitt's hobby, get it all in the papers."

"What hobby? Now, Mrs. Coles, I must say this all comes as—"

"Man's dirty hobby," she blurted, embarrassment vying with anger. "And that's all I'm going to say, so you don't need be doing no more now-Mrs-Coles-ing. And I ain't sitting no dead man's feet up on a chair. I'll wait for you to get out here." I heard a loud click and the hum of the dial tone.

I drew another box around "rescue squad" and glanced at

my watch. It was not quite ten. I dialed Directory Information
and got the rescue squad number in Waterston. I punched in
the number but hung up when the dispatcher answered. I
drummed my pencil on the edge of the clipboard. Sonofabitch.
I put the clipboard and a few papers into a briefcase. Then I
grabbed my suit jacket and told Anita on the way out that I'd
return late afternoon. Maybe.

By eleven when I turned onto Route 65, the overcast sky had
given way to a steady drizzle. A few minutes more and I was
in the piedmont, forty miles to the east of Waterston. The road,
narrower and with sweeping curves, was flanked by dairy farms.
The rolling hills on either side of the road were dark green,
punctuated by scattered rock outcroppings, muddy ponds with
eroded basins, and clusters of black-and-white holsteins huddled
together against what was now a hard rain. The Dodge's wipers
were streaking badly. I debated pulling into the next gas station
and having them replaced.

I didn't know what to make of what Mrs. Coles had said. I
replayed the conversation, recognized my condescending manner and regretted it. I decided to apologize, sort of anyway, to
Mrs. Coles once I arrived at Chez Niles, the name Niles had
given to his home. Mrs. Coles was a serious woman, a deacon-
ess in some sort of church, I seemed to recall Niles once had
told me. She might have overreacted, but she thought she was
doing the right thing. That was the key. Reward her for showing initiative.

I long had suspected Niles had a few kinks and quirks. So
Mrs. Coles's reference to a dirty hobby hadn't come as a shock.
Probably a collection of porno flicks, I guessed. I imagined
Mrs. Coles coming upon Niles sprawled amidst the lurid covers
of triple X videotapes he had ordered through the mail. Niles
probably had a post-office box rented in a fake name. Probably
had his student assistant pick up the plain brown paper parcels.
Confidential research materials, Niles would have told him.

I sipped the last few cold ounces of coffee and tried to decide
what I felt. I didn't blame Niles. It wasn't his fault. What he

did in private was his business. I was just sorry Mrs. Coles had to find him.

Just the same, I decided I was glad Mrs. Coles had called me. I imagined the rescue-squad volunteers, probably young guys with white-collar jobs, finding Niles's movies and snickering. I hoped Niles hadn't gone in for animal stuff or anything too weird. The story would make the rounds of the town and then spill over to university circles. I winced at the possibility. No doubt about it, I said to myself, Mrs. Coles had done the right thing. I made a note to make sure she got paid a little something extra.

The rain was coming down in white sheets, which cut visibility to twenty or thirty yards, beating down hard enough to drown out the radio. From the gloom two ghostly beams the color of runny yolks suddenly emerged. Then I heard a honk and jerked the wheel to the right just in time to avoid being scraped by a cattle truck.

I pulled onto the gravel shoulder, cut off the engine, and pressed the "emergency flasher" button. I imagined I felt the pickup truck sway, battered by the torrent. The drumming on the cab was hard and angry but couldn't last at this rate. I reached behind the seat and found an old hunting jacket left from duck season. I balled it up, laid it against the passenger side armrest, leaned across the seat and rested my head on it.

I remembered to say a prayer for Niles. I prayed that God had taken him quickly, without pain, for Niles had suffered more than his fair share of pain. I turned my head so I could watch the sheets break against the windshield and let my memory wash with the rain.

My grandmother was supposed to have been as rebellious as she was tall, homely, and bookish. She waited until she was thirty and then, in the expression of her day, married beneath her station.

The father, John Pierce Nesbitt, whom Niles shared with Mother, was by trade a bookbinder. Mother rarely spoke about her father, who died when she was eleven. Once she said he had published poems in an obscure quarterly. She claimed she couldn't remember the name of the periodical. But I have always suspected she was lying, possibly for a reason far more interesting than the poems, if there were any.

Pierce (pronounced "Pearse") was said to have received during the twenties orders for custom bindings from as far away as New York. He did well enough to hire two assistants and stockpile exotic leathers, some of which lie moldering in a wooden chest in the boathouse of the camp.

But his business had been an early and predictable victim of the Depression. The family farm, what little hadn't been sold off, hadn't been worked properly for years and the machinery was rusted and broken. Besides, Pierce was said to have been delicate, in contrast to the robustness of his wife.

In the mid-1930's, having failed at milling timber from the hickory copses which dotted the farm and, perhaps, as a husband—a supposition I based on oblique fragments of conversation spread over several decades—Pierce took the bus to Norfolk. An old friend, never identified, was said to have arranged a job for Pierce as a file clerk at the shipyard. Pierce's position paid enough for a bed at a rooming house, the occasional money order for his wife, and gin for amnesia. He never returned to Lassington.

In 1941, Pierce died of pneumonia compounded by alcoholism. In the same year, Niles, eleven, contracted polio and spent the better part of a year in an iron lung in the children's polio ward of a Richleigh hospital. Upon his return in a wheelchair, Niles was instructed at the farm by his mother and a haphazard assortment of tutors paid by the school board which, bowing to public sentiment, refused to permit Niles to enroll in the county schools. The school board cited safety concerns arising from the many and steep flights of steps as the pretext for its decision. Fear of polio was the actual motive.

Niles's education was separate but more than equal. He later claimed to have taught himself Latin and Greek, but Mother said that was an exaggeration. Niles refuses to give credit, Mother said, to all those who bent over backward to help him. Dr. Pauley, the rector at Redeemer, drove all the way out to the farm, using up his precious rationed gas, to teach Niles

Latin and Greek. Of course, no one bothered to teach me, Mother lamented. I was always little Miss Second Fiddle. I was just the doormat everyone stepped on in the rush to help Niles.

Niles at sixteen did well enough on qualifying exams, particularly in Latin and Greek, to be awarded a scholarship to Winston-Rhone College, a small—never more than four-hundred men— liberal arts college near Richleigh supported for the past century by the Episcopalian church. Having been elected to Phi Beta Kappa as a junior, Niles was graduated at twenty as valedictorian with a BA in philosophy. Winston-Rhone had a long standing and proud tradition of sending its outstanding graduates to seminary. Niles, after first having accepted, rejected a scholarship offered by Southern Episcopal Seminary. He sought and received a scholarship from the university law school.

In his first year, Niles authored a law review note about arbitrage which was reprinted in *Annals of Municipal Finance*. In his second year, he was appointed editor-in-chief of the law review. In his third, he received the offer of a clerkship at the United States Supreme Court, which he accepted. After his clerkship, Niles returned to the law school to teach.

I saw Niles once in a while during the sixties, occasions which coincided with football games at the university. Our visits with Niles usually ended in to-do's, as Mother called them. Mother and Niles persisted—and perhaps delighted—in dredging up grudges and raking slights from the forties. Mother and Niles bristled like alley cats when they discussed family history. But I sensed there was camaraderie, if not comfort, in their contention.

With tenure, scrimping ended. A good salary, virtually an annuity, supplemented by modest royalties from two textbooks and immodest consulting fees from Wall Street firms, enabled Niles to indulge. No more reproductions. No more paperback editions. No more off-the-rack suits. No more jug wines. No more wholesalers' no-name brands of Scotch.

I saw Niles infrequently during my college years. By then, Niles had developed what he called a gentleman's paunch and jowls. He claimed his suits were tailored by the Savile Row shop which had served T. S. Eliot. Niles wore tortoiseshell half-lens fitted to a braided gold chain. All traces of a southern accent purged, Niles spoke in a clipped manner which more than hinted at an English accent. He looked and talked like a don at Balliol in good standing at White's.

During this period Niles superintended the construction of Chez Niles on the crest of a hill overlooking Waterston. The long, single-story house was constructed of native fieldstone. The rear exposure was formed entirely of floor-to-ceiling glass panels. The open spaces, necessary for easy maneuvering in a wheelchair, lent the house an austere, elegant style. Incorporated in the home was a one-bedroom apartment, which Niles planned to make available rent free to a student assistant in return for tending the grounds and running errands.

When I learned in the spring of 1973 of my acceptance to the university law school, I let Niles know I would be interested in occupying the apartment. Niles assented, but in August, too late for me to make other arrangements, he withdrew his agreement (never quite firm, to be fair) with neither an explanation nor an apology.

With tenure, Niles acquired some bad habits. Or maybe they had been there all along, suppressed until he attained the security of tenure. Rather than attempt to restrain, Niles began to preen his arrogance. He bullied those who did not share his opinions, justifying impoliteness as ruthless honesty.

Niles did not require of his guests that they share his opinions in matters of art, music, or literature. But he demanded a vigorous defense of differing opinions in a manner which suggested it was owed to him. As to the law, which Niles increasingly deemed beneath him, the more so as he was recognized as an authority, Niles did not project arrogance. Legal issues he would discuss with a lassitude which precluded debate. This was taken by some as patience and even courtesy. Niles would change the subject as soon as possible, which was taken as humility.

During my last semester, Niles and I grew closer. He realized I was not interested in his assistance in advancing my career nor, for that matter, did I appear particularly interested in advancing it by any means. I had matriculated for lack of a better idea. That I succeeded in law school with slight effort endeared me to Niles. It shows there's hope for you to have a life after law, he told me.

I hadn't talked to Niles for several years until one late night in the late seventies. I was drinking by myself and phoned Niles for no particular reason. Niles, as it turned out, was drinking by himself and glad to hear from me. We rambled on about family history, resurrecting obscure cousins long dead and old, embarrassing rumors. This call led to other, similarly fueled late-night calls, which eventually resulted in my doing odds and ends of legal work for Niles and in what amounted to friendship, for lack of a better term.

Niles, hopelessly at sea when it came to managing his finances, didn't regard a bill as due until he received a letter from a collection agency threatening to destroy his credit. Beginning in the 1980's, Niles either was not being offered or was turning down consulting jobs. I guessed it was the former reason. I had heard through the grapevine that Niles's work habits had gone from bad to worse, and he had been censured by the president of the university for unexcused absences, a necessary precursor to revocation of tenure. Nile's cash flow, which had been sufficient, but with little margin, for his version of the fundamentals of life began to ebb. He was reduced to reliance on his salary which, while considerably more than modest, was not sufficient to underwrite the style he had cultivated. He hinted at bad investments and worse habits, but I never followed up on his hints.

One night in the spring of 1986, Niles telephoned. He said he needed twelve grand to pay off a loss he had taken on a high-flyer issue he had bought on the margin. His securities broker was threatening to file suit to collect if Niles didn't make good on the shortage. There was an edge of desperation in his voice which led me to make the loan even though I suspected he was lying about the stock loss.

Niles experienced an esophageal spasm in 1988 which he had mistaken for a heart attack. He telephoned not long afterward to ask me to send a form for a simple will. He brushed aside my reflexive admonition that there is no such thing as a simple will. Cut the bar association bullshit, Niles said. Send me a goddamn form. I did.

The sky seemed to have lightened. I sat up, switched on the wipers, and looked down the road. The rain was still heavy, but now I could see the double yellow line disappearing at the crest of hill, two hundred yards to the west. Muddy water angrily rushed in the little gully separating the shoulder from the macadam. I bumped the Dodge over the gully and headed west.

It was about noon when I arrived at Laurel Ridge Hill, the domain of the university elite. I followed the road uphill, past a succession of little "Tara's" on two-acre lots, to Niles's home, identified by a brass plate as Chez Niles.

Mrs. Coles opened the door when I pulled into the driveway and parked behind Niles's Jaguar convertible. I covered my head with the hunting jacket and sprinted up the flagstone path toward the door, which Mrs. Coles held open.

"Just wait here," she said. "Don't be dripping on the hardwood, no."

Mrs. Coles left me. She returned a minute later and handed me a thick towel. She remained to make sure I complied. She face me, her shoulders braced, holding herself—all five feet— as erect as a Marine honor guard. She was wearing a starched white dress with an old-fashioned, high collar and well-worn oxfords which looked to have been whitewashed. Cracks in the leather showed through the chalky, caked polish.

I heard the crunch of gravel and turned to see a BMW enter the driveway and park beside the garage.

"That be Neal somebody," Mrs. Coles said, taking the towel from me. "New student assistant."

"Who's that with him?" I asked, watching a slender man in denim cutoffs and sandals climb out the passenger side and pop open a yellow umbrella. He walked around the BMW and held the umbrella for Neal. We watched Neal and the man, holding the umbrella together, hurry up the brick walkway and turn the corner of the garage. The walkway, I remembered, led to the student apartment.

"Friend, alls I know," she replied as they passed out of

sight. "Been here since June, hmph." Mrs. Coles shut the door and dropped the catch of the security chain into its slot.

"They know about Niles?" I asked.

"Best hope not." Mrs. Coles sucked in her upper lip and shook her head slowly. "Hmph."

"You ready?" she said, folding the towel over her arm.

"I want to thank you for . . ."

Mrs. Coles curtly nodded acknowledgment, turned, and paced briskly down the hall.

I followed Mrs. Coles into Niles's bedroom. Built-in shelves, stuffed with books arranged haphazardly, lined two walls. Lurid paperbacks, their pages yellowed and dogeared, their spines split and rippled with age, were interspersed among classics finely bound by my grandfather in exotic leathers. Beside the low, kingsize bed was a chest-high stack of old newspapers.

I tried to imagine what Niles must have experienced when death suddenly interrupted what should have been another Saturday night like so many others. But quickly I shied away. Thinking about death is like looking at the sun. I wanted to believe my daily routines were proof against death, that death dare not disturb my rituals of ordinariness. Perhaps that was why the tableau was so unsettling.

Mrs. Coles pulled back the drapes. She stood before the plate-glass panels, her back to me. The rain had stopped. A broadening swath of blue outlined the steeples of Lassington and the rolling hills to the west. Rays of sunlight raked the still-dark clouds, seeming to draw a fine mist skyward from the close-cropped lawn, which sloped to a far border of oaks, their foliage so densely green as to shimmer in the fresh light.

"All this, the hand of the Lord God triumphant," Mrs. Coles said, her back still to me. "And still it wasn't enough. Umm. Umm. Ummph."

"Lord have mercy," Mrs. Coles said slowly, in a voice which told me she meant it as a prayer. She turned, nodded in the direction of the master bathroom, then turned again to take in the view. She took no notice of me. I stole a glance at her eyes, which, glowing with unshed tears, seemed to stare into a distance seen only by her.

I pushed open the bathroom door and saw Niles lying crumpled beside his wheelchair. He was wearing an intricately patterned white-on-white silk dressing gown and nothing else. His neck and face were tinged with a light blue-gray. His eyes were staring. I knelt and felt his carotid artery for a pulse. I picked up his hand, blue and cold. His fingers were stiff.

Beside the wheelchair was a bottle of Moët & Chandon and a half-filled flute. I picked up the bottle and flute and put them on the vanity. Light appeared to be coming from inside the medicine cabinet built into the wall just above the vanity. The mirrored door of the cabinet was open. Glass shelves had been stacked beside a handful of stainless-steel brackets. A sheet of white-enameled metal rested on its edge beside the chest.

I stepped over Niles and leaned so that I was eye level with the cabinet. When I peered into it, I saw Neal and his friend, both shirtless, propped up by a pile of pillows, on a double bed, each intent on a section of newspaper. They sipped from teacups and reached without looking for thin slices of brown cake laid out on a plate between them while they read. As I watched, they traded sections of the paper.

I was close enough to read the lead story, which described a proposal championed by Elliot Dean for cleaning up the Shenley River. Were it not for the glass plate which formed the back of the cabinet, I could have helped myself to a slice of the brown cake.

I had been in the student apartment enough times to know what was on Neal's side of the glass: a mirror. Only a few feet from the bed was an alcove which contained a little built-in refrigerator below a stainless-steel sink. Above the sink, a mirror extended to the ceiling. A wet bar in the bedroom was a custom touch, one which would appeal to any student.

When Neal draped his arm across his friend's lap, I picked up the metal-enameled plate and quietly pressed it into the chest. It clicked precisely into place, covering the glass. I twisted in the screws which anchored the corners of the plate, snapped the steel brackets into their slots, and slid the glass shelves into place over the brackets.

I inspected the results of the reassembly. The medicine cabinet looked so ordinary, I had to suppress an impulse to remove the shelves and the plate to make sure I hadn't imagined the two-way mirror.

I knelt, rolled Niles onto his back, closed his robe, tied the sash, and folded his arms across his chest. I said a prayer in Latin I hadn't thought of in decades, then I made the sign of the cross. Then I left the bathroom and shut the door.

I found Mrs. Coles in the library. She was dusting the upper shelves with a long-handled feather duster, as if this were another Monday. I waited until she turned.

"No point in calling the rescue squad," I said. "There's supposed to be a death certificate before the undertaker will take the body. I think so anyway."

"You's the lawyer man," Mrs. Coles replied.

"I'm going to call the coroner's office," I said. I shuffled through the correspondence on Niles's desk, uncertain as to how to begin.

"Mrs. Coles," I said. "Can we talk a minute?"

"If you're fixing to ask me if I can keep a secret, it won't take no minute. Fact, you don't need to ask."

"All right, then, I just . . ."

" 'Fore you go calling, you best see something else." Mrs. Coles laid down her duster and left the room. I followed her down the hall into Niles's study.

"Back in there," Mrs. Coles said, pointing to the closet. "Old leather-strap tote."

At the back of the closet I found what looked like an old sea chest. I dragged it out and opened it. It contained a video minicam, extra lens, battery pack, light meter, and a collapsible tripod.

Below the battery pack I found an unopened mailing folder addressed to Niles in graceful italics just below where "Par Avion/Air Mail" had been stamped in smeared red letters. I removed the folder from the trunk. The return address, penned by the same hand, was Brauner-Zweig, 11 Konigstrasse, Munich. I opened the folder, slid out a white plastic case, snapped it open and found a videocassette.

*   *   *

I found Mrs. Coles in the kitchen washing dishes. I showed her the videocassette.

"You know if Niles had any other videotapes?" I asked.

Mrs. Coles looked up from the sink and pointed to the window. "Out by the rose garden. Trash can 'longside mulch pile," she replied.

I went out the kitchen door and followed the brick path which led to the garden. Glistening yellow roses cascaded from the lattice arches, intertwined with thick, thorny vines, which spanned the path. At the end of the path I found a discolored, galvanized trash can beside a pile of mulch. Behind the pile was a jerrycan with a missing screw cap. I shook the jerrycan and sniffed the opening. It was empty but reeked of gasoline.

The interior of the trash can was blackened with soot. Lumps of what looked like hardened ash were stuck to the bottom of the can. I picked up a gardening trowel and pried loose a knob from one of the lumps. With my penknife I scraped off the ash and cut into the substrate. I broke the knob in half and held up the smooth edge. The sun glinted on black plastic.

I put the piece of black plastic in my pocket and returned to the kitchen. Mrs. Coles was sitting at a butcher-block table drinking a cup of tea. She had laid out a cup and saucer for me. She lifted the teapot and raised her eyebrows in invitation.

"Thank you," I replied.

"I found this 'longside the mulch pile," Mrs. Coles said. She reached into the drawer of the table, pulled out a white plastic case, and handed it to me. Imprinted on the spine of the case was the Brauner-Zweig logo.

"He burned the tapes?" I asked.

"Somebody did. Sometime 'tween suppertime Friday and this morning."

"Did you keep that trash can out by the mulch pile?"

"See that little green shed out by the garage?" Mrs. Coles pointed without looking. "Shed is whereas the cans be."

I considered the likelihood that Niles in his wheelchair moved a heavy-gauge steel trash can from the shed, a five-gallon jerrycan of gas from the garage, and videotapes from the house along an uneven brick path to the end of the garden. It was possible but would have taken a determined effort.

"You think Niles burned the tapes?" I asked after a moment of silence.

Mrs. Coles carefully dunked a cookie in her tea. She nibbled on the cookie.

"Man gotten so he wouldn't do nut'in' for hisself," she replied after a minute.

I spent an hour searching for videotapes. Around four I gave up, took the trunk, and put it in my truck. Then I called the coroner.

The mortician's assistant called the next day to tell me the coroner had ascribed the death to "coronary infarction/arterial sclerosis." Then he said he presumed the family wanted a coffin consistent with the status of a full professor. I asked if the model without tenure was cheaper.

Two days after the funeral, a small voice, which identified itself as belonging to a Mr. Arthur Hewins, called me to let me know that Niles's will had turned up in a safe-deposit box at Waterston Commonwealth Bank, which, not coincidentally, had been designated by the will as co-executor of Niles's estate. I was fairly sure of the answer but I asked anyway. Mr. Hewins told me I was the other co-executor.

CHAPTER 4

I got an early start on Tuesday, July 6, 1989. *Tidewater Tire City* v. *Chirkie Tire Mart* was in its second day of trial. On Day One, John Threll produced a twisted and shriveled tread which resembled a scaly black snake. Perhaps a water moccasin. When John stretched out the tread, then held up one end, the other end twitched, as if writhing, before obligingly twisting into a coil. The jurors cringed when Threll brought Plaintiff's Exhibit 1 within ten feet of the jury box.

I needed to review recent cases on disclaimers. Father always said when the facts are against you, find some friendly law. I didn't have any doubt the facts were against us. When I told Waylon, he complained I let Mrs. Cullen, whose Alligator Gripper All-Weather tread had peeled off as she was driving her two daughters to a Brownie den meeting, off easy. Should have took aholt and lit into her, Waylon said. You let her get away with saying she was driving only fifty. Them ones with shifty legs are leadfooters.

A few miles south of Lassington I passed the boarded-up storefront of Chirkie Traction & Implement Company. The ''For Sale'' sign stapled to the front door for over a year was almost as faded as the ten-foot-tall Indian, supposedly a Chirkie brave, who held his bow over his head as he rode the weather-beaten silhouette of a John Deere tractor on the roof of the cinderblock structure. The words printed on the cartoon bubble attached to his lunatic grin were illegible, but I knew them by heart. "Got My Deere! You-um Got Yourn?"

When Peyton's father, P. Harold Winifree, died two years ago, Chirkie Traction & Implement Company went into a tail-spin. Ship went down with the captain, Porky had remarked, lamenting more the prejudice to CS&T's collateral than the loss of the captain.

A ruddy, robust barrel of a man, P. Harold, for thirty years, had managed Chirkie Traction & Implement Co., a purveyor of new and used harrows, balers, tractors, threshers, bush-hogs, combines, plows, aerators, mowers, and chainsaws. The firm also sold ceramic bunnies, squirrels, leprechauns, and elves created (from precast molds) by P. Harold's wife, Janet, an artist whose chosen medium was lawn decorations. Mother once said Janet must have baked her brains in her kiln.

After the Second World War, P. Harold enlisted as a sales rep for The John Deere Company. Eight years later, P. Harold, by then a successful salesman but having come to hate spending four nights per week in motels, learned Chirkie Traction & Implement Co., one of his accounts, was 180 days in arrears, despite having the second highest sales volume in the Tidewater, and was about to be placed by The John Deere Company on a cash-in-advance basis.

Mindful that the business could not survive without credit and that skimming was the likely reason for the shortfall, P. Harold invited Amos Grady, Jr., to have a few beers. P. Harold was said to have told Amos there was good news and bad news. The good news was that P. Harold was willing to invest five thousand dollars and had obtained a commitment from The John Deere Company to reinstate the line of credit if P. Harold personally guaranteed it and took over running the business. The bad news was that if Amos did not sell him a controlling interest in the business, he would inform John Deere that Amos was skimming from his customer's installment payments.

Not long after P. Harold assumed the position of general manager, which enabled Amos to spend afternoons at the country club bar trying to determine whether his gratitude to P.

Harold for rescuing the business exceeded his hatred of P. Harold, there appeared on the roof the silhouette of the Indian. P. Harold, everyone agreed, was a real crackerjack just like Amos, Sr., had been. Just the kind of go-getter the business needed.

P. Harold and Janet spent the next eight years scheming to gain membership in Chirkie Golf & Country Club. They assiduously cultivated the crusty strata of "good families" which both expected and were contemptuous of the courtship paid by the trade class. Occasionally, when the club needed capital, an invitation was extended to a successful merchant who had proved his worthiness by years of slavish devotion to civic and philanthropic causes chaired by his social betters.

P. Harold annually led the Chirkie Lions Club in sales both of brooms and lightbulbs. Janet set (and annually topped) the PTA record for door-to-door sales of fruitcakes. Mother said Janet did so well because the first rule of selling was to identify with your product.

P. Harold and Janet, to improve their odds, forsook the Baptist Church and became Episcopalians, where, Mother said, they did everything except lick the pews. Whatever treasures might have been laid up in heaven by such labors, P. Harold and Janet had to wait until Amos drank himself to death before they were invited to join the club. Everybody knew Amos blackballed P. Harold every time his name came up. Amos said he had to talk to that slick-mouthed sonofabitch during the day but would be hog-tied and double-damned if he would do it at night.

My view, at the time, was that by dying to make possible the advent of Peyton in a two-piece at the country club pool, where I worked as the assistant lifeguard, Amos Grady was redeemed. I said a little prayer for Amos every time I saw a bush-hog.

I parked in the CS&T lot, walked down the alley to Fran's Diner, and picked up a coffee to go. It was just past seven. I used my key to let myself into the lobby of the building and took the elevator to the penthouse suite, as Porky Bryan refers to it whenever he discusses the lease. My law office consists of four rooms, including a private bathroom, on the top floor of the Chirkie Savings & Trust Building. A turn-of-the-century building of five stories, it was until five years ago the tallest in Lassington, not counting the silos.

The dimensions of the CS&T building are the same as its limestone blocks, a correspondence too exact not to have been deliberate. This identity of scale causes the building to seem either harmonically balanced or squat, depending on one's taste. The twelve-foot ceilings, solid oak woodwork, and marble floors reflect a culture sure of itself. To the perimeter of the lobby is bolted a heavy brass footrail with ornate cuspidors in the corners.

I opened the door to my office, looked upon a scene from the lawyer's Book of the Damned, and almost dropped my coffee. Thousands of manilla files littered the floor, spewing their contents. Drawers gaped open from a row of file cabinets which, overbalanced, had tilted onto the conference room table scarring the walnut. The drawers from my desk and credenza lay up-ended in a pile. Probably in a search for a wall safe the intruder had ripped from their cases the books which lined the reception area and library.

I flipped the light switch. There was no power. I checked and found the utility closet at the end of the hall had been broken into and the line cut. Only a professional would have thought to cut the power to the alarm system from a remote source. This was not the work of a county drunk looking for antiques to pawn.

I telephoned Anita to forewarn her. Her voice sounded like she was sleeping on the other side of eternity. Then I dialed the sheriff. The crime scene investigative team arrived before Anita. I left them to their work and went to the bar association library.

When *Tidewater Tire City* v. *Chirkie Tire Mart* recessed at noon, I returned to my office.

The debris had been coated with a fine, light-gray dust. A deputy, whose name I couldn't recall, was on his knees working over my desk drawers with an air puff. A halo of gray dust was raised each time he squeezed the rubber bulb. No one spoke to me. Anita, smoking for the first time in a year, was seated on the edge of the receptionist's desk, twisting tresses with her free hand.

There was a woman I didn't recognize in the library. She was seated on the conference table, talking on the phone. Press, I guessed, phoning in her story. I leaned against the doorframe and took in her profile. She looked to be in her early thirties. Shoulder-length red hair, left to its natural curl. Freckles spanning a turned-up nose. Freckles on long, thin legs. Dark-blue Eton jacket and matching skirt. She hung up the phone and turned in my direction.

"You ought to know better than to sit on a table which is going to be dusted for prints," I said.

She put her notepad in her handbag and looked up, inspecting me for flaws with cool, gun-metal-blue eyes.

"Mr. Wilkinson, I presume. Hello to you, too. The table was dusted about an hour ago. Negative. I'm Colleen Mulkerrin. I signed on as an assistant district attorney last week. This is my first case. Mr. Vecchio wanted me to become familiar with the crime scene investigative team."

Her first name struck a chord. I remembered Bobby had mentioned he had hired an assistant DA who would make you want to commit a felony just to be interviewed by her. Sweet lass, Bobby said in a thick imitation of an Irish accent, from the auld sod of County Brooklyn.

"First case here or first case ever?" I asked. She looked too old to be fresh from law school.

She read my look. "First case. Virgins make you nervous?"

"Sorry. I shouldn't take it out on you. Look at this mess." I waved my hand. "CSIT's probably wasting its time. The pros don't leave prints."

"Why would a professional ransack a lawyer's office? What's the market for hot lawbooks?"

There was a pleasing lilt to her voice. Her accent was definitely not southern. She probably could say "good morning" in fewer than five seconds.

I didn't have an answer to her question, one that had been bothering me all morning. I checked my watch. I had a half-hour to grab a sandwich and get back to court.

* * *

After the jury retired to deliberate, the litigants finally got serious about settling. I told Waylon Rumpert for the fortieth time that justice was God's problem. Our problem was that while the law was on our side, if the case went to the jury, they likely would ignore Carey's instructions and find in favor of Tidewater Tire City. The problem, I told Waylon, was that a peel-off which looks like a dangerous snake makes more of an impact on a jury than a disclaimer in 6 point italics on the back of a receipt. Waylon finally, grudgingly, offered to refund five thousand dollars and haul away the remaining tires. Charlie Gilbert accepted, on the side condition that Waylon's son stayed away from his daughter.

Carey was experienced enough not to be irked (at least not to show it) when Threll and I went to chambers to announce the settlement. Carey once told me a case that settles after the jury retires is the judicial equivalent of *coitus interruptus.*

I forced myself to return the jurors' cold stares when Carey told them the litigants had agreed to a settlement. I could read their minds: goddamned lawyers wanted to max out their fees before forcing their clients to settle this bullshit case. It's great belonging to a revered profession. No wonder Lenin and Castro left their law practices for revolutionary politics.

When I returned to my office, CSIT had departed, leaving fingerprint dust all over the office. Anita was on her knees trying to put scattered utility bills back into the right settlement files. When I offered to help, Anita waved me off.

I changed into shorts and T-shirt and went out to jog along the Pascamany. It was hot, humid, and hazy. The sweat drained out the tension and I felt more like my normal sardonic self. The bridle path along the river was deserted. I stripped off my sopping T-shirt and lodged it in the crook of a willow tree, planning to pick it up on the return route. The path between the Pascamany and Ottawomack Marsh is narrow and draped by willows laden with Spanish moss. Watching an old barge wheeze upriver, I almost ran into Colleen Mulkerrin.

She was wearing a slate blue navy T-shirt which had it not been soaked might have been sky blue. I couldn't make out what the white letters said. Her hair was pulled into a ponytail which looked like a small drowned animal. She was hyperventilating and flushed. I didn't think it was because of me.

"The latitude here is the same as Cairo," I said. "Get a cotton fishing cap with a high crown and a long bill. Soak a sponge in ice water and put it inside. It helps."

"Maybe you should put one in your shorts," she replied. "It says 'Fordham Law.'" She stretched out her T-shirt. I hadn't realized I had been staring. She smiled, then resumed jogging.

Bobby Vecchio was probably the only DA in the South who recruited at Fordham, his alma mater.

"Hey, Peckerwood," Vecchio said, answering my phone call. "I hear Threll's given up law for snake handling."

I don't know what Peckerwood means. It was Vecchio's nickname for me. He said it's Italian slang for a guy with a big pecker. It doesn't sound Italian. Maybe the guys in Brooklyn got it confused with peckerhead.

"Any leads on the break-in?" I asked.

"Negative. Dusting didn't turn up diddly. That all you wanted?" He chuckled.

"No," I admitted.

"Law review at Fordham, divorced, and thirty-three. And, no, I'm not. Anything else?"

"That'll do," I replied.

"Listen, buddy, we gotta talk sometime about the Dufault case and Peyton. You know what I mean?"

I wondered to how many of her dearest friends Peyton, half into a bottle of Chablis, had poured out her heart. She took seriously self-help columns which promoted "talking it out" as the cure for all ills short of cellulite bumps. She was a sucker for "self-diagnostic" multiple-choice tests, one-day-wonder-makeovers, exercises-to-flatten-your-tummy-in-ten-days, and other fairy tales for aging girls.

"I know," I said. "We will. Just not now."

"Toodle-loo, tiger," Vecchio said, and hung up.

During his tour as a JAG officer at Statler, Vecchio had met Marie Turner, who in the eighth grade had been my number-one girlfriend, and ended up marrying her. One day in the summer of 1980 he stopped by to ask if I had any overflow work. I've hung up my uniform and hung out my shingle, he said. Your dogs are my lions.

I liked Vecchio from the start and threw some work his way. Junk stuff, really. Deadbeat collections, third time at bat motions for alimony increases, and insolvent estates. I didn't do him any favors.

Vecchio was a hustler. I had to give him that. He ran down titles, did leg work for the indisposed guys, wrote appellate briefs for the indolent guys, and spent a lot of time hanging around court. Carey got to know him and started giving him indigent misdemeanors to defend. Before long he had moved up to felonies and was doing collections for GMAC. Brooklyn Bobby, the yankee fireass, George Carey once called him, meaning it as a compliment.

Vecchio had two kinds of suits. Dark blue and navy blue. He was an apostle of power dressing in a jurisdiction where lawyers still wore seersucker jackets, chinos, and penny loafers to court.

When Custis Carter got divorced, suddenly resigned as DA, and enrolled at Virginia Episcopal Seminary, I thought about running for DA. But neither very long nor hard. The job only paid fifty grand and required regular office hours.

Vecchio angled to get the endorsement of the county Democratic committee, succeeded, and tossed his hat in the ring. The Republicans waited until the last minute to recruit a candidate, for the sake of appearances. Vecchio won easily.

Vecchio had not been opposed in 1986, but I gave a fundraiser for him anyway. Crabs and kegs at the camp. Soul music by Rufus and the Dixie Cats, guys in their sixties in kelly-green suits with silver sequins. Fifty bucks a couple. After Bobby won, we spent the money on a fishing trip in the Gulf.

Everybody agreed Vecchio had a good shot at being appointed circuit court judge when Carey retired. That was supposed to be a boon for me—if it happened. Against Vecchio I had a won–lost record in drug cases far better than I (and my clients) deserved. He went out of his way to be fair, giving in at times on evidentiary points which were too close to call. Once or twice Carey had looked askance but held his peace.

Sometimes I wondered if Vecchio made me look good because of our friendship. I knew he had done me a favor three years ago when he *noll prossed* a marijuana distribution case against Tim Dugan. Tim's a character, not a criminal, Vecchio confided, over beers at the club. Prosecutorial discretion means never having to say you're sorry.

I vacillated for a week before I got around to inviting Mulkerrin to lunch at the club. When I started to give her directions, she said she had been there. I didn't want to examine why that vexed me.

The Chirkie Golf & Country Club is about five miles west of Lassington. The driveway winds gently uphill through the apple orchard separating the seventh and fifteenth fairways. In the spring it is strikingly beautiful, the sun-dappled white blossoms a gossamer canopy and the fairways luminous with new grass.

The initiation fee is up to twenty grand. Mother assigned her membership to me when she bought the house in Sarasota four years ago. The club, she told me, is more important than your office. Don't forget that.

The clubhouse, native fieldstone with a red tile mansard roof, was constructed in the 1920's. On summer weekends a buffet lunch is served on the broad, shaded porch. The fare is billed as heart-healthy, nouvelle southern cuisine. As far as I can tell, the only difference is the green beans are no longer simmered in bacon grease. Not the ones served to members, Thaddeus told me huffily.

I poured an iced tea, settled into a white wicker rocker, and rested my feet on the low stone wall. Plus fours, for some not very good reason, were making a comeback. In lurid tones, no less. Just what overweight, middle-aged golfers need. I watched Porky Bryan, resplendent in neon green with yellow diagonals, settle his two-tone spikes into the sand of the trap guarding the twelfth green. Porky had inherited the presidency of CS&T

when his father dropped dead in the middle of his backswing two years ago, keeping his elbow locked to the end.

Watching a father and son prepare to tee off on Number One made me remember golf with Father. Father would stand to the side, lazily stretching his shoulders and hamstrings while providing a critique of my practice swings. Just before I ascended the tee, as if it were a scaffold, he would share his sudden insight as to the cause of my slice.

Only the stirring of the breeze would break the silence as I prayed to the pristine white, dimpled apotheosis of hope which, resting on its little throne, stared upward implacably at me. If any of the waiting crowd broke the silence, I instinctively would shudder in anticipation of Father's sibilant to hush the malefactor.

Then, bearing in mind Father's advice to close the club face, pinch my right elbow to my side, lock my left elbow, bend my knees slightly, sit back on my heels, roll my left knee inward without lifting my toe, hold my head immobile, keep my eyes steadfastly on the ball, and *relax*, I would slowly sweep the driver to my right, carefully drawing it upward with a steady rotation of my shoulders until I was in perfect equipoise. Time would stop. Perfect so far.

But I still had to hit the little white sucker which would grin at me just as I began to uncoil. I invariably would give the ball a sidespin so vicious my stroke should have been studied by a physics lab. The ball usually would travel straight as an arrow for fifty yards before suddenly veering to the right at a ninety-degree angle and landing in the parking lot.

A guttural whine broke my reverie. I turned and watched an Alfa Romeo thread its way up the drive. The only Italian steel in the county of which I was aware had olive oil in it. I guessed the car belonged to Mulkerrin.

I watched her park and walk up the flagstone path to the porch. She had on a pastel-blue shirtdress with white pinstripes and high-heeled white sandals. I rose to meet her.

"I checked the obits before I drove out here," I said.

"I survived summers so hot muggers won't chase you," she replied, fluffing out her damp hair.

I led her to a table at the end of the porch in the deepest shade. Ancient live oaks wicked away the heat.

"Nice little men," Mulkerrin said. In reply, I nodded in the direction of the foursome in plus fours who looked like they escaped from the Mad Hatter's Tea Party. Mulkerrin shook her head and pointed to the two cast-iron statues of grooms holding lanterns who stood guard at the end of the flagstone path. After an acrimonious debate, the executive committee voted 4–3 to have the statues painted sky blue, which somehow made it worse.

"The lights work," I said. I wasn't a connoiseur of intergenerational guilt. I had enough of my own to keep me busy.

We served ourselves from the buffet. Thaddeus came around with a pitcher of iced tea with mint leaves thick as seaweed. She took a swallow and grimaced.

"Southern style. Pound of sugar per quart," I said.

"You were right about the prints," she said.

"Bobby told me."

"Any guesses who would want to ransack your office? Old girlfriends looking for love letters?"

"No one writes anymore, and I erase the messages on my answering machine." I laid down my fork and listened to the strumming of grasshoppers. A little breeze came out of nowhere.

"I've got a hunch the break-in at my office was related to the murder of Roger Dufault," I said.

"I'm listening," she said, leveling her eyes on mine.

"Roger had an angle on everything. Some angles are so sharp they cut." I took a sip of tea.

"Roger lived in the shadow of his dad. Vista Mer was going to be the big score that would cut him loose. He bought the Rivero track, ten acres of oceanfront, on spec for condo clusters. Other developers wouldn't touch it because it bordered a wetland. But someone had leaked Roger a draft of a corps of engineers report which said high-density development wouldn't hurt the wetland if a pumping station was put in.

"He counted on the report and political clout to get the permit from the Environmental Control Commission. Elliot Dean, the lieutenant governor, serves as chairman *ex officio* of the ECC. Roger had raised big bucks for Dean's campaign.

"Roger counted wrong. The ECC stalled him. By May, he was barely holding on. Roger needed fifty grand for interest payments and a second environmental impact study. CS&T refused to put another dime into the deal and no other bank would touch it.

"My guess is Roger went to see some guys who aren't FDIC insured. Guys who charge interest at fifty percent and make sure it's paid on Fridays. He couldn't make it. The wiseguys figured Roger wasn't good for the money but dead was a good example. Nothing personal. Just good business."

"So?" she asked, buttering a roll.

"So they find out I'm the administrator of Roger's estate. They hire some guys to break into my office to try to find documents which might tie Roger to them."

My theory didn't foot. I knew it as soon as I explained it. I had the sensation a trial lawyer gets when the jury starts looking at the ceiling fan during summation. Mulkerrin watched me for a while before speaking.

"Why the motel?" she asked. "Why run the risk of Mom and Pop in the next unit hearing Roger's head whacking the wall while they're watching Johnny Carson? Maybe they complain to the front desk guy who calls the cops. Set an example, sure, but don't wake the neighbors. Screw a silencer on a .22 semi. Makes about as much noise as a popcorn fart."

"That the kind of stuff they teach you at Fordham?"

Mulkerrin smiled and looked away.

She was right. Whoever had taken out Roger had made a mess of it.

"Besides," she continued, "what kind of document did they think they would find? A copy of a note made out by Dufault to the Federal Loan Shark Bank?"

My theory was as finely shredded as the cole slaw on my side plate.

"You made your case," I acknowledged.

"We got the coroner's preliminary report yesterday. Dufault was pistol whipped."

"That the cause of death?" I asked.

"Cause of the concussion anyway," she said, looking away.

"What else can you can tell me?" I asked.

"CS&T found a videocassette case. No tape. Just the case. We traced it to a firm in Germany, Brauner-Zweig, which makes videotapes specially engineered for low light. They run about two hundred dollars per."

I felt like somebody had rubbed dry ice along my spine.

"High-tech stuff," I managed to say.

"Not the kind of videotape you use to film your kid's birthday party. Unless you're having it in a bat cave."

She looked at her watch, frowned, pushed away from the table, and stood up.

"I've got a flight to meet at Richleigh," she said. "I'm not going to come close to making it if I don't leave this minute and forget about staying alive at fifty-five." She thanked me and was halfway down the steps before I could stand up.

I walked to the end of the porch to watch her hurry down the flagstone path to the parking lot. She looked good in a hurry. I thought about counting the freckles on her legs. It took my mind off considering that the Brauner-Zweig coincidence was just that.

The late-afternoon sunlight was slanting as I climbed the rise to the swimming pool. The generations still changed at five, just as they had when I had been the lifeguard in 1966.

A foursome of sweaty golfers, beers in hand, bellies jiggling, stripped off soaked shirts, unlaced spikes, and collapsed on lounge chairs to total their scores. Their wives, having slipped into one-pieces with skirts to shelter their thighs with more blue lines than topographical maps, migrated from the clubhouse veranda to the pool, carrying their gin and tonics, bridge hands, and gossip.

The mommies and kiddies had departed, leaving a film of peanut butter and chocolate on the tables near the wading pool and trash cans full of soggy diapers. The sunlight, filtered through the chain-link fence, cast a shadow of rhomboidal checks over the cracked concrete apron of the pool, making me think of mesh hose on bad legs. The hue of the chlorinated water deepened from pale blue to royal cobalt.

I had the lap lanes to myself. I swam a mile at a lazy pace, thinking about Peyton despite myself.

Midway through the summer Peyton's two-piece was replaced with an abbreviated version, the waistband of which failed to cover completely. It was a close enough resemblance to a bikini—or what passed for one in Chirkie County in 1966—to merit a letter from the executive committee to her parents. The old two-piece reappeared but Peyton defiantly rolled down the waistband.

I moved to the gentlemen's bar after a dinner of grilled shrimp and sautéed asparagus. I had a few beers to lay a foundation for sourmash. Whiskey on beer, never fear. I told myself that I wouldn't do it. That I would go directly home and get an early start on Sunday. (On what I didn't know.) But I knew the more I drank, the more likely it was that I would do it. And I wanted to so I had another double to make sure I did.

I called Peyton from the pay phone in the locker room. She sleepily said ''hello'' on the sixth ring. Kids are asleep, she said. Take off your shoes this time. Kitchen door isn't locked.

CHAPTER 5

I tried to work a hideously insistent buzzing into a dream I was having about babbling brooks and cool glades. The noise didn't fit. Peyton rolled over, smashed something, and the noise stopped.

"You, sir," Peyton said, a moment later, "are a user." She pulled on her panties and walked to the dresser. She shook a cigarette loose and lit it.

I pretended to be asleep.

"You hear me?" she said. "You're a goddamned user."

It was growing light. I shook a crumpled sheet, hoping my underwear would pop out. I wanted to be long gone before her kids woke up.

I also wanted the NFL All Pro defensive line to stop taking cha-cha lessons in the back of my head. I vaguely recalled having a few bourbons at the club, calling Peyton and having a few more with her in bed.

"C'mon, Peyton. Not even six," I said, wincing at the alarm clock. "Let's do this later."

"That's what you always say. Do it later. Put it off."

"I promise. We'll have a real talk. Soon." I motioned sleepily with my arm. "Come here."

She was sitting on the vanity, one leg drawn up under her chin, the other dangling, her heel angrily tapping a half-opened drawer. She reminded me of the general's mistress in a black-and-white French movie I had seen twenty years ago.

Peyton was wide-awake and ready to have at me. I guessed she had been on a low boil since before dawn. That I had been sleeping soundly made it worse. I could tell she had thought up some good lines while I dreamed of forest streams. I knew I wasn't going to get out of her bedroom without hearing them.

"Don't give me that 'come here' shit. You aren't going to fuck your way out of this. Not this time."

"You ever see this movie? Bardot plays this general's girlfriend? Filmed maybe in . . ."

"You're one of those men," Peyton said, ignoring me, "who are afraid of intimacy, who are incapable of making a commitment."

"No, I'm not," I said meekly, a second later recognizing the ambiguity in my answer.

"You know what they say about men who can't commit?" Peyton said.

"Where's my underwear? You seen it?"

"They say they're latent."

I was on my hands and knees, reaching under the bed, doing the underwear grope. I was considering suggesting there might be some antigravity phenomenon in her bedroom that dissolved jockey shorts when something hit me in the rump.

"What's this?" I said, picking up a fuzzy bedroom slipper with an animal's face on the toe. There were all kinds of weird things in her bedroom. Now they were flying around, attacking me.

"Latent, as in being a secret fag," she continued, ignoring me. I resisted the impulse to comment on the profundity of Peyton's analysis. Peyton's faith in the psychobabble she learned in beauty-and-fashion magazines was unshakable.

I studied the face. It looked like a bear, I decided.

"You," Peyton said with exasperation. "Not the frigging bunny slipper." She dropped her cigarette into a tumbler half full of whiskey and water.

"You mind giving me a hand here?" I asked as I rooted in a pile of dirty clothes beneath the window. The first, thin edge of the sun was peeping over the pine trees. Roger's black Lab managed a husky bark of greeting.

Peyton noisily sighed, angrily tossed her hair, and walked over. I slipped my arm around her and pushed her back on the bed. She started beating my shoulders, calling me a sonofabitch. Then she giggled, kissed me, arched her back, and slipped off her panties.

I reset the alarm for eight, left her sleeping, and slipped out the kitchen door. As I came around the side of the house I ran into the paper boy. He pretended not to see me. A small-town secret is an oxymoron.

I slowly drove south to the camp in the clear, early-morning light on old 723, a gravel track paralleling the Pascamany. I pulled over at Freer's Point and strolled down to the river. Limestone cliffs veined with quartz bounded the Pascamany at Freer's Point. I stared at the cliffs and yielded to the illusion they were flowing upstream. The concept of motion exists only because we supply the streambed of time. But, I wondered, when time itself is the stream, what is the streambed?

Peyton was wrong. It wasn't that I was incapable of making a commitment to her. She had been a part of my life for so long that it never occurred to me to make a decision to "commit." We had passed together from childhood to middle years. Memories of Peyton of various seasons and ages were indelibly part of myself, forming an unconscious bond more enduring than any contract of marriage.

Even when I was married to Renee—indeed, all the more so—I never stopped thinking of Peyton. Memories of first loves form a counterpoint to the melody of marriage which inevitably becomes a domestic refrain. When the refrain grates, we find refuge in memories saved from routine's scouring.

✳

The Friday which marked the end of Horton Military Academy's fall term coincided with the 1965 Christmas Cotillion. I didn't have anything else to do, so I yielded to Mother's urging that I attend. But I defied her instruction to sit in the backseat of the Chrysler when Olmie drove me to the club. You're just being contrary, Mother scolded. You know full well you're old enough now to sit in the backseat.

I wore my dress uniform, complete with brevets, marksmanship (first class) medal, and sash. That I did not give it a second thought and none of my peers thought it untoward speaks volumes about the South of 1965.

I hung out with the stags, clustered around Tim Dugan, who knew the combination to his father's liquor locker. Tim was negotiating favors in return for the liquor we knew he would steal anyway. Finally the price was set: Porky Bryan promised to try to grind Lucille Prentiss the next time a slow dance was played and I swore I would ask Mrs. Dufault, one of the chaperons, to dance the twist. Tim grudgingly departed, pretending to have been raped by the bargain, after receiving Porky's further agreement that a grind meant both hands on Lucille's substantial rump, girdled as taut as a snare drum.

I downed a half-tumbler of Coca-Cola and mostly rum to brace myself for honoring my promise. Tim, always one to squeeze a bargain, informed me that my promise implicitly obliged me to pivot on my toes and shake my butt at Mrs. Dufault. I was considering what General Horton would think of a cadet in dress gray shaking his butt (up and down and sideways, Tim demanded) at a middle-aged lady when I heard giggles from a bevy of girls clustered around Peyton, resplendent in a red satin gown. Two strands, the diameter of six-pound test nylon filament fishing line, kept Peyton's crimson gown from being an illegal strapless. Her hair was piled up and tied with a matching bow. She was wearing satin high heels of the same hue.

Peyton never lacked for retainers, so grateful to bask in her glory, they failed to notice their presence served only to accentuate her beauty. Peyton drew an endless succession of plain girls, moons to her sun, into her orbit. Decades later, emboldened and embittered, these same girls would remember their homage and hate Peyton for it.

I watched Peggy Flynn cross the ballroom and hand a folded note to the disc jockey. A minute later the opening notes of "Soldier Boy" mingled with giggles from the girls' side. Pey-

ton, her eyes locked on mine, crossed the parquet and took my hand. I would have walked onto the floor holding my glass of rum and Coke had Tim not grabbed it.

Peyton had a teasing aloofness about her which hinted at reckless possibilities and challenged you to call her bluff. Peyton's eyes let you know that, notwithstanding Tri Hi Y, Library Council, Christian Youth Fellowship, and Girl's State, she really wasn't a nice girl. Just dare me, her eyes said. But I never did, keeping a proper six inches as we slow danced. I kept silent, not trusting my intuition and afraid of making a fool of myself; afraid of Peyton pushing away from me, tossing back her head and laughing, then regaining her composure and saying, I don't believe you really said that, Lawd, I don't. But my greater fear was guessing right and hearing her whisper, yes.

❋

Mother, freshly divorced and traveling in Europe in the spring of 1966, wrote long letters, which wryly described improbably comic situations into which she had fallen and from which she, plucky ingenue of forty-two, cleverly had extricated herself. She applied a touch of self-deprecating charm as if it were blusher to take the hard sheen off her can-do attitude. Mother declined to mention with whom she was traveling, but I didn't really care.

Mother returned to Lassington in late April and told me she was engaged to marry Dr. Richard Stealey, a nationally prominent urologist and her distant cousin from Atlanta whom I knew had been her companion on the Grand Tour. Richard had been called to consult to President Johnson, she explained, as if there were a connection between Dr. Stealey palpating the President's prostrate and winning her hand.

Mother mentioned Peyton was wearing Roger's class ring and Mrs. Dufault was having conniptions. I sensed Mother knew—although I had never hinted at any interest in Peyton—I would be more interested in the latter than the former news. Peyton had no idea, of course, that every wind sprint I ran, I ran for her.

I wrangled a home pass to coincide with an interprep cross-country meet held in May. Horton Military Academy had been invited to the Cupp Challenge, hosted by Lancaster Academy located in the tony west end of Richleigh. To get the pass, I had expanded Father's promise to try to attend the meet to the assurance, conveyed to Captain Pendergast, that my father would pick me up at the meet and drive me to Lassington.

I finished a close second. Father was nowhere to be found. I quickly changed into civies and left by the back gate before Captain Pendergast could revoke my pass. A few minutes later, I hitched a ride on a milk truck which took me most of the way to Lassington. I hadn't called, hoping to surprise Mother. I learned from Olmie that she was in Washington with Doctor Dick the dick doctor, as Olmie delighted in calling Dr. Stealey. Olmie fixed me a skillet of scrambled eggs, tomatoes in corn-meal, and scrapple.

After supper I sat on the side porch. The breeze was cool and redolent of burning leaves. I went for a walk and ended up at the State Theatre where a James Bond movie was playing. It wasn't until I was in line that I noticed Roger and Peyton. They were holding hands, twenty feet ahead of me.

Roger every now and then would turn his head and whisper to Peyton who would toss her hair, push Roger away, laugh just for him, and then, after a few seconds, reach again for his hand. Finally something Roger said caused Peyton to form her red lips into an ''O'' of mock protest, fold her hands across her pink angora sweater, and pirouette away from him. Peyton saw me and waved merrily. She grabbed Roger's arm and pointed to me.

Peyton whispered to Roger, who seemed to hesitate before giving me the thumbs-up sign. Roger flipped a bill to the counter girl and picked his way through the line to greet me. He slapped my back and pressed a ticket into my hand. You're sitting with us soldier boy, he commanded.

The three of us—Peyton between us—sat in the darkest part of the balcony. Around us, couples groaned and twisted in im-possible contortions, struggling to overcome armrests. I glanced to my left and saw that Roger had draped his arm around Pey-ton's shoulders. Under cover of my jacket I gingerly probed with my left hand below the armrest.

Roger's attitude, I later realized, made me do it. I sensed

Roger's expansiveness was premised on his assurance I posed no threat to his relationship with Peyton. Had he shown a modicum of respectful wariness, maybe all of it never would have happened.

I probed gently with my fingertips until I touched Peyton's hand. She took my hand, then twined her fingers with mine. I waited what seemed an eternity to cast a glance at Peyton. She was staring at the film, her profile silver in light reflected by the screen.

Peyton must have felt my glance. She gave me a smile so quick I might have imagined it. Then, with her gaze fixed steadfastly on the film, Peyton drew my hand under her skirt and pressed it deep between her thighs.

Get your ass down here for Chuggers Week, Roger had demanded during a late-night phone call. Fix you up with a little honey, friend of Peyton's, who can suck a tennis ball through a garden hose. We'll take the KA barge out on the lake and have a hell of a time. Guarangoddamnteed.

Roger's invitation was perfectly timed. By mid-April, 1969, I had stood all I could stand of the dithering, stalling wet season which in New Haven passed for spring. A few crocuses had poked shy heads from muddy beds. That and the lengthening of the days were the only changes marking winter's end.

My sophomore spring at Yale had been marked by the publication of my essay on "Faulkner and Southern Romanticism" in The Yale Review *and a hot-cold, topsy-turvy relationship with Renee Randolph, of the lesser but richer Richleigh Randolphs, which had me commuting between New Haven and Northampton. Renee and I had just broken up for the third time in as many weeks.*

Remington State University, where Roger and Peyton had enrolled—he to play football, she to lead cheers—was located in the mountainous southwest corner of the state. RSU was famed as a party school, a reputation enhanced by Lake Traynor, the result of a hydroelectric dam which in 1962 flooded Craver Creek Valley. Protests by families that for centuries had farmed the narrow valley had been drowned out by campaign contributions from pulp mill owners desirous of cheap electricity and property owners (rumored to include friends and family of Governor Traynor and Senate Majority Leader Randolph Higgins) cheered by the prospect of recently acquired acreage fortuitously becoming the shoreline of a twelve-hundred-acre lake.

I drove along the Blue Ridge Parkway. The southern highlands were awash in pink and white dogwood petals. I took my time, stopping at overlooks, overwhelmed by the beauty of the Appalachian spring and wondering to what form of dementia my decision to go north to college could be ascribed.

I arrived at the north shore of Lake Traynor in the early afternoon of Good Friday, 1969. Roger's directions were not exact and it took me a half-hour to find the A-frame he shared with Peyton in the hills above Lake Traynor.

When no one answered my knock, I walked around to the deck which overlooked the lake. Peyton was lying facedown on a low chaise covered with a Confederate battle flag fashioned from terry cloth. Her head, turned toward the lake, rested on her folded arms. A pair of sunglasses, resting in the center of a textbook, kept the breeze from turning the pages. The planks creaked when I stepped onto the deck. I coughed. Peyton didn't move.

I started to call her name, but held back, stirred by the graceful sweep of her naked back, dappled by sunlight filtered by the towering pines. A fickle breeze riffled her long blond hair and whipped the dangling strings of her bikini top. I watched her until I could detect the almost imperceptible rise and fall of her breathing.

Two whiskey barrels holding dense clusters of jonquils marked the corners of the deck. I stepped between them and gazed at the lake below. The teal-blue water, scalloped by the breeze, yielded to the smoky blue of the far hills, which segued into a cloudless sky of robin's-egg blue. I listened to the whisking of the pines, hearing taunts in their whispers.

The stillness was strangely charged. It was one of those rare moments when the present, viewed as the past from the perspective of the future, is suspended.

After what seemed minutes—but it could have been seconds—Peyton turned her head toward me and slowly opened her pale-blue eyes. She showed no surprise. She met my gaze with an intensity I can shut my eyes and still feel, a burning sensation behind my eyelids.

Peyton lazily turned on her back and slipped off her bikini bottom. "It's all right," she said, holding out her arms.

✳

Roger married Peyton in June 1975. Renee and I missed the service but arrived in time for the reception, along with two hundred guests and a band which played swing and soul.

Peyton pulled me on the floor when the band struck up "Sunday Kind of Love." You know, she whispered, I was waiting for you. But I should have known I wasn't good enough for the likes of you. After you went and got engaged to that Richleigh society bitch with pencil legs, I gave up. But giving up don't mean you forget.

I mumbled something about how we could always be friends. Fuck being friends, Peyton whispered, leaning away from me and smiling demurely, as the music died.

✳

After I graduated from the university law school in 1976, I accepted a position as an associate at Calley & Penderson, the second largest firm in Richleigh. Despite misgivings I decided to give it a try because of prestige and Renee who, Richleigh born and bred, regarded Lassington as an outpost on the frontier of society. Two bad reasons, as it turned out.

I was assigned to work with Mr. Calley, supposedly an honor due to my law-school record. Mr. Calley, who always wore an expression which made me think he was constipated, shamelessly claimed credit for the briefs I wrote even though he rarely changed a word. He promised me courtroom experience, but in two years the only courtroom I saw was when I was carrying a partner's brief case. I spent my days in the library polishing memoranda while Renee polished her backhand at Foxwood Country Club, the preserve of old money Richleigh. Her mother detailed Cornelia, who had been Renee's nanny, to take care of Martha, born in the summer of 1978.

I was so bored I used to make bets with the other associates on the end of day readings on the photocopiers. I ended up getting involved in more than research with the assistant law librarian who had an apartment a half-block from the office. My job and marriage both folded in 1980 and I moved back to Lassington so I could live rent-free at the camp. But, deep down inside, I knew it was more than that.

The real-estate work Roger referred got me started in my own practice. At the time, I hadn't known an easement from an encroachment and told Roger so. But it hadn't mattered to him. Learn on the job, he told me, and I did. I relished being self-employed and was grateful to Roger. As General Development Corporation prospered, so did my law practice.

I saw a lot of Peyton. More than I wanted to, maybe. But there wasn't any way to avoid it, Chirkie County society being as incestuous as the Hapsburgs. Our social kisses and hugs had lingered too long. There had been more touching than could be explained even by the breezy manners, founded on whiskey and flirting, of country club society. If we weren't fanning flames, Peyton and I at least were poking embers. But it was play-acting, I had thought. There were lines that couldn't be crossed, limits that kept it safe.

✵

There is no logic to memories, no accounting for why we recall vividly odd fragments of conversations or scenes extracted seemingly at random from days devoid of significance. We are left to turn over and over in our minds these exemplars of the banal, left to wonder why these few and not others from our millions of impressions have been heaved from the unconscious to the crannies of our conscious minds where they strangely lurk, perhaps as runes.

I remember a Sunday morning in the fall of 1981. Peyton had given birth to Ann Clair in the spring of the year.

"Sweet Jesus save us," Mother had whispered as Peyton and her mother, Janet, passed our pew, halting a few yards from the communion rail, waiting their turn at the Lord's Table. "Sheath skirt to matins. I declare. How does Janet think she's going to kneel in that thing?"

I didn't respond. I was entranced by how the little raspberry-colored, kidney-shaped birthmark on Peyton's left calf seemed to change shape as she shifted her weight from one high heel to the other. I had studied Peyton's legs for years but had never noticed that before.

" 'Course, maybe that's the point,'' Mother whispered as Peyton and her mother moved a few steps closer to the rail.

Peyton suddenly turned her head and caught me staring. She smiled over her shoulder and winked. I flushed. It happened in a half-second, but Mother didn't miss it. She didn't miss much.

"Look at you,'' Mother whispered. "Ought to be ashamed. Communion wine wet on your lips and lust burning in your heart.''

"Hush, Mother,'' I hissed, staring straight ahead, feeling the heat in my face. I held my breath as Peyton knelt. I caught a glimpse of the back of her thighs before she smoothed out her skirt. Mrs. Winifree managed to fold slowly into a kneeling position without splitting her skirt.

"Cupcakes,'' Mother confided. "Pair of cupcakes. One's stale and the other's icing has been licked by half the county.''

"Enough, Mother.''

"You got more sense than that, don't you,'' she demanded. I ignored her.

"If you had enough sense to pass it up, you ought to have enough sense not to regret it.''

I focused on the stained-glass window behind the altar, keeping my eyes off Peyton.

"She's not of our class, dear,'' Mother added, patting my hand.

"Plus she's married,'' I hissed. "So what in hell are you worried about?'' I jerked my hand away.

"If she weren't married, I wouldn't worry,'' Mother replied. "You don't think I'd worry about you being serious about her, do you?''

One warm June evening two years ago, Roger, Peyton, Eileen Goodmae, and I were cracking crabs at Wooster's Crab House. Picking crab meat is tedious work justified only as an excuse for drinking pitchers of beer. One pitcher per dozen crabs is the standard pace. We were well ahead of schedule that night, with Roger accounting for most of our lead.

Midway through our fifth pitcher of beer, Peyton kicked off her sandal and, under cover of the red-and-white checked oil-cloth which draped to the sawdust-covered floor, massaged my crotch, not looking at me, talking to Eileen all the while about how stuck up the new PTA president was. A few weeks later, I came home to find Peyton in bra and panties, drinking beer and watching TV in my bedroom. The Braves lose because they don't know what they want, she said, clicking off the set. I do. We presented bills for years of teasing. Hard and fast, verging on violent, then sweet and lulling. A raging sea or a moonlit, glass-smooth bay.

We became a bad habit that neither of us could kick. Every two weeks or so Peyton would telephone, always late at night, and I'd meet her the following afternoon. Before we began, we would swear to each other that this was absolutely, positively the very last time. That we imagined we were sincere spurred our passion. Afterward we would drive in silence to Peyton's Range Rover, parked behind the little AME Zion church, two miles from the camp, at the end of the dirt road. She would get out quickly without looking at me. A week or two would go by. Then the phone would ring late at night. Peyton would say four o'clock and hang up.

CHAPTER 6

On the last Tuesday in July I decided to drive to Waterston.
I wanted to check the inventory of Niles's estate and law school
yearbooks. About twenty miles east of Waterston the billboards
appear. They advertise the University Lodge, University Diner,
University Dry Cleaner, University Podiatrist, University
Plumber, and so on. I parked in the University Parking Garage
and ordered a grapefruit half at the lunch counter of the University Rexall. I took the grapefruit out of the bowl and examined
the rind to see if it had University stamped on it.

I paid for my coffee and grapefruit and walked across the
campus to the law school. The Legacy of the Law, which
adorned the foyer above the marble paneling, greeted me when
I entered Milton hall. The overwrought panels of the mural
were rendered in the diverse styles of a WPA project.

A very large and white God hands down the Ten Command-
ments to a frail Moses who looks like God's grandfather. In the
next panel, Moses passes on scrolls (through some anonymous
intermediaries with beards and tunics, then clean-shaven and
togas) to a guy with blond ringlets topped by a laurel wreath.
Caesar passes a scroll to a troll-like creature with a furry shield
whose brows need landscaping.

This creature, probably an Irish artist's depiction of a Saxon
king, tenders a sheaf to an English gentleman, recognizable by

his pursed mouth, disdainful expression, white stockings, and powdered periwig tied with a red ribbon. The gentleman presents a bound volume to a man in buckskins who looks like he cut his hair with a broadaxe. The frontiersman, in turn, delivers a set of volumes to a somber delegation of men and women (in the rear, wearing bonnets) who appear to be refugees from a convention of pension actuaries.

I climbed the stairs to the law library. It took me a few minutes to find the yearbooks. I started with the 1973 edition of *Bellies to the Bar* and worked through the years, in a manner of speaking. The 1989 yearbook was the first to be paperbound, an economy emblematic of the new age of austerity.

I made a list of Niles's student assistants. Then I crossindexed names with addresses in student directories for the corresponding years. Niles's student assistants had resided at the apartment at Chez Niles. Each had been single, white, law review, male, and had amassed a block of credits in fine print.

I skimmed the pages of the 1976 edition of *Bellies to the Bar*, recognizing more faces than names, until I found my photograph. Big grin, Buffalo Bill mustache, and T-shirt. Screw the tie. Be the Wild One.

I looked up Rosalyn Cubertson. Skin the color of café au lait, jet-black hair and eyes, regal forehead, and thin, enigmatic smile. Cleopatra as a third-year law student, posed above a quarter-page listing of honors and accolades. I surprised myself by remembering most of them. But then Cubertson was hard to forget. She made sure of that.

Cubertson had been president of the Madison Society, the elite debating society almost as old as the university but arguably more prestigious. Mad Socs kept to themselves, hanging out at the Federal period three-story townhouse owned by the society's foundation. Being elected president was a singular honor which Cubertson trumped by being elected as a black, female neoconservative. Her achievement made the front page of the *Richleigh Journal*. Cubertson's subsequent criticisms of affirmative action were lauded by the national conservative press.

Cubertson, who had been chairlady of the Young Republicans, and Elliot Dean had been political rivals, but without rancor. There seemed more than détente between them, perhaps understanding and, maybe, secret winks. But that was supposition on my part.

I flipped through the pages until I found the photograph of Elliot, who had been Niles's student assistant during 1975–1976. Dean's credits almost ran off the page.

I studied Dean's photograph. Purposeful young man on the way up was the message. The photograph was a half-profile view, the same pose Dean later used for his campaign posters. An upward tilt of his head, combined with a quarter rotation toward the camera, deemphasized Dean's nose, a little hooked, his only bad feature. Neatly trimmed blond hair, tie properly knotted and drawn flush against a button-down collar. Thin, clean-cut face with prominent cheekbones. Flash of white teeth lighting up a shy smile, the same smile Olmie had admired in the *Standard*'s photograph of us.

The Rotarians had asked me to wear my Horton Military Academy dress uniform to the honors luncheon, which I finally did, after sparring with Mother for two days. Just do it for your old Mother, she had pleaded. It was the last time I wore a uniform. Elliot, valedictorian of the graduating class at Chirkie County High School, wore a blue suit with lapels which spread almost to the shoulder seams. It looked like a leftover from the Kefauver hearings.

The photographer for the Lassington Standard *had posed us shaking hands in front of the white satin Rotarian Club banner which draped the podium of the Holiday Inn banquet room. George Carey, soon to be Judge Carey, beamed down at us. I whispered to Dean, "This is ten pounds of crap in a five-pound bag," which made Dean smile just as the shutter clicked.*

The next day when I came down to breakfast, I found Olmie seated at the kitchen table studying the front page of the Standard. *I looked over her shoulder and saw the photograph, midway down the page. The story ran under the headline, "Brainy Buddies Take Top Honors: Dean and Wilkinson are Valedictorians." Just look at that Dean's smile, Olmie said. Natural born politician for the life of me. Now just look at you, Olmie*

*scolded. Shame on you. Looks like you was fixing to swallow
a furry tongue.*

✳

Mother, together with the rest of the county, somehow assumed that Dean and I, by virtue of both having been valedictorians, were locked in mortal competition. For what, I had no
idea. Perhaps for top honors in life, whatever that is supposed
to be.

After I enrolled at Yale, Mother made a point of keeping me
posted on Elliot's latest achievement at the university. Although
her transparent motive grated, I looked forward to her reports.
I was curious about Dean, but in a way not altogether whole-
some. My curiosity was akin to that which secretly draws fans
to stock car races. I had a sense Dean was wound too tightly,
that he was on the verge of crashing and burning. I had taken
up writing, which furnished me with an excuse for wanting to
have a front-row seat when it occurred.

No telling, Mother said, what that Dean boy might amount
to, if he had all the God-given advantages you take for granted.
Poor boy's daddy ran off when he was ten, leaving him with
a chippie for a mother and hardly a pot to pee in. Yet look at
all that boy's accomplished. Phi Beta Kappa as a junior and
president of the student government at the university.

Just like Jesus said. The good steward takes his talents and
invests them and reaps a harvest. The lazy one buries his talents
in his backyard. You know what happens, don't you?

His dog digs them up, I said.

The master returns and demands an accounting from the lazy
steward, the one with all the God-given advantages. Lesson
there to take deep into your heart. As the Bible says, if the
shoe fits, wear it.

The Bible doesn't say that about the shoe, I said.

Nothing in it either about a dog digging up the master's
talents, but that didn't stop you, Mother replied.

Wouldn't hurt you one little bit to have ambition like Dean.
Of course, now you're a literary gentleman, you look down on
trying to get ahead, going after honors, getting elected student
government president, common things like that.

Résumé padding is all it is, I said. Mickey Mouse crap.

Just the same, Mister High and Mighty, it wouldn't hurt your résumé one bit to get elected to a few things. Particularly if you're planning to go to law school.

I don't know what I'm planning. I know I'm not going to kiss ass just to add a few lines to a résumé.

Son, Mother said, that kind of attitude might be fine at Yale College. I know that's what they teach up there. Search for meaning and only do meaningful things, twenty-four hours a day, seven days a week.

It's called cutting out the bullshit, I replied.

It's called romantic nonsense, Mother said. With that kind of attitude, you end up picking petty battles in the name of grand principles. You end up fighting banalities and becoming banal as a result. It's the very reason I tried to dissuade your poor, bedeviled father from sending you to Yale.

I didn't reply. When Mother was on a roll, there was no stopping her.

You know the difference between you and Dean, she asked.

I've had all the advantages, you keep telling me.

True, Mother replied. But, in another way, compared to the Dean boy, you suffer from a great disadvantage. Dean doesn't give a second thought to what you call Mickey Mouse crap. And, of course, you're right. It *is* crap. But that's not the point, is it?

You don't need to tell me again about Dean's ambition, I answered.

Dean pays no mind to what you want to turn into a matter of high principle. Dear, don't you understand that an ambition on fire burns off the dross?

An ambition on fire is a fuse, I replied, without thinking.

※

Dean spent his second and third years at the law school as Niles's student assistant researching topics on limited partnership syndications, research which led to a job at Banks & Worth in Richleigh.

With income tax rates topping out at fifty percent (seventy percent on investment income), tax shelters were hot issues in the seventies. The economics of real estate didn't matter as much as finding structures that on paper could be divided into components depreciated on aggressive schedules. With a two to one write-off, the deal broke even for investors in the fifty percent bracket even if there was no cash flow.

Partners at Banks & Worth didn't do the detail work. The wordsmithing was left to worker bees like Dean who churned out billable hours, weekend after weekend, while the partners guzzled on G&T's at their beach houses.

Dean was in too much of a hurry to wait in line for eight years with the other associates on the promise of a turn at the trough. He had mastered the offering circulars, partnership agreements, and the rest of the boilerplate. All he needed was product, a CPA willing to do the financials on spec, and marketing reps.

There was no time to waste. Eventually, the supply of doctors eager to attend seminars at Ramada Inns on "tax sheltered investments" would dry up. Or hard questions would be asked about what happens when tax benefits are depleted and the mortgage still has twenty years to run. A seller's market in unreality couldn't last. Of course, no one could foresee that unreality would be carried to a splendid new level with Reagan's Tax Reform Act of 1981. That for Dean was simply a lucky break.

Dean found an ally in Charles Varret, a junior partner in the Richleigh office of Westin & Rhodes, a national CPA firm. Varret was thirty, the only child of a Richleigh grand dame, and bored to death with anything which remotely involved financial accounting standards. Dean, Varret & Co., formed in time to ride the last wave of the Carter-era tax shelters, was able to obtain a broker/dealer license not long after it opened its door.

✳

I borrowed the alumni directory from the reference librarian and looked up the sixteen names on my list of Niles's student assistants. Besides Dean, many were names in the news. Remmer was a federal judge. Niles's SA in 1979, Mike Ryan, was the United States attorney for our district. Billings was undersecretary of state for economic affairs. Bushnell was executive editor of *USA Insights*. Travis was a syndicated columnist. Two were congressmen. The rest were partners in white shoe firms, law professors, and investment bankers. Niles had a knack for picking winners.

I left the law school and walked the eight blocks to Auburn Square where Waterston Commonwealth Bank was lodged in faux Greek-revival splendor. I told the receptionist I had an appointment with Mr. Hewins. A secretary led me to a windowless third-floor office.

Niles's estate hadn't been large enough to rate a vice president. The young man behind the toy desk looked like a Boy Scout working on a merit badge in estate administration. Mr. Hewins had a handshake which felt like a small fish wiggling. He fumbled through the papers on his desk and found a copy of the preliminary accounting and inventory. It was neat, thorough, looked better than preliminary, and didn't mention either Vista Mer or Addio.

Hewins was crestfallen when I asked if he possibly could have overlooked shares of stock in a corporation known as Addio or a joint-venture certificate for Vista Mer. In response he pulled out a loose-leaf notebook and gave me ten minutes on the thoroughness of trust department procedures. Just the same, I said. Let me know if any assets have the nerve to show up uninvited and ruin your preliminary accounting. Hewins said he would. He was twenty-five going on fifty, the kind of detail-oriented, dutiful person who makes civilization possible for the rest of us. I considered telling him so but held back, fearing Hewins might pull out another manual.

I made it back to Lassington by three, in time to stop by the office, return a few phone calls, edit the letters and pleadings Anita had transcribed, and ease my conscience by putting in enough billable time to cover my overhead for the day. Then I phoned Tim Dugan and talked him into meeting me at the club for tennis.

I had been playing tennis with Tim for better than thirty years. I beat him when he was lazy or hung over, which meant

I won better than half of our matches. Peyton said Tim would make a fine ne'er-do-well if he had more energy.

I had been Tim's lawyer on a few occasions. I had never sent him a bill and he had never offered to pay, although after I got Bobby Vecchio to *noll pross* the marijuana distribution rap, Tim had offered to set me up with a hot babe in Richleigh. Tim probably regarded that as payment of sorts, but I turned down the offer, which eased both our consciences.

Mother once remarked that if there had been more unity of purpose to Tim's meanderings he at least could have claimed he was trying to find himself. I told her Tim had never lost himself. The unfolding process of being Tim was fascinating to Tim, the jewel in the lotus. Unaided by mantra or koan and, apparently, guilelessly, Tim had attained a state of self-absorption in equipoise. In a more tolerant and spiritually richer culture, Tim might have been appreciated as a buddha. But in the mercantile culture of Chirkie County, Tim was generally regarded as an indolent, narcissistic cad who at forty continued to sponge off his mother, rumored to be even wealthier than she tried to appear.

Anyone with a good, top-spin backhand can't be all bad. Tim beat me 6–4, 3–6, 7–5. I didn't quibble about a few of Tim's line calls at 5–5 in the third set that had a foursome watching from the nearby tee shaking their heads and groaning. I was playing to burn off the University Special, not win the Queen's Cup. Besides, I had in mind having a few beers with Tim and talking about Vista Mer.

In the locker room, Tim reached ahead of me to take the last clean towel.

"Only fat golfers sweat a lot," Tim said, which I took to be an apology of sorts.

"Gotta fully extend on your overheads." Tim twisted the towel between his toes. "Getting sloppy."

"I'll buy you a beer," I replied. "Meet me at the bar when you're through."

"No can do. Got one waiting with her oven on." Tim slowly picked at his gnarled toenails with a paper clip he had straightened. I hoped for her sake the oven was turned down low.

I told Tim I had a few questions about Vista Mer, which elicited a complaint about Peyton's unwillingness to honor Roger's promise to split a commission.

"Ever hear the name Niles Nesbitt?" I asked.

"Cracker? Wheat woven together?" Tim asked absentmindedly. "Mind moving out of the light?" He had reached the acute stage in cuticle surgery.

"How about the name Addio?" I asked.

"As in 'Addio Amigo'? Sure," Tim said.

"It's 'Adiós Amigo'," I replied.

Tim rattled off a few phrases, which, given my limited knowledge of Spanish, I interpreted as the expression of a desire to ride a wet donkey.

"Know what I just said?" Tim asked.

I declined to supply my translation.

"It's what you say to close a hot señorita," Tim said, in a tone which meant he had won the point. He picked up the paper clip and resumed work.

"Speaking of señoritas," he continued. "I caught Roger 'crossing' couple of days before some 'ol boy beat his head into hamburger. High-yellow gal."

"Who was she?" I asked.

"No idea. Pass me your towel."

"Where'd you see Roger?" I asked.

"Laurie and I drove out to Vista Mer, figuring to blow weed on the beach. Laurie likes to zone out and grok waves. Real turn on for her. Get her hips pumping. You know what I'm saying?"

I replied I got the picture. Tim thought of himself as a subtle devil.

"So we pulled in the back section and goddamned if there wasn't a red 280SL sitting there. One I would kill for. I recognized Roger right off. I said to Laurie, sumbitch's going for a header. 'Cause there ain't enough room for anything else. In the Benz, I mean."

Tim looked at me until I nodded to show I understood.

"So we pull up beside the Benz," he continued. "Check and see who the babe is. Keep track, you know?" I nodded again.

"Roger tells me to get the fuck away. His gal turns her head away. Uppity bitch. All I see is black hair, wraparound shades, and earrings. Noticed one thing, though. Richleigh sticker on the windshield.''

It was getting late. I thanked Tim for the tennis and zipped up my gym bag.

"Hey, Ken-dog,'' Tim said as I was leaving. "Be a pal. Show me a copy of Mom's will. We're buddies.''

Tim suddenly appeared downcast. I guessed he was lamenting his mother's robust health.

I had a hearing in the morning. My client, Arnold, a sheet metal mechanic, had been several hours late returning Missy to Mom on two consecutive weekends. On the last occasion Arnold had whiskey breath and was accompanied by his new squeeze, who was not much older than Missy.

Mom had retained Elizabeth Rhodes. She wanted Carey to enter an order suspending Arnold's visitation rights.

Carey was more interested in Mom's testimony about the whiskey breath than the tardiness. Arnold, ignoring my advice, couldn't resist expounding on his theory that whiskey makes for safer driving. See, Judge, a pop or two chills me out. Like I'm not minding when a dude be riding up on my tail. Be cool and drive cool.

It turned out during cross-examination that Arnold and his girlfriend had been passing a pint back and forth waiting for the drawbridge to close. Carey entered an order which provided for suspension of visitation rights if Arnold so much as had a light beer when driving Missy back to Mom.

After Carey left the bench, Arnold asked what the fuck went down, implying what the fuck was wrong with me for letting Rhodes get away with this outrage. I asked Arnold if he ever heard of breath mints. Ain't no way the judge could smell my breath from way over there, Arnold replied.

After lunch I went to see Brenda Stern, who had been deputy clerk in charge of Chirkie County land records since the day the Lord caused the waters to recede and looked with favor on the land. She loved her records and her Juicy Fruit. Brenda's idea of goofing off was an extra cup of coffee at her Monday-morning break. Every lawyer in the county had immense respect for Brenda. She was at least a rock if not our salvation.

She brought me the books I needed. I checked the grantor-grantee indices and did a perfunctory bringdown on the title of Vista Mer. Neither Niles nor Addio appeared in the chain of title.

I returned to my office and asked Anita to check with the Corporation Commission in Richleigh. She reported a few minutes later that there was no record of Addio, Inc., either formed under state law or as a registered corporation.

I placed a call to Rosalyn Cubertson. My only contact with her since law school had occurred four years ago when I had succeeded in enjoining a foreclosure by her client, a New Jersey mortgage firm, on a small farm owned by two elderly spinsters. Cubertson was in conference when I called. It was half past five and I was on my way out the door when Cubertson called me back.

"So how are the weird sisters?" Cubertson asked in a clipped, accentless voice. "Still hunting toads to toss in their pot? Double, double, toil and trouble?" Cubertson laughed. When I didn't say anything she added, "Shakespeare."

Her voice sounded like it was coming from a cave. I could hear her rustling papers.

"Ethel and Hilda crossed the bar two years ago," I answered. "Within six months of each other."

"Bit old for law school, weren't they?" she asked.

"Tennyson," I said. "They're dead."

"Oh, dear. Well, on that cheery note, what can I do for you?"

"I'm calling about a corporation named Addio. Ever hear of it?"

"Addio," she repeated slowly. "Should it?" Her voice suddenly was clear and close. She had picked up the handset. "No. I don't recall that name."

I started to mention the letter from Niles I had found in Roger's office. But, for some reason, I held back.

"You heard Niles died three weeks ago," I said.

"Of course," she replied huffily. "I tried to rearrange my

schedule so I could attend the funeral, but I couldn't get loose. Success can be a prison, can't it?''

"Niles told me in June about a real-estate venture he was involved in," I replied. "He said you were helping him. I think the name was Addio. Something like that.''

"I don't recall any Addio," Cubertson said slowly. "Niles rang me up now and then to cadge a freebee, try to find out if I knew any LBO in the works so he could hitch a ride on the stock of the target. That kind of thing. But I don't recall the name Addio.''

"Niles ever mention an investment in Vista Mer?" I asked.

"Project down your way that had environmentalists hot and bothered," Cubertson asked. "Ended up taking the big B, right?''

"That's the one," I said.

"Never," she replied. "My turn?''

"For what?" I replied.

"To ask questions.''

"Sure," I agreed.

"What are you looking for?''

"Nothing specific," I said. "Just trying to help straighten out Niles's affairs. I'm co-executor of his estate. Tie down some loose ends.'' I waited for her to respond. When she didn't, I thanked her for returning my call.

"Give me a cite," Cubertson said.

"To what?''

"That Tennyson line. I can work it into speeches. Passing the bar as crossing the bar. Self-effacing humor. Lay audiences will eat it up.''

I said I would send her a copy of the poem, thanked her again, and rang off.

CHAPTER 7

My client, Clarissa Joiner, was forty-five, the wife of a sergeant at Statler and charged with embezzling $2,257.32 from Mel's Home and Garden.

During our initial interview, Clarissa ran through a repertoire of mannerisms as stylized as t'ai chi. She held up her cigarette expectantly until finally I reached in the bottom drawer, came up with a Dunhill (one of Roger's), and gave her a light. She inhaled deeply, cocked her head, slowly exhaled a plume, put her hand on mine, and asked if I realized I was her only hope. I asked a background question on her training as a bookkeeper which she took as a cue to detail her martyrdom as the artistically talented wife of a noncom whose sole passion was to finish his twenty years and get his pension.

I guessed she probably had pulled the same story on Mel. I could see him being attracted by her fatigued, frail prettiness. Bottom-feeder guys like Mel are suckers for bruised vulnerability. Mel wasn't bright enough to realize he was being cast in a supporting role. Mine, I guessed, was Bogart to her Bacall.

Clarissa admitted she had given herself loans from the cash drawer. She claimed Mel encouraged her to make little loans to herself. She said Mel was always hanging around, asking if her neck was stiff from bending over the ledgers and offering to give her a massage.

I told Vecchio that I was authorized to offer a guilty plea if he would reduce the charge to a misdemeanor. Vecchio replied he could have papered his office with the printout he got when he keyed Clarissa's social security number into the fed's computer. Just for you, Peckerwood, he said, I'll go restitution, five-hundred-dollar fine, ninety days in the county cooler, and two years on probation.

Not great, but it gave me a little to work with. After I gave Clarissa a frank assessment of her chances, she sniffed and told me to cut a deal so long as it didn't involve jail time.

I started to tell Clarissa that Bobby's offer was a steal but caught myself in time to say it was a good deal. I explained I'd have to call her to the stand to get into evidence her story about the loan invitations and massage offers. Problem is, I told her, you take the stand, state's going to have a field day examining you on your priors. All twelve of them.

Misunderstandings, Clarissa huffed. I can explain them, she added. If they put me on that starchy jail diet, I'll never get it off my hips. I'm almost thirty-six. That's when it starts sticking.

Vecchio assigned Mulkerrin to prosecute. Smart move, not to play the heavy and run the risk of the jury feeling sorry for Clarissa. We were doing okay until Mulkerrin called Mel's CPA, who used the cash register tapes to document that on five occasions Clarissa had overstated receipts to hide cash withdrawals. In my cross-examination the best I could do was suggest that if Mel had invited Mrs. Joiner to make loans to herself, it would be logical for her to gross up the tallies so when she repaid the loans the books would balance.

Mel was a better witness than I expected. He didn't wear his rose-tinted wraparounds and planted his wife in the first row. He reached behind the rail to squeeze her hand when he was called to the witness stand. Nice touch. I wondered if Mulkerrin told him to do it.

I cross-examined Mel about the massage offers. His story was Clarissa asked him to get her a drink and massage her neck. He brought her an aspirin instead, Mel testified. I succeeded in getting Mel to admit that he had told Mrs. Joiner he wanted to be her friend. Friend, I repeated, arching my brows in mockery, letting the insinuation pend heavily, hating myself.

When the evidence closed, the state was well ahead. I had punched a few holes in the state's case but none were big enough for Clarissa to sashay through. Summations would be critical.

I stressed the "friendship" between Mel and Clarissa. To convict, I told the jury in my most somber voice, you must be absolutely convinced to a moral certainty the prosecution has met its burden of excluding all reasonable doubts as to the innocence of the accused. I described again and again the burden of proof, using different combinations of grave adjectives, trying to build a mountain in the jurors' minds. I ended each description with the refrain of "all reasonable doubts," which I syncopated with three slow knuckle raps on the jury rail.

Mulkerrin had reserved five minutes for rebuttal. She stood close to the jury box. She looked at each of the twelve jurors and paused for a long moment. Then, speaking gravely, she asked why, if Mrs. Joiner really thought she was making a loan to herself, she hadn't left her IUD in the cash drawer?

Judge Carey tried to turn his guffaw into a cough but fooled no one. The jurors exploded in laughter. Finally, Carey started banging his gavel and calling for order.

The jury was out for two hours. Clarissa gave me a hug and a wink, neither of which I wanted, when the forelady announced the verdict of not guilty. After the jury was discharged, I walked over to the state's table.

"You know she's guilty," Mulkerrin said angrily before I could get a word out. She was slamming legal pads and law books into a litigation case.

"So what?" I replied with a shrug. "We're lawyers."

"You really think it's that simple?" she asked.

"No, but I like it better than the other option."

"That being?"

"That being inquisitions instead of trials," I said. "Let's get out of here. I'll buy you a beer at the Arcade."

"I guess cynicism takes practice," she said.

"I wouldn't know. I was a prodigy."

"My screw-up will be all over the county bar by tomorrow morning, won't it?" she asked.

I considered telling her it wouldn't, but her malapropism was too rich. It was already on the grapevine, spreading through the sheriff's department, rippling through the clerk's office.

"We're all supposed to be famous for fifteen minutes. It's your turn."

Mulkerrin shook her head, laughed, and said yes to the beer.

We walked across Courthouse Square, descended the steps to the Arcade, and found a high-sided corner booth. Merle Haggard and the clicking of billiard balls mingled with the play-by-play of a baseball game.

Margaret, a solid, black mountain of a woman, came over, wiping her hands on a dishcloth. She had been serving me drafts for over twenty years.

"ID her, darling," I said to Margaret. "I just picked her up at the Greyhound station. I've got more at stake than you."

Margaret sternly eyeballed Mulkerrin.

"Miss, don't pay no mind to this no-account," Margaret said, slapping the back of my head with her dishcloth.

I ordered a pitcher of Pabst and a plate of onion rings. The first shift at the rendering plant had let out at three and the regulars were trickling in.

I debated saying anything. Let it drop, I said to myself. Niles and Roger were moldering in their graves and Vista Mer was a mortgagee's memory.

I had probed as far as I could, using as an excuse my status as Roger's administrator. That was the reason enough to stop. But I couldn't stop cobbling inferences into theories. I was suffering from unfocused anxiety. I kept experiencing the sinking sensation you get when halfway to the airport you suddenly are convinced you forgot to pack something essential but can't remember what.

I filled our glasses. I leaned back and listened to the hiss and pop of the grill punctuate Loretta Lynn's song about her daddy's hard times in the mines.

"You ever see the final autopsy report?" I asked.

Mulkerrin shook her head. "Vecchio moved the Dufault files into his office, said he's handling this one personally."

"Bobby's not into heavy lifting," I replied. "Makes me wonder why."

"I hear you know everybody in the county," Mulkerrin said after a pause. "White gloves to white trash."

"What else did Bobby tell you?"

"Maybe we can trade," she said.

"What?"

"Information."

"What kind?"

Mulkerrin pretended to pinch a joint and take a hit off it. She puffed out her cheeks and held her breath.

"An old-fashioned girl," I said.

"Momma said to know your herbs." She smiled. "Introduce me to the right people. People I can trust. Let them know I'm okay."

I didn't reply. Mulkerrin took a swallow of beer.

"I'm not asking you to score for me. Just make a few introductions. No big deal."

"Let me think about it," I replied. Mulkerrin slid out of the booth. I folded a ten-dollar bill and slipped it under the pitcher.

We crossed to the alley where she had parked her Alpha Romeo. The limestone of the courthouse was bathed in violet shadows. Mulkerrin tossed her briefcase in the backseat and turned to me. She extended her hand. I took it and leaned to kiss her cheek. She turned her head and kissed me on the lips. I moved my hand down the back of her skirt and pressed her against me. She pushed me away a few seconds later.

"We don't want to make the merry widow sad, do we?"

"Where did you hear about that?" I asked.

"Where do you think?"

"Bobby."

"You are quick. He said that, too."

"We're old friends," I said.

"You and Bobby?"

"Me and Peyton," I replied, then added, "Christ, Bobby, too."

Mulkerrin opened the door of the Alpha and slid behind the wheel.

"Keg party at the Marina," I blurted, reversing the decision I had made ten minutes earlier. "Saturday. People there you can meet."

Saturday night was hot as tweed, thick as velvet, and close as silk. The saline smell of the receding tide mingled with the sweet-sour scent of spilled beer and spiced steam from the fifty-gallon pot of boiling crabs. The steam, drawn by a milky, full moon, licked through the vents in the red-and-white striped awning.

"Ol' Renny's got a mouth on him like swamp gas," his younger brother, Gamper Gilkerson, told me, chuckling. He pointed with his pint of bonded toward Renny, who was huddled with Colleen Mulkerrin at the end of the wharf. Renny had his arm around her waist, just north of where her low-slung white shorts began. Renny was gesturing with his free hand at a twenty-eight-foot Marlin with twin, turbocharged inboards.

Renny and Gampy were co-owners of Aimes Point Marina Services, which was holding its annual "appreciation" party for captains and crews of the head boats which docked at APMS.

APMS, which occupied one of the rehabilitated warehouses at Aimes Point, did business as a chandler, yacht broker, and sales and service center for marine engines of all makes, models, and capacities—from electric trollers the size of soup cans that could barely raise a wake to Chryslers with enough muscle to make a launch dance on its stern at fifty knots. It was hard to come up with any good reason, at least any legitimate reason, for that much power. Add a specially designed tank holding 100 gallons, also sold by APMS, and it was harder still.

Aimes Point Inn occupied the other warehouse, the second story of which had been converted to guestrooms the Inn never had to advertise. The party was being held on the deck of the Inn.

"Breath and words to match," Gamper said, pointing again at Renny. Gamper handed me his pint.

I wiped mucous off the screw threads of the bottle. Gamper

pretended to watch Renny. I could tell he was keeping tabs on his pint out of the corner of his eye. I quick-tipped the pint and passed it back to him. Gamper took a long swallow and wiped his mouth on his shirttail. His faded madras shirt, missing several buttons, gaped open over his pot belly, exposing a tuft of hair just below his navel. Gamper put the pint in his hip pocket and hitched up his denim cutoffs.

"Best get your gal while you can," Gamper confided. "You know how ol' Renny gets."

I nodded, put my cup of beer on the railing of the wharf, and walked over to Renny and Mulkerrin.

" 'Bout ready to go?" I said to Mulkerrin.

"Leave us be counselor," Renny said. "Just telling the lady about how those twin bangers are for high-speed water skiing." He pointed at the Marlin and gave me a wink.

"And the five brands of papers you sell really are for rolling cigarettes," Mulkerrin said.

Renny got a kick out of that, giving Mulkerrin a little bump with his hip and a squeeze.

"You gave her the tour?" I said to Renny, pulling Mulkerrin away. Renny was fifty something with a chest like a sack of wet grain and a grizzled fringe around his cauliflower ears. He was half drunk and somewhere between mean and happy. I'd seen Renny mean and it wasn't pretty. Renny packed a gaff handle and a filleting knife. He pumped iron four nights a week at the Atlas Gym located in the Trak-Auto Shopping Center. The other nights he hung out at the UCT Hall on 33 hoping a young truck driver would wise off about his age, belly, or bald head.

Renny scowled at me, hunched back his shoulders, and spat into the water. Then, staring at me, he gave Mulkerrin a pat on her butt, waited a moment, patted her butt, spat again and headed back to the tent.

"He did that to see if I'd swing at him," I said as Mulkerrin and I were walking to the parking lot.

"You drive," Mulkerrin said, handing me her keys.

The Alpha Romeo's exhaust popped and echoed against the old brick of APMS. I turned left at the gate, deciding to take the long way. I looked over at Mulkerrin. She was slumped down in her seat, staring at the stars.

Mulkerrin lived in a rented townhouse in Ocean Pines, the last development of Dr. Dufault before he died of a heart attack. The townhouses had been sited in clusters around Whilley Creek, which was really just a backwater of the Pascamany.

It was just after midnight when we parked. Mulkerrin reached over the console and pulled the key out of the ignition. I put my arm around her shoulder. She turned toward me and arched her neck. I kissed her long and hard.

"I'm going to need a chiropractor, we don't stop this," Mulkerrin said, pushing off. "The gear shift is about to crack my spine." She sat up and brushed back her hair.

"Put your top up?" I said, looking at the swirling clouds.

"You can do that inside," Mulkerrin replied.

The sound of a dull crash followed by the sound of tires squealing woke me up. The green, glowing dial on the alarm clock on the dresser said it was 4:30 A.M. I looked at Mulkerrin. She was sound asleep. I walked to the window and looked out.

The light of a single spotlight barely illuminated the parking lot of the townhouse cluster. But the clouds had dispersed. In the moonlight I saw something sticking out of Whilley Creek. Then I realized it looked like the rear half of a car, a little car. I looked at the spot where I had parked the Alfa and read on the asphalt the stenciled number of Mulkerrin's townhouse.

I shook Mulkerrin awake and pulled her to the window. She leaned out the window and looked where I pointed.

"Shit," she said, covering her eyes. "Shit."

"I'll call a wrecker," I said. "It's going to sink in the muck if we don't."

"No," she said. "I'll do it. I don't want you here. I'll have to call the sheriff." I nodded.

"You got insurance?" I asked.

"Everything," she said. "Just go, okay?"

"That sonofabitch Renny," I said.

Mulkerrin had the receiver in her hand. She started to say something to me when she stopped and spoke instead into the receiver. She gave her name and address in cool, clipped tones, the ones I had heard in my office what seemed like years ago.

I got in my truck and stared up at the townhouse. The light was on in the bathroom and I thought I could hear the shower running. But maybe it was the night breeze I heard.

I switched on the headlights. Then I saw smeared crimson letters across the top of the windshield. "Meow," they spelled.

Thirty minutes later I dialed Peyton's number from the pay phone at the Shell station west of Lassington.

"Meow," she said huskily, answering the call on the first ring.

"Damn you to hell." Peyton giggled and made a purring noise.

"Goddamn you," I said, louder. Peyton in reply turned up the volume on the purring.

"That sounds like a vacuum cleaner." A peal of laughter answered me, little, merry silver bells. I held firm for a second before laughing, too. I started to cover the receiver so Peyton couldn't hear me laugh. But I didn't. I could learn a lot about myself from what I don't do, if only I paid attention.

"I've had it with you," I said, trying to make it sound final and stern.

"I guess that means you don't want to know what I found in the glove compartment," Peyton replied.

"Whose glove compartment?"

"Mulkerrin's, or whoever she is."

"Don't tell me anything. I'm not going to lie for you."

Neither of us spoke for a minute. Then Peyton started purring again, softly this time."

"Stop that, damn you," I said. "I'm through with you. You've gone too far. I really mean it this time."

"You think so?" Peyton asked in a small voice, managing to sound contrite.

"What do *you* think? Bumping Mulkerrin's car into the creek. Good Christ, Peyton." I felt angry again and it felt good. I liked sounding tough.

"I meant, do you really mean it," she replied, her voice soft.

"Goddamn right I do." I looked at the first streak of sunlight, a hot-pink strip. I could hear Peyton breathing into the phone, blowing away my resolve. Then I heard what maybe was sniffling.

"Get some steel wool," I said after a minute. "Wipe off your bumper, all of it."

"Whole thing?" Peyton sounded sweetly incredulous.

"They can pick up paint flakes now so small you can't even see them," I said. "And Peyton." I summoned conviction, letting my voice trail off.

"I know," she said before I could continue. "You really do mean it."

"I do, this time." I looked to the east. A layer of Popsicle orange had sneaked under the pink strip. The Protestant spires of Lassington were no longer silhouettes. It again occurred to me that Lassington was the kind of sleepy town that gives you insomnia.

A flock of cawing starlings suddenly swept down from the Confederate-gray sky, so close I felt the thick, cool air pulse on my hot forehead.

"That was supposed to be your hang-up line," Peyton said after a minute.

"I got distracted."

"By what?"

"Birds," I said, lying, thinking about Peyton's thighs and how easy it would be to slip over to her house. I struggled to banish the vision as I glanced at my wristwatch to calculate how much time we would have.

"You want to reboot and try again?"

"I'm serious," I said, hating the weak words and the meek way I said them.

"You're many things, darling, and I love all of them. But that you're not. You ought to accept it as one of your charms." Peyton laughed softly.

Her laughter gave me a jolt of anger which I turned into the words, "I am," and strength to hang up the phone. I realized I had almost said, "I am, too," and was glad I hadn't.

*   *   *

The Motion's Day Docket, for as long as anyone could remember, was called on the second Friday of the month. It allowed the circuit court to hear contested pretrial issues and enter
uncontested orders. Motion's day was the lawyers' market day,
a sanctioned excuse for the county bar to gather once a month
to close old files and start new rumors.

On the second Friday in August the gossip seemed split
evenly between the Dufault investigation, who likely would replace George Carey when (as rumored) he retired at the end of
the year, and what the hell Vecchio thought he was doing when
he hired a woman as good-looking as Colleen Mulkerrin.

I was seated in the jury box, waiting to argue a motion for
alimony *pendente lite*, when Warren Closter, Carey's bailiff,
handed me a note.

Warren had the countenance of a moribund basset hound
having a blue Monday. He had been Carey's bailiff for so long,
the rumor had circulated they had purchased adjacent gravesites.
Closter's tombstone was going to say "Oyez, Oyez. All Rise."
Warren lived by himself in an apartment over what had been
the Western Auto store, rarely venturing out except to cross the
square to the courthouse, attend church, and walk to the Careys
for Sunday dinner to which he had a standing invitation.

Since no one knew how old Closter was and none dared ask,
Warren had gained a *de facto* exemption from the county's
mandatory retirement rule. Brenda Stern once told me Warren
had been near retirement when Carey was appointed to the
bench twenty years ago. Stringy old buzzard back then, she
said. Same as now.

Nor did anyone, including Sheriff Cane, Warren's nominal
superior—as bailiff, Warren was, technically, a deputy sheriff—
dare question Warren's habit of following Carey to chambers,
ready to run errands for Carey or his wife. It was common
knowledge that Warren was Carey's ear to the ground and back-
alley channel.

I unfolded the note. Warren had scribbled: "Meet me in the
canteen after your motion."

I found Warren in the canteen, sipping a coffee. He handed

me a coffee, took me by the arm, and led me to a table in the rear.

"Fish been biting?" Warren asked, without looking at me.

"Been too hot," I said.

"Before dawn, ain't too hot." Warren sipped his coffee. "Ought to do your fishing then. What I hear, you're up and out anyway."

"What do you hear?"

"Hear what I hear." Warren studied the box scores. "Braves lost again. Had it won and blew it. Relievers ain't worth a damn. Maybe they been up partying all night, too."

"Tell me," I said.

"Some of those relievers. Might be good if they took time off. Maybe went away for a while. Wear your arm out, going for it night after night. Get away for a spell. Make their arms last. Maybe even save their careers." Warren folded the newspaper and fixed rheumy brown eyes on me.

"C'mon, Warren. No more ring-around-the-rosy."

"Listen close," he said in a hoarse whisper. "Don't be messing with that Mulkerrin gal."

"Jesus," I said, irritated. "Tell Carey he's no longer my frigging Sunday school teacher."

"Sometimes things ain't what they seem, son," Warren replied, standing up. "You think about that long and hard."

Before I could say a word Warren was halfway out the door.

CHAPTER 8

Staunton Yester's phone was disconnected. I stared at the To Do List with which my computer greeted me. The hell with it.

I phoned Richard Bernhard and got his agreement to a two-week extension for Mrs. Cringline to answer Food Ranch's interrogatories. I told Anita to reschedule Mrs. Cringline for next week.

I didn't want to listen to Mrs. Cringline whine about the lumbar injury she sustained when she slipped on a patch of "mysterious moisture" (her deposition testimony) near the salad bar at the Food Ranch.

She had a winnable negligence action. I could prove water was leaking from the compressor which chilled the salad bar. Unfortunately, from an economic perspective, she only had a soft-tissue injury. I had booked it as having a settlement value of eight grand, max. It was one I was going to settle. If I put Mrs. Cringline on the stand, I figured the jury would reduce any damages award by five hundred dollars for every minute they had to listen to her. She could end up owing Food Ranch.

I had suggested to Mrs. Cringline at our initial interview that she keep a pain-and-suffering journal. I hadn't called it that, of course. I referred to it as a diary to record her condition. Mrs. Cringline regularly kept Anita posted on the status of her pain and suffering. They discussed entries in Mrs. Cringline's P&S journal.

Some cases pend for two or three years. Plaintiffs, particularly older persons and those not gifted with rich imaginations, tend to forget just how bad the pain really was. The shy plaintiff—I have had three in sixteen years—who has trouble speaking forcefully, despite rehearsals in my office, of excruciating, wrenching, agonizing, jolting, and debilitating pain need only identify the P&S journal and testify that entries were recorded contemporaneously with pain.

The foundation thus laid allows me to get the journal admitted into evidence which enables me during my summation to read, with appropriate dramatic flair and gesture, the choicest entries. There are always a couple even if Anita has to dictate them.

The key is to make evidence come alive for the jury. Any good thespian knows the way to do that is to make it concrete and vivid. See that pernicious patch of mysterious moisture lurking like a serpent in the shadows of the salad bar. Feel poor Mrs. Cringline's synapses flood with pain and her lumbar muscles howl in spasms of agony.

Some clients, the Mrs. Cringlines, misconstrue my suggestion to keep a P&S journal as an invitation to disclose their deepest longings (a new Barcalounger that the Rev. Thomas Duke Cringline is too cheap to buy) and disjointed observations on life in general and selfish spouses of children in particular. ("Sept. 8. Fonda is too vain to take time to appreciate the good qualities of Tommy. She was a greedy little girl who acted up in my Sunday school class and she still is. I am in agony from the pain in my back. It hurt so much I couldn't even get out of bed to go potty. I just lay there about to bust.")

I stopped at the 7-Eleven on 201 and filled up with gas and coffee.

Harston is a pleasant three-hour drive to the west if you follow 201 to 43 to 17 to 181 or an unpleasant ninety-minute drive if you take Interstate 62 to the exit for 181. I almost invariably avoid interstates, which I rank a close second to VCR's as enemies of the irenic soul.

Late September in the tidewater offers up several weeks of

cool, sunlit beauty so profound as to be almost overpowering. It is as if the haze of the summer was a cataract to our senses, now suddenly restored. The sky was cloudless and a perfect shade of Delft blue. Dazzling white steeples soared above maples touched by the slightest hint of rust, and oaks by the merest suggestion of pale gold. Pastures and lawns were painted a deep, dense shade of green. Corn stalks, weathered to ocher hues, stood at attention in close rows, drying in the still sunlight for a week more before surrendering as fodder.

As I drove west, I glanced out the side window. Fence posts zipped by in a blur. Motion is the physical expression of time. That, I guessed, is why journeys make me pensive.

The law and I have a love-hate relationship, I decided. I was self-employed. For that I was grateful. I had been spared performance reviews, mentoring, departmental quotas, weekend retreats to prioritize priorities, bickering over diagrams of boxes and arrows (ego maps dignified as ''flow charts''), scheduled coffee breaks, and dress codes.

It had surprised me when I discovered I had a talent for trial practice. For the first several years, it was invigorating having the power to move a jury. Then it became an increasingly lucrative indoor sport as to which I maintained a professional's detached, yet uncynical, perspective. Then it became a job which I would defend if challenged (particularly if by laity). Now it was somewhere between being a boring routine and drudgery. Cynicism had replaced detachment, and I suspected self-loathing was next in line. Strutting and fretting on the stage, generating sound, fury, and judicial results, if not justice, had lost its charm. Sometimes people mistake an old lawyer's sourness for wisdom. Usually it's moral dry rot. I saw it happening to me.

Good trial work demands that the lawyer be steeped in banal detail, immersed in minutia. I have learned how new treads are melded onto scarified carcasses and why salad bar compressors leak due to condensation. Oddities. Hardly the storehouse of a great mind. This, I suspect, is what Disraeli meant when he said immodestly he was forced to choose between being a good lawyer and a great man.

The realization that I could have done more was shading into the criticism that I *should* have done more. I had sold myself short in a bull market. I had let my mind wallow even as my abilities as a trial lawyer were honed by experience.

Once in a while, dinner-party conversations veered from the seemingly obligatory topics of interest rates and how many tenths of a second one's ten-year-old had shaved off his best time in the fifty-meter free style or, depending on the season, other equally salient blazes on a predestined path to renown. Occasionally, someone inept or inebriated would dare to steer conversation toward a cultural or philosophical issue. Whatever I would contribute all too often would be summoned, vintage port from a cobwebbed cellar, from what I had learned at Yale better than twenty years ago. I had allowed professional success to excuse intellectual laziness. I read "serious" novels now and then, mainly as a change of pace from the histories of the War Between the States to which I was addicted. I subscribed to a few highbrow journals to counterbalance *Sports Illustrated, Southern Living* and *Field & Stream* on the coffee table of my reception room.

I had broken the promise I made to myself when I left academia for the so-called "real world." I had abandoned the serious business of being an intellectual. I was a captive of the evening newscast and front page just like every other fool. This was hardly a fresh insight. I saw it happening when I was in my twenties. In my thirties, I tried to pretend it hadn't happened. (That was when I subscribed to the highbrow journals.) Now in my forties, I was mad at myself for letting it happen.

For a long time it had seemed I had all the time in the world. Then I woke up one day and it seemed like the world was running out of time. My world, anyway. Or perhaps the problem was that I had a fear of running out of motives. I imagined waiting for a motive and finding a void rather than resolve.

I felt both oppressed by the accumulated weight of foreclosed options and desperate to hold open the ones which remained. Peyton was right. I was reluctant, unable to strike out, to set forth, to cut loose. It takes guts to take your dreams seriously, she said. The problem was mine too often were nightmares, and I did. Tethered by childhood memories of foreboding, I held back, testing, measuring, observing, waiting for a clarity of purpose that eluded me. Or maybe I shrank from denouement because I suspected what the purpose was. I let Father's mantle serve as his shroud. I remembered a skit, part of a silent movie from the twenties. An actor tries madly to find an open door in a hall of mirrors. He keeps running into reflections. That was how I felt, except I kept running into memories.

As soon as I hit 17, the gradient changed perceptibly. The slopes of the Cannama Range were no longer just a blue ridge on the horizon. Signs of autumn became less subtle as the elevation increased.

Route 17 climbed Peddler's Ridge—the easternmost ridge— of the Cannamas. I parked at the same overlook where Father and I had parked that September afternoon in 1964. I got out and looked to the west. The crenelated towers of Horton Military Academy soared in the distance above the Roman arches that capped the battlements of the fortress. The citadel, crafted from ruddy sandstone blocks quarried in the valley below, appeared to have been designed by a mad *patissier* for a reception of a million. Seen from a distance, the Academy looked like a monstrous, multitiered pink wedding cake delicately balanced on a spiny ledge, which, jutting from the principal ridge of the Swannonona Mountains, resembled the upturned hand of a server.

HMA had percolated in the mind of Brigadier General (CSA Ret.) Lucas Pellam Horton for many years before its cornerstone was laid, with much fanfare, to coincide with the twentieth reunion of the brigade General Horton gallantly had led. Ten years were to pass, and several fortunes (the general's included) were to be squandered, before the cast-iron portcullis was raised to admit the first corps of cadets.

The construction of HMA had required the building of a rail spur, which the general just before his death at ninety-two ordered destroyed. Only a traitor, the general was reported to have said to a trustee who demurred, would suggest retaining it. Any damned fool can see the spur could be used to support a siege. The general had personally sighted the artillery emplacements and calculated that one good battery of Napoleons could hold off a regiment of Yankees. But in his last days, the possibility of a siege—HMA was dependent on water from the valley—tormented him.

It was common knowledge that the general was deranged. But, as was true of certain saints, his insanity was viewed as proof of a vision so profound and apocalyptic as to burst the sordid chains of the mundane, the practical, and the legal. (The general occasionally fired live artillery rounds into the valley.) Well-to-do parents clambered to send their sons to Horton to be inspired by the general's vision, never precisely defined, but grandly expressed in architecture, uniforms, marches, and manners.

HMA in 1964 had been a good five-hour drive, for the most part over old 234, a narrow road constructed from concrete slabs, which Father said would have resembled a Roman ruin—the Via Hortonus—if the WPA engineers had been half as good as their Roman counterparts. Father sipped from a half-pint and quietly cursed the asphalt seams, which, protruding a good inch above the slabs they joined, caused his '58 Cadillac to pitch and yaw like a sloop in a heavy sea, the thump of each seam sounding for all the world like the slap of a wave across a bow. The softly sprung Cadillac tacked through hairpin turns, its heavy chassis swaying across the center line, forcing lesser vehicles, their honks sounding like angry gulls, onto the shoulder.

Don't hold this against your mother, Father said, when we pulled into the overlook and I first saw HMA. It was my idea, I replied. Bullshit, he said. You don't know beans about women yet.

At HMA I learned to spitshine shoes, polish brass with toothpaste (which worked best), keep my white webbing from twisting, and field strip a M-1 carbine. I ran cross-country on a course so notoriously hilly, the Horton athletic director was hard pressed to find opponents, none of whom ever returned. I ate scrambled eggs made from powder, biscuits made from scratch, bacon as thick as bootsole, and gained fifteen solid pounds.

We observed the military hours, called by the venerable chaplain who also served as the bugler. The Right Reverend Dr.

Martin claimed—no one believed him—to have served under General Horton. He played his dented bugle with such sweet, haunting clarity that at times the last note of Taps, drawn out endlessly, infused even the stones of the citadel with elegiac longing for what could not be named.

Captain LeConte, rumored to have sought refuge at Horton from the French Foreign Legion, taught French and fencing, at the same time. We practiced conjugating verbs while practicing lunges and parries on the parapets, weather permitting. To this day I speak French in a rapid, breathless manner, as if I am about to be run through or fall to my death.

Math finally made sense. Calculating artillery trajectories and optimal fuse lengths gave a sense of purpose to geometry and trigonometry. The history we read tended to be from a military perspective and a southern one at that. The Industrial Revolution, for example, was depicted as an unfair advantage enjoyed by the North.

Horton provided a peculiarly eclectic education, a mixture of the bizarre and the brilliant, in homage to its founder, whose lifesize portrait in Confederate dress gray adorned the vestibule of Horton Hall. (The general did not suffer from false modesty.)

I never once, then or since, regretted my years at HMA, an institutional time capsule which preserved the nineteenth-century South. Or perhaps Horton preserved the myth of a South which never existed and thus could never die. Perhaps, it later occurred to me, the general's eccentricity was calculated for that purpose. When I returned to Horton for the twelfth reunion of the Class of '67, I stared at the painting of Old Lucas. I am convinced I saw him smile in recognition that I had divined his secret. But it could have been the bourbon talking to me. I was drinking a lot back then just after my divorce from Renee.

I reached Harston at noon. Nothing had changed but the signs. I stopped at the old general store, renamed Griswold's Gas-and-Go, and asked the proprietor for directions to Staunton's trailer. Follow 865 to Peen's Ford and look for the church, he finally said, after a few moments of silently debating the pros and cons of giving a stranger directions to any spot other than hell. Yester's place is up in back behind the graveyard.

Not far beyond Harston the macadam patchwork ended and gravel began. County Road 865 twisted sharply uphill. The pickup by turns skidded on loose gravel and shuddered when it gained traction on the limestone outcroppings that crossed the narrow road at irregular intervals. Two years of beer bottles clinked together under the front seat, reminding me of background music in Chinese restaurants.

Honeysuckle entwined the barbed-wire fences so thickly on both sides of 865 that I rarely had any view save for, at most, several hundred yards of rutted, ascending right-of-way before the road was lost in the elbow of the next curve. Finally, the Dodge bumped to the top of a stony ridge. Ahead in a glade was a little whitewashed, clapboard church. A handpainted sign identified it as the Peen's Ford Gospel Church. Behind and up the hill from the church was a small cemetery.

I parked in front of the church. The whitewash was new but the limestone foundation was eroded and old. The vista from the church embraced miles of shadowed valleys and verdant ridges. Down the hill from the church there were several buildings and a sign with a vaguely familiar logo I couldn't quite make out. Either Neiman-Marcus or Wonder Bread. The air was still. I could hear the murmur of rushing water below me.

I followed the dirt road which climbed past the cemetery. I was about to give up when I saw in the distance the outline of a satellite dish. When I got to the trailer I recognized Roger's Eldorado.

Roger had given Yester his Eldorado when Vista Mer went into bankruptcy. Roger told Porky Bryan that if he were hellbent on repossessing it, he could look for it in the hills where a repo man had a life expectancy measured in days.

Staunton was a legend among dirt salesmen. Used to be, Roger once said, stressing the past tense, Staunton had more moves than a truckload of snakes packed in grease.

Staunton met Roger in April 1970, soon after Roger dropped out of Remington State. Staunton at the time was sales manager for a developer pushing "chalets" on half-acre lots in an "exclusive country club recreational community" in the mountains above Lake Traynor.

It had been, Staunton told me, one of those deals where the developer exhausts his line of credit to build a gatehouse that looked like a scale model of the White House, lay down a driveway of paper-thin macadam, and throw up a display model with cardboard walls. The rest was left to a good salesman's imagination.

One morning Staunton heard a knock on the door of his trailer. He opened it and looked down at a clean-cut kid, in a pressed suit. The kid had blue eyes as big as half dollars and held steady eye contact. Staunton told him to go back to college, don't mess up the crease in your pants. The kid replied he was sick of jerking off pencils.

Staunton stuck his face up close so the kid could count the stubble on his lip and smell the overlay of antacid on last night's bourbon. Then Staunton lectured him for ten minutes on why only one man in ten thousand has the right combination of balls and brains to really sell.

Staunton had a gut instinct the kid could sell. He had a polished manner that would play well with doctors' wives. (Get the wife, you got the hubby, Staunton was fond of saying.)

Within a few weeks, Staunton knew he had a natural on his hands. When the season ended, Roger took his share of escrowed commissions and bought a yellow Cadillac convertible as bright and cheerful as high school cheerleaders used to be.

I heard hard, dry coughing inside. I knocked again and the door opened. Staunton's cheeks were slack as an old hound's jowls and covered with the salt and pepper of several days' growth. The whites of his eyes were as yellow as the nicotine stains on his fingers. The trailer smelled of stale butts, cheap whiskey, and sour piss.

"Lawdy, I swan," Staunton said, shaking my hand. He gave my shoulder a feeble squeeze.

"A-joinin' me?" Staunton said, shuffling to the counter

where a 1.75 liter plastic jug of cut-rate bourbon rested beside a pile of dirty dishes.

I said it was too early. He didn't hear me. The TV in the corner was blaring. I made a twisting motion with my hand and pointed toward the set. Two men were excitedly discussing the results of a contest involving girls in spandex shorts and rollerblades. I guessed it was one of those sports invented to make twenty-four-hour programming possible and America rich in culture.

"Cut the sucker off," Staunton said, handing me a coffee mug half filled with bourbon. "Take a load off." He pointed toward a recliner resting on three legs and half a cinder block.

The preliminaries were not a strain. I was fond of Staunton. I asked how he was and if I could get him anything. I meant it. He laughed a short, dry laugh, which turned into wheezing. Finally, the wheezing became short, rapid pants. Staunton took a sip of whiskey, cleared his throat, and stumbled over to the sink to spit.

"Sure can. A new pair of lungs and forty good years," he croaked.

I guessed in a year, maybe in a few months, there would come that time when he would start wheezing, struggle for breath, fail to catch it, and end in convulsions amid the litter. The whiskey held the future at bay. I decided I wanted a drink after all.

"You didn't drive way the way hell out here to inquire about my health. If you did, it'll be a mighty short visit. And I know you didn't come so you could bill a day to Roger's estate, which ain't got enough to pay for your gas. So lean back and speak your mind."

There was no point in being indirect. You can't sell a salesman as good as Staunton. Either he would tell me or he wouldn't.

"Ever hear the name Niles Nesbitt?"

"Name I could have heard," Staunton said, after a moment of silence.

"This ain't part of your job as lawyer for Roger's estate, is it," Staunton said. It was a declaration, not a question. I shook my head anyway.

Staunton poured himself a slug from the bottle on the floor beside the sofa. His hand trembled.

"Some things are best left be," he continued. "You ain't getting paid and you ain't getting laid for whatever you had in mind when you came out here. That ought to tell you something."

"No good reason," I admitted. "Just curious."

Staunton studied me, reading me as he had countless thousands in four decades of selling.

"Sometimes no good reason can be the best reason." Staunton took a quivering sip, splashing bourbon on his chin. He wiped his mouth on his sleeve.

"You, I can see there won't be no reasoning with. Lot of men, soon as they hit their forties, damned if they don't go piss away their money on a big ol' boat with a ton of brightwork. I reckon that won't fix what's ailin' you. But I'm warning you, a boat'll be cheaper in the long run."

"I already got a boat," I replied.

"You got a diddly jackshit skiff that ain't fit for frog-flashin' when the water's flat. You're too damn cheap to get something decent," Staunton said.

It was a standing joke. Staunton had borrowed my boat so regularly he treated it as if he owned it. He had knocked out the dents, scraped rust from the gunwales, and fitted it with an electric trolling motor. Staunton did as well with fish as with marks, maybe better as he got older.

"I'll tell you what I know," he said. "But I don't want no part of that pot you're stirring. You walk out that door and you forgot who told you what. That plainly understood?"

I nodded. Staunton shook a Pall Mall loose and tamped it on the arm of his chair. The slanting sunlight, refracted through Rolling Rock empties, cast lime-green rays across the grimy linoleum floor.

"Rog gambled on gettin' the permit for Vista Mer," Staunton said, watching the blue smoke twist through his cupped fingers. "Fool paid too much for the land. Numbers didn't work, lessen we could put in condo clusters. But you know all that." I nodded in reply. Staunton took a slow drag on his cigarette.

"Last October, I think it was," he continued, "Roger and I went to see the head engineer for the Environmental Control Commission. Chickenshit sonofabitch by the name of Whitley. Roger said his buddy Elliot Dean set up the meeting.

"Whitley said the ECC had just gotten a draft of a report by the Army Corps of Engineers saying there weren't no adverse impact on that swamp they now are calling a wetland so long as a pumping station was put in. Whitley asked us to keep it confidential. He said that information could be worth a hell of a lot of money to somebody who knew how to use it. Then Whitley gave us a shit-eating grin.

"Roger thought he had a license to steal the land on the cheap. Couldn't hardly contain his fool self, so het up he was.

"Fool wanted to rush back to Lassington, storm into Johnny Rivero's office and sign a contract on the spot.

"Gotta know your shot, Roger tells me. Upside on ninety units nigh on two million, he says. Can't take the risk of the corps' report getting out. That sucker gets leaked, Rivero's gonna to have developers hiding in his hedges, sticking contracts at him when he picks up his paper off his step.

"I told Roger, 'Son, don't close until all your permits been signed by everybody from the Pope on down. Make that a condition to closing.'

"Roger said he had a vision. I told him dirt is dirt. Didn't listen. Damn fool said he had something to prove.

"Johnny Rivero, whose family had owned the land since Adam, said no contingencies. Shit or get off the pot, he said. Rivero claimed he'd have a buyer on the next plane from New York if Roger didn't want the deal. Rivero started acting like he didn't want to sell. Wouldn't return Roger's phone calls, chilled him out. 'Course, I could see what was happening.

"I said, 'Roger how many times you used a bait-and-chill to sell a lot? Don't matter if it's a third of an acre or ten acres of oceanfront. Same old game. Sit on your heels. Make Doctor Johnny call you. You chase him now and he'll have you by the balls and be a-twistin'.'

"Roger said Rivero, for chrissakes, was a dentist. Don't know squat about selling. No way he was pulling a bait-and-chill. Roger figured Rivero must have gotten wind of the Corps' report.

"Rivero all of a sudden goes out of town and Roger's fit to be tied. Called Rivero all weekend. Worked himself into a tizzy. Losin' my shot, Roger said. Losin' your head, I told him. Finally, Roger reached Rivero at his office on Monday early and said he was ready to sign. No conditions.

"Problem was financing. Banks wouldn't take the Rivero tract as collateral. No way, they said. Not until you get the ECC to sign off on the development permit. Roger had to pledge his equities, even his and Peyton's place, to get Porky to bankroll the deal.

"So CS&T came up with the money and we had that goddamned awful closing . . ."

I told Staunton I knew this part. I was the closing attorney. The closing took two days. Roger and Rivero turned my conference room into the O-K Corral. They hadn't liked each other to begin with and ended up with blood in their eyes.

Staunton obliged me and skipped ahead.

"We got the architects up from Richleigh. Got the engineering plans drawn to show the EEC. Plans just happened to include a pumping station that cost a bundle. I came up with the marketing plan. Exclusive club. Security checkpoint, uniforms with brass buttons and braid. Wine-and-cheesers on the clubhouse deck. Pay some college gals three bucks an hour to wear aprons over short skirts, serve jug wine, and yessir and yesmam the marks.

"Upscale marketing from the get-go. Ads all gonna say: for a few qualified purchasers only, by invitation. Gonna do a first-rate snob sell. Make 'em apply, see if they qualify. Hell, we'd have half the docs and attorneys in Richleigh lined up, wearing blazers and white britches, seeing if they're good enough to join, checkin' out my college gals' tails.

"*Richleigh Journal* ran a piece on Vista Mer. Printed some quotes from Roger about it being a luxury project for people who knew enough to appreciate first-class living. Roger hit it a bit hard, the class stuff. Quiet-money people get embarrassed by that kind of talk. Half the fun of having all that money is not having to talk about it.''

The green rays cast by the Rolling Rock empties were fanning out, turning a deeper shade. Staunton tamped another cigarette.

"Well, I reckon I can cut to the part you want, let you get out of here 'fore the sun drops behind yonder ridge.

"Not long after the article ran in the *Journal,* seemed every ducklover and swampsucker in the state started raisin' hell about how we were fixin' to destroy this precious wetland, this fragile habitat for waterfowl, which is what they're calling ducks these days.

"Stinking swamp's all it ever was. Calling it a wetland don't change nothing. No one paid a lick of attention to it before, 'cept to throw tires in and shoot muskrats. 'Sides, it's better'n a mile to the west.

"Rog and I get to the ECC hearing. Room was packed with longhairs trying to see if Rog and I had horns and tails. Whitley sat there lookin' like he'd eaten raw a piece of bad fish. Wouldn't look at us. I knew what that meant.

"I took Rog out in the hall. 'Son, this ain't our party,' I said. 'Tell Whitley we want to withdraw the application, do another study or something.

"Fool wouldn't listen. Kept telling me Dean knows what to do. Delay'll kill sales. Can't afford to miss this season.

"Turned out it weren't just sewage runoff that had the ducklovers' bowels in an uproar. No, sir. All kinds of eco things had them upset, eco things so goddamned delicate they'd break if you farted and didn't ask the ducks' pardon.

"Whitley didn't know which side was up. Some lady wearing sandals made out of truck treads would ask him about an eco this or eco that. He'd thank her and agreed whatever it was she was bitching about needed more study. Time we got outta there, list of crap needing more study hardly fit in Roger's briefcase.

"Way out, all's I could do to keep Roger from popping this

little reporter who kept asking Roger if ducks knew how to appreciate first-class living.

"Roger said, Dean'll straighten out Whitley. But Dean wouldn't return Roger's calls."

Staunton refilled his jelly jar, wiped his nose on his sleeve, and caught his breath.

"Roger, being Roger, hadn't planned for enough working capital to deal with delays, much less'n all those studies.

"Roger's calling Dean five times a day, leaving messages about messages. Dean finally had some secretary call back. Procedure this, procedure that, she says. Shucked him.

"Monthly interest payments started coming due, eating us up. Then Porky gets nervous and sics this dink AVP on us. Boy's supposed to hound us, make sure we don't impair no CST collateral.

"Finally, in May I reckon it was, Roger, out of the clear blue, gets a phone call from Dean. Come on down to Richleigh and let's talk, Dean says. Bring your blueprints.

"Roger can hardly wait until morning. So het up he can't get the plats in order. I rolled up the plats, made sure he knew which was which. I couldn't go, Roger said, on account of Dean telling him it was a confidential meeting.

"Next evening, late, I run into Roger at Aimes Point Inn. Rog saw me come in and damned near knocked over a row of bar stools coming over to give me a hug. Rog is buying drinks all around with money he don't have. Telling everyone who'll sit still that Vista Mer is locked, cocked, and ready to rock.

"I take him aside and ask what in hell is going on. Dean's going to cut through all the ECC bullshit and get us the permit, Roger tells me.

" 'Sounds like Christmas,' I said. 'What's your present for Dean?' Roger says Dean don't want nothing. Says Dean wanted to help all along but the time wasn't right. Dean's gal is going to fix things with the ECC. I told Roger that a politician who says he don't want nothing wants everything."

It was getting dark. The sun was a red crescent above the ridge. Staunton took a long drink before continuing.

"Couple of days later I get to the office after breakfast and find Roger loading something in his briefcase. He sees me and snaps it shut. 'What's the hurry?' I say. 'Not noon yet. Early for you.' Roger says he's gonna meet with an investor. 'Investor in what?' I said. 'All we got left is a stack of concrete footers.' Roger looks at me funny, like he wants to say something. But he shuts his case and heads out without a word, which ain't like Rog.

"Next day I run into Rog at the marina bar. I wait till Roger gets a few bourbons in him. Then I ask him about this investor.

"Roger says the investor is a professor at the university, man named Nesbitt. Then he gets all fidgety and clams up, which ain't like Roger. So I order another round of drinks. But I couldn't get another word out of him.''

"Who was Dean's gal?'' I asked.

"Don't know. Lady lawyer is all Rog said.''

Staunton said he didn't know anything else. Whether he was tired of talking, too drunk to remember, or had decided he'd said enough, I couldn't tell.

I thanked him and made him give me his phone bill so I could get service reinstated. I didn't like the thought of Staunton unable to call for help. How fast it would come, if at all, here in the hills, I didn't know. I also had a selfish reason. I wanted to be able to talk to Staunton without having to drive to Peen's Ford.

At the bottom of the hill I put two hundred dollars in an envelope and stuck it in Staunton's mail box. What Staunton had told me was worth considerably more than two hundred dollars. To whom, I wasn't sure.

CHAPTER 9

Anita stuck her head in the door and scowled.

"Guess what?" she asked, rolling her eyes toward the reception area.

I put down the newspaper and looked up.

"The Honorable Olive Oil is here to see you," she said. She stuck out her tongue and pressed her finger against it.

"Christ, Anita," I said. "Bobby's not all that bad."

"Not to you, maybe he's not," Anita said. "You ought to wear a skirt and see what he's like. Hon, this. Babe, that. Leans all over me. Picks up my phone. Doesn't even ask."

"A minute, then. All right?"

"I can manage maybe a half-minute with that ass," Anita replied. "Speaking of which, if he doesn't get it off the edge of my desk, I'm going to stab it with a letter opener."

I knew Anita well enough to know her threat wasn't idle. I sighed and walked to the door. Vecchio, in a pinstriped navy suit, was sitting on the corner of Anita's desk. He had her telephone nestled against his shoulder and was scribbling notes on her steno pad.

"Hey, Bobby," I said. Vecchio held up one finger and waved it. Then, still talking, he leaned in my direction and stuck out his hand, in so doing dragging the phone cord across Anita's Rolodex which fell to the floor, spilling index cards across the carpet.

"Oops," Vecchio said, covering the speaker with his palm.
"Sorry, babe," he whispered to Anita. Smiling, he put his hand
on his head and hunched down, as if to protect himself from
an imaginary overhead blow.

"The one in the library," I said, shaking his hand. "Take it
in there." I pointed to the phone on the conference-room table.
Vecchio whispered, "Half sec." I looked at Anita, who was
fuming, to make sure there were no sharp edges within easy
reach.

I returned to my office and sat down on the couch. So Vecchio dropped by to talk about Peyton. So what, I told myself,
fine-tuning my attitude. I figured I'd play it brassy. I'd use
Vecchio's expression on him: a nothing deal, I'd say. But talking about Peyton made me uneasy.

"Peckerwood, my main man," Vecchio said, sauntering into
my office ahead of Anita, who shut the door on us with a clap
just shy of a slam.

"Fuck's her problem?" he asked, hooking his thumb toward
the door. "Time of the month or something?"

"Something to do with you sitting on her calendar."

"Touchy, touchy. You mind?" Vecchio pointed at the tufted
leather high-backed desk chair that once had been Father's.

I minded but nodded assent.

"So this is the life of the private bar?" Vecchio rocked back
in my chair and put his feet on the corner of my desk. He
played with the white carnation in his pocket. "Nice, real nice."

"Offer's still good," I said.

"Yeah, but I'd have to do all that civil crap you do and I'd
hate it. I mean, can you see me talking to some old biddy
about her will? Not Bobby Vee's style, Peckerwood, but thanks
anyway. Who knows, though? Maybe someday."

Maybe if you don't get appointed circuit court judge when
Carey retires, I thought.

"Got some news for you."

"About what?" I asked.

"News about your dear, dead and departed buddy Roger,"
he said, picking up my microcassette recorder, and clicking the
buttons. "Tommy Prescott called me yesterday afternoon."

"So tell me," I said, wary.

I heard my tinny voice commenting on a draft contract for a strip shopping center.

"Shut that damn thing off, will you?" I said.

"What's it about?" Vecchio let the tape run, turning the recorder around in his hand.

"Letter to Goldstein, Ephardt, in Richleigh about a contract for chrissakes. Damn it, shut the thing off. The red button," I said, standing up.

Vecchio managed to depress both the play and fast-forward buttons. My voice became a blur. I reached across the desk, took the recorder from him, and clicked it off.

"Jesus, you're like a two-year-old. You know that? Always fiddling with something."

"You've got all these toys lying around. What can I do?" He turned up both palms imploringly.

"Just tell me what Prescott said. And take your goddamned feet off my desk."

"What if I put them on the newspaper? Can't hurt anything. Am I right?"

"The floor," I replied sternly.

"What is it with you and Anita today?" Vecchio asked, sliding English cap-toed oxfords off my desk and onto the radiator. "I come in at the wrong time? Not your type, I would have thought. Little heavy in the buns. But, hey, the older they get, the more they appreciate it. Am I right or am I right?"

"For chrissakes, Bobby, just tell me what Biddle said."

"Ah yes, Mister Prescott, much esteemed Richleigh DA. Very honorable man," Bobby said in his all-purpose Oriental accent, placing his fingertips under his chin, pressing his palms together, and making a little bow.

"Honorable Prescott san inform me he have line on guy who did Roger. Doper named Jason James. Evil, much evil. Ring a bell?"

"Should it?"

"Where you been? Call boy dope case last spring." Vecchio made a fist and tapped it with my ruler. "Ting-a-ling?"

"All right. I remember now," I replied. "What's the angle?"

"The angle, my friend, is el flako. Mucho flako."

"Give me a break," I said. "Roger a dealer? Get out of here."

"No lie, big guy. Roger needed major-league bucks to keep Vista Mer afloat. Where else would he get that much green?"

"Where did Prescott hear that crap?"

"Twinkie at the Richleigh lock-up celling with James tells his lawyer James confessed to offing Roger. Twinkie's lawyer peddles the story to Prescott, tries to cut a deal for his hero."

"Bullshit story," I said. "Who's the lawyer?"

"Jack Burger," Vecchio replied. "Ever hear of him?"

"Yeah," I said. "Jamming Jack the Jopley hack." Jack Burger, all three hundred pounds of him, worked out of the basement of his house in Jopley, a Richleigh suburb. He hadn't tried a case in years. He was famous—or infamous, depending on whether the perspective was that of the prosecutor or the defense bar—for once pleading out six felonies back to back in under an hour, picking up $150 each.

"So the Jammer has a chat with Tommy P., who might as well wear a sign saying he's planning to be the next attorney general."

"Who's going to be the Demos' hero?" I asked. Bobby's name had been bantered about and I wanted to check his reaction.

"Some forlorn sonofabitch from the Southwest, probably. Some slow-talking hillbilly with no baggage. Davey Crockett type." Vecchio hummed a few bars of the Davey Crockett song and then sang, " 'Got drunk in a bar when he was only three, Davey, Davey Crockett . . .' "

"I think it's 'killed him a bar,' " I said.

Vecchio hummed the refrain several more times. "Who the hell knows what's going to happen?" he said. "We've got what? Fourteen months to the '90 election? So far's, all that's certain is your buddy Elliot Dean's got a lock on the nomination for governor. The rest of it? Who knows?"

I didn't say anything. Vecchio looked at me expectantly.

"Why?" he asked. "You hear something about somebody trying to get the Demo nomination for AG?"

"I heard your name mentioned once or twice."

"Run against Prescott?" he said. "No way. He's been riding the law-and-order circuit for years, preaching the gospel of the electric chair. Cure for all ills, if you listen to Tommy boy. But he's got a problem, Tommy does."

"That being?"

"That being, Tommy P.'s supposed to have cut a deal with James, put the boy to work for the good guys. Problem is, James ain't doing any heavy lifting. Fact, he ain't doing squat." Vecchio laced his fingers together and wiggled them up and down. "Blown and flown.

"Boy's long gone is what I hear," Bobby added, picking up my cordless pencil sharpener.

Anita buzzed me on the intercom to tell me my eleven o'clock appointment was there. I replied I'd be a few more minutes.

"So the bottom line, Mister Billable Hours, is we're going to wait and see if Prescott gets a line on James."

Bobby inserted a pencil and ground off a half-inch.

"Sorry, guy. Meanwhile, we work the Roger-dodger-the-dealer angle. Round up the usual suspects, get you a little business, am I right?"

"Don't tell me you believe that crap."

"I don't know what to believe. I hear things about you I know I don't believe."

"What kind of things?" I said, feeling the muscles in my throat.

"Chill, my man. Chill," Vecchio said, chuckling. "Anonymous tip. Woman phoned me last Friday. Says ol' Kenny's been a bad boy, been dealing flake for the country club set. Can you beat that? What's going down? You piss off a girlfriend or something?"

"That's crap," I replied, putting more emotion in my voice than I intended.

"Hey, buddy, you don't have to convince me," Vecchio said, pointing at his chest. "That's exactly what I told Mulkerrin. Actually, I think I said 'crock of shit.' Close anyway."

I looked at my watch.

"I know. You've got the president of Westinghouse in the waiting room, pacing the floor, worrying whether you'll take his antitrust case against General Electric."

Vecchio stood up, patted his lapels, and buttoned his suitcoat. He turned and looked out the window at the courthouse.

"Just the same, Peckerwood—we're talking images here, big guy, just images—you ought to stay away from the Dufault mess. You know where I'm coming from? If it gets sticky, I don't want you getting an invitation to talk to the grand jury. Just doesn't look good. Besides, who know's what you might be asked, if you follow me." Vecchio winked, clucked his tongue against his cheek, and gave me a big smile.

"I'm administrator of Roger's estate. What am I supposed to do? Close out probate without taking a look?"

"That why you're driving way the fuck out to Harston?"

I didn't reply.

"Keep it light and easy is all I'm saying," Vecchio continued in a soft tone. "Want my advice? Do a once-over on the inventory and get your final report to Carey. Close it out. Nothing but debts anyway, am I right or am I right?"

"Probably," I acknowledged, wondering how Vecchio knew I had visited Yester.

"So what's the problem? Big five, my man," Vecchio held out his palm. I slapped it.

"One other thing," Vecchio said, turning in the doorframe. "You see any ghosts with little horns, look out for your pecker." He winked at me and shut the door.

CHAPTER 10

The Vecchios lucked out. The squall had headed out to sea earlier than predicted. The early-October evening sky, lit by a harvest moon, was clear as a martyr's conscience. The evening was made to order for the Vecchios' Columbus Day dinner, just cool enough to counter the hot gas of political speeches.

A week or so in advance of the dinner, Bobby imports his mother and at least one aunt from Brooklyn, along with half the stock of a trattoria. Enough pasta is rolled out to cover a tennis court. If I had my way, I would ban the oratory and glad-handing. It is sacrilegious to count votes in the presence of homemade fettucini al fredo and ice-cold Corvo Blanco.

What started as a dinner for the staff of the DA's office and a few members of the defense bar evolved into a cornerstone event in the agenda of the Chirkie County Democratic Party. Four years ago the governor attended and the Vecchios' Columbus Day dinner became a fixed event on the state party calendar, an essential appearance for any Democrat considering a run at statewide office.

I remained a Democrat because the Republicans burned our cornfield in '64 and put a Minnie ball in my great-great-grandfather's knee. I figured it was a better reason than most had.

The keynoter this year was Elliot Dean. That Dean was planning to seek the nomination for governor in the spring was an open secret. When a politician says he isn't ruling out further opportunities to serve the people, it doesn't mean he's going into charity work.

Dean's only competition for the nomination was Peter Biddle, the attorney general. Biddle was at a disadvantage because he had a job which forced him to make policy choices. This prevented Biddle from pleasing all the people all the time, a handicap not inherent in the ceremonial office of lieutenant governor.

Last February, I'd had a few drinks with Biddle after the Jefferson-Jackson Day dinner in Richleigh. 'Tain't fair, Biddle had lamented. All that sonofabitch got to do is speak at the high school graduations the governor turns down. Ten minutes of corn and candor in the boonies, shake hands, climb back in the limo, roll down the road, and do it again. That and hand out ribbons at 4-H fairs in counties so far in the west the governor thinks they're in Tennessee.

I might as well be running against Miss Congeniality at the Miss America pageant. Smiling and shaking's all Dean's got to do. Bastard works the press like a fiddle while I've got to run an office of sixty lawyers, half of them convinced they could do a better job than I'm doing.

Dean's been running nonstop for governor ever since he trashed Petit in '86. For nigh on four years now the sonofabitch's had his computer cranking out congratulation cards to every high school graduate, birthday cards to every old biddy who ever gave a dime to the party, and kiss-your-ass cards to anybody who holds a door open for him. What am I supposed to do? You tell me, Wilkinson.

I didn't have any advice, except to tell Biddle to scrape off his five-o'clock shadow and learn to air-kiss instead of landing wet willies which left ladies frantically grabbing in their handbags for Kleenexes.

When Rodney S. Petit, who represented Richleigh in the state senate, had announced his candidacy for the Republican nomination for lieutenant governor in the spring of 1986, so-called prominent Democrats, who had been considering a run, ran instead for cover. Petit had been quietly campaigning for the nomination for over a year. He was reputed to have the heavy money guys in his corner and the conservative press in his pocket.

Tommy Harris, the state senator from Prentiss County, who for nine months had been "exploring" the possibility of seeking the Democratic nomination, suddenly discovered he had "family obligations" which came as a shock to the party, his family, and his mistress. After Harris dropped out, the executive committee of the party made up a list of probables and possibles, but, one by one, they all found reasons to decline. That left at the bottom of the list Elliot Dean, whose only qualifications were his service as vice chair for finance and net worth.

If Dean, Biddle told me while we were having our drinks, caught fire in the boardroom of the state party, the executive committee would let him burn for a while before they bothered to piss on him. Even then, Biddle said, they probably would have aimed to miss. The committee nonetheless concluded Petit had to be challenged and Dean would have to do as the offering.

At least Dean had his own money to throw away, so the only risk to the party was an embarrassing loss. Since Petit would be heavily favored, that risk was manageable. To deflect criticism of the executive committee, quotes from anonymous "party activists" could be leaked to the press to place the blame for the coming disaster at the polls on Dean's lack of experience.

Not long after the delegates at the convention in June 1986 unenthusiastically nominated Dean as the party's candidate for lieutenant governor, Dean spent three hundred thousand dollars for a statewide prime-time TV buy. Dean's TV spot, which ran in the last week of October, turned out to be political dynamite. Dean somehow had learned that Petit owned a disguised interest in a trust which quietly and cheaply had optioned land throughout the state. The pattern of the optioned acreage appeared so oddly configured as to be random. But when a transparency of the State Highway Department's planned right-of-way for Route 53 was overlaid on a map on which the optioned acreage had been shaded, the implication was plain. The shaded areas were strategically located at planned interchanges.

No one knew how Dean had discovered Petit's secret interest in the trust. When Dean had purchased primetime, he was thirty points behind Petit and could count only on yellow dog Democrats, baseline support equal to about twenty-five percent of the vote.

After Dean whipped Petit by over twenty points, the executive committee claimed as much credit for the victory as the gullibility of reporters would allow. It hadn't surprised me when Dean won. I knew how much he hated to lose.

❆

In 1960, Statler kids were a separate tribe, in our land but not of it, transported to and from R. E. Lee Elementary School in a blue Air Force bus.

Mrs. Grady didn't seem to notice the new boy in our fourth-grade class. She was accustomed to Statler kids enrolling at odd intervals and then suddenly disappearing. It was hard to keep track of them. The new boy was skinny and crew cut, like the rest of the Statler boys who sat together at the rear of the classroom. Mrs. Grady didn't notice him until he raised his hand and provided correct answers, in rapid-fire succession, to thirteen times thirteen, fourteen times fourteen, and fifteen times fifteen.

Mrs. Grady told the new boy to put his hands in the air and keep them there. Ruler in hand, she walked to the rear of the classroom, stopped behind the new boy, and leaned over his shoulder to see if he was cheating by looking in the back of the book. She realized he wasn't because he didn't have a book. Then she made him stand up and tell us his name and where he came from. Elliot from the base, 'mam, he said.

During recess, Grevey Rails kicked Elliot in the shins for smarting off. I was delighted to have a smartoff to distract Grevey. But Grevey didn't forget his duties. He made time for the smartoff and the niggerlover. Our shared persecution resulted in a common, if ineffectual, defense, which led to a friendship of sorts.

I taught Elliot to play chess. He taught me the performance specifications for every plane in the Air Force. Elliot knew a lot of things. He already had lived in four states, the last being Maine, which he said was so cold he had to oil his shoes to keep the leather from splitting.

Mother reluctantly permitted me to visit Elliot, telling me not to forget those people haven't had your advantages. But she refused to drive me to Statler after a sentry leaned his head in the window of our station wagon to check her ID. Sonny, she said, my driver's license isn't down the front of my dress. Thereafter, Olmie had to drive me to the base. She was glad to have a reason to get out of the kitchen.

Elliot lived in a two-room apartment beside the hangars. Elliot's father, paunchy but with forearms cabled with muscles, wore fatigues streaked with grease and black boots which stopped just below his knees. Sometimes he would come home while Elliot and I were playing chess. He would enter without speaking, grab a quart of beer from the refrigerator, strip to his undershirt, plop down in front of the TV, unlace his boots, and throw them into the hall. He acted like we weren't there. His dad, Elliot said, was a maintenance guy but was studying to be a fighter pilot.

Elliot's mother's hands were ceaselessly in motion, making jerky, birdlike movements. She made a lot of noise slamming drawers and complaining to Elliot in a thin, high voice. She always seemed to have her hair in curlers, a cigarette in her hand, and on the verge of screaming. She did housework in a dingy slip which gaped open when she knelt to pick up bottle caps. Once she left the door of the bedroom open and I saw her in bra and panties lying on her bed painting her nails. Elliot punched me in the shoulder and said to pay attention to the game. We both blushed.

Sometimes while we played chess, I would overhear Elliot's parents yelling in the bedroom. Elliot never looked up from the board and invariably won those games. I told him they didn't count because he was used to the fighting. Elliot said the harder it gets, the more you have to concentrate. Louder, you mean, I replied. Both, he said.

One Saturday, Elliot made me wait outside the apartment

*while he got dressed. He said his mother wasn't feeling well.
We spent the afternoon collecting pop bottles to cash in at the
PX for deposits. Elliot wasn't talking much, which wasn't like
him. When I told him I was going to leave, he seemed relieved.
We walked back to the apartment to get my chess book. When
we reached the parking lot across from the apartment, Elliot
told me to wait there. As Elliot was crossing the lot the door
to the apartment opened. Elliot's mom, whose hair seemed a
lot blonder, was saying goodbye to a man, when all of a sudden
they started kissing and grinding. They didn't seem to notice
when Elliot pushed past them. When Elliot came back with my
book, they were still hugging in the doorframe. Dad left, Elliot
said, with a shrug. He handed me the book. Then he sprinted
in the direction of the PX.*

✴

On breaks from HMA, I would stop by to see Elliot. He and
his mom lived then in a little clapboard house next to the Gulf
station on 2nd Street. I couldn't tell if we still were friends.
Once I caught myself thinking that my visits to Elliot were sort
of Christian charity, seeing as how he didn't seem to have any
friends. The truth is, I was curious, in a detached sort of way,
to see how Elliot would turn out.

Elliot wasn't a lot of fun to be with. Everything he did, he
did intensely. I didn't know anyone so intense. Goddamn it, I
once said to him, when he turned down an offer to play a little
pool at the Arcade. What better you got to do at nine on a
Friday night? Think about what I'm going to do on Saturday,
Elliot replied. And about how I'm going to do it better.

Sometimes Elliot would take a pack of Marlboros from the
carton his mother kept over the refrigerator. He'd chain smoke
while we played chess, often accompanied by the angry hiss of
air drills and the clanging of hammers on tire rims. I told myself
I lost because of the racket from the Gulf station next door.
But I knew better. Elliot just flat out beat my pants off, which
probably was good for me because I was used to beating everyone at HMA.

I wouldn't have minded losing so much if Elliot hadn't been
so cocksure. He never said anything, but sometimes he would

offer to let me take back my move. I would tell him to take back his own goddamn move. Elliot wouldn't say anything then, either, but there would be anger in the quick way he would move his pieces and I usually would be checkmated in a half-dozen moves.

The little house always reeked of cigarette smoke and burned coffee. You ought not smoke so much, I said to Elliot. It's going to cut your wind. Elliot said smoking keeps you alert, helps you concentrate.

During Easter break in 1966, Elliot showed me a map of Vietnam tacked up beside his bed. Pins with different colored heads had been stuck in it. Elliot could talk for hours about Vietnam, about how it was important to check the commies there. Sometimes he would name his chess pieces after Marine units. He never mentioned the Air Force, except to say that air superiority didn't mean a damn thing if you couldn't hold the ground. The guys with guts aren't the pretty flyboys, he would say. They're the grunts on the ground.

I'm enlisting in the Marines as soon as I graduate in the spring, he told me. Bullshit, I said. You're going to be valedictorian. Everyone knows that. No way they're going to let you enlist.

They can't stop me, Elliot said. Yes, they can, I replied. You don't know how things work. You'd best pay attention I added. I've got Saigon or whatever your king's supposed to be in check. You sure you want to make that move, Elliot asked.

Elliot's mom worked as a teller at Chirkie Savings & Trust. Sometimes she would come upstairs, sit on the end of Elliot's bed, kick off her high heels, rub her feet, smoke, drink a beer, and watch us play chess on the carpet. She looked good dressed up, even though she was in her late thirties. I tried not to look up at her. It broke my concentration just knowing her legs were nearby. She wore a name tag which said, "Helping Chirkie County Grow by Helping You! My Name's Marilyn G. Dean."

When I made deposits for Mother, I made a point never to get in Mrs. Dean's line. She never looked at me, either. It was as if we shared a secret, but I didn't know what it was or why. One time I saw Porky Senior put his arm around her shoulders and whisper to her.

✳

Just before Christmas, 1966, it was so cold the bay froze over, which was supposed to happen once every century. Roger, Porky, Tim, and I were driving to the mainland in Dr. Dufault's Lincoln to look up some girls who worked the second shift at the cannery. Tim said they were sure things. And if we sucked gin up our noses we couldn't smell the fish.

I looked out the window at the ice. The night was so clear I could see the reflection of stars. But maybe I imagined that.

You listening to this, I asked Porky, pointing with my beer at Tim, riding shotgun, who was explaining to Roger why it was a proven, scientific fact that drinking beer with a straw gets you drunk faster. Roger's dumb enough to believe him, Porky said, shaking his head.

Tell me about Elliot Dean, I said to Porky a few minutes later. Not much to tell, he replied in a low voice, looking away. Dean don't do nothing but make A's and stock shelves at the IGA.

Tim suddenly turned around, leaned over the back of the seat, and grinned. Ask Porky about Elliot's mom, he said. He probably knows more about her. Ain't that right, Porky Dorky?

Turn around, Tim, Roger said. You're blocking the mirror. Turn around and shut up, goddamnit.

Yeah, shut your fucking mouth, Porky said.

Ask Porky what kind of deposit his dad's making down at the bank with Elliot's mom. Working late making those deposits, what I hear.

Tim was laughing so hard he didn't quit until Porky cracked him across the head with a longneck Pabst.

You wait until this car stops and see if I don't up and whip your fat ass, Tim said. Everyone in town knows your dad's dicking Marilyn Dean.

✳

Roger, unannounced as usual, dropped by my office one afternoon in the summer of 1979 and asked me to look over an offer submitted by Dean, Varret & Co., on behalf of a limited partnership to be formed if the contract was signed. Roger was wearing an off-white seersucker suit with broad, sky-blue stripes. He was florid from the heat, a post-lunch shot, or both. He dropped the documents on the pile at the side of my desk.

"Have much to do with Dean when you were at the law school?" Roger asked.

"Said hello in the halls when we passed," I answered, surprising myself by lying.

"Seems Elliot's done gone and traded in timesheets for spreadsheets. Wants the Traders Union warehouses. Asked me to convey his regards to you." Roger lit a Lucky and looked around for an ashtray. I pushed a Coke bottle across the desk.

The Traders Union warehouses, imposing brick structures built in the 1890's at Aimes Point, had been abandoned when Richleigh cigarettes replaced Chirkie plug tobacco as the drug of choice. There had been a desultory attempt by the county, which had succeeded to ownership of the warehouses due to unpaid real-estate taxes, to develop the warehouses as emporia for dealers in antiques and curios, but they were too far from main roads, and the channel was filled with algae, weeds, and silt. Their windows shot out by duck hunters years ago, the warehouses' principal use was to shelter vagrants and teen-aged lovers.

The county had given General Development Company a listing on the warehouses. Until Dean suddenly appeared, Roger hadn't had a nibble.

"Last I heard, Dean was at Banks and Worth. I haven't seen him in years," I replied.

"Last time I saw Dean was high school graduation," Roger said, flipping Dean's business card across the desk. "All of a sudden, guy in a custom-made suit pops in my office and shakes my hand like I was his long-lost brother. Barely recognized him. Damned if it wasn't Dean."

Roger put his tassel loafer on the edge of my desk and buffed the vamp with his handkerchief.

"If Dean thinks he can raise a million dollars for those warehouses, we can do business. Make him put up a twenty-five-thousand-dollar deposit. Try to make it nonrefundable."

I tried but couldn't. Dean said okay to the price but insisted that closing be contingent on tax-exempt-bond financing. Lots of luck, I said, knowing the county sooner would issue a bond to finance a cathouse with a neon sign on Main Street.

Dean surprised me by applying to the state Maritime Industrial Finance Agency, an obscure agency which existed to finance harbor improvements, including dry docks. Dean had figured out that MIFA didn't specify a minimum volume of dry-dock business. Dean, Varret & Co., used the bond proceeds to dredge the channel, convert one warehouse into a marine supply store and the other into an inn which made money the day it opened. The dry dock consisted of a secondhand hoist and an open-sided shed.

The Traders Union transaction cemented Dean's relationship with Roger. Dean became a frequent guest at Regent's Glebe, the eighteenth-century estate which Dr. and Mrs. Dufault had restored meticulously, down to the cut of the cedar shingles. Dean, abstemious and reserved, was the perfect counterpoint to Roger's gregarious and, after a few drinks, blowsy enthusiasm. When Roger introduced Dean as his "podner," Dean would flash his quiet money smile and raise his club soda in salute.

At times it seemed half the vice presidents for commercial loans in the Southeast were in attendance at the cocktail parties at Regent's Glebe. Dean was as perfectly suited in demeanor and style to pitch proposals for financing to bankers as Roger was to sell vacation lots to Mom-and-Pop types.

Even when Dean appeared to be acting spontaneously, there was a rehearsed aura to his mannerisms, as if they were planned in advance and critiqued as performed. Dean appeared as serene and unflappable as a yogi, but I sensed his emotions were screwed down a turn too tight. What others saw as cool confidence I saw as anxiety under wraps.

Dean had mastered the shoptalk of internal rate of return, net present value, and compounded cash flow. His tentative manner appealed to bankers to whom the hard sell was anathema. Dean did not request financing so much as to hint it might be in the interest of the bank to propose it. Bankers took to Dean's aloof manner like largemouth bass to May nightcrawlers.

Dean's modern buzzwords and Roger's ancient bourbon swept all before them. They were making serious money turning old farms into quarter-acre lots, generating more work than I could handle. Roger delighted in reminding me that I was stuck on the timesheet while Dean had moved onto the spreadsheet.

Dean, Varret & Company was doing well in areas of the state other than Chirkie County. DV spearheaded the rehabilitation of the old cigarette factories in Richleigh after it had the area certified as historic, which meant tax credits were available to underwrite a large part of the renovation. DV, which had previously optioned many of the factories, made a killing.

By 1982, DV was one of the leading syndicators in the Southeast. The following year, DV went public in an offering which sold better than expected. Roger told me Dean's shares were worth almost three million dollars.

As soon as the holding period expired, Dean began to sell his DV stock in small blocks. By the end of 1984, Dean had sold almost all of it and reinvested in blue chips, sleepers paying two percent dividends, which quadrupled in value during the Reagan bull market. In 1983, Dean became a star fund raiser for the state Democratic Party and a regular on the rubber-chicken circuit.

The party pros regarded Dean as another Jack Kennedy wannabe, a guy with too much hair and too many teeth who had made a bundle too soon and too easily and was hell-bent on losing it in politics. They were glad to help. Dean was touched by every Democratic candidate for every office from dog catcher to governor. He had contributed with a smile, gladly and again. Finally there had been nothing to do but appoint him in 1985 vice chairman for finance.

Dean made no secret of his ambition for statewide elective office. No one took him seriously, but everyone liked his checks. So all the laughing went on behind his back.

When I arrived at the Vecchios' home just after seven, a pair of overweight state troopers with yard-long flashlights were directing motorists to park in the hayfield across the road. A black Cadillac limo was parked in the driveway. The split-rail fence bordering the side yard had been draped in red, white, and blue bunting. Japanese lanterns cast a soft glow over shift-

ing huddles from which emanated murmurs punctuated by
whoops, belly laughs, and shouted first names, the Greek chorus
of politics. My name was called several times as I got close
enough to smell the smudge pots and hear the clinking of ice
cubes.

I got in line at the ticket table. Marnie Linden, handling
registration, was one of those wiry, little women with short,
tightly permed gray hair who make a second career of being a
professional volunteer for the party. Volunteers like Marnie,
who had walked in Father's campaign, were the backbone of
the party. They didn't pontificate or promise. They knew organi-
zation, not oratory, won elections. They were the foot soldiers
who updated registered-voter lists for possibles, probables, and
diehards, worked the phones to get out the vote, went door-to-
door for lit drops, and never got the credit they deserved for
victories. That some governor once had thrown his arm around
her shoulder and addressed her by her first name was reward
enough. Recognition, even if prompted by an index card deftly
slipped to the governor by an aide, not ideology was what
mattered.

Marnie gave me a big smile. I kissed her on the cheek. We're
waiting for you, she told me. Hell, it's only ten past, I said. To
run, she replied, winking.

The "suggested contribution" had jumped to fifty dollars, up
from thirty-five last year. I wrote my check and stuck a name
tag with a gold border to my shirt pocket. Other tags had blue-
and-red borders.

I asked Marnie why I rated a gold border. That's the VIP
tag, she said. In your case, it means I like you, even if you
don't listen to me. I've been listening, dear, I said. Just not
doing, she replied. It also means you get to attend the private
reception for the lieutenant governor.

I entered through the kitchen and made my way to the recre-
ation room. Dean, flanked by an aide with a notepad, was working the room. Dean had a light tan set off by a heavily starched,
brilliantly white shirt. If there were a pattern woven into Dean's
maroon tie, it was so subtle it would take a cryptographer to

find it. The white, maroon, and navy were set off by gold cuff-links with the state emblem as insets and a gold collar pin.

His blond waves were trimmed with just the right touch of deliberate irregularity to convey a hint of casualness even when sprayed rigidly in place.

Bobby Vecchio pressed a plastic cup of bourbon and ice into my hand and pulled me aside. Look at that glorious sonofabitch, he whispered, pointing with his drink. You mean Dean, I asked, puzzled. No, stupid, Vecchio said, his suit. Check out the lapels.

"So what? Blue labels. Blue suit."

"The roll," Vecchio said.

"Roll what?"

"Christ, you crackers can't tell Savile Row from Sears Roe-buck." Vecchio shook his head.

"That's a drop-dead English custom. There's only one way to get that lift to the lapels with that long, soft roll down to the middle button."

"What's that?"

"Baste and shape with prewar five-pound notes." Vecchio punched me in the arm and slipped into the milling crowd.

I hung out beside the pool table and watched Dean work the room with a professional's rhythm. The men got a quick squeeze just above the elbow with Dean's left, followed by a firm, lingering right-hand shake, followed by a left arm across the back and a few huddled words. The women got a kiss on the cheek, a soft shake of their cupped fingers, at least one compliment, the afterglow of Dean's smile, and a wink.

Every now and then, Dean turned to whisper to his aide, an earnest-looking young man in a khaki suit with flat lapels, who nodded and scribbled on a little notepad. Once in a while the aide passed a handkerchief to Dean. These were the only inter-ruptions to Dean's flow, so regular it would have seemed cho-reographed if it hadn't also seemed stale. Dean's movements were more mechanical than balletic, as if beneath his airy man-nerisms and fixed smile was grim machinery. Cast-iron gears below the merry-go-round.

Dean paused, accepted the handkerchief offered by his aide, winced, and mopped his brow. I considered suggesting he leave the sweat beads in place. The human touch wins votes. But Dean, I decided, was way ahead of me. He probably practiced the human touch on Mondays, Wednesdays, and Fridays. On Tuesdays and Thursdays he practiced appearing spontaneous.

Dean's aide nudged him. The aide whispered to Dean, then tilted his head in my direction. Before I could put my drink on the rail of the pool table, Dean was grabbing my elbow and reaching for my right hand.

"Elliot," I said. "We need to talk."

"Sure we do," Dean replied. "Been way too long. You keeping the boys straight down here?" Dean slipped his arm around my shoulders and seemed glad to be out of the traffic in the center of the room, if only for a moment.

"Be a pal. Trade me," Dean suddenly whispered. He handed me a plastic cup of soda water and took my glass of bourbon. He glanced at his aide who was talking to Jamie Higgins, covering the event for the *Standard*. Dean gulped what was left of my bourbon and I handed him back his club soda.

I took a closer look at Dean. He was breathing too rapidly. There was a pallor hiding below the tan and a raw redness in his eyes that drops wouldn't erase.

Dean's aide appeared expectantly at his side. The aide pointed at his wristwatch. Dean turned aside to confer. Then he turned to me, wearing a fixed grin a cannonball couldn't dent.

"Law treating you well?" Dean asked.

"Still paying the bills."

"Need a change, come next year, let me know, you hear?"

I nodded, wondering to how many others Dean had alluded to a state job if he won the election.

"Catch you up later, old buddy? Tommy here has promised an exclusive to this lovely lady." Dean nodded to Jamie Higgins.

"Sure," I said. I got in the buffet line behind the guys already in for third helpings. Bobby Vecchio climbed on the dais and tapped the microphone, which emitted a cough you could hear two states away.

"Let me make one thing perfectly clear. There possibly may be a few, short—and I mean *short*—extemporaneous speeches tonight. But this is first and foremost a party for our friends.'' Laughter exploded from every corner of the half-acre lawn.

"Hey, do I deserve that?'' Bobby said, in an exaggerated, plaintive whine. Louder laughter. But the crowd of about three hundred was paying attention and had turned toward the dais.

"We are here tonight to honor the memory of that great Italian brickmason, Antonio Vecchio, who discovered Brooklyn,'' Bobby said in a sincere manner, getting only a few laughs. Deadpan humor is wasted on political groupies, who above all else fear losing face by an inappropriate response.

"I can see some of you are students of history. Thank you very much. Then one hundred years later Christopher Columbus discovered Wal-Mart.'' More laughter this time.

Bobby tried a few more one-liners before introducing his wife, mother, and aunt, who received a prolonged round of applause. Then he turned over the mike to Deneale Worthy, the chairlady of the Chirkie County Democratic Committee. Reading from notes, she fumbled through a long-winded introduction of dignitaries down to the level of den mothers. This segment of the program was regarded by the crowd as the bar break.

Finally, Worthy turned over the mike to George Carey, who introduced Dean as our native son, in whom we have great pride, from whom we expect great things, who with our sincerest blessings has departed the sacred soil of Chirkie County to serve all the people of our state and, perhaps, someday our nation.

Dean on cue briskly stepped onto the dais, grabbed Carey's outstretched hand, raised it, and waited for the applause to subside.

"I'm glad to be counted among the good friends of Bobby and Maria. There's nothing like a few good friends and forty gallons of marinara sauce to make me feel at home.'' The crowd responded with laughter. Smart, I thought, to pick right up on Bobby's opening line. Instincts like that can't be taught.

Dean opened with references to local politicians and county issues. Storm sewer improvements. Widening Route 201. Dean got a round of applause when he said the congestion on 201 had gotten so bad it wouldn't be long before you would need a reservation just to get on the road. Good advance work, I thought.

"As I look around I see a few of you are old enough to remember Walt Kelly's cartoon strip, Pogo. Don't worry. I'm not going to ask you to raise your hands." Dean paused for scattered laughter.

"In one episode Pogo and his friends are madder than hell about trash in the swamp. So they form a search party to find the mysterious enemies who have been dumping trash. Finally, Pogo notices the litter the search party has been dropping and tells the other animals, 'The enemy is us,' " Dean paused.

"I'm here to tell you the enemy *is* us. We blame politicians for the incompetence of our government. But the politicians we elect year after year are our politicians. The system is our system. The enemy is us.

"For a long time America was rich enough to muddle through, to slap together half— I can't say *that* can I, Jimmy?" Dean turned to his aide, who vigorously shook his head from side to side.

"Half-*baked,* then, I can say that, can't I?" Jimmy nodded as the crowd broke into laughter. It was as rehearsed as Newton at the Nugget but no one seemed to notice.

"Half-baked *problems,*" Dean continued, "once they get so big they can't be ignored any longer. Even by politicians. The days of Band-Aid politics are behind us. Yet our politicians are still looking for the painless quick fix to make our problems go away. Or at least stay off the front page until after the first Tuesday in November."

Dean paused and scanned the crowd, trying to make eye contact with each.

"When I grew up here, I used to attend Trinity Methodist Church out on 43." Heads nodded.

"I remember preachers talking about the sins of omission. They were the tough ones. The sins of commission were easy to spot. Murder. Stealing. Lying. Adultery.

"But the sins of omission were slippery devils. They were the not-doing sins. Not helping a neighbor in need, not taking the time to care, not bothering to notice our brother's need, our sister's pain.''

Dean paused and looked at the crowd. All I could hear was Jamie Higgins scribbling on her stenopad and the grasshoppers strumming in the hayfield.

''I'm here to tell you that in politics there are sins of omission. When our representatives year after year play the reelect-me game rather than trying to find principled solutions to our problems, they sin by omission.'' A chorus of amens swept across the yard.

''And when we the voters let them get away with it, time and time again, that is *our* sin of omission.

''If we fail to honor the trust placed in us, if we fail to set high standards and hold our representatives accountable to those standards, then this noble experiment in self-government—of the people, by the people, and for the people—will fail. And it will be our fault.''

Dean paused. The breeze picked up, causing the bunting to flutter, the lanterns to flicker, and napkins to blow off tables.

''The enemy does not have to be us. But the choice must be made by us.''

The crowd was silent for a moment as if waiting for the benediction. Finally, a few people started clapping, igniting a longer and louder round of applause than I had heard in many years. I clapped along with the rest. There seemed in Dean a pure flame burning amidst the rubbish of glad-handing and back-slapping.

I decided to skip the follow-up remarks. I headed to the bar to pick up a road beer. I almost bumped into Jamie Higgins, still scribbling notes.

''Comment?'' she asked, lifting her pencil.

''Let me ask you a question instead,'' I said.

''Shoot,'' Jamie said.

''That guy who gave the speech. He the same phony I saw working the reception?''

Jamie smiled and walked away.

CHAPTER 11

On the Wednesday after Columbus Day, Porky Bryan telephoned. You hear about Yester, he asked. A falling sensation swept over me. I knew what Porky was going to tell me.

"Old boy bought the farm two days ago."

I said a prayer for Yester. It was turning out to be a good year for praying.

"Graveside service's tomorrow at ten. There's supposed to be a little cemetery at Peen's Ford behind a white church. Thought you might want to know."

"I can find it."

"You going?" Porky asked.

"I'm going."

"Do me a favor, will you? Check on Roger's Eldorado. We've still got four grand hanging out on it."

Thursday morning came with drizzle and threats of worse. The rain picked up as I drove west. The sun seemed to have taken a peek at the day and retreated. I fiddled with the radio dial until I locked on to a Remington station. The forecast for the Harston area was heavy rain with possible flooding. A traveler's advisory was in effect.

I opted this time for Interstate 62. The rain slowed traffic to the speed limit. I reached the exit for 181 and crossed the Shenley which was swift, swollen, and viscid. Caramel fudge at twenty knots.

West of Harston the rains had worsened the rutting of 865. I kept the Dodge in first gear. A few minutes before ten I crested the ridge and parked the truck in the gravel lot in front of the church.

I put on a poncho and slogged uphill through the driving rain in the direction of black umbrellas and huddled shapes. When I was halfway up the hill, one of the shapes turned toward me and then the others did, waiting.

When I was a dozen yards downhill, an old man met me, shared his umbrella, and escorted me to the grave. Without a word the half-dozen mourners turned toward the open grave, the preacher nodded in my direction, slid his hand out of his Bible, and resumed reading, in a thin tenor, a passage from Paul's letter to the Corinthians. For we shall return as bodies incorruptible.

The preacher looked like a young farmhand. His huge hands, red even in the darkness of the day, made his Bible seem a puny thing. His face was very long and very white, pitted but without a wrinkle. His black hair formed a widow's peak over a tall brow.

The remainder of the service was soon concluded. Then the preacher handed his Bible to an old woman, picked up one of the shovels from the pile of mud, and handed it to the old man, who handed me his umbrella. The preacher took up the other shovel and the two men fell into a swift, practiced rhythm.

"It'll need to be hepped up and tamped down, but it'll hold her for now," the old man said to me when they finished. I followed them down the hill and into the vestibule where the women had laid out cupcakes and slices of nut bread beside a coffee urn.

I introduced myself as a friend of the deceased. The old man said he was Staunton's first cousin. Once removed, one of the women added. She said she and her sister were cousins, too. On his mother's side, the other woman added. Then the old man formally thanked me on behalf of the family for paying my respects. Then conversation foundered, sputtered ehs and ah-hems seeking to form themselves into words, failing, and dying away. We gave up and stood in a half-circle, looking at the floor, as if the grave still yawned before us.

The preacher appeared at my side and asked if he could have a word with me. I followed him to a little room behind the pulpit. Choir robes hung from hooks along two walls. He lifted the top of a chest and removed a little box wrapped in newspaper.

"I attended Mr. Yester in the time of his final troubles," he said, looking at the box. "He said if you paid your respects to give this to you and, if'n you didn't, to drop it off the bridge.

"Here you be. And here you are," he said, handing me the box. "He was hard a-dyin', but he had you in his mind."

I took the box and thanked him.

"May God make his face to shine upon you and be gracious to you," the preacher said as I was leaving.

I waited until I was east of the Shenley before I pulled over, opened the package, and found an audiocassette.

I made good time, arriving before sunset at the forest of tall pines just south of the turnoff to the camp. I turned onto the rutted, pebbled road, almost swallowed by pines, which led to the promontory where my home, a rambling wooden structure, built at the turn of the century by a Richleigh sportmen's lodge as a fishing camp, stood watch over the bay. The camp, as Father always called it, and its two hundred sandy acres, covered with saw grass, golden rod, cedars, live oaks, and yellow pines, had been deeded to me by Father the week before his death. I didn't find out until after his death.

Other than fencing it with barbed wire, now rusted into flakes and splinters, to keep out hunters, I had left the land to nature's designs. The pine planking of the lodge I had allowed to weather unpainted in the salty air. Five years ago, when the cant of the bayside deck reached twenty degrees, I had shored it up with new timbers. The camp creaked in a stiff breeze and groaned in a gale.

After a microwaved dinner, I poured two inches of bourbon, slipped the cassette into the tape deck and pressed the play button.

The voice of Roger, earnest and pleading, filled the room.

I've got to have it now, goddamnit. Too late now to chicken out. It's a done deal.

The other voice, Nile's, clipped and huffy, interrupted. Goddamn your badgering. I'm not going to be rushed. Do you understand that? Are you listening to me?

Then Roger's voice again, softer and slower. We've done been over this. I'm the guy whose tit's in the wringer, not you. No way it can be traced back to you.

Then Niles's voice, weary and labored. I don't know. I just don't know. I've got to think about it. I need more time.

Just listen to me, Roger replied, his voice tense. We've tromped up and down and all over that same old field. It's a done deal now. No backing out.

Then a long pause and the sound of breathing. Finally, Niles's voice, weary and resigned, saying, all right, all right, for Christ's sake. Don't tell me what you set up. No more calls to the law school. Never call me there and don't ever come to my home again. I won't stand for it.

Then Roger's voice again, saying I understand, receiving only the hum of a dial tone in reply.

I rewound the tape and played it again and again. I concentrated on tones and sounds, as if hidden behind the words there was a message from the dead.

Two days later I called Cubertson. She's in conference, her secretary told me.

"I'll be in Richleigh tomorrow. I only need to see her for a few minutes."

"I'm afraid that's impossible, Mister . . ."

"Wilkinson. Kendall Wilkinson."

"Wilkinson," she continued. "She's booked solid. All day."

"Slip her a note. Tell her it's about Addio. I'll hold."

"If you insist," she snapped, and put me on hold. I listened to the greatest hits of Mantovani. The recording had just started to play through for the third time when Cubertson's secretary broke in.

"Ms. Cubertson says she has a slot open at one-fifteen if this is truly urgent."

I resisted replying she could save her slot for someone else, that I just wanted to talk. Instead, I thanked her and said I'd be there on the dot.

On Friday morning I crossed McAllister Memorial Bridge and headed southwest toward Richleigh. I followed old route 45 which long ago had been the Richleigh Turnpike. When Interstate 79 was completed in the late sixties, 45 turned overnight into a gallery of relics linking ghost towns, a river of history flowing past banks of Americana. Along 45, Union and Confederate troops had advanced and retreated in the tango of war. South on 45 to Richleigh, flat trucks laden with cured leaf for almost a century had trundled. Some still did. North on 45 after the First World War, the great migration had passed.

The gas stations not boarded up had been converted to antique shops and the banks to video rental stores. I passed the Wig Wam Motor Court. Tiny wooden cabins, facades crafted to resemble tents, were bunched around a weed-infested gravel crescent. Most were boarded up. The gaudy paint of the totem poles at the entrance had weathered to faint pinks, barely-there yellows, and hints of sky blue. A Coca-Cola sign had been left to fade to a shade of deep pink which takes forty years of weather. An Oldsmobile with more primer than paint was parked beside one cabin.

I arrived in Richleigh well in advance of my meeting with Cubertson. Richleigh named a chapel after Robert E. Lee. That tells you a lot about Richleigh. At least about the Richleigh that was. The present Richleigh, marred by discontinuities, was as ill at ease as a gracious old lady in a turquoise pant suit. Atlanta again had fallen first. Richleigh was barely holding on, her idiosyncrasies under siege and sure to fall to national marketing, national media, and what passes for a national culture.

Banks & Worth occupied the top two floors of a recently constructed, twelve-story building which towered over the dome of the eighteenth-century capitol. The reception area was paneled with a densely grained, luminous wood the color of old bourbon. Intricately patterned rugs, blends of deep purple, dark gold, and hunter green, were bordered by tufted leather club chairs of a cherry shade so deep the red was discernible only where brass studs melded seams. In the center of each rug a dark-gold oval framed a purple monogram, B&W.

The reception area was spacious and cool, illuminated by small brass wall lamps above antique paintings of fox hunting scenes. I half expected a steward in a riding habit to emerge from the shadows and offer me a hunt cup of Madeira and brandy. The interior decorator hadn't bothered with understatement. The pitch (power, class, and money) was slow, down the center, and chest high. Abstract art makes old, rich people insecure. Give them The First Blooding from 1796 and bill the hell out of them.

The young blond receptionist didn't have a desk. She sat behind a small table which looked too delicate to support her steno pad and little gold pen, the only items on it. In keeping with the decor, the receptionist had been buffed and polished to perfection.

I asked if she had a pair of sunglasses I could borrow. She flashed a bright smile which clashed with the theme of the room. After a few minutes, a secretary, who looked like she worked weekends as an undertaker, emerged from the wings to lead me to Cubertson's office.

I crossed the threshold precisely at one-fifteen and was greeted by the tall, leather back of a desk chair. A pair of crossed, trim ankles extended from the side of the chair. They ended in gas-blue, lizard skin pumps which rested on the upholstered window ledge. The contralto tones emanating from the depths of the chair I recognized as Cubertson's. She was talking about a leveraged buyout.

When her secretary rapped on the doorframe, Cubertson spun the chair around and held up an index finger to indicate one more minute. Then she spun the chair back to face the window and took five more.

Cubertson had the usual trophy wall. In addition to framed certificates, commendations, appreciations, and sheepskins, there was an arrangement of power photographs: Cubertson shaking hands with the former governor, Cubertson standing at a lectern receiving the presentation of a gavel the size of a softball bat,

Cubertson accepting a large, shiny plate from a lady in a print dress who looked like Betty Ford.

I studied a photo of Cubertson seated at a small table before a committee of heavy, jowled men in dark suits arrayed in a raised crescent. I recognized Randolph Higgins in the center of the committee. There were no drawings by children nor, for that matter, any photographs of children to take the edge off her power archive.

Cubertson rang off and swiveled the chair around to face me. She was wearing a knobby silk jacket, in a shade which matched her pumps, with white piping to which was pinned a small corsage of white carnations. Her glossy black hair was done up in a French braid. Her face was angular but striking. Her eyes were big, black, and bold.

I decided you first were struck by Cubertson's intensity. Then all of a sudden you realize she's dropdead beautiful. It comes as a surprise, like a left hook, sneaking in behind the right cross you see too late.

"So what's so urgent?" she asked me as soon as the door was shut. "I told you I have no memory of Addio, whatever it is."

"I thought you might want to see this." I pulled a photocopy of Niles's letter to Roger from my pocket and handed it to her. She unfolded it, read it, and flicked it dismissively toward me.

"So what?" she said, looking up.

"I thought it might refresh your recollection."

"Even if it did, the question is still pending."

"Why don't you repeat the question?" I replied.

"So what?"

"I thought I answered that."

"No. You gave me some trial-lawyer crap about refreshing my recollection. You didn't tell me why I should give a damn."

"I thought maybe you could tell me that," I replied.

"Nesbitt, Dufault, and Vista Mer are all dead," she replied softly. "Do as Jesus said. Leave the dead to bury the dead."

"Dufault and Nesbitt, in a manner of speaking, are alive," I said.

"How's that?"

"I'm their personal representatives, charged with the duty to carry out the wishes of the decedents."

"And what do you think they are?" Cubertson asked.

"Just desserts," I said after a pause.

"You're wasting my time," she snapped. "Attorney-client confidentiality follows the client to the grave. You knew I couldn't comment. You came here to see what my reaction would be when you gave me this letter. I hope you're satisfied?"

I didn't respond. Our eyes locked.

"You don't know what you're getting into," she said. "Let what came to past belong to the past."

"The past is prologue," I replied.

Cubertson started to buzz her secretary. I told her I knew my way out. I exited to the parking lot with ninety minutes to kill before I picked up Martha. The teenaged attendant had balanced his stool on its back legs and was rocking. After a moment he pushed up the visor of his LA Raiders cap and removed his earphones.

I said I'd been in a rush and might have dinged a red Mercedes convertible. I couldn't remember where the car was. I wanted to check and leave a note on the windshield if I had clipped it.

"There be only one," he said. "It be on A, over near the elevator." He pointed out a red Mercedes 280 SL in the corner, below the sign which said the section was reserved for Banks & Worth.

"If I dinged it, maybe I'll go up to Banks & Worth and give the owner my insurance stuff. Get it out of the way."

"That be Miz Cubertson. Ice fox."

I thanked him and walked over to pretend to examine the fender. When I returned to tell him there wasn't a nick, he looked relieved.

Charlie and Renee lived in Mosby Woods, a fashionable enclave renowned for its boxwoods. In our state, old boxwoods are revered as an essential cultural expression, as much so as miniature bonsai trees in Japan. Charlie last spring won a prize for a sculptured hedge. I told Renee to name it Boa Constrictor with Cramps.

Blue blood and boxwood sap, Mother once said, scolding me for my neglect in pruning the boxwoods at the camp, rise in the spring. I have an intuitive understanding of the alchemy between bourbon and horse sweat, the other protean elements of our culture. The one between blue blood and boxwood sap eludes me.

When I was growing up, Mother seemed to believe in a myth, the key elements of which I was able to infer over time from the scoldings I received.

Once upon a time there was an Episcopalian lad, who minded his parents and didn't slouch, from a well-respected, venerable family. He was an outstanding graduate of the right schools (not more than one of which was in New England and none in California) and fell in love with a virgin, more or less, of equally distinguished lineage, who was a graduate (or at least a sophomore) of one of four expensive, private women's colleges in our state.

Following an eleven A.M. wedding held on Lee-Jackson day, officiated by a bishop or better, the newlyweds rode thoroughbreds until their (the humans') loins were lathered, drank ancient bourbon, and consummated the marriage in a four-poster bed strewn with cuttings from boxwoods from each of our state's fifty-three counties. From this mating, a messiah would be born and the South would rise again. There is supposed to be a foundation for this prophecy in the Revelation of St. John along with the prediction of a hole in the ozone layer.

When I pulled into the circular driveway, Charlie put down his pruning shears by way of greeting. He was my senior by a few years. Charlie had pretty much surrendered to the flesh. Let it fall out, grow slack, or spread as it may, his appearance seemed to say. Charlie was the kind of guy who was born wearing tassel loafers. An eight-ball had more edges than Charlie.

Gardener, prune thyself, I thought, feeling self-righteous, redeemed by my push-ups and other tortures, and pleased Martha was old enough to appreciate the contrast. Civilized rivalry is the best that can be hoped for between a parent and a stepparent of the same sex.

I followed Charlie to the poolhouse. He found a few beers behind the bar and tossed one to me.

"Renee's at the club. Semis of a doubles tourney. Martha's still packing. Down in a few moments."

We settled into wicker chairs in the gazebo, drank the beers without speaking, and listened to the bumblebees at work in the roses.

"Keep in touch with Dean?" I asked.

"Went to the inaugural ball. Last time I saw him. 'Nother?" Charlie said over his shoulder as he ambled toward the bar.

"Still working on this one." He came back with two cans.

Martha, ten years old going on fifteen, hot-pink duffel bag slung over her shoulder, crossed the terrace. She was thinning out, losing baby fat, about to enter the on-deck circle to womanhood.

I didn't know when she was scheduled to stop being a little girl and start being something adolescent. I suspected the onset coincided with a training bra. It was happening too fast. I wanted a second chance.

I wanted more time to patch the fissures caused by my selfishness and that of Renee. We had been sixties children, coddled first, then spoiled, and finally stranded by the neap tide of narcissism, left to rot with our obsessive quests for personal fulfillment. In the smithies of our souls we forged golden calves.

"Hey, tiger."

"Daddy."

I hugged her and held her to my side.

"Ball was a gay affair." Charlie laughed and rolled his eyes toward me.

I cringed when Charlie gave Martha a little hug and told her to behave herself.

On the way to Lassington, Martha told me she wanted to go fishing with me. She said she would rather do that than almost anything. I hung on her words, as grateful as if I had received a papal benediction. Except for listening to the new album by UB40, she added a few minutes later.

CHAPTER 12

I was the courthouse canteen's last customer. I tapped what was left in the urn into a styrofoam cup and studied the result. An iridescent globule shimmered on the surface. I snapped on the lid, laid two quarters on the counter, and stepped into the basement hall. I pushed open the fire door which led to the back stairs, reserved, according to the stencilled lettering, for Official Use Only.

The stairs ascended to a landing just outside the robing room. I pushed open the jury-side door to the darkened courtroom and took a seat in the jury box. I opened my briefcase and took out a clipboard and a pen. I drew a line down the page. One column for facts, the second for inferences.

The late-afternoon sun struggled through cracks in off-kilter Venetian blinds. Planes of light more sepia than gold cut intersecting swaths through the shadows. I rocked back in the swivel chair, which creaked in protest, the sound echoing in the empty courtroom. I sipped the acrid coffee and let the shadows turn into ghosts.

That day I had been sitting two benches back from the defense counsel table. It had been so hot I burned my chin when I rested it on the back of the wooden bench. But maybe I had imagined that. Remembering is like looking at a stream through a hand-blown pane. It's hard to tell if the ripple is in the water or the glass.

I looked at the oak lectern, standing sentinel in the center of the well, its sides stained dark from the sweated palms of generations of lawyers. I looked away. When I looked again, Father was gripping the sides of the lectern leaning forward, seeming to overwhelm the lectern, cross-examining Dr. James Barone, the coroner. Jimmy Bones, as everyone called him. Bones to dust, years ago.

From the way Father cocked his head toward the jury box, I could tell he finally had extracted the admission he sought. Father stepped away from the lectern and turned to the jury box, letting the silence pound, not looking at me. I believe only in the ghosts I deserve.

The jury deliberated—long enough for a catered lunch before returning to acquit Sanders Trent of murder, finding he acted in justifiable self-defense when he shot his wife's lover, a lieutenant from Statler armed with a nail clipper, in the parking lot of the IGA. The verdict provoked an editorial in the *Atlanta Constitution,* which, ever mindful of the South's image in the eyes of the North, both condemned the acquittal and blamed it on Father, backhanded praise that mightily pleased him.

A good trial lawyer, son, Father said to me after he read the editorial, is an alchemist who can dissolve the obvious. Never forget the obvious is mutable, the momentary precipitate of an unconscious perspective.

Mindful of Father's advice, I picked up the clipboard and started scribbling notes.

Like a billiard player lining up combinations, trying to decide on the percentage shot, I tested angles on Dean and Roger, drawing possible connections. The angles were long-ball combinations which had scratch written all over them. But I had a sense this was the last shot I was going to get.

Dean planned his chess moves six in advance. The day after he was elected lieutenant governor, Dean would have started lining up pledges, chatting up activists, and honing issues in preparation for a run for the governor's mansion in 1990.

During the 1986 campaign, Roger had been Dean's envoy to the state Builders and Developers Association. Roger had been

a one-man phone bank, dialing every number in the BDA directory to let the boys know that Dean, notwithstanding the usual
environmental claptrap required of a Democrat, was a regular
guy who put the bottom line first, not some flake who remembered snail darters in his prayers.

Dean wouldn't have forgotten that. He would have counted
on Roger's help when he ran for governor. Of course, Roger's
help wouldn't be as critical in 1990. By then, Dean would have
nurtured his own ties to key BDA leaders. Still, Dean would
not have wanted to throw away Roger's help. Smart politicians
are environmentalists; they never forget to recycle old friends,
even if their value wanes. But they never hesitate to cut them
cold and never look back when old friends become more of a
burden than a benefit. But Roger in 1987, when he dreamed up
Vista Mer, hadn't become a burden to Dean, not yet.

Roger counted on a payback from Dean who by virtue of
being lieutenant governor became chairman *ex officio* of the
Environmental Control Commission. Roger, who believed in the
natural law of deals, was oblivious to the subtle minuets of
political favors, to the delicate subterfuges required lest the trust
of the public be lost and the dance come to a halt. To Roger
politics was a species of business, another game played with
markers known as debits and credits. If price tags weren't
openly affixed to the markers, the rules were the same.

Roger would have told Dean about his plan for the oceanfront
tract before he had gotten too far into negotiations with Rivero.
Dean wouldn't have said no when Roger brought up the need
for a condominium development permit. Decisions foreclose options, the coin of politics. A politician is as reluctant to decide
as a businessman is to plunk down hard dollars. Remaining
noncommittal is the political equivalent of preserving capital.

Roger wouldn't have understood that. For Roger, a friend
was a friend, not a cipher in a chess game. In Dean's bland
"we'll see," Roger would have heard a promise. A few months
later, when some local environmentalists started a low wail of
protest, Roger would have sought assurance from Dean before
closing. Maybe this time Dean said no, but not emphatically,
while at the same time frowning and winking, as if to chide

Roger for being a bad boy but one who was going to get his cookie anyway.

Had the wail from environmentalists not swelled, Dean might have put in a word for Roger. But Vista Mer, in part due to Roger's foolish remarks to the *Richleigh Journal* about the "exclusive" nature of the development, took on a symbolic importance as a "have *versus* have-not issue" which transcended the environmental debate. Dean would have seen the storm brewing, or, rather, the brouhaha storming. He would have reassessed Roger's value and found him more of a liability than an asset.

Maybe Dean recognized he had held the Roger card too long before flicking it onto the discard pile. Maybe Dean realized that if he had nipped Roger's hope in the bud, it never would have become an expectation, far less a claim. Maybe a twinge of regret, born more from recognition of a tactical error than from any moral sense, caused Dean one night to toss and turn for a few sleepless hours.

I put down my pen and looked over my list. So far, so good. The flow of events was consistent with the law of political survival, my working hypothesis. That Roger stood to be beggared by the law would have troubled Dean no more than the destruction of a family farm by a railroad right of way would have troubled a robber baron. Dean would have blamed the law while exonerating the application.

But there was a hard fact that refused to be explained, contrarian grit that jammed the gears of my theory. Dean had invited Roger to a meeting in Richleigh in mid-May. Roger returned from the meeting sunnyside up. There was no reason to doubt Yester's account. Nor was there any reason why Dean would have scheduled the meeting.

Dean made a habit of wringing his feelings through cold rollers, squeezing out emotions which might skew the dictate of logic. It made no sense for Dean in mid-May, when Vista Mer was moribund, to inflate Roger's hopes falsely. Dean was cynical, not gratuitously cruel.

Nor could Dean's decision to meet with Roger be explained by assuming Dean had been touched by Roger's desperation and, belatedly recognizing his passive complicity, experienced a change of heart. Intervening with the ECC posed for Dean a risk that far exceeded any possible gain to be derived from Roger's gratitude.

Two uneventful weeks of a fine Indian summer rapidly passed by. It was my weekend with Martha. On Friday, I was scheduled to meet Renee at our standard drop-off point, the Stuckey's at Exit 43 on Interstate 79. A dark-blue Jaguar with vanity plates, "RCV-Jag," was parked in front when I arrived.

I gave Martha a kiss on top of her head. "Daddy," she said, surprised, looking up from a chocolate sundae.

Renee's air kiss, aimed in the general direction of my cheek, left a wake of perfume which made me think of yellow roses after a heavy shower. Renee looked like she had escaped from the show window at the Laura Ashley shop in Richleigh. Matching alligator pumps and clutch. Wraparound skirt of navy suede, heavy silk blouse in a shade of rich vanilla ice cream, cut low enough to show off a knotted cluster of pearls, slate-gray Eton jacket with navy windowpane checks.

Her chestnut hair, which seemed to have lost the sheen I remembered it had when it was thicker, was pulled back and fastened with a gold monogram clasp which matched her gold monogram earrings. Her face was sharper now, the skin somehow too shiny and taut across her cheekbones. There was a pinched look to her mouth which pastel lipstick couldn't soften. Her skin seemed to have slipped, just a bit, off her chin. She was fighting her forties, gallantly holding her own. Still beautiful, but now also courageous, her demeanor seemed to suggest. And still expensive, of course.

"All this for me?" I asked.

"Just the pearls," Renee said, reflexively fingering the strand of discolored little pearls. Then I recognized the pearls as the ones I had given Renee. Christmas 1968. Father with a laugh had loaned me a hundred dollars telling me a bottle of fine bourbon was a damn sight cheaper and more likely to work. Toss in some kind of underwear thing, he had said, and you're

still fifty bucks to the better. She read my expression and
blushed. Then I blushed. Just as we had then.

"Maybe it's because they're knotted," she added, discom-
fited by the memory we alone shared.

✳

*I met Renee at a mixer at Smith. By October of my freshman
year at Yale, I was an accomplished liar, having discovered
Yankees were willing to credit any lie about the South so long
as it involved dementia, lust, violence, and dark, piney woods.*

*I invented gothic tales which would have made Faulkner
blush. I experimented until I came up with the right mixture of
lust and violence. There is a lost land, I would say, of gargoyles
and grits, where crimes of passion are so admired they are
judged along with hand-hooked rugs, heifers, and home canning
at the county fair.*

*I discovered it always seemed to help, for some reason, to
work in a cattle prod. Ivy league women seemed to want to
believe southerners were always fooling with cattle prods. I
had never seen a cattle prod, which allowed my imagination
free rein.*

*I said some prods were as small as a ballpoint pen and had
a little clip so they wouldn't fall out of your shirt pocket. Others
were called toe prods because they were designed to slip over
the toe of a hob-nailed piney-woods boot. Folks too poor to
afford a store-bought cattle prod were forced to carry around
an electric eel in a gunny sack. (I didn't know what a gunny
sack was, but it sounded Southern and no one ever ques-
tioned it.)*

*I was explaining to a half-dozen Smithies how back home in
Chirkie County we still used our servants as beaters to flush
game in bad weather. Can't risk using a good dog when hunting
wild boar in a ground fog in a dark, piney wood. Might use
an old dog you're going to have to put down anyway, but not
a good dog.*

*I had just gotten to the part where I shot a beater by accident
and Father, as punishment, made me learn by heart the twenty-
fifth chapter of Genesis, which lists the descendants of Abra-
ham, when the prettiest girl—the one I had been watching out*

*of the corner of my eye—put her hands on her hips, rolled her
eyes, hissed, and stamped her scotch-grain loafer.*

*I figured the problem was I hadn't worked in a cattle prod.
So I switched to a tale which never failed to work, one involving
a termite-ridden shack in a cypress swamp, a pregnant prom
queen, a free will Baptist deacon snakehandler, and a cattle
prod. I was getting to the good part—where the girl's father
strangles the deacon with his own rattlesnake—when, in an
accent I recognized, she told me I was so full of shit my eyes
were brown.*

"From Richleigh or thereabouts, ma'am, I presume," I said.

*"Presume all you please," she said, "but you probably
ought to stick with lying. Seems you're right good at it."*

*The other girls looked at her and at me. Then, after a pause,
she sighed and said I should at least know what the hell I was
talking about. The guy strangled by the girl's father wasn't a
deacon. He was a fat, ugly deputy sheriff named Cecil. The girl
who was murdered was just a prom princess, not the queen.
And, for chrissake, she said, any countrified fool knows that
cypresses don't grow in swamps. They grow in bogs. If you're
going to tell it, she said, you might as well get it right.*

*I was in love with her before she finished pirouetting on the
hand-stitched genuine moccasin toe of her classic Bass Weejun.
It occurred to me, after we had been married for several years,
that we never were again to attain timing so perfect. I became
a prisoner of our finest moment.*

*I followed her tartan plaid skirt down a brick sidewalk split
by bulging oak roots. Wait up, I said. Mister, you are full of
shit, she replied, over her shoulder, dragging out "shit" into
two heartrending syllables. Just leave me be. You hear? I came
up here to get away from the likes of fools like you.*

✳

"Things okay?" I said as Renee picked up her clutch from
the counter and slipped out a bill.

"Sure. Why not?" She laid a ten on the counter, shut the
clasp with a snap as sharp as a .22's report, and gave Martha
a kiss on the cheek.

"See you here Sunday at ten to seven," she said to me.

"Why not seven?"

"Because you were ten minutes late," Renee said, taking out her mirror and popping open her lipstick. "Used to be you were always ten minutes too soon." I turned in time to catch the reflection of Renee's eye in the mirror, watching for my reaction. She snapped the compact shut and dabbed her lips on a tissue. She gave me a goodbye smile which I didn't return.

"That your bag, Tiger?" I said, after a moment, gesturing at a large, blue denim roll by the coat rack.

"It's called a duffel, Daddy," Martha said, hugging me. She put on her baseball cap and flipped up the visor.

"There's no rush, honey. Finish your sundae."

"It's Mom's. She gave it to me when she saw you drive up." Martha beamed a grin, knowing all too well it was the kind of detail which amused me.

The dying sun had just finished painting the low bank of cumulus clouds in shades of rose and magenta when we arrived at the camp. I heated up a salt-cod stew and fried tomatoes in cornmeal. Martha and I bundled up, carried our plates onto the deck, and settled ourselves into eighty-year-old rocking chairs. We ate in silence, watching the full moon slip and slide between swirling piles of clouds, listening to wind-driven, flood tide combers slap the limestone cliffs below.

After I put Martha to bed, I poured a drink and listened again to Yester's tape of Roger and Niles. I rewound it and played it again, focusing on inflections and cadences. Maybe I had it wrong, I decided. Maybe Dean didn't invite Roger to the meeting. Maybe Roger had lied to Yester. Maybe Roger forced the meeting. It was a possibility, an ugly one.

I slipped on my HMA varsity jacket and carried my drink onto the deck. The thin layers of clouds, buffeted by gentle updrafts from the bay, seemed to vibrate in the moonlight. The distant clanging of a channel marker answered the sibilants of the white pines. I sipped the bourbon, feeling its glow rise as the pit of my stomach fell.

CHAPTER 13

I arrived with Martha at the Howard Johnson's at 7:00 P.M. on Sunday. Renee arrived at 7:10, planning to teach me a twenty-minute lesson, which I cut to a ten-minute wait. I returned to the camp and turned in early.

I woke up at four with my mind racing. I took a couple of aspirin and silently chanted Om-Mani-Pad-Me-Om, focusing on the syllables, letting them resonate.

I'm not sure where the mantra came from. I have a vague recollection of learning it during my freshman year from a town girl with shoulder-length corkscrew curls, tie-dyed bib overalls, a water bong, and all of Ravi Shankar's LPs.

Meditating on the mantra is supposed to banish nettling, half-thoughts, the ones that scurry like cockroaches whenever you try to concentrate on them. It seemed to work until I began to worry about getting stuck on Om-Mani-Pad-Me-Om, which would be worse than getting stuck on "Oops, there goes another rubber tree plant," a fragment of a Sinatra song from the mid-fifties that haunts me. Suddenly, it hit me. As representatives of the estates of Roger and Niles, I had access to their phone bills.

When I got to the office, I made copies of the orders appointing me as administrator and co-executor of the estates, respectively, of Roger and Niles. I sent a letter to Bell Tidewater requesting copies of bills for December 1988 through June 1989 for GDS's phone, Roger's home phone, and Niles's home phone. In the letter, I explained I was adjusting between the two estates credits and debits for long-distance call reimbursements.

Ten days later, a box with a Bell Tidewater logo and a Richleigh address arrived at my office. I put it aside, figuring to save the fun for a rainy day. I took it as a sign when around three o'clock clouds rolled in from the Atlantic, in defiance of the forecast, and loosed a heavy downpour.

The records for GDC's phone were the thickest even though GDC's phone had been disconnected for nonpayment in April. There were several dozen calls to two Richleigh numbers which I guessed belonged to the office of the lieutenant governor and the Environmental Control Commission. I dialed the numbers to make sure I was right. I was. The other long-distance calls were to numbers I didn't recognize, many of them out of state. I asked Anita to dial the numbers and make a list of the owners.

She gave me a list forty minutes later. Almost all of the out-of-state calls were to banks and S&L's. When I looked over the list, I could hear Roger pleading the case for a take-out loan, offering to pay double origination points and escrow the interest in advance. Roger, cradling the phone, cajoling some jaded assistant vice president who at thirty had heard it all too many times.

The records for Roger's home phone predictably showed a surge after GDC's phone was disconnected. On May 23, there had been a fifteen-minute call to the Richleigh number of Banks & Worth. There had been a twenty-two minute call to Banks & Worth at 3:00 P.M. On June 6. On that same day, at 4:30 P.M., there had been a five-minute call to Dean's office. The June bill showed a forty-three minute call at 11:35 P.M. on June 11 to a Richleigh number I didn't recognize. When I dialed the number I received a recording telling me the number was not published. There had been a nine-minute call to this same number on June 14, the day before Roger's death.

On May 28 at 11:20 A.M., there had been a call to the main number for the university, followed, three minutes later, by a call to the law school. The call to the law school occurred on the afternoon following Roger's return from his meeting with

Dean. On May 30, there had been a call at 7:09 P.M. to a nonpublished number I recognized as Niles's home phone. In June, there had been five calls to Niles's home, three of them in the week before Roger's death.

I started on the records for Niles's home phone. There had been no calls to GDC, nor to Roger's home. Niles had made four calls to Dean's office during the six months covered by the records.

Niles had placed six calls to Banks & Worth during the last week of May and first two weeks of June. Niles had made a seventeen-minute call at 11:12 P.M. on June 11 to the same nonpublished Richleigh number which Roger had dialed. On June 17, there had been a twenty-three-minute call at 10:54 P.M. to this same number.

I counted thirty-seven calls which had been placed by Niles during December to March to a Richleigh number I didn't recognize. The last call had occurred on March 11. The calls, for the most part, had been made late at night and for durations in excess of ten minutes, with a half-dozen exceeding an hour. I dialed the number and got a disconnect message with no forwarding number.

I dialed Directory Information for Richleigh. The operator declined to give me information on numbers not currently in service. She referred me to a billing accounts manager who seemed satisfied by my explanation that I was trying to locate a missing heir. He put me on hold.

"Mercury Express mean anything to you?" he asked when he returned to the phone ten minutes later.

"Got an address?" I asked.

"203 Cory Street," he said. "We talking big bucks here?"

"Why do you ask?"

"Because Mercury Express owes Mamma Bell two grand, in round numbers," he said. I said I'd let the probate clerk know, thanked him, and rang off. I buzzed Anita on the intercom.

"Mercury Express mean anything to you?"

"Sounds like a delivery service," she replied.

"Call the Corporation Commission. See if Mercury Express was incorporated. Most delivery services are, for liability reasons. Get the CC to pull the most recent annual report and give you the names of the directors.''

About twenty minutes later, Anita handed me a slip of paper on which she had written, ''Jason James, 203 Cory Street, Richleigh.''

The name struck a chord that vibrated gently for a few seconds before I remembered what Vecchio had told me. I didn't say anything. Anita read my expression.

''Mother lode?'' Anita asked.

''Maybe fool's gold. What else?''

''James was the big enchilada,'' she replied. ''Sole director, sole officer, and formerly the registered agent for Mercury Express, Inc.''

''Formerly?'' I asked.

''The corporation was dissolved on June 1 for failure to file its annual report and pay the registration fee. Last annual report was of 1988. I checked with Directory Information. There's no telephone listing for a Jason James, nor any for Mercury Express. Want me to call Allied Process and order a skip trace?''

''No,'' I said. ''If Tommy Prescott can't find James, Allied's not going to have any luck.''

I let a few days go by before I telephoned Mulkerrin and asked her to have lunch with me at the Jade Garden. I hadn't seen much of Mulkerrin since the summer. It wasn't that I intentionally had heeded Warren Closter's warning. It had just worked out that way.

The tenth day of November rode a zephyr sweeter than a memory of May. Sunny and seventy. Lee Yin gave me the front booth, my usual, which afforded a panoramic view of the truck traffic on 202. The Jade Garden was the oldest Chinese restaurant in the county, a claim the other one never bothered to contest. I studied the menu stained with samples of most of the entrees.

''No broccoli day,'' Lee Yin said, setting down a second pot of tea. He hadn't bothered to clip the Safeway tag from the tea bag steeping in the still wet, stainless-steel pot frosted with dishwasher powder, green-and-white beads baked onto the spout and lid. I sipped plain tea from a chipped thimble on which faded scarlet dragons were dueling and waited for Mulkerrin to show up. Apart from the clinking of tableware behind the counter, I was left in a silence which befitted my melancholy. Over the past several days, I had spent a lot of time thinking about time, space, and death, and whether there was a Woody Allen movie with that title. I had a classic case of the ol' ontology blues about which John Lee Hooker had sung for so long and so well.

Mulkerrin arrived a few minutes later, wearing a pale gray suit with a very pale blue silk blouse cut low. She looked so good I forgot my wounded pride. But when she slipped into the booth and her pleated, short skirt rode to midthigh, I remembered freckles and it began to ache again, throb anyway.

"Not exactly Mott Street," she said, picking up the menu. "Fried rice with shrimp, chicken, or beef."

"Old Chinese saying. Few choices lead to right choice."

"They make their own MSG?" She wrinkled up her nose.

I told her the Lee family operated the Jade Garden and the Kwik-Clean next door. I suspected an interior passageway. Several times the counter girl at the Kwik-Clean had borne an uncanny resemblance to the waitress who had served me.

Lee Yin brought the chicken fried rice. Mulkerrin poked at it with a chopstick before sampling it.

"Different. Kind of a smoky taste."

"Secret's the spot remover," I said, pouring tea. "I need some information."

"Business with the entree. That the gracious southern style?" she asked.

"That went out with air-conditioning," I replied.

"What kind of information?" she asked.

"Sheet on a guy from Richleigh."

"Guy got a name?"

"James. Jason James," I said.

"What's the connection?"

"James and my uncle—my dead uncle—played phone tag a lot."

"What makes you think there's a sheet on James?"

"Bobby stopped by the office a few weeks ago," I said, pausing to take a sip of tea, "to tell me the SBI has an angle on Roger's murder. James was the angle."

"News to me. But I already told you Vecchio's working this one himself."

"Bobby said he heard Roger was dealing coke to keep Vista Mer afloat. This James guy is supposed to have confessed to his cellmate that he took out Roger when the deal went bad."

"Believe it?"

"Roger had a motor mouth sober," I replied. "Worse when he was drinking. Roger joined the fifth-a-day club when Vista Mer went bad. Everybody in the county knew that. No dealer in his right mind would do serious business with Roger."

I waved at Lee Yin, still sorting tableware, managing somehow to make as much noise as a crane operator stacking I-beams. Lee Yin bought a fresh pot of scalding water and two new Safeway tea bags. He gave Mulkerrin a little bow, me a sly smile, and removed our plates.

"What else did Vecchio tell you?"

"Nothing," I said. "Why? You hear something?"

"Your buddy have a thing for dry-cleaning bags?" she asked, after watching me for a long moment. "Somebody wrapped a dry-cleaning bag around Roger's head while he was unconscious. Cause of death was suffocation."

"Where'd you hear that?" I asked.

"Never mind where I heard it. You just forget you heard it. The official story—at least for now—is Roger died from a concussion."

Mulkerrin laid a five on the table.

"By the way," she said. "Rennie never left the marina that night."

"Who says so? Gamper?"

"Ten solid citizens according to the sheriff," Mulkerrin replied. "Know anyone who hates Italian cars?" Mulkerrin gave me a smile that was just shy of a smirk.

"This is a patriotic county. There's a lot of 'Buy American' sentiment."

"Bimbo emotion is more like it," Mulkerrin said under her breath.

I poured the rest of the tea into my cup. Lee Yin had stopped clanging silverware. The silence was edged by the low rumble of tractor trailers on 202. Lee Yin set down a vermillion tray. Two fortune cookies rested on the check, the oil from the cookies staining the loden-green paper on which Lee Yin had penciled Chinese characters and arabic numerals. I passed a fortune cookie to Mulkerrin. "What's your fortune?" she asked.

I cracked open my cookie and untwisted the slip of paper.

" 'Keep your friends close but your enemies closer,' " I read.

"Good advice," Mulkerrin said. "If you can tell the difference."

"How about the sheet on James?" I asked, handing Mulkerrin her five-dollar bill. I laid a ten on the tray.

"I'll think about it," Mulkerrin said, standing up. "Do me a favor."

"What?"

"Keep that ditz away from me."

Two days later, I ran into Vecchio. He asked me to stop by his office after I argued a motion for an accounting in a trust case.

It was just past three when I rapped on the doorsill of Vecchio's office. The door was open. Vecchio was standing in front of the window.

"Starting," he said, pointing to the window. I joined Vecchio at the window. We looked down at the intersection of Main and Court.

The teenagers in the box of the lead pickup truck were waving blaze orange hats and holding up hooves, which looked to have been torn rather than cut from the buck which, lashed to the hood, stared glassily upward. The littlest one, a freckled-faced boy of maybe nine, was swinging a tawny foreleg over his head. There was a swath of dried blood, as broad as his grin, on his forehead.

His father and four of his favorite uncles, squeezed into the cab, were passing a fifth back and forth to celebrate Junior's blooding. Now and then, one of the guys in the middle leaned across the driver to yell at someone on the sidewalk.

"There's fifteen, maybe twenty," Vecchio said. "In this pack anyway. More at the weighing station."

The light changed and the caravan of pickups and four-by-fours turned onto Court Street to circle the square.

"How long is this crap supposed to go on?" Vecchio asked.

"Until they run out of whiskey, the married ones anyway," I replied. "After they honk, hoot and holler and circle the square a few times, they'll park in the town lot and pass around a bottle. After a while they'll light a fire in a trash can. Then someone will dress out a kill and hack off strips to twist around coat hanger wires. 'Round nine their wives will collect them if the whiskey hasn't run out earlier."

"I know the routine," Vecchio said. "I meant, how long is this tribal shit supposed to go on?"

"Been like this on opening day as long as I can remember," I said, watching a half-dozen pickups approach. "Anthropologist would have a field day studying a tradition like this. Maybe it's sociologist since they're not dead."

"Psychiatrist is more like it," Vecchio replied, returning to his desk and picking up a sheet of paper.

The light turned red, halting an old Ford pickup, a relic from the mid-fifties, below the window. A tawny doe about the size of the German shepherd riding in the cab was stretched out on the front fender, her feet roped to the bumper. Her tongue was coated thickly with bloodfoam from a lung shot. The little trickle of blood that ran from the edge of her maw fanned out when the light changed and the Ford lurched forward, its old horn wheezing bleats more fatigued than merry.

"Speaking of which," Vecchio said. "Maybe you need a check-up from the neck up." He pushed the paper across the desk.

"What's this?" I said, picking it up.

"The sheet you wanted on James."

"Guy's got a prior," I said nonchalantly, scanning the sheet.

"Two. Both chickenshit," Vecchio said. "Misdemeanor possession of weed in '85. Fine. Possession of a half-gram of cocaine in '88. Thousand hours' community service and probation.''

I folded the paper and slipped it in my pocket. I turned toward the desk, then pivoted toward the window, drawn by a dull thump followed by the sound of glass smashing and wild laughter.

"Hell's that?'' Vecchio asked, jumping up from his desk chair.

"Looks like the boys riding in the back of the Ford tossed a whiskey bottle at the Chevy with the two bucks racked on the fenders,'' I replied, pulling back the curtain to get a better angle. "Good, clean fun.''

"Long as they don't start shooting,'' Vecchio said. "I told the sheriff I was goddamned well going to prosecute this year even if they're shooting at the moon. Discharge within town limits is illegal no matter what they're aiming at, I told him.''

"Part of the tradition,'' I said.

"Part that used to be,'' Vecchio said, emphasizing "used.'' "Your anthropologist can begin work on that part, get a head start on a dead tradition.'' I considered telling him that in the South the deader the tradition, the more revered. Instead, I said nothing.

Vecchio resumed his seat and propped his feet on his desk, taking care to put his heels on the blotter. He leaned forward to pull up his socks and pluck the crease in his slacks.

"Kenny, Kenny, Kenny,'' he said. "What am I going to do with you?'' Vecchio smoothed back his thick hair with both hands and then held them out, palms up and shiny. "What did I tell you?''

"So I wanted the sheet on James. So frigging what?''

"So frigging what?'' Vecchio mocked, drawing out "what,'' letting the "t'' drop an octave and trail off. He slapped the side of his chair with his palm. "C'mon, big guy. You know what the 'what' is. You're the buddy of a guy dealing coke, guy who just happened to be your client as well, guy whose wife, for good measure—just to keep it interesting—you just happened to be fucking. I *implored* you, for your own good, to stay the hell away. Do you bother to thank me?''

"Thanks for the sheet," I replied, turning to leave.

"Hey, that, too," Vecchio said softly, holding up one finger. "Explanation, though, is what I had in mind."

I turned to look out the window.

"What's the problem?" he said. "You want to check with Mulkerrin? You want to use your secret radio ring or something? I'll leave the room, let you have a little privacy."

"Leave her out of this," I said, turning to face him. "I asked her for a favor."

"Hey, Peckerwood," he replied. "You know who did you the favor?" Bobby pointed at his chest. "Bobby Vee, your buddy. You know what Mulkerrin wanted?" Bobby let out a little snort, smirked, and shook his head, before locking his black eyes on me.

"Too much trouble to speak, just nod 'yes' or 'no,' " Vecchio said after a moment.

"So what did she want?" I asked, settling into the chair across from the desk. Vecchio swung his feet off the blotter, sat up in his chair, leaned forward and rested his chin on the bridge made by his intertwined fingers.

"She told me we ought to play you, give you what you wanted," he said slowly, keeping his eyes on mine. "She said she wanted permission to keep close to you, see where you would lead us."

"Lead you where?" I asked.

"I told Mulkerrin she doesn't know Kenny the way I do," Vecchio said, rocking back in his chair. "I told her Kenny's a guy born with a silver spoon in his mouth, not up his nose." He waved off my protest before I could speak.

"Don't bother," Vecchio continued. "You don't have to convince me. I told her Kenny gets a kick out of hanging out with guys on the fringe, playing badass."

Vecchio stood up. He rolled his shoulders and rocked his head from side to side. He took a pill from his shirt pocket, popped it in his mouth, and chased it with a swallow of coffee.

"Crick in my neck," Vecchio explained. "Went one on one with my kid. Thirteen years old and already scoring off me with either hand. Down the alley. Jumper from the key. Gonna make the varsity next year as a freshman. Bet on it. So where was I?'' He looked at me expectantly for a moment before shrugging his shoulders and continuing.

''That's just Kenny's karma, I told Mulkerrin. Try a little of this. Do a little of that. Nothing serious. But, like I said, Mulkerrin, she doesn't know Kenny the way I do.''

''What does Mulkerrin think?'' I asked.

''She thinks Kenny may be a dealer. She thinks Kenny's interest in James is a smokescreen, just Kenny's way of staying close to where the investigation is heading. Want some free advice?''

''I'm guessing I've had it before,'' I replied, feeling my pulse in my face.

''Stay away from Mulkerrin. Lady doesn't look like it but she's hardcase. Poison for an existential kind of guy like you.'' Vecchio looked out the window.

''That smoke?'' Vecchio said, standing up.

''From the parking lot,'' I replied, moving to the side of the window to get the northern angle.

''Kenny,'' Vecchio said. ''You know what your problem is?'' He gave me a little punch on the shoulder. ''You gotta learn who your friends are, big guy.''

After I got back to my office I pulled James's sheet from my pocket and studied it with care. Circuit Court Judge Abel Henry had ruled on March 14 that James qualified as an indigent. Henry had appointed Cornell Campbell as defense counsel. Coming full circle, I said to myself.

CHAPTER 14

"Guess who absolutely, positively must speak to you about something personal?" Anita rolled her eyes in disapproval.

Grateful for any distraction, I told Anita to put her through.

"Guess what I'm doing," Peyton said cheerily.

"Watching Donahue," I said, looking at my watch.

"Standing on the scales naked as a jaybird. I'm down to 125 again. I'm going to throw out all my old underwear. But not yours." She giggled. "What you gave me, I mean."

When Fitzgerald wrote there are no second acts in American lives, he hadn't consulted Peyton. It was as if Roger incorporeal no longer weighted down her spirit. For Lassington's opinion leaders this was altogether too evident. There had been a few remarks in the bar at the club I had been intended to overhear.

To celebrate returning to a size six, Peyton made a reservation for Saturday at the Magnolia Redoubt, a Victorian-era hotel near the state capitol. After we checked in, we took a walk on the brick sidewalks of Minor Hill. The morning clouds had dispersed to reveal an azure sky. Peyton stopped to admire late-blooming geraniums set off by copper window planters. She talked about taking up painting again. I surprised her with a set of watercolors I found at an arts and crafts shop on Capitol Square.

When I awoke on Sunday I found Peyton, my suit coat over

her peignoir, on the balcony of our third-floor room finishing a painting of the governor's mansion, located on the other side of the square. I ordered a large pot of strong tea, buttermilk biscuits, and blackberry preserves. I was halfway through the *Journal* when Peyton presented me with her watercolor.

Remarkably good, I told her. She inscribed, signed, and dated it. Then we made love on automatic pilot as we had so many times before, without speaking, without thinking, consciousness surrendered to ageless instinct, the fuse that drives the flower.

Driving back to Lassington on Sunday afternoon, Peyton tried to steer conversation to considerations of the future, considerations that chafed both of us, but in different ways.

She invited me to supper at her home. She said she wanted me to spend some time with her kids. I felt suffocated by the idea and tried to beg off politely.

"I really don't think I should."

"You mean you really don't want to. At least be honest."

"Okay. I really don't want to."

"I'm just a piece of ass. That's all I am to you. That's all I ever was and all I'll ever be. I'm too old to delude myself, get taken in by that stuff you say in bed."

Peyton stepped on the gas and accelerated more than was needed to overtake a logger's truck. She swerved too soon back into the right lane, eliciting a long, angry honk.

Peyton dropped me off at the CST parking lot where I had left my truck. When I tried to kiss her, she developed rigor mortis. She wouldn't face me and wouldn't say goodbye. We'd played that scene before. My role was to slam the door. Her's was to spin rubber. I did and she did. In a minor degree, I was as relieved when Peyton left as she had been when Roger, in a manner of speaking, set her free.

I went to my office to check for phone messages. Chirkie Video Barn reminded me to return *Twelve Angry Men,* which was three weeks overdue and somewhere under the seat of the Dodge. I decided to pick up rice and chicken breasts at the IGA and head back to the camp.

Shortly after I turned onto 33, I looked in the mirror and saw the flashing of twin red lights in the grill of a tan Ford. I pulled over, irritated, wondering why in hell I was being stopped.

In the oncoming lane, a green-and-white Chirkie County Sheriff's Department cruiser appeared, blue lights flashing. It crossed the road and parked in front of my truck. From behind me an amplified voice told me to get out slowly, put my hands on the hood, slide my palms forward and keep them flat on the hood.

I did as I was told. I turned my head to my left and recognized Deputy Sheriff Lonnie Ackerman and a new deputy named Earlene something. I turned to my right and saw a state trooper approaching.

"You mind telling me what in hell this is all about?" I asked. Lonnie didn't respond. Earlene was practicing her hard cop stare. She unsnapped the safety strap on her holster as she approached.

"Mr. Kendall Wilkinson?" the trooper asked. "I have a search warrant for your vehicle." He put a typewritten document on the hood beside my still-outstretched arms.

"Sir, I'm going to ask you to remain motionless," he said quietly, but with a hard edge. I tried to read the document while he frisked me.

"Sir, you can take that with you. Go with Deputy Harrelson and have a seat in the back of the car." Earlene motioned for me to precede her. I climbed in the back of the Ford.

I read the onionskin carbon of the form. Signed by District Court Judge Peterson, the warrant authorized a search of a vehicle identified as a blue 1977 Dodge pickup truck, license YTH-435, registered to Kendall Scott Wilkinson. The objects of the search were identified in standard boilerplate as controlled substances and paraphernalia.

Through the steel mesh which separated the seats I watched Lonnie crawling under the truck. Then he levered off the hubcaps and placed them in a row. The trooper was in the bed, rummaging through the utility box. After twenty minutes, the trooper returned. He opened the door and told me to get out and put my hands behind my back.

I felt steel bite into my wrists. The trooper asked me to turn around. He had a little card in his hand. I resisted the urge to comment on his inability to recite the *Miranda* warning from memory by this point in his career. He told me I was under arrest for possession of a controlled substance with intent to distribute. He read me my rights and asked if I understood them.

"This is a frame," I replied. "That's all I understand."

The trooper pushed me toward the rear seat. With my hands pinned, I was off balance and struggled to keep from falling into the backseat. The door slammed. The trooper made a U-turn and headed toward Lassington followed by the deputy sheriffs.

I was put in the holding pen with two drunks. Six hours later I was brought into Peterson's office.

"You can thank Vecchio for this," Peterson said, handing me my belt, shoelaces, wallet, and keys. "He waived surety on the bond. Sign here."

I signed the forms Peterson gave me, initialed the receipt for my possessions, and checked out of jail. I made it home at midnight. Sleep proved impossible. I replayed Cubertson's warning, again and again. I was certain that I had been set up to keep me from making up the past. But I didn't know by whom or why. I guessed whoever it was figured that if I were nailed for distributing cocaine, my credibility would be destroyed. I'd come off like every other inmate eager to trade a far-fetched conspiracy for a few years off his sentenc. Memories I had run from ran me down. Yet, strangely, I welcomed them, for in the jostling of old memories and new fears, there was the prospect of communion with a spirit with whom I had never made peace. Father, too, had been framed.

✳

A month before the 1958 primary election, Tidewater Produce filed a complaint against Father with the state bar ethics committee. The complaint, leaked to the press, made front page news. It accused Father of conspiring with Payne's Markets to defraud Tidewater Produce and other wholesalers of $28,500, "which sum, upon information and belief, has been secreted by virtue of having been deposited in the trust account of Wilkinson & Campbell."

Father testified the $13,500 had been pressed on him by

Hewitt Payne, an old friend and long-time client. Payne, Father testified, told him he owed the $13,500 to the IRS for withholding taxes and wanted to remove the temptation to spend it. Besides, Payne told Father, if you are going to work out a settlement with the IRS, you might as well hold the money.

At the hearing before the committee, Payne lied. He testified that when he told Father that his stores were insolvent, Father advised him to run up credit balances, discount inventory to sell it quickly, and stiff vendors by transferring the proceeds to Wilkinson & Campbell in payment of "legal fees." Payne claimed Father agreed to split the money with him as soon as he was discharged from bankruptcy.

That left Father's partner, Cornell Campbell, to rebut Payne's testimony. Campbell testified he saw nothing, heard nothing, and knew nothing. Pressed by bar counsel, Campbell conceded Father was not keeping up with his share of the firm's expenses and had lost several important clients.

I remember it was raining hard when Father returned from the hearing. His suit was soaked, his tie was missing, his face was ashen, and he reeked of bourbon.

He staggered across the hall, tripping on the umbrella stand. I didn't think he saw me. But he stopped and hugged me for a long time. He pressed my face against his chest and I heard the rasping of stifled sobs. Then, without saying a word to Mother, Father entered his study and locked the door.

I remember Mother weeping, dialing a number, speaking in hushed tones, then dialing another number, hesitating and slamming down the phone.

I remember Olmie taking me down to Clarence's and her room in the basement, where they had a TV. Missus say you can watch all TV you want but you can't go up there, no. Olmie made popcorn on the hot plate beside the bed.

I remember waking up on the sofa. Olmie and Clarence were huddled on the bed, uniforms on and fast asleep. I tiptoed upstairs, drawn by voices coming from the entrance hall.

I remember peeping through the crack between the door and the frame. I watched Mother pound the study doors. Don't talk like that, she said, in a hoarse voice, to the seam where the double doors met. Don't you dare talk like that. Don't even think about it.

Reverend Oakley stood silently behind her. George Carey leaned against the stair railing, a teacup in his hand.

❧

I finally dozed off toward dawn, only to wake an hour later with the realization that no matter how it turned out, nothing would be the same ever again. I picked up a coffee on the road and was waiting at Vecchio's office door when he arrived.

"What the hell's going on?" I demanded as soon as Vecchio stepped from the stairs into the hall. He scowled, unlocked his door, and motioned me into his office. Vecchio slipped behind his desk and pulled out a file.

"Hey, you think this was easy for me?" Vecchio asked. "I agonized over it. Let me tell you."

I didn't respond. I was having a hard time working up empathy.

"You don't believe me? Ask Maria. Tension was killing me. I was grinding my teeth so badly she made me sleep in the guest room. You know what that does to crown work?"

He loosened his tie, massaged his temples, looked up and fixed cocker spaniel eyes on me.

"What could I do, buddy? Just tell me."

"There was no probable cause for the arrest," I replied. "I was set up." I picked up the folder Vecchio pushed across his desk, opened it, and scanned the affidavit in support of the search warrant.

" '. . . based on information,' " I read, " 'which the under-signed affiant has reason to believe is credible, supplied by a reliable informant known to the undersigned affiant, whose information was detailed and precise, which information was corroborated by information supplied by the informant regarding the suspect's habits, background, and known association with the target of an ongoing investigation into the sale and distribution of controlled substances in the County of Chirkie . . .'

" 'Anonymous, reliable informant.' Cop bullshit." I tossed the affidavit of State Police Corporal Deale across the desk.

It was impossible to know if an anonymous informant existed, except in a cop's imagination. The wariness of the Founding Fathers as to cops' imaginations had been the reason for the Fourth Amendment. Glib, tough-on-crime demagoguery sold because the average voter had no more knowledge of history than of astrophysics. Understanding is contextual. When the voters' context consists of the sports pages and thirty-second beer spots, it's easy to sell a bill of goods at the expense of the Bill of Rights. Less Thinking. Feels Great.

"Kenny, what could I do?" Vecchio spread his palms outward and moved his hands apart, the supplicant seeking a blessing.

"Had enough guts to make Deale get further corroboration."

Vecchio got up, moved to the front of the desk, propped up his thigh on its edge and leaned toward me.

"I've had about enough of this," he said quietly. "The sonofabitch only wanted a search warrant for your truck." He began pacing.

"Your goddamned truck was all, not a body cavity. What am I supposed to tell Deale? That I can vouch for Ken Wilkinson because he's a buddy? I'll tell you what I didn't do."

Vecchio pointed at his chest with his pencil. "I didn't tell Deale about the lady who phoned in the tip that you're Dr. Dope for the country-club cotillion."

He had a point. I couldn't expect special favors.

It had been humiliating to appear before Carey at the arraignment, alone at the same table where I stood beside defendants. I could bear neither the studied politeness of deputy clerks nor the fervent, but, in some cases, I suspected, feigned declarations of solidarity from comrades at the bar who accosted me in the halls of the courthouse, nor the murmurs from the courthouse regulars, mostly retirees, when I passed the benches where they congregated.

Jamie Higgins's piece on my arrest had been fair, balanced, but devastating nonetheless and on the front page. I got top billing. Dean's formal announcement, hardly news, that he would seek the nomination of the Democratic Party for governor had been relegated to the lower, left side of the front page.

Jamie had reported only the facts in the arrest record. They were bad enough. Half-kilo of cocaine found in a Dodge pickup truck registered to Kendall Wilkinson. Jamie quoted me as saying that I had been framed. But she also quoted Deale who, when asked for his reaction to my statement, asked rhetorically what Jamie would expect a guy to say when a half-kilo was found in his truck. There had been no sign of any tampering with the truck, Deale added.

No clients had sent me letters instructing me to deliver their files to other attorneys but they would come. It wasn't fair to expect clients to ride out the storm. Some would, I knew, despite my advice to seek other counsel.

"It ain't like the old days," Vecchio continued. "You know that. Now a guy burps, it's probable cause."

I nodded again, got up, and started for the door.

"Wait," he called after me. "Shut the door. People were watching me. Otherwise I would have done more."

"It's okay."

"McAllister," he said. "Little suckbutt's gunning for my job, scratching to find an issue, something to run on."

"I don't want to hear this."

"If there's anything I can do, within, you know . . ."

"Look, Bobby. I understand, okay?" I walked into the hall and softly shut the door.

A week later I received a phone call from Renee's lawyer, Greta Trolst, flagship or battlewagon, depending on to whom you spoke, of the Richleigh domestic relations bar. She was a polished, heavyset scrapper in her late fifties whose trademark was that the color of her cigarette holder always matched her nail polish and her shoes.

She conveyed Renee's sincere hope that everything would turn out for the best, a sentiment cloaked in ambiguity. Then the Troll volunteered that, having come to respect me, albeit constrained by our adversarial relationship, she felt sure that I would do what was best for Martha. I said nothing, listening to the Troll inhale, waiting for the shit in the velvet bag. For this reason, the Troll told me she hoped I would agree with Renee and voluntarily suspend my right to have Martha spend every other weekend with me. And the Christmas holiday, she added, almost as an afterthought.

Just until this blows over, she said. Do the right thing. Spare Martha the stress. Besides you can drop in at Renee's and Charlie's and visit Martha there. Just give a little advance notice, through my office, just for the time being.

The Troll said she would send me an order for my endorsement reflecting this temporary realignment.

I told her if I needed a realignment, I'd see my chiropractor.

I'm truly sorry for you, she replied, savoring the opportunity for condescension. You're making the mistake of a lawyer who represents himself. You're incapable of assessing your situation objectively.

My secretary will call you to arrange for a date for the hearing, she continued. A professional courtesy, although I would imagine your calendar should be quite open for the next two months.

CHAPTER 15

"The welfare of the child, of course, Your Honor," intoned the Troll, whose bulk smothered the lectern, "must remain . . ."

"Paramount," interjected Judge Henry.

"My very word, Your Honor."

"Your very word about five times now. Let me remind you, Miss Trolst, that I do not wish to be lectured." Henry's syllables fell ponderously, triphammer tones. Trolst hugged the lectern.

Judge Abel Henry, carved from black granite, would be a natural for the role of Othello if only he could tone down the force he projected. When irritated, Henry's eyes flashed cold fire and his voice dropped two octaves below his normal basso profundo. Two decades on the bench had given Henry an aura of dignified weariness combined with implacable self-assurance.

You know how some judges will finish your sentences, Arnold Levy, a Richleigh lawyer once told me. That sucker will finish your next five minutes of argument, rule on it, and goddamned if you won't thank him even if the ruling went against you. He's that good. But don't ever piss him off. You smartmouth at Henry, he's been known to come down off the bench and get in your face.

"Mr. Wilkinson," Judge Henry said in a deep, sonorous tone, somehow adding a fourth syllable to my name.

"Your Honor?"

"The cup, sir. Take it to the men's. The bailiff will accompany you."

"Sir?"

"The stack of plastic cups beside the pitcher on the counsel table. Surely you have observed it, Mr. Wilkinson."

"I'm aware of the cups, Your Honor. I was just . . ."

"I assume I shall not be compelled to spell out the procedure for you, Mr. Wilkinson."

"No, Your Honor, not that part. I would like to inquire of the Court . . ."

"Return the cup to Miss Trolst, sir."

"Your Honor," the Troll interjected, "if I may say . . ."

"No, madam, you may not. I have listened patiently to your allegations as to the character and deeds . . ."

"Those are not my allegations . . ."

A thunderbolt struck. The chandeliers swayed. Judge Henry put down his gavel and glowered at the Troll for a good minute before continuing.

"As I was saying before I was interrupted, I have listened to this lady's allegations as to the character and deeds of Mr. Wilkinson. And I am compelled to state that the circumstances appear grave. Grave, indeed, sir.

"Nonetheless, the merits of the matter pending in Chirkie County are not before this Court. The province of this Court is to determine if the welfare of the child would be compromised if Mr. Wilkinson's visitation rights were to continue unabated.

"This Court will reserve judgment upon your motion, Miss Trolst, until you produce a report of a certified urinalysis. The standard screen, Miss Trolst, will do. You will provide a copy to Mr. Wilkinson."

Henry gaveled court into recess. He slipped out the door behind the bench before the bailiff had finished saying "All rise." I returned to the courtroom a few minutes later, handed the Troll a brimming cup, and left without saying a word.

"You think you got enough in there? Why didn't you just take the trash can?" the Troll called after me.

I checked my watch. I had almost a hour to kill before my meeting with Cornell Augustus Campbell, Esquire.

The last time I had seen Campbell was at Father's funeral in 1972. He hadn't attended the service at Redeemer but showed up for the interment. He had gripped my arm, more to keep from stumbling than to convince me of the fervor of his promise to be there if I needed anything. I had waved away the whiskey fumes and said, sure, just like you had been there for Father at the ethics hearing.

After receiving notice of the Troll's motion I had arranged a meeting with Campbell for the same day. There had been neither an office nor residence listing for Campbell. Reasoning that if Henry had appointed Campbell to defend James, Henry must have had some way to get in touch with him, I called Henry's chambers.

"What you want with *that* man?" Henry's secretary had demanded. I told her I was a Lassington attorney who needed local counsel in Richleigh. "Not *my* business to say," she replied after a long pause. She gave me the number for the pay phone at the lawyer's lounge at the courthouse, adding, "Let that mother ring."

On the twentieth ring, someone answered who said he would get my message to Campbell. I figured ten to one against it was a smart bet. It had taken whoever it was five minutes to find a pencil. Then he kept repeating the numbers in different sequences. Several days later, I had been surprised by a call from Campbell. Give me your office address, I said. He gave me the name of a bar on 5th Street.

I walked along Beauregard Avenue in the direction of 5th Street. A sharp, wet wind from the west added to the chill, unseasonable for early December. The intersection of 5th Street and Beauregard Avenue is five blocks to the south of the courthouse.

The vicinity is know for pawnshops, pool halls, Gospel missions, used furniture shops, greasy-spoon diners, perm parlors, prosthetic supply stores, chiropractor clinics, antiques emporia, secondhand book shops, consignment shops, and army-navy surplus stores not to mention bars.

Where 5th Street borders the Shenley, there are hints of gentrification. Several late Victorian iron-front office buildings have been sandblasted, patched, and painted. There are some ethnic restaurants (Mexican and Chinese) that have gained a following among the cultural vanguard of Richleigh. An old tool & die shop, where once musket barrels were lathed for the Confederacy, has been turned into an experimental theater. For Richleigh, this means a reprise of *Man of La Mancha*.

But these harbingers have as little effect on the down-at-the-heel atmosphere as gaudy neon signs in ground-floor windows have on the grimness of dark brick buildings, stained by the sweat of generations of brokers of slaves and tobacco. Their upper stories furnish cheap offices shared by criminal lawyers starting out and criminal lawyers ending up; soujourners on the career wheel, who trade services for rent, enthusiasm for experience, energy for knowledge, and innocence for wisdom. There are no marble-paneled lobbies with potted plants. The few lobbies are covered with the cheapest linoleum available in 1959. If there's a plant, it's algae. The typical foyer is accessed by a steel fire door next to a bar. There may be a plaque above it which says, simply, law offices. Behind the door is a four-by-four stair landing, with an office directory screwed to crumbling plaster. The occasional elevator is not for the risk averse.

Criminal lawyers share a bent toward anarchy and contempt for drones clustered in legal hives. Criminal lawyers are the one-eyed jacks. If law practice were a western, criminal lawyers would be cast as the mavericks.

The ones who deny it most vehemently share most deeply (as they all do in some degree) an identification with the outcasts it is their lot to defend. There is a queasy ambiguity to defense work reflected by the grammatical ambiguity of "criminal lawyer."

The good ones are imbued with understanding that never ascends to the airy offices of the uptown bar. The rabble for them is not an abstraction. Cases are not scattergrams. Cases are snapshots that once in a while mediate a detached empathy, an unsentimental knowing of the process of how Jay Bee, facing twenty to life for armed robbery, evolved in four years from John B. Martin, who sang in the choir at Avenger Baptist Church and averaged sixteen points as a sophomore.

The 5th Street "bar association," hangs out at the Barrister, a bar and grill located on the ground floor of a sadly dilapidated brick building. In second floor windows are signs advertising bailbonds, kung fu, electrolysis, nail-bonding, and legal services.

A few minutes before noon, I walked into the long, narrow, dark and overheated interior. The odor of stale beer was beginning to replace the scent of tired grease, aromatic tides marking the transition from griddle to tap. A little, whitehaired man with a creased fox face the color of old brick was seated at a small table at the far end of the bar, huddled over a plate of sunny-side ups and thick slices of grilled ham, mug at the ready

"Ah, lad, you're early. Be so good as to give that log a jump." He motioned with his fork in the direction of a poker beside the fireplace.

Campbell handed me the menu. "BLT's best in town," he said. I nodded and handed the menu back unopened.

Campbell waved the menu to catch the attention of the grillman. He wrote the letters BLT in the air with his finger and made a pumping motion with his fist.

"Not too early, is it? There's hair under the yardarm somewhere."

The BLT and draft arrived. There was a huge pile of bacon, probably what remained from breakfast.

"I've heard with sorrow about your case. Should I be able to render any assistance, I would . . ."

"Not mine, Cornie," I said. "One of yours. State versus Jason James."

Campbell leaned on his elbows and studied me. He sat up, dabbed at his mouth, and brushed a thick shock of white hair from his brow. In his seventies, there was yet an air of elfin quickness about him, an alertness as if he still were point guard waiting for the inbounds pass.

"You mind?" Campbell asked, pulling a cigar case from his pocket.

I shook my head.

"Case of the peddling pedaler," Campbell said.

"Hell of a good title," I said.

"Maybe a better story," he replied.

"I've got time." I pushed my mug over to him.

"Good-looking kid, about five seven, just shy of twenty-two," he said. "Smart, God knows he was. Is, for that matter. Boy could talk the bark off a tree." He drew a cigar from the side pocket of his tweed jacket, scraped off the ash and lit it.

"James spent two years at Tulane. Studied performing arts. On stage and off."

I nodded in reply to Campbell's sly smile.

"Say what you will about James's choice of performing arts," he continued. "Kid had gumption. Started a courier service with a bunch of secondhand bikes. Had them spraypainted with silver enamel. Decked out his boys in silver lycra. Got a metal shop to make aluminum wings to clip on pedals and helmets. Called it Mercury Express.

"Silver boys on silver bikes flashing through traffic. Great image. Press loved it. *Journal* ran a feature just before James was busted. Problem was, according to the grand jury bill, James's boys were delivering more than messages. Seems they peddled as they pedaled."

"Flake?" I asked.

"James said he didn't know his boys were dealing. I believed him, not that the jury would," Campbell replied. He relit his cigar before continuing.

"Started with personal services. Motto was: 'We got your message.' Went both ways, whatever the customer wanted. Smart cover and tax deductible. Regulars got billed monthly for courier services.

"One of his boys, kid named Cratter, got picked up with five grams of powder. SBI flipped the guy. Cratter went before the grand jury and finked on James. Took the grand jury maybe ten minutes to hand down a bill. James was picked up by the SBI before the ink was dry.

"I told James, straight up, the SBI had him nailed. Warrant good. Arrest clean. No holes.

"James didn't want to talk about a plea. All he wanted to talk about was bail. No doubt in my mind he planned to jump. No doubt whatsoever. Couldn't blame him. Given priors, James would end up doing a dime at Greenwood.

"James tells me to call a guy in New Orleans, guy named Garnet Thibodeaux." Campbell repeated the name, rolling the vowels with nasal exaggeration. Said Thibodeaux would stand surety for the bail bond, which Henry set at a hundred grand.

"I called the number James gave me. I go through a few secretaries and finally get to Thibodeaux. Turns out the T-Man is president of a bank."

"Family?" I asked.

"Personal friend is all James would say. My guess is Thibodeaux is a sugar daddy James used to lick.

"Thibodeaux played cat-and-mouse with me, asking if my client had an account. That sort of crap. I said, cut the shit. James needs surety to make bail. You're supposed to be his buddy.

"I give Mr. T the friend in need, friend in deed number. Mr. T stonewalls me, keeps harping on collateral and approval of the loan committee, that kind of runaround. Finally, I say, 'Garnet, or whatever the hell your name is, suppose my man makes a personal appeal to the loan committee? Suppose he says your cock is his collateral? Can't tell what a desperate man might do.' He hung up on me.

"I summarized for James the response of the good Mr. Thibodeaux. Kid takes it hard. Starts sobbing in waves.

"After a while, I tell him, 'Look, kid, maybe we climb the same ladder as your pal Cratter. We give Tommy Prescott the names of a dozen johns and cut a deal. Tommy's hot to trot politically and might go for a high profile deal like that.'

"Prescott believes—says so anyway, all the goddamned time—in setting examples for the community, all that deterrent crap. Always getting in a word to the press about how he believes the district attorney is not just a prosecutor. The DA, Prescott loves to tell 'em, is charged with protecting the morals of the community. Doesn't believe a word he's saying, but it makes for good ink.

"Prescott, I tell James, might get a kick out of seeing socially prominent johns on the first page of the *Journal*. Particularly if they're Democrats. Kind of moral example Prescott likes. Good for the community, good for the *Journal,* and good for Tommy boy. Likes to keep his name out in front."

"What I'm hearing," I said, "is Prescott is supposed to be humbly waiting for the Republicans to implore him to allow his name to be placed in nomination to run for attorney general. Playing the role of the good citizen who reluctantly allows himself to be talked into running for the good of the people."

"The sonofabitch's done gone and written his acceptance speech is what I hear," Campbell replied. The waiter brought the bill. Campbell pushed it across to me.

"James wouldn't even consider a deal," Campbell continued. "Said he'd see me in hell before he'd name his johns. Matter of personal honor, he said.

"I said, 'Son, I admire honor. Keep it bright and shiny. You'll need it when you're keeping house for Tyrone down at Greenwood. You're auditioning for the role of a stand-up guy. But your imagination of your worst day at Greenwood ain't going to be half as bad as your best day.'

"I met with James about a week later. Kid looks like hell. Fingernails chewed down to the second knuckle. He starts bitching about how he has to use bar soap for shampoo.

"I was up the creek. No bail, no deal, and no defense. Ever had one like that? You can't do a goddamned thing except figure out how to make bad news not sound as bad as you know it really is."

"Too many times to count," I replied.

"James tells the guard to move away. Says he has something confidential to say to his attorney. Goddamned if James doesn't up and tell me he needs to talk to the lieutenant governor. James says he used to deliver messages for Dean, Varret & Co. Says Dean may remember him and take a personal interest in his case.

" 'Helluva idea, son,' I tell him. 'Why not go for broke? Get

the governor, too. Meet with both of them. That way they can
share the limo, maybe get some ink for saving gas, car-pooling
to the lock-up to meet with you.'

" 'Look,' I tell him, 'best I can do is get a letter delivered
to Dean's office. Mark it personal and confidential. I'll run it
over to Dean's office.' Where, I'm thinking—but don't say—
some secretary will put it in the round file. Not good enough,
James says. Has to speak to Dean personally.

" 'Son,' I tell him, 'one, there's no way in hell I can set up
a private chat with the lieutenant governor. Two, even if I could,
there's not a blessed thing Dean can do for you. Not yet anyway. Only two politicians can help you: the governor and the
Richleigh DA. Problem is, the governor has to wait until you
get convicted before he can pardon you.'

"Prescott, now, I already done told you, can work you a
deal, even walk you. Magic wand called prosecutorial discretion. Change your mind about trading a few johns, I'll talk to
Prescott. Other option, of course, is to get convicted. Then,
assuming your buddy Dean gets elected governor next year, the
man can rush over and write a pardon on the spot. I'm sure
he'd be glad to do that, seeing as you used to deliver messages
for his banking outfit. Besides, pardoning a drug dealer's a
politically smart move. Kind of move helps your career along.
Dean's a bright guy. He'd realize that and probably thank you
for the opportunity.'

" 'Look,' I tell James, 'you write your letter. I'll get it to
Dean. In the meanwhile, think about trading with Prescott. Give
it some real serious thought.'

"Three days later I get a phone call from that sassy bitch
who works for Henry. She tells me to sober up—her very
words—trot my ass over to His Honor's courtroom, and wait
for His Honor to take one of his cigarette recesses. She hangs
up before I could offer a suggestion for her pleasure. I get over
there and slip in the last row. Henry's in the middle of a civil
suit. Damned if he doesn't declare a recess and call me to
chambers.

"Doesn't say a word, Henry doesn't. Just sits there smoking,
staring at the wall. Finally, Henry points with his cigarette to

a letter on his desk. I pick it up. Find out James has fired me. Says he's going *pro se*.

"Henry tells me he would rather watch a *pro se* root canal than a *pro se* defense. Ain't going to have no amateur hour in his courtroom, no siree bob, Henry says. Get your dough ass over to the jail and see what in hell's wrong with your hero. You can't straighten it out, you best talk that James boy into another court-appointed lawyer. Henry tells me he's going to hold me personally responsible if James puts on a *pro se* defense. Boy goes *pro se,* only appointments you're going to get are DWI repeats.

"So I head over to the lock-up and tell the hacks to bring me the twinkie in 4D. When they bring James to the visiting room, I let him have it.

" 'Got something to bitch about,' I say, 'you tell me first. Elsewise, I'm going to stop having sleepless nights because all you have for shampoo is bar soap. Split ends is going to be the least of what's going to be split, you get sent down to Greenwood.'

"James does his soft shoe on me. Says he made a mistake. Says he's changed his mind. Been thinking, he says, about what I said about prosecutorial discretion.

" 'Now, that's better,' I say, relieved. 'Now maybe we can do business with Prescott. You're a bright kid. I knew you'd come around.'

"Then James says no offense, but he wants to meet in private with Prescott. Gotta be just himself and Prescott or it's no deal." Campbell finished my mug of beer.

"New one for me," Campbell said. "Ever happen to you?"

"Once. About three years ago," I answered.

"How'd it turn out?"

"I told my guy whatever he said to Vecchio could be used against him, even used to indict him on new charges. I told him if he wanted to be a damned fool, that was up to him. No reason to change at this point."

"Vecchio meet with him?"

"Sent down an assistant with a tape recorder. Turns out all this guy wanted to do was to complain about me. Said I was insensitive to his feelings and used profanity. Vecchio played the tape at his Christmas party. Got a big laugh.''

"The damned-fool stuff is pretty much what I told James,'' Campbell said. "But he wasn't budging. Said if I couldn't set up a meeting for himself and Prescott, he'd stick to his decision to go *pro se*.

"My guess is some jailbird told James that Henry flat out will not stand for a *pro se* defense. Kid figured he could use it to put the heat on me. And he was right.

"I said I'd see what I could do. I run into Prescott that afternoon. Tommy, I say, you owe me. I'm calling one in. Tommy gives me his oh-shit look.

" 'You'll like this one,' I tell him. 'All you gotta do is take your recorder down to the lock-up and listen to my man James spill his guts. Guy wants to cut his own deal with you.'

"Prescott says he won't do it. Thinks James is trying to come up with appeal grounds. Ineffective assistance of counsel. I hadn't thought of that, I confess. It's the age. I'm slipping.

"I tell Prescott to write a disclaimer. Make it bullet proof. Put in it all kinds of stuff about the client having been fully advised and declining to accept his attorney's advice. I'll get James to sign it. Prescott finally says okay, like he's doing me a big favor. Next day or so, Prescott meets with James. You know the rest, don't you?''

"I heard Prescott cut a deal with James.''

"Word around the courthouse,'' Campbell continued, "was Prescott *noll prossed* the beef to get James to work the street. Least that's the official story Prescott came up with''

"Know where I can find James?''

"No idea,'' Campbell said. "James fired me a week after he met with Prescott. Haven't seen hide nor hair since.''

"What about Prescott? Think he'd give you a line on James?''

"You kidding? What am I going to tell Tommy? I want to send James a Christmas card? Besides, the word is, Tommy doesn't have a line to give.''

It was almost one-thirty. Regulars were lined up along the

dark side of the bar, knocking back a few shots before afternoon naps in their offices. I put a twenty on our checks and stood up.

"You never asked me why I had an interest in James," I said.

"I know enough not to ask some questions."

"Did you know enough not to answer some questions?"

"I told the truth, Kenny," Campbell replied, not taking his eyes off mine. "There was nothing I could have done to help your father at the hearing, short of lying. I thought about it, thought about it long and hard. But that would have made me no better than Hewitt Payne, the slimeball they used to set up your father."

We looked at each other through the haze of old memories.

"Let it go," I finally said, more to myself than to Campbell.

When I left The Barrister, the wind was whipping dark gray clouds into layers.

CHAPTER 16

I was lost in thought, head bowed against the wind when the bare dogwoods flanking Lee Boulevard suddenly blossomed. A constellation of tiny lights commenced to twinkle delicately amidst the boughs, an epiphany of hope set against a prematurely dark day. In the near distance, a ghost of a moon lodged in the angle formed by the dome of the capitol and the Banks & Worth building. The pale reflection of the sun was overwhelmed by crimson and green reflections cast skyward by merchants' Christmas decorations.

I drove north on Lee Boulevard toward the ramp to Interstate 79. The lights, shoppers, and the season depressed me as never before. I parked in the lot beside Trimbow's, once the finest department store in the South, and considered buying a present for Martha. But I realized I couldn't play the role of a light-hearted shopper, cheerily bantering with salesgirls and watching parents pick over toys.

The wind was at gale force. On the interstate I had to countersteer to compensate for side-slipping caused by gusts. I changed lanes to take the exit that led to Mosby Woods. At the last second I steered away from the exit, in doing so realizing that I had decided to grant the motion Henry had under advisement. I wasn't any good for Martha the way things were. She was old enough to be embarrassed by me, and I had too much pride to let that happen.

When I was a quarter mile from the camp, I heard a loud banging. The wind had ripped loose a rusted hinge. A shutter was whipping angrily, slapping the clapboards. I wedged a length of two-by-four over the loose shutter and drove in two nails. The deck was heaving like a boat in a rough sea.

In the great room a symphony greeted me. Groans from the joists and beams accompanied wind whistles, their pitches modulated by the gaps and cracks in the pine planking. I added kindling to the charred remnants of stump wood, poured in a dose of kerosene, and stood back from the hearth to savor the flame. You can fit a lot of wood into a five-foot fireplace and I did.

Pine burns fast with a hot, hungry flame. Soon the stack of wood was reduced to a pile of crackling embers and iridescent coals which shimmied in scarlet, gold, and pale-blue waves of heat. A fire's solace is intimate, legs of flame choreographed to music which only the imagination of the observer can supply.

I sat so close to the fire, the ice melted. I poured another bourbon, this one measured with a shot glass. I had caught myself drinking too much and resolved to cut out free-hand pouring. Except for the first drink and maybe the second.

In the morning I knocked on the door to Vecchio's office. A voice from within said, "Yo."

Bobby was reclined in his desk chair, pencil in hand, staring at a newspaper.

"Four letters. Superior Prude," he said without looking up.

"Prig," I said.

"Prig it is." Bobby filled in the squares, folded the paper, and threw it in the general direction of the trash can.

"I need a favor," I said, settling into the side chair.

"Should have called first. Technically, I shouldn't talk to you. Not alone, anyway. Office rules."

"When did you start giving a damn about office rules?"

Vecchio ran his fingers under his paisley suspenders, stretched them and let them snap against his pinstriped dress shirt. He looked out the window. The cast-iron radiator began to clank. He walked over, opened the valve, and kicked the intake pipe.

"Had maintenance up here a dozen times since Thanksgiving. I get here on Monday morning. Office's cold as a witch's tit in a brass bra. I call maintenance, tell Jenkins to hustle his ass up here. He says he'll get there when he gets there.

"So I run over to the K-mart and buy one of those electric three-bar heaters with a little blower, kind that burns one side of you while the other side freezes. Old Jenkins finally gets here after lunch to diddle with the radiator, sees my new heater. Sonofabitch up and tells me it's against the fire code, says it's got to go.

"I said sure, right away, boss. Next morning, goddamned if my heater wasn't gone. Jenkins had scribbled a note on my pad telling me he confiscated it for a continued violation of the fire code after a warning. Now I can't even get Jenkins up here to fix this antique." He kicked the pipe again. "I'm an elected official and I gotta put up with this kind of crap from a janitor."

I listened to his lament knowing it was not idle rambling. Years ago a lecturer at an American College of Trial Lawyers seminar had told Vecchio to use stories to make his points during summation. Much to the chagrin of the defense bar, who had to hear the same folksy anecdotes again and again, he had taken the advice to heart.

"The moral of the story?" I asked.

"Off the record, okay?" Vecchio waited until I nodded.

"The tom-toms are beating all the way to Richleigh. I've got about this much latitude with your case," Vecchio said, holding his thumb and finger a micrometer apart. "If you're gonna ask me to agree to a continuance, it's not in the cards." Vecchio looked at me expectantly. I didn't reply.

"Here's something else," he continued, leaning forward and lowering his voice. "So off the record that if you repeat what I'm going to tell you, I'm going to have to call you a liar."

"If you don't trust me, don't tell me."

"Had a call from our beloved attorney general," Vecchio continued, ignoring my response. "Biddle called me at home last Saturday. Asked how the missus was, how my golf game was, and when we were going to get in a round. That kind of shit. I played along like I was glad to hear from him.

"Finally, Biddle gets around to asking if I'd given any thought to getting Carey specially to appoint somebody to prosecute you. Maybe, Biddle says, as if it just came to him out of the blue, you get old George to appoint one of your assistants who's known to be a Republican. That way you don't risk potential flak if Wilkinson gets off. Sonofabitch didn't mention anything about us being pals, but that was implied, plain as a turd in a punchbowl."

Vecchio stood up and kicked the radiator again.

"Know what I think? That bastard McAllister's been on the phone. Little sneak's only got two speeds: kissing ass and kicking ass.

"The long knives are out," Vecchio continued in a stage whisper. "For both of us, big guy."

Even making allowance for Vecchio's penchant for melodrama, his last comment grated. I considered telling him facing McAllister in a truly contested election wasn't quite the same as being disbarred and doing five to eight. But the point would be lost. Vecchio was a politician.

"I didn't come here to ask for your agreement to a continuance."

Vecchio looked relieved but wary. He pushed back the salt-and-pepper hairs on his temples.

"I've got a lead I need to run down. But it's going to take me to New Orleans. I don't have time to waste on a hearing to amend the terms of my bail so I can go out of state."

I flipped a sheet of paper across the desk. Vecchio studied it as if it were rune.

"I've prepared a consent order. It says you don't object if I travel to New Orleans during December fifteenth to December eighteenth. Sign it and I'll run it over to Carey."

Bobby pushed the order back to me.

"Don't take this the wrong way, okay? Take my name off and put Mulkerrin's name on it. Tell her I said it was okay for her to sign off. You know where I'm coming from, don't you?"

"Preserving deniability, just in case McAllister tries to score points in November."

"No skin off yours. Am I right?" Vecchio turned his palms up and outward, cocked his head to the side, and gave me his patented sad smile, as if we shared an ironic secret.

I borrowed a typewriter, amended the order, and went looking for Mulkerrin. I found her in the cafeteria eating a crabcake sandwich. I handed her the order.

"Bobby says its okay to sign. You want to check, he's in his office."

She pushed her tray to the side and reached upward expectantly, sending a cascade of bracelets down her freckled forearm. I clicked a ballpoint pen and handed it to her.

"Bring me back a quart of jambalaya," she said, signing the order.

I took the order to chambers. Carey was tied up. I left the order with his clerk, Fennell, who had finished law school in June. Fennell suffered an attack of uncontrolled paper shuffling when I tried to make conversation with him. He probably believed speaking to me alone was an unethical *ex parte* communication. But he wasn't certain, so he was exceedingly polite to cover his embarrassment.

The following morning, I stopped in chambers at nine, hoping to find Carey, who didn't go on the bench until ten. He was smoking a double-bend briar pipe the size of a cedar stump. I rapped on the frame of the open door. He looked up and waved me in.

"You're a damned fool if you don't get a lawyer," Carey said, shaking his pipe at me.

"Don't put it off," Carey growled, rapping his pipe on a silver knob which protruded from the center of a crystal ashtray the size of a salad bowl. He glanced at the order, signed it, and pulled out his pocket watch.

"Show time," he said, striding across to the closet where he kept his robes. I thanked Carey and turned to go.

"Kendall, give me a minute," Carey said, fumbling with the zipper to his robe. He pushed his glasses down on his nose.

"Damn it, getting old, can't see to thread this little do-hickey. There, got it." Carey pulled up the zipper.

"Kendall, I'm not going to recuse myself, although I probably should. I'm going to make sure you get the benefit of any doubt and every break in the book because I think you're a fool." I started to speak.

"Don't say anything. I also think you're innocent."

Carey pulled a business card from his desk drawer and handed it to me.

"I don't know if you've ever run into this guy. Lewis Yancey put in ten years as the principal assistant U.S. attorney in the western district. Left in June to open his own practice. You need a top-notch legal technician, someone like Yancey who can come up with a hundred objections at trial. Give me something to work with."

Fennell, cradling a stack of files, appeared expectantly in the doorway. He coughed to alert us.

My trial was six weeks away. The odds of finding James were a thousand times longer than sucker odds at a dog track. All I had to go on was what Campbell had said about James and Thibodeaux. But I had a gut sense it was a solid lead. If James had gone once to Thibodeaux when he was desperate, he'd go again, no matter that Thibodeaux had stonewalled Campbell. James would reason if he couldn't rekindle the flame with blandishment, he would burn Thibodeaux with blackmail. Either way, he'd hit up Thibodeaux for the stake he needed.

I stayed late at the office, trying to finish a few wills and contracts before I left for New Orleans. My trial work, as I had expected, had slowed to a trickle. Referrals from lawyers had stopped altogether.

When I got home, Peyton's Range Rover was in the driveway. She was rocking in the swing on the deck, the tip of her cigarette painting an arc against the sky.

She took the fifth of bourbon from me, stood on tiptoe, and kissed my cheek.

"Long time, sailor. Thought you might stand a little cheering up."

I let us in and flicked on the light. Peyton poured drinks while I lit a fire.

Peyton was wearing a black leather jacket over a sequined, black cocktail dress, cut low in the back. Her stockings sheerly hinted at shadows. Her hair was turned up. A few strands had come loose from the gold clip.

"Where you been?" I took the drink and kissed her, tasting smoke.

"Benefit at the club."

"For what?"

"Some kind of foundation for some kind of disease I can't pronounce even if I could remember what it was. They can't stop me from going to benefits, though they'd like to."

"Good crowd?"

"Not much. Never has been. Same anyway. Goddamn them all to hell." Peyton patted the sofa cushion beside her. I remained facing the fire, waiting for the bourbon to kick in.

"Don't turn your back on someone who loves you. Didn't your momma tell you that?"

"All the time."

"You ought to listen to her." Peyton walked over and clinked her glass against mine. "You know, darling, I could help your prideful self if you just had the decency to ask." She looped her arm around my waist. "Don't even have to say please," she added.

"There's nothing you can do."

"Honey, you might be surprised what I'd do," Peyton said, taking my hand.

"I don't want to be. God knows."

"You're not still pissed about that little piece of shit car, are you?" She gave my hand a squeeze.

"Goddamnit, Peyton, that was stupid."

"I suppose it was," she sighed. "I know her type. I knew it wouldn't amount to nothing. It just pained me to see you take on airs, get your poor pride all worked up just to be knocked flat by that Yankee bitch.'' Peyton walked over to the side table, picked up the bottle of Wild Turkey and refilled my glass.

'' 'Course, I saw it coming. I told myself, 'Peyton, honey, just let him be. Just let him learn his lesson. He knows to come home when he's hurt, hungry, or horny. Like any old dog.' ''

Peyton poured what remained of the Wild Turkey into the crystal decanter.

"What got into you?" Peyton asked. "You think I'm getting too old to be your good ol' gal?"

"You're more than that," I replied.

"Am I now?" Peyton asked, freshening her glass with bourbon from the decanter. She looked at me expectantly. I looked away.

"Know what I found in her glove compartment?" Peyton asked, pouring herself a drink form the decanter. "A paycheck stub is what."

"So what?"

"So it was showing a biweekly gross of over three grand."

"Couldn't be Mulkerrin's," I said a moment later. "Assistant DA starts at thirty-six thousand and the county pays weekly."

"Well, I figure she must be one busy beaver," Peyton said. "No wonder her skirt's about to fall off her butt."

"What makes you say that?"

"Because I presume a county employee who gets a federal paycheck has to earn it, she replied."

Peyton laughed softly and clinked her glass against mine. I didn't respond. She clinked my glass again.

"Hear that?" Peyton whispered. "Sounds like someone's brain just got in gear."

"Jesus," I sighed, embarrassed, shaking my head.

"He ain't going to make you feel half as good as Peyton," she said, kicking off her high heels.

"Not freezing in here anymore, leastways." Peyton walked over to the fire, turned her back to it and wiggled her shoulders. She put her drink on the mantel.

"Help me," she said, reaching her hand expectantly behind her neck. I crossed over, put my hand on hers, and finished pulling the zipper. Her dress seemed to evaporate from her shoulders, deliquescing to form a shimmering blue pool at her ankles. She stepped out, hooked the bodice over her toe and kicked the dress in the direction of a club chair. It wrapped around the armrest.

"Bull's eye," she said, turning to me and starting to unbutton my shirt.

"Peyton."

"Don't talk, baby. You're just going to confuse yourself."

"Just imagine," Peyton said in the morning. She was wearing my Tar Heels T-shirt and standing over me with a mug of scalding coffee. "An old stone farmhouse on the bank of the Arles, surrounded by ancient vineyards."

She shut her eyes, frowned, and shook her head. Then she opened her eyes and smiled.

"Are you imagining?"

"I'm working on it," I replied, sipping my coffee.

"I'll wake you up with fresh-baked bread and coffee deeper and darker than a witch's dream. The sun will be mustard and mad just the way Van Gogh painted it, and all the colors of Monet—and, hell, Manet, too. I can't remember which was which. You'll write wonderfully and I'll paint the best I know how. We'll hike in the hills of Provence, make love in mountain streams, and drink Armagnac watching the stars explode in a blue velvet sky."

"That would be nice," I replied, wondering if I could get an erection in an icy stream. I did it once in the ocean in early June, but that had been twenty years ago and not quite icy.

"Nice," Peyton said, oozing contempt. "That *all* you can say. Don't you understand? It doesn't have to be a dream. All we have to do is want it *enough.*" Peyton slapped me on my chest to emphasize the second syllable in "enough."

"Darling, this is the only life we get. If all you do is watch yourself live it, your life is nothing more than a dream."

"Maybe that's all it's supposed to be," I replied. "Maybe we're supposed to come to terms with that."

"Don't do one of your philosophical wimp-outs on me," Peyton replied. "They're just fancy excuses for losers."

"Define winning," I said.

Peyton snorted, rolled her eyes, and gave me her fake mean look.

"You poor sonsofbitches," she said. "You men have to shore up middle-aged lives with philosophical poses. We only have to cut our hair."

CHAPTER 17

The 737 passed through a heavy layer of clouds and emerged in brilliant sunlight. The top side of what from the ground had seemed roiled, dense, slate-gray clouds, appeared as interlocked tufts of airily spun cotton. A shaft of sun transected the angle formed by the wing and the fuselage and exploded against the seat back.

Someone who sounded like Greta Garbo told us to return our seat backs and tray tables to their full upright and locked positions in preparation for landing. Flight attendants, eyes darting, patrolled the aisle. A few sips of coffee remained in my cup, which I protected from seizure by hiding it under *The Richleigh Journal*, folded open to the editorial page.

The lead editorial, captioned "Moderation in All Good Things," began by reminding readers of the *Journal*'s unstinting dedication to protecting the environment. Then the editorialist castigated Dean for his "extreme and unbalanced" proposals to strengthen environmental laws. Dean was reminded "there's no free lunch." The editorialist warned that Dean's "radical and single-minded" strategy to clean up the Shenley would force pulp mills to move to states "which understand families depend on jobs." The editorialist did not explain why dumping tons of acid waste in the Shenley was essential to the health of the pulp industry.

The plane bumped, shuddered, and bumped again on the tarmac of New Orleans International. Airports are theme parks for alcoholics. Turn a corner and there's another snuggery, intimate, cool, and dark, where it's happy hour even at ten in the morning. There's always someone to drink with in the morning: mechanics coming off the eleven-to-seven shift; an off-duty flightie nervously waiting for her lover to bring in the red-eye from LA; garishly attired, middle-aged couples, Caribbean bound, getting a head start with rum; rumpled salesmen, refugees from a night in the departure lounge looking for an eye-opener; and hookers shopping for johns with a few hours to kill between flights.

New Orleans International goes one better. Vendors hawk spicy bloody marys, fresh strawberry daquiris, and Dixie beer from pushcarts. I passed up the first two carts but surrendered, at the third, to a bloody mary in a hurricane glass. Most of a seafood salad, along with a celery stalk the size of a fern, had been stuffed into the glass.

Certain as Providence to burn a hole in your gut, the gatekeeper at the rental lot said, as he handed me back the contract for a well-used Ford Tempo. He pointed to crypts in a cemetery across the highway. Them stone houses, he said, pointing at the bloody mary, is where they ends up, thems that mix up their liquor. I didn't argue with him.

Driving east on I–10 I went over my plan, so simple as to be pathetic. I was going to stake out Garnet Thibodeaux's home and see if anyone entering or exiting matched James's description. I had an address and hope born of desperation. I also had a problem with an opening line, assuming I saw a young, blond male about five seven leaving Thibodeaux's home. I envisioned several scenarios. They all began with James being as glad to see me as the Hound of Hell and ended with him making various exits.

I turned off Claiborne onto Canal, then made a left onto Royal. After a few blocks I saw the Laffite Hotel where I'd made a reservation. The assistant concierge gave my blue jeans and battered one-suiter a disapproving glance, marking me for a low tipper.

My room overlooking Royal was furnished with a four-poster bed, a crystal chandelier, and fireplace with a bubble-gum pink marble mantel. I half expected to find the coronation robes of Louis Seize in the antique armoire, carved walnut with cherry inlays.

I had a shrimp po-boy and chicory coffee in a little cafe before heading west on Magazine. Garnet Thibodeaux was supposed to reside at 1423 Garland Street, a side street off St. Charles Avenue in the Garden District. I found Garland without difficulty and drove past 1423. If this Thibodeaux didn't have taste and money, some other Thibodeaux had. That much was apparent from the imposing Greek revival-style mansion surrounded by an ornate cast-iron fence.

I parked the Ford on Prytania and walked the few blocks to Garland, which ran for three blocks past meticulously restored antebellum homes with lush lawns which looked to have been groomed with nail clippers. Stately Corinthian and Doric columns, soaring masts of dazzling whiteness, supported broad galleries, bordered by intricate patterns traced in wrought iron.

Mid-December is far from the peak of the tourist season. Even in season, comparatively few tourists visit the Garden District, an exclusive domain of private homes exactingly restored to ante bellum elegance. A few gardeners and maids eyed me suspiciously, causing me to pull my guidebook from the pocket and pretend to check my bearings. I was as conspicuous as a cockroach on a slab of angel food cake. It occurred to me that if I leaned against a lamppost for more than ten minutes, a NOPD patrol car would appear. The tolerance of officialdom for slack behavior on Bourbon Street is measured by miles. Here I had the feeling it was measured by inches.

Garland ended in a "T" intersection with St. Charles. I took a left on St. Charles, planning to walk a few blocks before heading back to Prytania. I had gone about a half-block before suddenly, for no reason, I decided to retrace my route. The afternoon was fading. Shadows climbed columns which only minutes ago had been radiantly white. This time no one attempted politely to shield a stare. I had gone about a half-block when a clanging of metal caused me to shift my attention from scroll work on balconies.

Two hundred yards or so ahead of me a man with long blond hair, carrying a small duffel bag, was shutting the iron gate to the side garden of 1423. Then he turned around and walked rapidly toward Prytania. I doubled my pace and closed the distance to about one hundred yards by the time he turned right at the intersection with Prytania. When I reached Prytania I crossed to the opposite side of the street and, maintaining my distance, continued a parallel course. Homebound traffic on Prytania provided a screen. Shadows were flattening out and deepening. At the intersection with 4th Street, he crossed the street, giving me an unobstructed profile view, looked once to his left, in my direction, and continued his brisk pace down 4th Street, which I turned onto just in time to see him make a right onto Coliseum and vanish from sight.

I broke into a jog. There were only a few minutes of daylight left. When I reached the intersection with Coliseum he was just over a hundred yards ahead. The streetlamps came on. I watched him knock on a side door which opened immediately to admit him to Maison Verde, which occupies the corner of Coliseum and Jefferson.

Maison Verde is a rambling, culinary cathedral. Several years ago, I had gotten lost in the maze of dining rooms and halls trying to find the men's. If the guy I was following had any suspicion he was being tailed, his strategy for losing me was brilliant. There could be several hundred diners at the Maison Verde, even on a midweek evening, and dozens of exits.

I reached the side door, a solid sheet of steel unrelieved by handle or knob, on which he had rapped. A notice in block letters had been stenciled: "Fire Exit Only. Use Main Entrance on Washington Ave." Below the sign, a red arrow pointed in the direction of Washington Street. I glanced at my watch. It was just past five-thirty. Someone had been waiting for his knock, which meant he hadn't suddenly decided to duck in a fire door to shake me. It also meant he planned to stay a while.

I lingered across Jefferson from the main entrance. I watched a sightseeing van with more glass panels than Cinderella's coach pull into the parking lot. Twelve Orientals disembarked and formed a file of pairs. The dark suits of the men made me consider my appearance. I looked like a roustabout fresh from an offshore rig.

I considered trying to bluff my way past the maitre d', telling him that I was rejoining my party of four, haughtily admonishing him for his failure to recall that I was the diner summoned to turn off the headlights on the Lincoln with Mississippi plates UYT-876. But I had the feeling the maitre d' was a case-hardened pro. He probably first had heard my story the day after it was invented and knew by heart the thousand variations developed over the next thirty years. He'd politely give me ten seconds to move on before pressing a floor button to call security.

Somewhere inside, a blond male who from a distance of several hundred yards seemed to fit the general description of Jason James, who possibly might have information which conceivably might be of value, was probably getting into ravigote of crabmeat. I was getting chilled and nowhere. I also had attracted the attention of a NOPD patrol car which slowed the second time it passed me. On the third pass it would stop and I would be summoned to show ID.

I tried to walk inconspicuously along the side of the parking lot. I wished now I hadn't missed the law school seminar on how to case a joint. Two short men in baggy white pants and white Eisenhower jackets emerged, jabbering in a language I didn't recognize, from the rear of the Palace. A few minutes later, a kid with a ponytail gunned a Vespa into the lot and joined the two guys in white. They were smoking now. One checked his wristwatch periodically. An old Fiat pulled into the lot and parked beside the Vespa. Two guys got out and joined the group.

It was getting close to six. The evening shift was about to relieve the afternoon shift. Two more junkers parked at the far end of the lot. Guys were banging open the rear door of the Palace, unsnapping their white jackets and shaking cigarettes loose as they came down the steps. They were young, slight, and seemed Hispanic. Busboys. The bottom rung of the ladder.

Browbeat by waiters and burdened with rubber trays holding sixty pounds of dirty china, slops, and scraps.

What the hell, I thought. I fell in with the new arrivals and followed them up the steps. There was a changing room with lockers inside the door. In the corner stood a stack of fresh uniforms. I grabbed the biggest one I could find, ripped off the wrapper, and shook out the uniform. The lapels hadn't been shaped and basted with prewar five-pound notes, but it wasn't a bad fit for a sack of coarsely woven, heavily starched cotton.

No one paid any attention to me. I buttoned up the jacket, put on a paper fatigue cap, cocked it at a jaunty angle, and followed the evening shift into the kitchen, the size of a hockey rink but with more shouts, shoves, and slapshots.

Stainless-steel sinks lined the far end of the kitchen where we milled about, loosely forming a double row. A little coffee-colored man, lithe and whippet-quick, wearing a chef's cap and double-breasted white jacket, inspected our ranks, jabbing in the air with a pencil as he shouted out numbers in French.

A couple of guys in the front row were goosing each other and giggling. With his clipboard, he slapped one on the head. Then he called the roll. When no one answered to "Mirabar," I said "Sí." He pointed at me and shouted, "Third East."

We broke ranks and scrambled to fill silverplated pitchers with crushed ice, water, and lemon slices. After loading twelve pitchers on a serving tray, I hoisted the tray to my shoulder, hoping to make it out of the kitchen before I dropped it. Once past the swinging, double doors, I put my tray on the first serving stand I found, picked up a brass peppermill the size of a Louisville Slugger and got as far away from the kitchen as I could.

I extended the peppermill in front of me, holding it at eye level the way drum majors hold their batons. I adopted a calm but purposeful expression appropriate to the ground pepper emergency to which I had been dispatched. My cover was the image of a serious man in a controlled hurry, armed with a lethal weapon.

I started with the dining rooms on the second floor. Waiters in tuxedos and starched aprons were scrambling to serve the six o'clock seating. I tried to avoid eye contact as I walked quickly between the closely spaced tables.

The only young, blond men I saw in the upstairs dining rooms were accompanied by mom and dad. The six o'clock seating seemed reserved for families, retirees, and group tours. Champagne corks weren't popping. Pitchers of iced tea outnumbered ice buckets twenty to one.

Then it occurred to me James hadn't come to the Maison Verde at five-thirty in order to get a good table near the party of twelve representing the Rotary Club of Jackson. James was the kind of guy who didn't get out of bed until noon on his good days. He probably thought dinner before midnight was gauche. Hors d'oeuvres were lunch for James. I decided to check the lounge.

The hundred crystal pendants seemed not to refract so much as absorb the pale light from the antique chandelier. The gas flares in the courtyard garden cast a spectral light through the floor-to-ceiling windows. Opposite the windows were a dozen booths upholstered in black leather. Flickering wicks extending from crystal bowls of perfumed oil speckled teardrops of light onto the marble tops of cocktail tables.

I passed quickly in front of the booths. One was occupied by beefy, middle-aged businessmen loudly recounting the day's adventures in capitalism. The next contained a trio of chain-smoking, middle-aged women dressed too young, surrounded by shopping bags and huddled over daquiris. The wives, I guessed. In the end booth an attractive blond woman wearing a black strapless was snuggled beside a distinguished-looking older man in a dark suit.

The bartender, a younger version of the maitre d', displayed a broad red cummerbund over a boiled white shirtfront from which a mainsail could have been cut. If the cummerbund had been smaller, it could have doubled as a sumo wrestler's ceremonial sash. I turned to leave and caught a stare which could etch steel. I was running out of luck and time.

Then it hit me. There had been a duffel bag on the floor beside the May-December couple. I pivoted to take a second look. Just then she laughed softly and turned her head to the side to exhale, giving me a profile view. Then I felt something like a forklift clap me on the shoulder and spin me around.

" 'Fuck you staring at?'' the bartender said in a harsh whisper.

"Get your sweaty palm off me. I'm delivering a message to Mr. Thibodeaux.''

"Don't be eyefucking his gal. Tell him and get back to yo bussing. This ain't no breaktime, boy.'' He lifted his hand.

I walked to the booth. The older man looked to be in his late fifties. His silver hair was raked in waves over his high forehead. Delicate features had been chiseled into his thin, elongated face. He let me stand at attention for a long moment, ignoring me, while he explained why the new Beaujolais was inferior.

"What is it?'' he finally said in an irritated tone, peering at me over the rim of his goblet. I leaned forward as if to whisper discreetly a message in his ear. I could sense the bartender's cold eyes on the back of my neck. He scowled, then angled his ear toward me.

"Mr. Thibodeaux?'' Thibodeaux made a clucking noise, then hissed, "Yes?''

"Look up at me and smile,'' I whispered. "I'm not a cop. That's the good news. The bad news is, I don't get what I want I'm going to turn you in for harboring a felon. And I'm going to tell the cops where to find candypants.'' I nodded in the direction of his date.

Thibodeaux flushed, clenched his jaw, then started to speak.

"Don't talk. Nod your head. Smile and keep smiling. I need some honest answers from James. That's it. I get that and I'm out of your life. Both your lives. I don't, I'm going to take you both down. Your choice.''

Thibodeaux hissed something in French to his date, who was wearing a tight smile which made Mona Lisa's seem like a country grin.

"Give me one of your cards,'' I whispered.

Thibodeaux hesitated, then extracted a little silver case from his breast pocket. He handed me an engraved card which said he was president of Monmarte Trust Company.

"Got a pen?"

He pulled a little, cloisonné mechanical pencil from his vest pocket and handed it to me. I scribbled the name of my hotel and room number on the back of his card.

"Call me before ten. I don't hear from you, I'm calling the FBI and James's buddy, Tommy Prescott." I handed the card to him. "Now give me a tip."

I bowed my head deferentially and said, "Merci, Monsieur," when Thibodeaux handed me a five.

On the way out, I stopped at the rail, folded the five, and slid it over to the bartender.

"Your turf, your tip."

The bartender covered the five with a palm the size of Kansas and eyed me for a moment. Then he poured a double Stolichnaya in a shot glass, passed it to me and winked. I winked back, downed the shot, and headed for the side exit.

CHAPTER 18

I played with the remote, clicking through channels. Then I did sit-ups, push-ups, and stretched out. None of it made the waiting easier.

It was almost ten when the phone rang. I lifted the handset before the first ring finished.

"Got a pencil?"

The voice was soft and mocking.

"Go ahead," I replied.

"Lamont Industrial Park. Payphone at the corner of Tremont and 9th. Wait there."

I borrowed a street map from the concierge and located Lamont Industrial Park, situated across the river not far from the Interstate 90 bridge. I jotted down directions and crossed Royal to the parking lot. I sat in the Tempo for a while, listening to the radio, trying to come up with a reason, other than setting me up for a hit, why I had been directed to a pay phone in an industrial park.

I followed the Interstate 90 bridge over the Mississippi and made a right onto 7th Street. Only a few streetlights were functioning. The macadam roadway was badly rutted. Halos of white dust were kicked up when oncoming cars hit potholes partially filled with sand and oyster shells. Apart from a few forlorn motels and hard-hat bars, the area was dark and deserted, the

skyline marked by cranes, boxcars, and container ships silhouet-
ted by the lights of the French Quarter across the river.

Compounds bordered by twelve-foot-high sections of chain-
link fence crowned with razor wire occupied the south shore
near the bridge. A few spotlights displayed artifacts of the industrial age. A collection of propellers rested against the up-
ended hull of a shrimper. Gargantuan spools of cable were
stacked like Tinkertoys against a warehouse. Oddly shaped concrete castings littered a gravel lot.

Lamont Industrial Park consisted of wire grids, corrugated
steel sheds, and fenced and chained storage lots served by a
rail spur and marine terminal. I made a right at 9th Street,
turned off the headlights, and followed it into the park. At the
intersection of Tremont and 9th, a streetlight cast glaucous light
on a boarded-up Southex Gas station. Waist-high weeds poked
through the cracked apron where pumps had once stood. At the
base of the streetlight was a pay phone sheltered by a translu-
cent hood bearing the logo of Southern Bell.

I parked the Tempo beside a loading dock about two hundred
yards away from the gas station and got out. Were it not for
the dueling barks of guard dogs in the distance I could have
heard my watch tick. Or my heart pound. Suddenly, the thick,
moist air was shattered by a shrill ring. The rings became pierc-
ingly insistent, deflected from the thousand hard-angled surfaces
abutting the gas station, finally seeming to echo mercilessly in
the back of my head. I launched the Tempo down the street
and skidded it to a stop beside the pay phone. I reached out
the window and lifted the receiver.

"It's the retro ambience," the same voice said, "that appeals
to me. So evocative. Warehouses as crypts for the American
Dream." The voice was relaxed, in control.

"James?" I said in a hoarse voice. My mind raced, mistaking
every twitch of tensed muscle as the shredding of flesh.

"Go slow, fella," the voice said. "Don't be in a rush to get
your rocks off." He laughed softly. I took a deep breath.

"Why don't you hop out of the car so I can see you?" the
voice asked.

I let a minute go by, then reached for the gear-shift lever with my free hand.

"You don't need to see me to talk," I said into the receiver.

A harsh crash erupted to my left followed immediately by a distant thunderclap which trailed off in ripples of echoes. All that was left of the exterior mirror was a jagged chrome stump.

"Hope you didn't decline the property damage coverage," the voice said. "If I wanted to kill you, you'd be a stain on the seat right now. Get out of the car."

I laid the receiver on the shelf of the phone booth, slowly got out, and lifted the receiver.

"Stand over against the streetlight so I can look at you." I moved three feet to the left.

"Take off your jacket and throw it in the car," I rested the receiver on top of the pay phone and did as I was told. The chilled air lapped at my soaked shirt. I retrieved the receiver.

"How are those pecs and lats?"

I pulled off my shirt and tossed it in the car.

"I don't see a wire," the voice said.

"I'm on my own. No wires. No tapes."

"Put on your jacket," the voice said. "You're shaking like a leaf. The crosshairs are jumping all over you, giving me a headache."

"Long-range killing. That's your style?" I asked.

"Verily it's not, not that I haven't the eye for it. Daddy used to make me hunt, but I'd shoot high on purpose. One time he snuck up on me at the club and saw me fairly well drill every skeet before it got head high. Pissed him something awful. But you can't tell. Maybe at this range, using a scope, it wouldn't be so bad. Kind of abstract."

"Before I left the hotel, I sent a fax to my office," I said. "I told my secretary to get it to Prescott if I don't call in the morning."

The lie came easily.

"Prescott," he repeated, then laughed. "It really doesn't matter what anyone does at this point. There's a Janis Joplin song. Lousy song, but it's got one great line. 'Freedom's just another name for nothing left to lose.' That's how it is. I'm just letting go, cutting loose what doesn't matter, getting things as simple and straight as I can. That's why GT's been good for me, just letting me have time to get ready.''

"For what?" I asked after a long pause.

"For what?" he mocked in an exaggerated drawl. "Where you been, boy? Ain't you preparing your spirit for the Sugar Bowl?" He laughed. The breeze from the Mississippi had picked up.

"How long you planning to keep this up?" I said, breaking the silence.

"Funny now you'd be asking that. Seems as I recall from somewhere your cameo as the great white busboy. Upset poor Garnet so badly he had to put a nitro under his tongue. All because you wanted to talk. That's what we're doing. Talking. You ought to be careful what you wish for. Now, what's your wish?"

"Honest answers," I replied.

"That pathetic old drunk Campbell let me know you'd been to see him. I thought you might come calling."

"Did Campbell tell you the SBI is laying off the Dufault murder on you?" A long pause followed.

"He did. 'Deed that's the only reason I'm talking to you, sweetstuff. What you think about that?"

I didn't reply.

" 'Course," he continued, "it was no surprise. I suppose I shouldn't care what those scum-sucking pigs lay on me." I heard a rasp followed by a slow exhale.

"But I suppose I do," he continued. "I've got the family name to consider, silly as that sounds. It's hard to leave off thinking southern no matter how hard you try."

"Maybe we share an interest," I replied.

"Two little white lambs. Baa, baa, baa." He snorted a dry laugh.

"Tell me about my uncle," I said softly.

"May he rest in peace but screw Niles anyway. I didn't owe Niles anything. I wrote him a letter after I was arrested, asking if he could help me swing bail. At least put in a word for me. I knew Niles spent money faster than he made it. But he did consulting for law firms which thought nothing of blowing twenty grand on a Christmas party. Take it out of petty cash. So I wrote Niles, asking him to call in a favor, maybe interest some do-gooder foundation with megabucks. I knew it was a long shot. Just asked him to see what he could do. Never heard a word from him. Not even a sympathy card.

"Only good thing about being arrested was getting away from your crazy uncle. Man was driving me crazy, driving himself crazy. Wouldn't leave me alone.

"One night, December a year ago it was, I was at Niles's place. I was dead on my size eight feet. I'd filled in for one of the boys who'd let a john talk him into staying over. I must have pumped that bike up Minor Hill fifteen times if I did it once. So I shook out a few lines, just a pick-me-up. Niles says he wants to try some. I told him to stick with the Story he was working on. Man wouldn't take no for an answer.

"So I let him hit a couple lines. Major-league mistake, let me tell you. Niles gets wired and has a bad case of first-timer coke mouth. Can't stop talking. Man started going on about plumbing the depths of our souls and not flinching. All this crap about ruthless honesty, about the secrets about ourselves we most fear are the ones we must face. Forthrightly and foursquaredly. Kept saying that. Man gets all weepy.

"I'm thinking, holy shit, what's this sucker fixing to confess? In the business you learn real fast to run when some dude starts working up to confess. Sonofabitch might tell you he strangled some boy—accidentally, of course—in a B&D scene twenty years ago. Wants you to say it's okay, accidents happen, don't worry about it. Next day he's going to sober up, remember his confession and come calling. You don't need that. So I told Niles I'm going to skip dessert and head on back to Richleigh.

"All of a sudden Niles wheeled himself off and down the hall. I did a line in the bedroom, got dressed, and headed for the kitchen, figuring to grab a road beer and slip out the back door.

"On the way down the hall, I looked in the library. Niles had switched on his VCR. Niles didn't look over, but I can tell he knows I'm standing by the door.

"A little voice, which sounded peculiarly like Mama's told

me to keep my sweet ass in high-gear and out the door. Man's secrets are liable to stink like a week-old mackeral wrapped in a dirty diaper. But my fool self couldn't resist. Just like Lot's wife, I had turn back and look.

"So I walked in and stood behind his chair. Niles doesn't say a word, just rewinds the tape and hits the 'play' button. Film was gray and grainy with bands of snow rolling across it. Niles adjusted the tracking and brought the film into better focus. Not great, but good enough. Two ugly little guys are going at it. At first I thought Niles had gotten jipped by some porn dealer. Then all of a sudden I recognized the interior of the student apartment and said, 'Oh, shit, Niles.'

"Niles gives me a bad-boy grin and begs another line off me. While I'm chopping it up for him, he starts in on this monologue about the problem of low light and how he had to order specially treated film from some place in Germany.

"I tell him he's the Fellini of sneak flicks. 'You ought to enter your best film at Cannes. Go for the video voyeur prize,' I told him.

" 'This one,' Niles says, holding up a tape. Niles rewinds the first film, which is about over. One guy is trying to find his glasses in the cracks between the sofa cushions.

"Niles plays the second tape. He tells me to notice the sharper focus. I recognized Dean right off and damned near choked on my beer. He was thinner then with longer hair, but it was Dean all right. No doubt about it. I'd seen him enough times when I picked up jobs at Dean, Varret.''

James let the silence pend. I heard a guard dog whimper. The edge of a half-moon peered from a break in the clouds. A barge churned slowly upriver.

"I was going to find some way to kill myself rather than do a dime at Greenwood. When I told Campbell to put me in touch with Dean, I wasn't planning to threaten Dean. I wanted to trade favors, that was all. I was going to promise Dean I'd get the tape, somehow, from Niles if Dean would get me out of the jam I was in.''

"But you figured out Dean couldn't help you,'' I said.

"I spent a few days thinking about what that meant and not

liking the answer I came to. Not liking it one damn bit. But I can't say I agonized over it.

"It boiled down to a choice between Dean's career and my life. That didn't make it much of a choice. Politicians, even right-thinking ones like Dean, are like trains. There's always another one coming along. Politicians pop out of circumstances. Always have and always will. The tides of times throw them up and wash them back. I respected Dean, but there'd be another Dean to take his place."

"So you made Campbell set up a meeting with Prescott," I said.

"Prescott said he didn't want to talk about it. Even hear about it. 'You take note I said that,' Prescott told me, putting his hands over his ears. But Prescott made sure he heard enough.

"Three days later, early in the morning, the keys woke me up and took me to a holding cell in the basement. A guy was there, waiting. Little over six feet. Midforties. Thinning blond hair slicked straight back. Wearing a double-breasted blue suit that showed off his shoulders.

"He's got his back to me. Doesn't look at me. Says 'Sit.' Not sit down. Have a seat. 'Sit.' As if I'm his dog.

"After a while he turns a chair around and kicks it close to me. He straddles it and gives me a hard look. Sits there staring at me, arms folded over the chairback. Drums on the chairback with his Citadel ring.

"Man tells me he's a detective assigned to the special investigations branch of the attorney general's office. I almost laughed. This guy has fake written all over him. Cops go for a suit with a nice shine to it. One of those polyester jobs that looks like it was injection molded. Real cop wouldn't be caught dead in a custom-tailored, tropical-weight worsted wool even if he could afford it.

"I play along like a good boy. Nothing else I can do. I 'yessir' and 'no, sir' him, letting him know that I might be a purveyor of faggot whores who corrupted the burgers of Richleigh with dangerous narcotics but, by God, my mama taught me good manners.

"Doesn't take him long to start asking about Dean. Wants

to know if Dean was a customer. I tell him the truth. Dean, Varret was strictly a business account.

"He presses me hard. Am I sure about that? Think back. It would be helpful to the attorney general if you had a more precise recollection. Read my lips. Helpful to you, too, you dumb little queer. Talks about lack of helpful cooperation, stressing 'helpful,' just in case I'm so obtuse I haven't gotten the message. I tell him my memory doesn't need editing.

"He gives up. Asks if I know anything about other crimes. 'What other crimes?' 'Whatever you have in mind,' he says. 'You mean like dirty movies?' I asked. 'We take pornography seriously, very seriously,' he tells me.

"So I tell this guy I might know something about a professor who makes his own dirty movies.

"I finish my story, telling just enough to make sure I had this guy hooked. He gets up, gives his crotch a good tug, and bangs on the door. The guard opens it and he leaves without a fare-thee-well."

"Who was the guy?" I asked.

"You're messing up the flow. You want to hear this or not?"

"Proceed."

"Proceed. By you leave." James laughed.

"About two weeks later, the keys take me back to the holding cell. Same guy's there. Have a seat please, he says, smoking. Give me a stick, I say. He asks if menthol is okay. I tell him I'd prefer sensimilla but I'd take whatever he's got.

"He slips out a monogrammed silver case, flips it open, and flicks me a Benson and Hedges. He clicks a switch on the side of the case and gives me a light.

" 'The attorney general,' he says, 'expressed grave concern when I reported to him the tapes you described. If what you told me is true, not only has a state law been broken, but, as you can appreciate, the existence of the tape creates the possibility of extortion involving an elected official. We want your cooperation in obtaining the tape. In return the attorney general will intervene to reduce the charge on which you've been indicted.'

"To what?" I asked. 'To maybe time served, depending,' he

says. 'Depending on whether I get the tape?' 'All the tapes,' he answered. 'We're interested in results, not procedures.' 'You mean you don't give a shit what I have to do.' 'That,' he said, 'and we don't want to hear about it.' I said okay, let's do it. I didn't trust the bastard, but figured they'd have to let me out of this dump, give me a shot at skipping. Wasn't much but better than I had.

"Two days later, a guard takes me back to the holding cell. The same guy is waiting. Sporting two-hundred-dollar French wraparounds. Sandwashed silk suit in a shade of bleached bone. A short guy is standing a few steps behind him. I'm thinking maybe he brought his little brother. Field trip to view faggot felons. Learn how to recognize them so you can avoid stepping on them in the woods.

"Junior's tricked out in a satin silver-and-blue Dallas Cowboys jacket. Got himself a pair of Air J's with contrast laces loose and slopping out, homeboy style. Junior's wider than tall with bulging trapezoids instead of a neck. Chrissakes, I say to myself, not another short, mean bench-press freak. I thought all of them were in the lockup with me. Up close I see Junior's a good ten years older than I thought. Maybe thirty. Junior done lost the zits war. Left his face looking like a pepperoni pizza which caught fire. Then somebody put it out with an icepick. Mean little ice-blue eyes.

"Junior pulls out a pair of handcuffs and tries to clamp a ring on me. I jerk my arm free. Don't lay a hand on me, dogbreath, I tell him. Junior looks like he's going to stomp me.

"The dude looks at me and shakes his head, sad like. He puts his arm around Junior, who's still revving up, and tells him to chill.

" 'You're not going to see me again,' he says, taking off his Vuarnets. 'What's more, you're going to forget that you ever saw me. Ricky here is going to monitor your progress in securing the evidence we discussed.' "

James paused. I heard the rasping of a match. Another barge slowly chuffed its way upriver. The wind whipped grit into swirls at my feet. I glanced at my watch. James had been talking for almost twenty minutes.

"Ricky had a '76 Coupe De Ville with primer for detailing. He told me to get in and head toward Waterston. Every time Ricky saw a 7-Eleven, he'd say, swing her in queerbait and get us a cold one.

"About halfway to Waterston, Ricky says 7-Eleven ho. I pull in and pick up another quart of Bud. This time I also pick up a box of sleeping pills, gel-capsule type.

"When I come out of the 7-Eleven, Ricky's over by the dumpster, doing a little dance, singing to himself, having a hell of a good time pisspainting the dumpster. So I break open a dozen capsules and pour the gel into the quart Ricky left on the console. I swirled it around good and gave it a little shake.

"We'd gone a mile or so when I see Ricky tilt back his head and chug the rest of the quart. Slow down, queerbait, and pull to the right, he tells me, mean like, kind of growling. I do what he says, figuring he's tasted the sleeping pills and is going to kill me. Then Ricky yells, third and long. He leans out the window and throws the bottle at a railroad crossing sign.

"By the time we get to the turnoff for Waterston Ricky's mumbling to himself. About the time we get to the hill where Nile's place is, I hear a noise like a chainsaw chopping up a stack of wet newspapers. Ricky's slumped against the door.

"I drive up the hill, park in Niles's driveway, and take the keys. I beat on the door. Finally, Niles opens it. He pretends in this huffy, fake British way he has that he's glad to see me but he's extremely busy. He's wearing his demi-glasses and has on a velvet robe. I can tell he's as glad to see me as a boil on his ass.

" 'I'll make it quick,' I say. 'I need money. Serious money.' Niles gets nervous, says something stupid about co-signing a loan for me. 'I mean now,' I tell him. 'Or I'll invite the pitbull in the Cadillac to help me look for your videotape collection.' I fill Niles in on enough background to let him appreciate the situation.

"Niles doesn't say a word. He rolls down the hall, opens the safe, and takes out a roll of twenties and stack of videocassettes. I drag a trash can into the yard, out behind the rose garden, and dump in the tapes. I find a can of gasoline, soak them good, and burn the suckers.

"Then I climb back in the Caddy. There's a reservoir a few miles down the road from Niles's place. I was going to lean a rock against the accelerator and send Ricky and the De Ville to the bottom. But I couldn't do it.

"Instead, I pulled into a rest area on Interstate 75 and rolled Ricky out. Two hours later, I reached Richleigh International and caught the next flight to New Orleans."

"Who was the guy playing detective?" I asked.

"It took one phone call to find out." He paused and laughed softly.

"Guy was dumber than a fence post. First visit he beats the table to death with a ring the size of a golf ball. Says right on it: Citadel, '66. Next time he gives me a light from a cigarette case with RSP engraved on it.

"Day after I settled in with Thibodeaux, I called a boy I knew over in Charleston and asked him to check the 1966 Citadel yearbook. He phones me back and says there was only one senior with the initials of RSP. Rodney Sempert Petit. How's that for a meaty, mince pie, as my mama used to say?"

"Sonofabitch," I said.

"Thought you'd like that," he said, laughing. "I called Prescott and told him if anyone came after me, I'd give the *Journal* a story to scorch the front page. 'What story?' he asks. 'Try this one,' I say. ''DA Loans Call Boy Drug Dealer Suspect to Ex-Senator Petit.'' It's all written in my safe-deposit box.'

"He got real quiet, Prescott did. Then we had a nice talk. I told him I'm already under a sentence. When the blotches come, I'm gone. Seconal and Southern Comfort. All you have to do is make sure I'm left alone.

"Prescott says there's a lawyer from a hick town doing some freelancing. Then he tells . . ."

The report of a high-powered rifle shattered the night, sending echoes careening, followed immediately by a second shot, echoes chasing echoes. I thought for a minute I was dead. Then I realized I was the one saying "Hello, hello" into the receiver.

Seconds later, NOPD cars, blue lights twirling, raced down

the street and lurched to angled positions in front of me. A cop wearing a helmet and padded vest rolled out of the second car and pulled me to the pavement. The heavy, muffled beats of a helicopter grew louder.

A few minutes later, I heard the cop's radio crackle and spit. Then a voice said, "Code Green. Repeat, Code Green."

The cop beside me unbuckled his chinstrap, flipped off his helmet, and sat up, leaning against the bumper.

"What's Code Green?" I asked.

"That means the situation's done been resolved."

"Resolved?"

"The sucker drawing down on you," he said lazily, looking at me for the first time, "just got his ass resolved. For keeps. You ought to thank your friend."

"What friend?" I asked.

"Mr. Thibodeaux."

CHAPTER 19

At the airport in Richleigh I picked up a copy of the *Journal.* I found the story on the second page under the headline, "Richleigh Kingpin Slain in New Orleans Shootout." The *Journal* had mixed in filler from its archives on Mercury Express and James's arrest in March.

Prescott was quoted: "James went from dabbling, to dealing, to death. I hope our young people take to heart the lesson James never learned. When you're on that slippery slope, it's already too late. You're only safe if you don't start. Just say 'Never' to drugs." It was too pithy a quote to be extemporaneous.

I phoned Jamie Higgins to ask a favor: access to the *Standard*'s file on the Investment Equity Trust scandal. She told me to stop by that afternoon around three.

Snow flurries were swirling, ghostly dervishes on the macadam of the parking lot, when I arrived. The lot was empty, save for a battered, muddy Chrysler station wagon with "Holly Hills" stenciled on the front doors and no hubcaps. The editorial offices were located in a one-story cinderblock building, painted white with a big, red door and plastic shutters to match. The front door was not locked. I wandered down the hall, poking my head in empty offices, until I found Jamie, jodhpurs propped on the edge of a file cabinet, thumbing through a thick sheaf of clippings. Her dark hair was pulled back into a ponytail that trailed over the collar of her leather jacket. She was about the size of a seventh grader but wirier and with twice the energy.

Jamie was about thirty, I guessed, and, according to Tom Kennelly, the editor, had turned down a dozen offers from major dailies. Won't think of leaving, long's her daddy's still kicking, Kennelly said. I'm praying for that mean old son of a buck. I'd hate to lose the lady. Ain't much to look at. But she's got ink for blood.

"Five pounds of cold scandal," she said, handing me the file. "Keeps better that way."

"I really appreciate this."

"Bibliography of all articles in the MediaNet database on Investment Equity Trust or Petit," she replied, handing me a printout. "Need help. I'll be down the hall, third office on the left."

I listened to the heels of her cowboy boots echo on the cinder-block walls of the hall. Then I spread open the file on a scarred and ink-stained oak table, a relic from the days of linotype. I started with the lead article in the October 26, 1986, edition of the *Richleigh Journal.*

Dean's TV spot had exposed Petit's secret interest in Investment Equity Trust which through a dozen nominees had optioned farmland adjacent to proposed interchanges. The two-minute spot was an instant sensation and, abetted by the press release issued by Dean's campaign, was front-page news.

Petit attempted to defend his interest in the trust as a legitimate business deal. He was arguably correct, as the sidebar which accompanied the *Journal*'s article stated. No law prohibited a legislator from using information about the likely right-of-way for a new highway to make a killing.

Once in a while a zealous or unseasoned (the adjectives tended to be synonyms) legislator with a hyperactive conscience would decry the lack of a code of ethics stronger than a gentleman's tacit sense of honor. But these jeremiads, being as predictable as ineffectual, were treated by the old hands as annoyances and pissbreaks.

Dean had made enactment of a code of ethics a major theme

of his campaign for lieutenant governor, but his bill never got out of committee. Within the club even those legislators who privately denounced profiteering from access to insider knowledge declined to make the practice a crime. Haggling publicly about ethics tarnished the image of incumbents, a flagrant breach of the first rule of politics. (The second is that there are only two parties which matter: incumbents and others.)

Besides, the old hands warned, trying to link a member's visionary real-estate investment to an exploitation of insider information was an exercise in metaphysics, the legal equivalent of chasing the will-o'-the-wisp. Worse still, it was a snipe hunt which could be turned into a witch hunt by the party which succeeded in capturing the office of attorney general. The result would be more vendettas in Richleigh than in Rome in the sixteenth century.

It's better, they counseled, to chastise privately over a glass of old bourbon those members too greedy to be discreet, an error better analogized to crude table manners than to a crime. Better to inculcate *savoir faire* patiently, through example and measured admonition, than to enact an unwieldy statute rife with potential for vindictive prosecutions. When the boat rocks, we all get wet.

The *Journal*'s editorial argued Petit shouldn't be crucified for feasting from the same trough as Democrats. Dean would have done the same thing, the *Journal* contended, had he not been busy "making millions by hyping tax shelters to keep fat cats from paying their fair share of taxes." The editorial unctuously ended: "Let he who is without sin cast the first stone." Measured by even the high standard of casuistry maintained by the *Journal*, the editorial, a strange mixture of urbane acceptance of lust for lucre as man's fate and righteous condemnation of hypocrisy, was a masterpiece of twisted logic in the service of ill-conceived public policy.

There was, however, as subsequent articles in other newspapers disclosed, a fine, perhaps ephemeral, line between a legislator using his own capital to profit handsomely from information gained by virtue of elected status and selling such information. The latter practice (together with the complementary practice of purchasing such information) fell within the vague ban of a nineteenth-century public corruption statute.

Further examination revealed this statute had been enacted to deter competition from carpetbaggers, the apparent rationale being that new corruption should be funded only with old money. Given that millions in old money had vanished when the Confederate war bond market went South, a modest degree of home-cooking, affirmative action to aid patriotic investors, doubtlessly had seemed justified to the legislature of 1878.

Petit's problem was that his money was neither old nor was there much of it. Wife and children in tow, Petit held a press conference to denounce hypocrisy and announce his support for a "realistic" ethical-practices statute. Petit claimed the "pie-in-the-sky" version favored by Dean was designed to be unenforceable, thereby allowing wily Democrats to continue lining their pockets.

In response to questions from the press, Petit cited examples of swindles and scandals by Democrats. Some wag from the press, noting that the Democrats cited by Petit had held office in the nineteenth century, remarked we had more to fear from live Republicans than dead Democrats.

At the press conference, Petit contended he innocently had invested the meager funds of his young family in the trust at the suggestion of Eddy Carnes, a fraternity brother who fortuitously happened to be the investment advisor to the Trust. Petit reminded the press that he and Eddy had been paired as the offside guard and tackle ("two regular guys with our noses in the mud") on the only winning team fielded by the university in the past twenty years. Implicit was the message that high-stepping, hip-swiveling backs might engage in financial hanky-panky but not steadfast stalwarts of the line, honest yeoman caked with God's good earth.

It was later said by self-styled "political analysts" that had Petit not called the press conference he would have lost the election but that would have been the end of it. But his bravado in calling a press conference to proclaim his innocence and subsequently failing to produce a check drawn on his own funds roused popular outrage to a fever pitch. Finally, Howard Shenfield, the incumbent attorney general and ticketmate of Petit, stuck a wet finger in the wind and decided to yield. Shenfield recommended that the governor appoint a special counsel to determine if the statute had been violated.

Former guard Eddy Carnes again pulled; this time, however, a deal with special counsel Molly Dotoli. Eddy talked. Eddy walked. Petit was left with his nose in the mud. Petit lost the election and was sentenced to six months in jail, suspended on the condition that he complete five hundred hours of community service. Judge Abel Henry, in sentencing Petit, commented he was disturbed by the vagueness of the statute that had been invoked in only one other prosecution in the twentieth century. He also noted the disbarment was severe punishment in and of itself.

Jamie appeared in the door. She stretched her back against the frame. I slipped a rubber band around the file and stood up.

"You didn't find what you wanted," she said, reading my expression.

"No," I admitted.

"What were you looking for?"

"How did Dean find out about the trust?"

"Never came out, publicly anyway. Case never went to trial. Carnes cut a deal and Petit pled no contest."

"Nolo contendere," I said. "Crapping out sounds better in Latin."

She slid out the file tray and riffled files, taking more time than needed to return the file to its holder. Finally, she closed the cabinet and turned to face me. She seemed to start to say something but didn't. We walked across the parking lot. I whisked a dusting of snow from the windshield of her station wagon and held open the door for her. She slid in and switched on the ignition. Then she turned to me.

"Stop by for a drink," she said. "Around five. We'll talk."

The snow stopped by the time I got back to the camp. A white sun glinted on fields of diamonds. The perimeter of my acreage adds up to just over three miles. I jogged the property line, adding my tracks to those of deer, rabbits, squirrels, and foxes. I stopped now and then to reattach strands of barbed wire pried loose by hunters oblivious to "No Trespassing" and "Posted No Hunting" signs. A few years back I put up a "Danger: Radioactive Waste" sign, but it hadn't made any difference.

Just after four, I left for Holly Hills. Twelve miles north of Lassington I turned left, toward the Pascamany, on the unmarked gravel road which led to the estate. It had taken the Higgins family a century to piece together the parcels which made up Holly Hills. It took another fifty years after Reconstruction to reconstruct about one-third of the original estate. The rest had been lost, first to speculators who had hoarded US coinage, then to punitive taxes imposed by the Carpetbagger government in Richleigh, and finally to strip centers and subdivisions.

The rump redeemed included limestone bluffs overlooking the Pascamany. The bluffs were said to be the ancient burial ground of the Chirkie tribe whose generosity to the invader, as in the case of the Pequod in the Bay Colony, was rewarded with obliteration. Thirty years ago Roger, Porky, Tim, and I had trespassed with the impunity of youth on the bluffs, spending summer days digging for artifacts, finding occasional arrowheads and pottery shards.

The gravel road threaded past limestone outcroppings and ancient live oaks whose thick limbs formed a bower. After better than a mile, the road led past a low stone wall, under a wrought-iron archway, over a cattle grate, and, paved now with cobblestones, turned into a circular drive.

Two wings, one per century, had been added to the Georgian-style manor which, situated on a landscaped rise, commanded the approach. I parked my truck and ascended a flight of uneven brick steps slippery with moss and snow. At the top I turned to the west and took in the view of the Pascamany, its serpentine course purple against a dark-red sun pending just above the horizon.

A drainpipe was partially detached. The bricks which formed arches over the bay windows badly needed repointing, the mortar having surrendered to relentless roots of ivy. The white paint on sills, frames, and columns was chipped and scaling.

The effect on me was not dilapidation but, rather, dishabille, the architectural equivalent of a slight tear in a lace slip. The flaw that makes perfection. I decided not to compliment Jamie and her father. My justification for letting the camp remain somewhere between barely maintained and gone to seed was not universally appreciated.

I lifted the bronze celtic harp and let it fall against the striker plate. Jamie opened the door a moment later. She was wearing a long skirt and had put her hair up.

"Speak up when you talk to Dad. He's too vain to wear a hearing aid."

She led me through a dark, cavernous center hall and into a side parlor. A fire burned in the hearth. Randolph Higgins used his cane to push himself as far erect as possible. He retained the frame of the large man he had been. His hand trembled when he lifted it and quivered when I shook it. He was wearing a gray herringbone jacket over a plaid flannel shirt with a mustard stain on the collar.

For over thirty-five years Higgins had represented Chirkie County and part of Somerset County in the state senate, rising through the ranks to serve as chairman of the appropriations committee, and, finally, as majority leader. Higgins had announced his retirement following the adjournment of the legislature in the spring of 1987. I guessed he was in his early eighties.

"How are you, sir?" I asked, shaking his hand.

He moved closer to examine me. White stubble covered his chin. His grey-green eyes were rheumy and bloodshot. Sagging folds of flesh made them appear to bulge.

"Parkinson's," he replied, holding up his hand. "Goddamned nuisance. Sit down, sit down." He pointed with his cane in the direction of a captain's chair.

"We've got bourbon," he said. "Some decent gin, too. Left over from a reception I gave years ago for Governor Traynor. Wasn't Governor Traynor then. Senator Sammy at the time. Only martini drinker I ever knew. Not a credit to the breed, I must say. May he rest in peace." He lifted his glass in salute.

"Bourbon's fine," I said.

"Jamie, get this gentleman a drink. Water?"

"That's all right," I said, rising. "I can help myself."

"I don't doubt that. You look fit enough." Higgins used his cane to block my way. "However, you're a guest in this house."

Jamie didn't look at me when she placed a silver tray laden with drinks on the coffee table.

Silver- and gold-plated cups and trophies of various descriptions and dimensions, with red, gold, and blue ribbons taped to them, were crowded together on the mantelpiece. The wall above the sideboard was covered with framed photographs, all in equestrian settings, of Jamie as a little girl, adolescent, and young woman.

Jamie was the only child of Higgins's brief marriage to a woman I knew as Becky. In the early sixties, Becky had been in charge of junior tennis and making sure the bar was stocked. Her official title was assistant manager of the country club.

I had lived for those moments when Becky would cradle my shoulders with her arm, lightly pressing her breasts against my back, to make sure I fully rotated on forehands. The sudden, startling whiteness of her panty when she stretched to cover a sharply angled ball flashes still, twenty-eight years later, a supernova in my constellation of memory.

There had been talk that Higgins had ruined his career when he eloped with Becky. But it hadn't mattered to the voters. Callous bastards, Mother said, not even trying to suppress a smile, made hay of it. Men admired him for getting in pants when they had failed and women forgave him because he did the right thing after he got the silly girl pregnant. No one liked Elizabeth anyway. Comeuppance served her right, snotty as she was. Randy's marriage to that girl didn't last as long as his third term. Longer than anyone thought.

A short, broad white terrier mottled with liver spots wandered into the room. He looked up at me quizzically and sniffed my boots. Satisfied, he crossed the room and hunched expectantly, licking his muzzle, in front of Randolph Higgins.

"Well, say, I'm just a worthless, fat, white dog with a trash-mouth and I want to lie on your lap,'' Randolph Higgins said in a hoarse whisper, leaning forward to address the dog and pat its large, flat head, which rocked in timing with the ticking of a truncated tail.

"Hop up here then, you old bastard,'' Higgins said. He put his knees together and patted them. A split second later the dog jumped into his lap and curled into a ball.

"Pass gas and I'm going to throw you down the cellar stairs. You hear me?'' In response, the dog slowly rolled onto its back.

"You didn't give this dog beer, did you, Jamie?''

Higgins snapped his thumb against the dog's taut belly. Had the belly been a cantaloupe, the sound produced, a deeply resonant thump, would have been a sure sign of ripeness. The dog, its eyes shut, tongue lolling, seemed to grin.

"Get off,'' Higgins said a few seconds later. "You're making me too hot.'' He dropped the terrier onto a soiled, crocheted comforter which covered the seat of the adjacent armchair.

"I want to know why you came out here.'' He pointed at me with his glass, serious now.

"I want you to tell Kendall about Petit and the trust business,'' Jamie said to her father.

Higgins looked at Jamie, shook his head, snorted, and turned to me.

"How's your mother? Still kicking up her heels and raising hell?''

"Runner up last month in women's over-fifty-five singles at her club.''

"Madeleine's a piece of work.'' I didn't say anything. He looked at me. "Piece of work,'' Higgins repeated. "Work, I said. Shakespeare.''

"Hamlet,'' I replied.

"There you go. Tell Madeleine I think of her often and fondly. She'll like that.''

"I'll tell her,'' I said, knowing I wouldn't. In the early sixties, Higgins and his first wife, Elizabeth, spent a lot of time with my parents. Father, after he was disbarred, sought solace in bourbon, which Mother seemed to accept too readily, if not actually encourage.

I had a child's memory of a game of touch football in the backyard. I vaguely recalled Higgins drilling Father with a pass, hitting him so hard in the chest that he fell backward, landing squarely on his butt. Everyone laughed. I tried to remember that I hadn't.

"So you want to rake muck? That the only reason you invited Kenny?" Higgins said accusingly to Jamie, who silently mouthed words that made Higgins grin.

"Well, let's get it over with. What do you want to know?"

"How Dean found out about Petit's interest in the trust," Jamie answered. "Just that."

" 'Just that,' you say." Higgins snorted. He slid out the drawer of the coffee table and rooted through grocery coupons and loose tobacco until he found a tarnished cigar case. He fumbled with the latch, cursing under his breath, until he managed to snap it open.

"There's no 'just that' to it," he said. "Problem with you journalists is you think in headlines." Higgins removed a short black cigar from the case.

"Petit," he said, twisting the cigar in the flame from the match Jamie held for him, "I came to see personified vulgar ambition.

"Dean was every bit as ambitious as Petit, but—and this is interesting to me—Dean's ambition wasn't vulgar. And it should have been, for Dean didn't come from much whereas Petit had a measure of good breeding in his stock." He puffed rapidly and then pointed at me with his cigar.

"You know when ambition is vulgar?"

"Depends on the end to which it's directed," I replied.

"The difference lies in the transparency of ambition," Higgins continued without taking note of my answer. "And not the way you might think. That the more obvious the ambition, the more vulgar it is. Not true in my experience." Jamie put a ceramic ashtray in the shape of a horseshoe on the coffee table.

"Thank you, dear. I was referring rather to transparency in the sense of self-understanding. Every hack on the make convinces himself he wants power, not for the sake of power, but because of all the good things he can do for people once he has it.

"Definitions of what's good for the people, of course, vary all over the lot. But all politicians refract ambition through the same prism: doing good for the people. Some people, anyway. Four-buck-an-hour gutters at the rendering plant or hundred-grand-a-year rotters at the club.

"Fact is, you have to justify ambition somehow. Ambition is uglier than an ulcerated toad. Plainly begs to be dressed up in pretty principles.

"Good actor has to sell himself on the role before he can play it. Politician has to sell his ambition to himself before he can sell himself to the voters. Matter of practical necessity if he's going to project heartfelt concern.''

Higgins stopped to relight his cigar. Jamie poked the fire and added a slab of oak. The terrier yawned, arched his back, and stretched his legs.

"You should know about this, Kendall,'' Higgins said, slipping me a sidelong glance. "Lots of times recovering alcoholics will hide half-pints. Maybe put one in the tool box, another under the spare tire in the trunk. Little secrets between their good selves and their bad selves. Might never touch those bottles for years. But knowing they're hidden and ready gets them high, just thinking about how easy it would be to sneak a drink. Little secrets so bad they're sweet.

"That's how it is with politicians, the vulgar ones. They try to hide the high-proof stuff, the raw stuff, even from themselves. But, secretly, they know it's still there, covered up under all their fine talking about wanting power to serve the people, principle this, principle that. And just thinking about it gets them high.

"Most politicians lack the guts and the intelligence to deal with ambition openly and honestly. Can't bear the self-scrutiny. Can't look ambition in the eye and understand it for what it is, where it comes from, and why. That's when ambition is vulgar.

"Dean, now. I think Dean knows why he craves power. I think Dean has dug deep in the dark cellar of his soul on nights when the bats are screaming.

"He knows ambition is a fruit of blighted roots. But he's looked that devil in its red eye. Self-understanding for a politician means pain, not peace. But take away that pain and the rank weed of delusion flourishes. That's when ambition turns vulgar."

Higgins had been speaking to the embers. He turned to me and said: "You know what a demagogue is?" This time I knew better than to answer.

"A demagogue is a politician who believes his own lies. A common politician, someone like Petit, doesn't believe his own lies but won't admit it, even to himself. He sneaks down to that cellar to sneak a drink, not to dig. Dean, I think, is a digger more than a drinker. That's the difference."

Higgins started to say something else. He turned an indecipherable word into a cough and tapped his ash into the tray.

"In case you're wondering, dear," Higgins said, looking at Jamie. "I sure as hell never believed the ones I told myself. Other lies, they ranker yet. I may have to sweat them soon, despite all that money I've given to Redeemer's endowment."

"No one lives without regrets," she replied, breaking a long pause.

"Living with them, dear, is one thing. Dying with them is a mare of a different shade." Higgins rattled the ice in his drink. Jamie poured a shot into his glass. He turned toward me.

"Your mother like Florida, all those old farts passing out and crashing Cadillacs into palm trees?" Higgins laughed so hard he sneezed bourbon onto his lap.

"Dad," Jamie interjected gently, "we were talking about how Dean found out about Petit's interest in the trust."

"Summer of 1987," Higgins said, nodding in her direction, "I was down at the shore for a fund-raiser and ran into Fielding. He invited me for a round at his club. Still an old friend even if Fielding never saw a lie his toe couldn't improve.

"We had finished a lousy front nine at Culmore on a day so humid the balls wouldn't fly. We popped into the clubhouse for a few beers and never did get to the back nine. We got to talking politics and what effect the Petit scandal might have.

"Fielding's boy was on Molly Dotoli's staff. Deputy special

counsel or some such. Fielding made me promise I'd never repeat what he told me. And I haven't, except to Jamie, and that doesn't count. But Fielding passed in August, so I guess I can tell you.

"Molly served two terms in the Assembly before getting lazy and losing. That dog knows as much law as Molly, which is why Shenfield recommended her as special counsel to prosecute Petit. He knew she'd plead out the Petit case because just thinking about trying the case would make Molly wet her pants. Fielding said his boy had to do all the grand jury work. All Molly did was to pester him to cut a plea deal.

"I told Fielding I reckoned some do-gooder clerk on the transportation committee must have gotten wind of Petit's deal and leaked it to Elliott Dean.

"Fielding looks at me, shakes his head, and grins. No, sir, he says. Bastard makes me buy him a few more beers before he swears me to secrecy and tells me it was that high yellow gal who was supposed to be some sort of advisor to Petit's campaign, helping with minority outreach or whatever these days they call getting the colored vote.

"Excuse me, dear," Higgins said. He leaned over to me and whispered conspiratorially: "Ass like a sweet Georgia peach." He slapped my knee with a hand the size of a catcher's mitt.

"Fielding says his boy told him Dean had known this gal in law school and had kept up with her. Fielding's boy said there was a rumor that Dean cut a deal with her in return for information about Petit. Dean, the rumor had it, had promised this gal the next open seat on the Court of Appeals.

" 'Course, my thought when Fielding told me—and still is— is that this gal, if the rumor was true, was playing both sides, sort of a 'double-agent,' to make sure she was the winner no matter how the election turned out.

"Recall her name?" I asked, knowing the answer.

"It'll come to me if you let me talk. Woman did lobbying for the builders' and developers' association. Knew her stuff. Good talker. Better looker."

Higgins leaned back in his chair and covered his eyes with his hands.

"Name of suburb up near Washington," he said. "Woman's first name was something like it."

"Rosalyn," I said. Higgins stared at me.

"She pronounced the first syllable 'rose,' slow and sweet." Higgins imitated the pronunciation.

"I can see her now, seated at the counsel table. I don't remember what she said. But, by God, I remember she had legs to kick your heart out. Can't blame Petit. Hell, I might have gone for it if he hadn't got there first."

Higgins rambled on for a while after that, talking about deals cut, backs stabbed, and elections stolen. But I could see he was tiring out and Jamie wanted to put him to bed. When he came to a long pause, I took my leave.

Higgins insisted on walking me to the door. After we shook hands, he didn't release his grip.

"You won't forget," he said.

I didn't say anything. He squeezed harder.

"You won't forget to tell Madeleine what I said." It was a command not a question.

CHAPTER 20

Tidewater winters have a sense of humor. Temperatures sometimes rise at night. It seemed warmer when I left Jamie and her father just after nine. South of Lassington, I turned left toward Aimes Point, the project which melded the fortunes of Roger and Dean and, perhaps, their fates.

I parked beside a Crown Victoria with a Hertz sticker, the only other car in the parking lot of the Aimes Point Inn. A lonely yacht shrouded in foul-weather curtains bobbed gently in one of the guest slips.

I took a seat at the bar. The broiled captain's platter, double slaw instead of fries, and a long draft, I said to a weary, peroxided girl working on a wad of Double Bubble or Red Man. There was a little blue rose tattooed on her cheek which was sort of fetching. Probably a student, I guessed. Chirkie County Community College had done wonders for employers seeking part-time labor at subminimum wages.

The inn's juke box holds a collection of little-known sea chants. I fed in a quarter and selected, "Salty Shorts Make Me Stiff." The thirty-something couple in matching two-tone boat shoes huddled beside it didn't open their eyes or break off a kiss that hurt so much they were groaning. The guy was wearing blue corduroy slacks decorated with little lime-green whales. Maybe they were missionaries from Connecticut.

I carried my beer over to the window to watch the bay slop against the bulkheads below the ghost of a cold moon. When I looked again at the deck, I imagined I saw Roger in the mist, feet propped on the rail, bourbon in hand, regaling his coterie of fast-buck artists.

The chant swelled. "Billowing jib and straining brace, fifteen knots for a Sunday's pace, ice-flecked spray in my face, heel and hardabout through the race." I turned to check on the couple. Her chin seemed to have turned upward and slightly to the right.

When I looked out the window again Roger's ghost was still there, holding court, gesturing with his cigarette. Roger never told the same tale twice. It got bigger each time until it finally collapsed under the weight of embellishment. His promises followed the same pattern. Roger never lied. Not deliberately. He assumed everyone applied the same discount factor. Roger waged a one-man campaign against what he contemptuously called "banker facts," pedantic literalness devoid of vision. Truth for Roger was grander than numbers.

I returned to my table disconcerted, feeling stalked by an insight destined to be obvious in hindsight. I was already vaguely angry at myself for ignoring it, whatever it was. I tried to clear my mind from the preconceptions behind which it lurked. I flipped over the paper placemat decorated with nautical flags and sketched a graph on the reverse side.

I sketched a time line along the X axis. Along the Y axis I wrote the name of persons who had knowledge of Niles's video-tape. Then I plotted coordinates, charting back bearings. The trail of knowledge ran from James to Prescott and from Prescott to Petit.

I stared at the blank opposite Dean's name. I drummed the table, feeling teased. From the juke box the refrain washed over me: "Her slip was my port of last resort, 'til your bare midriff cast my heart adrift. Come sail with me in my leaky skiff, 'cause salty shorts make me stiff." A hand clapped me on the shoulder, causing me to spill my beer.

Tim Dugan draped his arm around my neck and whispered, "Gotta tell me how she likes it."

"How who likes what?"

Tim motioned conspiratorially with his head. I looked and saw Mulkerrin seated at a table near the door. She was wearing jeans, a denim jacket, and a disdainful expression.

"Just borrowing her for the night, ol' buddy," Tim said, giving my shoulder a squeeze. "C'mon back with us." I folded the placemat, put it in my pocket, and followed Tim, who walked as if he were fighting a port gale.

"Small world," Mulkerrin said coolly.

"In a year you'll be nostalgic for anonymity," I replied. "In two, you're going to think depersonalization is a virtue."

"Like a fishbowl here," Tim said, kicking out a chair for me, " 'cept the sand ain't white and the food ain't free."

"Maybe small worlds," Colleen said, looking at me, "are more intense."

"That's theory," I replied. "The reality is reruns."

Tim took a long swallow of beer, eased out a slow burp, put his hand on Colleen's, and swayed in her direction.

"Don't worry, darling," Tim said. "We swap roles once in a while to keep it interesting."

"Which is yours?" she asked him.

"Prodigal son," Tim said. "Young man with promise struggles to find his calling in life. Only his mama believes in him, but she's getting cheap in her old age. And this sonofabitch won't even show me her will."

"Tim's stale in the role," I said to Mulkerrin.

"While you were over there doodling," Tim said, "I was telling the lady about all the coves and tidal creeks we got. About how easy it would be—in theory, of course—to rendezvous with a tramp freighter, pick up a load of dope, and run it into one of those little coves." Tim gave me a wink that he made sure Mulkerrin saw.

"That so," I said, watching Mulkerrin.

"Never happen here, would it?" Tim said. "This is a law-abiding, God-fearing county. That's what I was telling the lady. You tell her, too."

I finished my beer and stood up.

"Where you think you're going? Sit your white ass down,

boy." Tim grabbed at my sleeve and missed, almost falling off his chair.

"Lady's got questions," Tim said, righting himself.

"I'd let her keep them if I were you," I said to Mulkerrin, who gave me a thin smile over the rim of her glass. As I left, I looked over my shoulder at the other couple. If there had been any change, it was glacial.

I walked along the pier, cross-hatched with empty boat slips. When I reached the end, I turned and looked at the Inn. The windows glowed in the mist which was turning into a fine, warm rain which somehow felt like cold sweat. A channel buoy tolled mournfully. A raccoon darted from under the slopsink at the end of the pier, startling me. Then the insight popped into my mind with no more fanfare than a suddenly recalled phone number. I had been blinded by a preconception. I had assumed Dean had learned of Niles's videotape independently. What if, instead, Dean was the last man on the knowledge trail I had charted? The odd man out.

The drive to Lassington took ten minutes. I parked in the lot behind the CS&T building and let myself in the rear door. I used my key to deactivate my new burglar alarm and opened the door to my office.

I carried the records for Niles and Roger's phones into the library and spread them on the table. I scanned the records until I found the unlisted Richleigh number they both contained. I figured it belonged to Dean's home phone. Calling Dean in the middle of the night was bad manners, but I was past the point of caring. Besides, if my guess was right, Dean wasn't doing much sleeping.

Dean answered on the second ring, saying hello pleasantly. He didn't sound as if he had been awakened, nor did he seem surprised or irritated to receive a phone call at midnight.

"Elliot," I said.

"Kenny," he replied after a pause. "What's up?"

"We need to talk."

"About what?" I could tell from his tone that Dean knew I hadn't called to discuss precinct operations.

"The ozone layer," I said.

"When?" Dean snapped.

"Tomorrow. You choose where."

"Pickwick Beach. I've got a place there. Number 2 Tern Lane. Garage code is 4356. I should be able to get there by five."

"Five then," I said, hung up, slid open the credenza's file drawer. In the back, I found the hip flask that belonged to Father. I shook it and was relieved to hear sloshing. I poured a shot into my coffee mug and examined the dented silver flask, almost black with tarnish.

Father, I remembered, used to keep his flask shiny, buffed by the satin lining of his jacket pocket.

I realized, being myself a heavy drinker, Father always had been a heavy drinker. Not that he got drunk. But after six he always seemed to have a highball glass in one hand and a book in the other.

The humiliation of disbarment pushed Father over the edge. It turned a bad habit into the expression of a death wish. Father stayed in his study—Mother had removed the rifles—and drank until he passed out. Then Olmie would call Clarence, and he and Olmie would carry Father into the downstairs guest bedroom.

Mother told me Father was sick and would get better if we loved him. She didn't try very hard. Maybe I didn't try hard enough.

I couldn't bear the way Father's eyes would get buggy when he was drunk. I hated it when he wouldn't bother to brush sweat-twisted locks of hair from his brow. I could tell when he was drunk by the meticulous care he took when speaking, as if each syllable had to be wrapped with his tongue to keep it from breaking. It made him sound like a sissy.

I tried to feel sorry for Father, but I couldn't help feeling betrayed. The harder I worked to summon compassion, the further away compassion slipped and the guiltier I felt. So I ended up trying to put Father out of my mind, a futile effort in which I nonetheless stubbornly persisted. I ended up hating myself and blaming him for it.

Around Christmas of 1963, Father packed his clothes into an old army trunk and moved to the camp, the run-down Victorian-era fishing lodge he had inherited from his father. After that I didn't see much of Father, who claimed to be traveling a lot on business. He became a ghost, hovering but unreachable. He flickered in and out of my adolescence, suddenly appearing out of nowhere to watch me run at a cross-country meet and then as suddenly becoming a postcard again.

I sipped the bourbon slowly, thinking about whether stillborn dreams were worse than living nightmares.

The phone rang. I somehow knew who it would be. I let it ring a while before I picked up the receiver.

"I suppose you might as well bring along that whiskey you're drinking," Peyton said.

"How do you know I'm drinking whiskey?"

"Sweetie, do you really think there's anything about you I don't know?" She hung up. I poured the whiskey in my coffee cup back into the flask and screwed on the cap.

CHAPTER 21

I must have dozed off about five in the morning, only to be awakened an hour later by a chain clanking. The devil was coming for my soul and I couldn't remember where I threw my underwear. Lord, give me another chance, I prayed, trying not to think about how many times I'd prayed for another chance, prayers that coincided with hangovers.

I looked out the window. Roger's fool dog—I still thought of the black lab as Roger's dog—had wrapped the chain to which he was tethered around his dog house. He was whipping the loose end back and forth.

I put the animal in the basement. He scratched at the door and whimpered. I couldn't find any dog food, so I opened a jumbo can of chili con carne and dumped it in a china bowl. When I reached the second story, I heard a loud thumping which at first I thought was caused by a broken part inside my head. Then I realized the brute was lashing the basement door with his thick tail.

Peyton, curled into the fetal position, had usurped my half of the bed. Her lips writhed like earthworms when she exhaled, making a noise like a death rattle. Peyton's hair looked like last year's bird's nest. Her face was ashen, except for her nose which had the texture of old brick and was larger than I had realized. The flesh around her eyes was puffy and wreathed in wrinkles.

What in hell are you doing in bed with this old woman? I asked myself. Then I remembered I was fifteen months older than Peyton. Some terrible mistake had been made. I decided to figure it out later when it didn't hurt to squint. I wrote a note on the bottom of a tissue box telling Peyton I'd call her later and slipped out the kitchen door.

The lane markers on Route 22 were oscillating. It took a while before my steering was syncopated with the rhythm, a hot salsa beat. I didn't mind the red snakes as long as they stayed on the windshield. But when I saw one trying to slither from the vent, I decided to pull into the Chick'N Haven truck stop.

A tractor hooked up to a stake-sided flatbed trailer stacked with white-and-purple stained cages was taking on diesel fuel at the center island. Angry red heads poked through the slats of the wooden cages. Thousands of beady eyes accused me.

Two pickup trucks were parked in front of a low cinderblock building which decades ago might have been painted a light color, maybe even white, festooned with faded signs for engine oils and poultry feed. Beside the building, empty cages caked with chickenshit were racked on pallets. Two pony-size mongrels the color of used motor oil were playing sniff-ass, cavorting among and over the cages. A white-haired, black man wearing a Charlotte Hornets sweatshirt, khaki shorts, and unlaced combat boots, was aimlessly hosing down the cages. As I got out of the truck, he pointed the nozzle at the dogs and let fly a string of invective which would make an LA rapper blush.

A sallow-eyed waitress in a too-pink overblouse, which sagged from the weight of a cluster of pens, gave me a knocking once-over and brought three aspirin in a paper thimble along with the coffee. My hand shook so badly when I tried to pick a five from my wallet, she told me to forget it. Dear heart, Johnny Cash wrote a song about the kind of Sunday morning you're having, she said, patting my hand.

I finished my coffee and headed south, waiting for the aspirin to kick in. I stopped south of Richleigh and took a nap. Then I drank a quart of grapefruit juice, which seemed to kill some of the toxins, and took a nap. I got back on the road around one and reached the bridge which led to Pickwick Beach just after three. "Welcome to Pickwick Beach, Incorporated 1927," the sign read. A half-truth. Omitted, maybe for lack of space, was the caveat: If You Have Megabucks. Pickwick Beach made Palm Beach seem like a Puerto Rican block party.

The City of Pickwick Beach ruled a barrier island, three miles long and a half mile wide, linked to the mainland by a drawbridge which spanned the Intracoastal Waterway. There was one category of residential zoning: single family with an acre-lot minimum. Diversity of architectural styles was encouraged, subject to a prohibition of any design which suggested Florida or California. Estates facing the ocean started in the millions. On the waterway side, occasional distress sales in the mid six-figures occurred.

I crossed the bridge, waved at the cop in the guard house who wrote down my license plate number, and drove to the business district, which consisted of a gas station, convenience store, and newsstand. I picked up a copy of the *Journal*, a turkey sandwich, and a cup of coffee.

Just to the south of the business district a jetty constructed of rocks, steel pilings, and reinforced concrete extended for several hundred yards into the Atlantic. For all its thousands of tons, it was a finger of folly, designed more to allay the fears of property owners than to retard beach erosion. An unintended consequence of the sea wall was the attraction of surf fishers. Because federal funds had been used to pay for the construction, the city had been stymied in its efforts to bar the public from the jetty.

The city made the best of the situation. Apart from five metered spaces (fifty cents for fifteen minutes) in front of the convenience store, public parking was prohibited which tended to restrict access to the M. K. Hardesty Public Beach, as the rocky little strand at the base of the sea wall was officially known. It was hard to imagine what Hardesty had done to deserve the honor. Maybe the city council decided to punish him for painting his shutters pink.

I had almost two hours to kill before my meeting with Dean. The afternoon was mild. Ignoring "No Trespassing" signs, I walked to the end of the beach and back to the jetty. Apart from the few dozen scattered among the rocks of M. K. Hardesty Public Beach, every grain of sand within the city limits was privately owned.

I arrived at Number 2 Tern Lane before five. It was at the north end of the island, the older part, where the homes had been constructed in the 1920's. Number 2's brick was weathered to a shade of dusky rose. Slender columns supported two tiers of balconies which overlooked a terraced garden and the Atlantic beyond.

I punched in the code Dean had given me. Seconds later I heard gears grind somewhere far away. A green light lit up on the control panel and the garage door retracted. I parked beside a jeep with balloon tires. An unlocked interior door led to stairs that ended in a hallway beside the kitchen, which looked like a transplant from a Loire chateau. From mission-oak ceiling racks dangled dozens of variously size burnished copper pans, and skillets with long porcelain handles patterned with royal-blue fleur-de-lis. In the cabinet over a restaurant-size stainless-steel gas range, I found a rack of assorted teas. I filled a copper kettle, put it on to boil, and walked into the study.

The walls of the study were twelve feet high and painted a shade of soft almond. The wainscotting, chair railings, sills, mantel, and French doors were white enamel for contrast. The furniture was fashioned of ivory leather, white wicker, and natural linen. The effect was an interior in search of a red wine accident. The kettle faintly whistled. I returned to the kitchen, made a pot of Earl Grey, and carried it into the study. I sipped the tea and watched the ocean turn purple. When I heard a cough, I turned. Dean was standing in the doorframe. He was wearing a charcoal-gray suit and a blue striped shirt. A paisley tie dangled from the side pocket of his jacket.

"This where populists go to get away from the people?" I asked.

Dean managed a thin smile, folded his jacket carefully, laid it across the back of the sofa, and left the room, to return a few minutes later with a squat bottle that looked like it was made of melted brown glass and two snifters the size of gold-fish bowls.

"Vile habit I swore I would never resume," Dean said, taking a cigarette from a silver box on the marble coffee table. Dean slumped into a wingchair, pinched the bridge of his nose, lit his cigarette and exhaled slowly. Dean's face was lined and drawn. The bags under his eyes rested on dark crescents. His hairline seemed to have edged backward on sharp, parallel angles. Dean seemed to have aged ten years in the few months since I had spoken with him at the Vecchios.

"I'm dead on my feet and scheduled for a live interview on Channel 8 at seven in the morning." Dean rolled his bloodshot eyes at me and sighed heavily. "Who in hell watches TV at seven A.M.? Tell me, Kenny."

I shrugged my shoulders. Dean watched me through the smoke.

"Come on, Kenny," he said, glancing at his wristwatch, yawning and rubbing his eyes. "Let's get to the bottom line."

"I don't need to start at the beginning, do I?"

Dean leaned forward to rearrange ivory chess pieces on the coffee table. "Do you? Why the fuck ask me? It's your show."

Dean lifted the bottle and raised his eyebrows in invitation. I shook my head.

"Too early?" Dean asked.

"Maybe too late," I replied, watching Dean cup the snifter in both hands, warming the cognac. He swirled it gently. A knot of nerves in the back of my brain, switched on by the bouquet, began to tingle and glow.

"You sign any documents that pertained to Vista Mer?" I asked.

"Assume hypothetically I did sign one. So what?"

"What kind of hypothetical document did you hypothetically sign?"

"Bureaucratic mumbo-jumbo. Meaningless crap," Dean said with a contemptuous wave. "Fine print took back what the first paragraph seemed to grant. No binding effect whatsoever."

"It looked official?" I asked.

"It had no more legal effect than *that*." Dean pointed at

a crumpled cocktail napkin beside the bottle of cognac. We implausibly stared at it for a long moment.

"If it looked official to Roger, it'll look official to the *Journal*. Maybe that was the point," I said.

Dean frowned, started to speak, then thought better of it. Instead, he picked up his snifter and walked over to the French doors.

"In any event, I destroyed it," he said, staring at the sea.

"Don't be naive. It's the one sin God won't forgive a lawyer. Photocopies could have been made."

A few minutes passed in silence punctuated by the almost inaudible slap of the surf. Then Dean returned to his seat. He poured two fingers of cognac in his snifter.

Dean stared at the chessboard. He moved black's bishop back and forth.

"Do-gooder exposed as a fraud," I said. "That's how the *Journal* will play it. Putting in the fix for Vista Mer while preaching the gospel of love for Mother Earth. High priest of ethics defrocked, revealed as one more cheap whore. The *Journal* will reprise your exposé of Petit and run a special edition on hypocrisy."

Dean took a long time grinding out his cigarette. Then he leaned back in his chair and studied me for a long moment. I met his stare.

"Why are you doing this?" Dean asked.

"Somebody beat Roger to death. Somebody planted a half-kilo of flake in my trunk."

"What's that got to do with me?" Dean asked.

"A blue movie, maybe," I replied, watching Dean's reaction. There was none. I decided to try again.

"I don't need to ask why you met me," I said.

"No? Tell me why," Dean said with a bored offhand tone, as if he were straining to be polite but wanted to make sure I knew he didn't give a tinker's damn.

"Because you're living a nightmare, wondering when Roger's murder is going to be traced to you."

"Look at me," Dean said, staring blankly. "I had absolutely nothing to do with that. Do you hear me? *Nothing.*" Dean spoke softly and very slowly, parading each syllable for me to admire. All politicians learn the technique, which is supposed to project dignity and candor.

"Who drafted the Vista Mer document?" I asked.

"Cubertson," Dean answered after a moment. "Ros said she needed it to get Roger to go along."

"Along with what?"

"With the deal, goddamnit." Dean said, swallowing his words along with the rest of his cognac. He glared at me over the rim of his snifter.

I stood up and put on my jacket.

"Where you think you're going?"

"I didn't come down here to play twenty guesses with you. I'm not one of your suckass aides." I headed for the door.

"No more bullshit," Dean said quietly. "Sit down. Please."

"How did Cubertson hear about Niles's videotape?" I asked, guessing.

Dean looked at me for a long time. He lit a cigarette, French inhaled, and blew a thin plume at the ceiling.

"Tommy Prescott told Ros what this scum, James, had said," Dean replied. "About a videotape Niles was supposed to have."

"Prescott and Cubertson are friends?"

"Friends?" Dean repeated with a snort. "Prescott used to be a partner at B&W. I suppose Ros and Prescott are on each other's Christmas card list, if that's what you mean."

"That's not what I mean."

"I *know* that," Dean replied. "I don't think she's gotten around to Prescott yet, but, hell, she might have. They finally had to let Cubertson join Foxwood. Ros bumps into Tommy at all those charity benefits."

"Prescott have any reason to lie to Cubertson?"

Dean started pacing the perimeter of the study. He stopped at each painting to adjust its frame by a few micrometers.

"Whether James lied to Prescott is more to the point," Dean said, pacing again. "Scum like that would say anything."

"You couldn't leave it alone, could you?"

"I *had* to know, goddamn it, Kenny," Dean said, turning to face me. "Niles was coming undone, unraveling. I couldn't invest the sweat and dreams of thousands of volunteers in a campaign that could abort the next time Niles hit a few lines with some rodeo boy. If Niles actually had the videotape that James claimed, I had an obligation to see it was destroyed. You can see that, can't you?''

"Who came up with the plan?''

"First Commonwealth Bank is a client of B&W. Cubertson found out FCB was about to foreclose on Niles's house. You know what that house meant to him?''

I nodded in reply.

Niles's home, specifically designed and equipped to accommodate his wheelchair, was his refuge, the one place where he did not have to confront his paralysis on brutal terms.

"Cubertson reasoned that if Niles had the videotape, he would use it to get the money he needed to keep from losing his house,'' Dean continued, looking away.

"So you set a trap,'' I said. "A trap to flush the tape, if it existed.''

"A test,'' Dean replied testily, lighting a cigarette.

"You don't bait a test. You bait a trap. You needed someone to plant the bait. That was where Roger came in. Dog-loyal, dumb, and desperate. The perfect patsy.''

"That's not how I saw it. You have to understand . . .''

I waved my hand, cutting him off.

"You promised Roger you'd cut through the ECC bullshit and get the permit for Vista Mer.''

"I wasn't there,'' Dean said in a voice that was almost a whisper. "I didn't want to know. Cubertson handled it.''

"But your help came with a price.''

"If it had worked out,'' Dean said wistfully, "I would have found some way to take care of Roger. I really mean that.''

"That's touching. That should impress the jury.''

My sarcasm hit Dean like a mackerel slap. He opened his mouth to say something but looked away instead.

"So Cubertson met with Roger,'' I continued. "She told him you had wanted to help with the ECC all along but the time wasn't right. She told Roger you needed his help to flush out a videotape. Right so far?''

"I guess. I stayed out of the details."

"Roger was supposed to offer Niles an interest in Vista Mer, an interest worth maybe a million bucks if—a big if—the ECC issued the permit. All Niles had to do was use his influence with his former student assistant, who just happened to be the lieutenant governor and chairman *ex officio* of the ECC, right?" Dean nodded and stubbed out his cigarette.

"But that's where it breaks down," I said. "Didn't you consider that Niles would be suspicious if Roger drops in out of the blue and makes an offer like that?"

"Not if you had told Roger about your uncle's financial condition and his influence with me," Dean said, studying his chess pieces. "That was how Cubertson told Roger to play it."

"You sonofabitch . . ."

"Look, Kenny . . . ," Dean said, standing up, holding his hands out, palms up.

"Tell me again about the sweat and dreams of thousands of volunteers and your obligation to them."

"Kenny . . ." Dean took a step toward me.

"Get away from me."

Dean looked at my clenched fists, shook his head, then sat down heavily in the armchair.

"Tell me the rest," I said. "I'm not up to cross-examining you."

"If we confronted Niles with James's story, he'd deny it," Dean said after a pause. "That seemed obvious. So we had to find some way to put pressure on Niles to use the videotape if it existed.

"Ros figured that Niles wouldn't have the guts to use the tape himself. But he might offer it—if it even existed—to Roger, let him use it to pressure me.

"Cubertson told Roger to tape his phone calls with Niles. If Niles brought up the tape, then we had him on a blackmail conspiracy rap, a felony. Cubertson would have a confidential chat with Niles, trade tapes, and put an end to the matter, quietly and privately."

"Let me guess the rest," I said. "Cubertson tells you Roger won't go along unless he has some assurance, something on

ECC stationery signed by you, to make sure you're on board. Cubertson says she's only going to show it to Roger to convince him the deal's for real.''

Dean tapped the black queen nervously on the chessboard.

"What's your deal with Cubertson?" I asked.

"We've been through a lot together."

"That's not your deal. That's your history."

Dean fidgeted with his tie, smoothing and resmoothing the silk.

"I heard she did you a big favor in '86," I said.

"What favor?" Dean said, watching me closely.

"I heard the payoff was she was supposed to be appointed to Jackson's spot on the Supreme Court of Appeals," I continued.

"Let's just say Cubertson was well qualified and her appointment was discussed when Jackson died last year," Dean replied after hesitating.

"Was that your deal with her?"

Dean nodded quickly, almost imperceptibly.

"And you welshed on it?"

"It just didn't work out," Dean answered. "The timing wasn't right. I couldn't get the governor to go along with it."

"You tell Cubertson when the time was going to be right?"

"Ros is a big girl. I didn't have to spell it out for her."

"I suppose that's fair," I replied. "She sure as hell didn't spell it out for you."

"What's that supposed to mean?"

"Why the fuck ask me? She's your pal."

"Touché," Dean said, leaning back in his chair and almost smiling.

"You never saw any videotape, did you?" My question was rhetorical, but I wanted Dean to say "no" anyway.

"I don't know if there ever *was* a tape," Dean replied.

"Tell Cubertson," I said after a moment, "that I telephoned. Tell her I told you I needed to meet privately. Tell her I said it was urgent and that you were to tell no one I called. Tell her I said I had the videotape, information about Petit and wanted your help to cut a deal with the SBI."

"That true?" Dean asked.

"That I have the tape? No," I replied. "Give me a road cognac. A big one." Dean found a plastic cup and filled it.

"I mean about Petit," Dean said, handing me the cup.

"Petit heard the rumor about Niles's tape before you did," I replied, putting on my jacket. "Maybe the tape's real. Maybe it's not. Either way, it worked as bait."

"Bait for who," Dean asked.

"Ouch. Try again."

"Bait for whom?" Dean said, with a half-smile.

"You've already figured that out," I replied. "That's why you look like death warmed over."

Dean found a notepad in the drawer of an end table and wrote down a number. "Private line to my office."

"Do what I said. Do it tomorrow."

"Still a grammar freak," Dean said, handing me the slip of paper. "Christ Almighty, Kenny."

"Gotta believe in something, Deano," I said, folding the paper and putting it in my pocket.

CHAPTER 22

Dean called me at the camp the following evening to tell me Cubertson had told him to stall, advice that proved nothing.

"Don't leave it open-ended. Tell her you've decided to meet with me."

"When?"

"Day after Christmas. Two in the afternoon. Tell her the anxiety was killing you. Say you couldn't stand to wait. Whatever."

"That's only three days away," Dean replied.

"That's the point. Force the play." There was another reason. I needed momentum to carry me past Christmas.

In prior years I had paid stoically the toll exacted by Saint Nicholas from divorced fathers. Jingle bells as a hymn of penance, candy canes for flagellation, and mistletoe as the bitter herb of failure. This Christmas, emotionally, my pockets were turned out and I had a lump of coal where a heart was supposed to be.

"Where's the meeting supposed to take place?" Dean asked.

"Your place at Pickwick Beach. Be sure and tell Cubertson that."

With a single bridge and more cops than visitors this time of year, Pickwick Beach was the locale for a hitman's worst-case scenario. Whoever it was wouldn't wait for me to deliver the tape to Dean at Pickwick Beach. They would come to the camp, secluded and accessible by water, road, or forest trails. The nearest cop was six miles distant and neighbor two. Anyone who heard a gunshot would assume it was a poacher.

Dean said he would play it by my rules, adding he hoped I knew what I was doing. Maybe for the first time in years, I said. I rang off and headed into town. I stopped by my office and left Anita a note telling her not to expect me for several days. I threw a few legal pads and what work I had into a briefcase. On the way home I purchased cable, screweyes, and groceries.

I spent the balance of the afternoon sawing deep wedges in the pine pillars which supported the deck. The wood was rotted where water had breached the creosote. They should have been replaced years ago.

I cut the wedges, leaving the angles open to the water, drilled holes into the opposite sides of the pillars, below the cuts, and screwed in heavy steel eyes. I strung a thick nylon cable through the eyes and connected it to the double pulley I detached from my boat. The pulley's cable led to a heavy-duty marine winch bolted to the bayside beam.

The winch generated enough force to lift a six-hundred-pound boat from the bay, twenty feet below, to the deck. I wound in the cable until it was as taut as I dared and locked the winch's ratchet gear. When I plucked the nylon cable, it vibrated over two octaves.

I crossbraced with two-by-fours the door which faced the driveway. The only other entrance was through the sliding-glass doors at the far end of the deck near the winch.

I nailed down the shutters on the first floor and bolted the windows. Then I cleaned and loaded three shotguns with buck-shot. I put the Remington pump in the upstairs hall, the old Winchester double barrel in the great room, and the Ithaca in the kitchen.

I checked the sensor which causes an alarm to sound when a vehicle turns into my driveway. That and the floodlights all worked. I had food on hand for a week and enough anxiety to oxidize it in three.

The wise men would have felt right at home with December 24. It turned out to be implausibly sultry, the gift of a high-pressure zone which extended west from Bermuda. Winter in the tidewater is more fickle than feckless, a season in search of itself. Some nights are so sharp that in the whisking of the white pines there seems the distant howl of arctic wolves. Yet the dawn might be so gentle the sea breezes carry the lilt of the calypso and the faint rhythms of steel drums.

It was a mercurial season that teases more than suggests, a season of potentialities instead of certainties. In the cool rustling of December's starched petticoats, in the sudden caresses of her sun-warmed touches, a dixie waterman finds the Balm in Gilead.

I spent Christmas Eve reading. I read the Gospel of Mark, the oldest of the four. Simple, declarative sentences. Mark was a reporter, not a stylist.

I sat on the deck watching terns glide, strike, and ascend. I was tense yet strangely content. My mind was clear, my memories vivid, and my thoughts concentrated.

It takes extreme circumstances to break the grip of the mundane, of the petty strivings and fears which make us opaque to ourselves. The ordinary is mistaken for the real, an error reinforced by—and essential to—popular culture. Buy that riding mower before it's too late to care. We equate self-consciousness with self-absorption, a pathological state which impedes getting on with the business of life. At the heart of our culture lies the cult of the instinctive life, as opposed to the ideal of the conscious life.

Anecdotes have come to satisfy our thirst for knowledge and sporadic acts of charity, our thirst for righteousness. The quest for justice has been supplanted by feuding over group entitlements. A national culture of slick mediocrity has become pervasive even as it has grown invasive.

Acquiescence is a decision made on the installment plan. I knew better but failed to stand fast. When civic virtue went out of fashion, I took up my hem along with the rest. Two roads diverged in a wood and I took the path of least resistance.

Maybe there were some potholes in the road Dean had chosen. But at least Dean's path led uphill, with sheer ascents and hairpin turns to make it challenging. Dean was not guilty of nonfeasance by default, of the passive selfishness which expresses itself in sterility, in nest-feathering. He stuck his chin out. Dean, born without privilege, had taken on duty. I had been born with privilege and forsaken duty.

Christmas augured to be balmy and bright. I sat on the deck, sipping black coffee, watching the dawn crack into gold-and-pink shards over the gently ruffled bay.

At nine I placed a call. I was grateful when Martha answered. She said she hadn't opened the presents I had mailed her because Renee and Charlie were still asleep. I told her to go ahead and open them. Do it while we're on the phone together. Renee won't mind if you open just the ones I gave you. She didn't reply. Go ahead, honey. It's okay.

Martha hesitated. I know, Daddy, but I want to wait. Why? I asked, persistent, hearing the edge in my voice. Because, she said, after a pause, I want Mom to be there when I make a big deal out of your presents. Do you understand now?

From the rush of emotions which came over me, a tremulous "oh" precipitated. Then I told Martha I loved her very much and she must never forget that, no matter what happens.

I poured another cup of coffee and returned to my chair on the deck. When I felt the first pangs of guilt, I started chanting my catechism. For the umpteenmillionth time, I doggedly assured myself that the divorce wasn't really my fault and that, anyway, even if it were, Renee and I were fundamentally incompatible, and children are better off when parents divorce rather than stay together and bicker.

We had obeyed the first commandment for wilted flower children. Thou shalt be true to your feelings. All of them. Always. The second commandment, a corollary, was: a feeling hidden is a sin committed against the holy ego. Ergo, better to bicker than suppress feelings (as did your foolish forefathers and foremothers), and divorce is better for children than bickering. Studies, I reminded myself, have proved this. You read about one in *Redbook* while in the check-out line at the Safeway. Remember?

I was trying to remember when I was interrupted by the buzzing of the alarm. Someone had turned into the driveway.

Because of the ruts, it takes a good five minutes to reach the camp. I slipped the safety off the Ithaca and put it behind the bunched up curtains framing the glass doors.

I heard the car before I saw it. The brush was thick. Branches slapped metal. Then a red Mustang convertible, top down, popped into the clearing. Tim Dugan waved, goosed the engine to kick up some gravel, and skidded the car to a stop below the deck.

"That driveway gets any worse, you're going to have to get yourself a mule team," Tim called.

"You got any cold ones up there?"

I nodded and pointed at the steps that led up to the porch.

"What's the occasion?" I asked as Tim stepped onto the deck. He was wearing an Army surplus field jacket, unzipped, over a T-shirt that claimed "Divers Do It Deeper."

"Lawd Almighty. Got us a grinch here." Tim went inside and sprawled in the middle of the sofa. I put a can of Pabst on the table in front of him.

"Ken-dog, got me a problem."

"How late is she?"

"Not one of those. Lord, remember that time . . ." Tim laughed, letting the sentence drift, then popped open the beer.

"Fact is," he said, "you've got a problem, too. Something about a videotape." I didn't reply. I didn't need to. Tim read my expression.

"Hey, hey, come on, buddy. Ain't no point in getting pissed at me. Messenger boy's all I am. I told them I could talk to you business-like."

"Who sent you?" I managed to say, choked by anger rising in my throat.

"Ken-dog, calm your ass down and just listen for a minute. I'm doing you a favor 'cept you're too dumb to know it."

I moved a step closer to the curtain.

"Christ," Tim mused, "if I had any sense I'd have stuck to selling a little homegrown to a few friends. Just like college, you know? Deal a little extra but keep the good stuff for yourself. Weren't no harm in that.

"But it sort of got to be more than that. Without me really

trying. Just happened, is all. And I sort of branched out without really meaning to.''

"You told me you quit dealing after I got Bobby to *noll pross* the distribution rap.''

"Hey, no fair guilt-tripping." Tim held up a palm. "I wasn't lying. At the time, I by God had quit. But later on, I sort of slid back into it without meaning to. You know how that goes.'' Tim looked at me hopefully. I didn't change my expression.

"Well, whatever. Then I sort of got to know some guys down at the marina who were into moving flake. And all of a sudden I was into it making more in a week than I used to make in a year. And we needed protection, which sort of got to be my side of the business."

"Bobby," I said, almost to myself, the realization hitting me like a body slam. I felt like a fool.

It made sense in a twisted way. Vecchio was the kind of guy who didn't feel alive unless he was testing the limits of his nerve. It was probably the risk as much as the bribes which made him do it. Riding the risk, controlling it, was the kind of challenge he relished. He thrived on intrigue for the sake of intrigue.

"Now, I ain't one to start naming names. You know me better than that. That ain't businesslike."

Bobby had given in too easily. The warrant arguably was defective. But he hadn't pushed hard enough. Carey had been surprised when the charge had been *noll prossed.*

There had been other dope cases I'd won when I shouldn't have, cases where I'd been able to cut deals too sweet, and indictments that had evaporated, vaporized by the force, I had thought, of my advocacy. You're a tiger, Bobby used to tell me. Damned if you're not.

"Let's just say," Tim continued, "Bobby has taken a renewed interest in the Dufault case and has learned from a reliable anonymous source that you might be in possession of material evidence."

"Which happens to be a videotape," I replied.

Tim took a swallow before continuing. "Now if you happened, follow me, to know where such a tape might be, I can give you my word that the beef pending against you will go away. That's a businesslike offer, now, ain't it?'' Tim watched me.

''How's that going to happen?''

His face brightened. ''Don't worry about how, pal. All kinds of ways. Say a witness might be found who saw a boy tampering with your truck just before you got picked up. Boy who had a plastic bag of white powder. Affidavit of a witness like that would be enough to cause Bobby to take the case off the trial docket and investigate further. After a while, it all goes away quiet-like, investigated to death. You follow?''

I edged a step closer to the curtain.

''What you got behind there, Ken-dog?''

From the side pocket of his jacket Tim's hand emerged with a revolver in it.

I looked first at the gun, then at Tim's eyes.

Tim walked over and kicked the curtain. The shotgun fell with a clang to the floor.

''God *knows* I'm sorry about this,'' Tim said. ''C'mon, Kenny. No more bullshit. Just give me the tape.''

''It's in the baitbox of the skiff.''

''That bait caught you one ugly dogfish.'' Tim stood up and motioned with the revolver. I didn't move.

''Be reasonable, Kenny. It's just a frigging tape. C'mon, move your ass outside.''

I led Tim onto the deck. I leaned over the railing and pointed.

''Skiff's down there. Hanging on cable. You want me to lower her down or reel her up?'' I pointed at the winch.

Tim extended his fist with his thumb up. When I crossed the deck to the winch, he moved behind me to the far edge of the deck, keeping his distance from me.

I unlocked the gear and flipped the bailer to the position to take in cable. Keeping one hand on the roof beam, with the other I switched on the power.

The motor groaned in protest, struggling. Just as Tim looked over the railing to see what was the problem, the groaning was replaced by sharp cracks as the uprights snapped. I grabbed the overhanging beam with both hands in time to watch the deck with a low roar rip loose and crash into the bay.

My mind's eye kept replaying a shot of Tim—one I knew I would see for a long time—mouth wide open, scrambling, the deck suddenly canted. Then he and the deck crashed into the bay.

I swung along the beam until I got a foothold on the base to which the deck had been bolted. Then I shifted to a handhold on the doorframe, and pulled myself into the kitchen and looked at the bay.

There was a gentle roll to the bay which made the debris bob. The impact had torn the deck apart. I didn't see any sign of Tim. The deck could have knocked him unconscious. He could be trapped him under the debris.

I hesitated, then cursed, ran to the shed, grabbed a hank of rope, and rushed to the landing, taking the shotgun with me. I could see no sign of Tim. I stripped off my jacket and jeans and waded into the frigid water. The debris was scattered in several piles fifty feet offshore. The water instantly took my breath away and numbed me as I swam toward the largest pile.

When I drew closer, amidst the rubble I saw something that appeared to be a mop. I swam a few more strokes and looked again. A tangle of dark hair. I shoved aside the splintered planks, ripping my arm on a nail and wrapped my hand in the hair.

I jerked Tim's head backward, forcing his face upward. With my left hand I reached around his neck, cupped his chin, and angled his nose and mouth above the surface. Tim wasn't moving, but, as I towed him to shore, I could tell there was air in his lungs.

I dragged him onto the muddy gray sand, flipped him onto his stomach, lifted his legs to my shoulders, and shook him. Water trickled from his mouth.

After a few moments Tim began spitting. I let go of his legs and picked up the shotgun. Tim rolled onto his side and vomited, gagged on his vomit, and threw up again. Then he started panting. He choked on every breath, expectorating more than exhaling.

I sat on the hull of the skiff, shotgun across my lap. Tim kept his head down and continued to spit the bay into the mud.

"Get up," I said after Tim's vomiting stopped. Tim stood

up, leaned over, put his hands on his knees, and vomited again. But it was a dry spasm this time. "Move. Ahead of me." I motioned with the shotgun. Tim slowly made his way toward the steps chiseled a century ago into the limestone cliff.

My left arm was covered with blood from the gash made by the nail. When we reached the clearing, Tim turned and gave me a sheepish look, as if this were just one more prank, one more fuck-up by ol' Timmy. In reply, I raised the shotgun level with his chest and motioned for him to keep moving toward the camp, which, stripped of its deck, seemed precariously perched on the cliff.

I considered calling Cane at his home. Merry Christmas, Sheriff. Tim Dugan pulled a revolver on me. No, I'm fine. See, I booby-trapped my deck. So when Tim pulled a revolver, I snapped the uprights and collapsed the deck and Tim into the bay. Then I saved his life. And now I've got a shotgun pointed at his chest. So, if it's no trouble, why don't you stop by and arrest him?

Cane would tell the duty officer I had sounded deranged and was armed. In ten minutes a dozen deputies would descend on the camp. Tim would tell them he had been trying to talk me into turning over evidence important to the Dufault case when I freaked out and grabbed a shotgun. Maybe the adrenaline was keeping me from thinking.

I wasn't thinking clearly. Maybe it was the sting of betrayal that unaccountably I experienced as shame. Maybe it was pride wounded by realizing Bobby had used me for years.

I realized whoever sent Tim could have sent a back-up with or without Tim's knowledge. Or a fisherman might have seen the deck collapse and radioed a report to the emergency hotline. I didn't like either scenario. Get away from the camp, as far and as fast as possible. It was an instinct more than a thought.

Tim noticed my preoccupation. He started walking slowly toward the Mustang.

"Get away from the car."

"Chrissakes, just want to put her top up. Looks like rain, don't it?" Tim replied casually, looking upward, as if this were just another day and another conversation between old friends.

He took another step, testing me, and put his hand on the door handle.

If I let Tim draw me into conversation, he would guess I wouldn't use the gun. Probably a good guess. But I didn't want to find out. I raised the butt and blasted a cluster of buckshot into the door. I pumped to chamber another round and pointed with the shotgun in the direction of the Dodge parked in the barn.

I made Tim drive. I sat half turned to Tim and kept the muzzle pressed flush against his side. When he started to talk, I shoved the muzzle hard. He didn't try again.

I told Tim to turn onto 201. North of Lassington 201 transects a series of small hills which, rolling to the west, end as bluffs overlooking the Pascamany. Once or twice when we came to a crest at the end of a straightaway, I had turned and seen a car a mile behind us, keeping the same distance.

Just before the turnoff to Pokamo State Forest there is a grubby little rest area with a pay phone. I planned to make the call to Mulkerrin from there. The rest area was deserted. I told Tim to park at the rear of the gravel apron near the metal picnic tables chained to pine trees.

A few minutes later, a 1975 Eldorado, the size of an aircraft carrier, with more primer than silver paint, lumbered to a stop on the opposite side of the highway. I tilted the mirror so I could watch the junker and the two men in it.

The occupants were wearing baseball caps, brims pulled low over their eyes covered by sunglasses. Spare the glare but there wasn't any. The sky had turned overcast.

The driver tossed a beer can out the window. It skittered across the road. The passenger seemed to be studying something. Maybe a map. Probably hunters, I thought. But I couldn't remember what game was in season.

"Look at the Cadillac. Those guys friends of yours?"

He adjusted the angle and studied the mirror. "Couple of rednecks out cruising," he said, shaking his head. "Never saw them before." He looked again in the mirror. "The guy on the far side just crawled into the backseat. Maybe they're taking turns with some babe."

I told Tim to start the engine. A half-minute later, I saw the Eldo creep in a lazy arc across the road.

"Cut sharp and head out slowly," I said.

When I heard the Eldo's engine growl, I looked over my shoulder. The guy in the backseat was leaning out the left rear window. He had his elbow braced against the quarter panel to steady a shotgun. I reached over with my left foot and mashed Tim's foot on the accelerator. I felt the pedal hit the floor as I heard the explosion.

The pickup fishtailed in the gravel. Tim swung the wheel in the opposite direction, accentuating the skid. The pickup pivoted a split second before the Eldo swept past, missing the fender by inches. I looked across Tim to see the guy in the backseat lean out the window, pump, and raise the gun.

I pushed Tim's head down. The rear window exploded. Nuggets of shattered glass rained on us. The buckshot punched holes, surrounded by spiderwebs of cracks, in the windshield. The Dodge clipped a pair of trash cans, bumped over a hedge, knocked down a railing, and lurched onto the highway.

The fractures in the windshield made it seem there were a dozen double yellow lines ahead of us. With the butt of the shotgun, I smashed out the remnants of the windshield and the rear window.

The Eldo exited from the far end of the parking area and, laying rubber, had turned at a sharp angle in our direction. The weight and soft suspension of the beast had caused it to wallow onto the right shoulder. The driver wrestled the Eldo back onto the macadam.

The Eldo was one hundred yards back, its grille a chrome grin which took up both lanes. The Caddy with its big V-8 held the advantage in power. But the truck had an edge in cornering and road clearance.

I suddenly recognized an unmarked gravel road just ahead on the left as the road which led to Holly Hills. I grabbed Tim's arm and pointed at the road.

Tim swung the wheel hard enough to set the truck over on her right tires. Behind us I heard tires scream in protest and turned in time to see the Eldo overshoot the turn and scramble for traction. We had gained maybe twenty yards.

The Dodge was airborne when it was not scraping its universal joint on ruts, bouncing off limestone spines or crash landing. We were kicking up a screen of dirt, grit, and dust. When we came to the top of a grassy hummock, I heard a shotgun blast.

The road twisted uphill, past ancient white oaks and limestone cliffs crowned with scrub pine and bramble. I looked to my right as we rounded a bend and caught a glimpse of the Eldo followed by a rooster tail of dust clearing a curve below us. For the moment we were safely out of range. But we had crested the ridge and in a few minutes would complete our descent to bottomland which extended all the way to the bluffs over the Pascamany. The road ahead, flat and straight, divided cornfields and pastures for a good half-mile before crossing the cattle grate. He wouldn't be able to sustain the quarter-mile lead we had built up crossing the ridge.

"Who the hell are those guys?" Tim yelled as the truck skidded around the final curve of the ridge. I could see the Higgins manor house and barns in the distance.

I didn't answer. I recalled James's story. The guy driving had to be Ricky. The guy with the pump action? Maybe some freelancer Ricky knew. Maybe Judge Carey. Maybe Jimmy Carter. Nothing would surprise me at this point.

I remembered suddenly the Chirkie village near the bluffs. The site had been excavated in the late 1940's by archaeologists from the university. Artifacts dating from the fifteenth to the early eighteenth century had been discovered preserved in layers of mud and ash, ordered integuments forming nature's time capsule. But the site had not measured up to early expectations. By the 1960s, the site, known locally as the Indian pit, had all but been forgotten. Roger, Tim, Porky, and I had caught scores of salamanders in stagnant trenches and climbed ladders abandoned by researchers, the rotted wood held together by honeysuckle vines, set against walls braced by timbers similarly reclaimed by nature. Then we, too, had forgotten the Indian pit.

"The Indian pit!" I shouted, pointing toward the bluffs. Tim glanced at me and nodded.

He swung the wheel to the left, heading for a path between harrowed fields. I turned and saw the Eldo emerge in a cloud of dust from the ridge's final curve half a mile behind us. The path came to an end in front of a sea of dried cornstalks, chest high, which sloped upward, at a gentle angle, for a half-mile to the bluffs of the Pascamany.

I told Tim to stop. I climbed out and stood on the running board. Looking as far ahead as I could, I located what appeared to be a darker area of the field. The Eldo turned onto the track, maybe a hundred yards behind us, just as I slammed the door shut. I saw the passenger hanging out the side window, drawing down on us.

I heard the whistle of buckshot to my right before I heard the shotgun blast. Tim hit the accelerator and the truck spun into the cornstalks. I pointed to the northwest. Tim aimed the truck and we crashed through the cornstalks.

I could hear the low-slung Caddy churning after us but couldn't see it. Tim was steering blind through the cornstalks. I told him to aim to the left of the cloudbank and hold the course. I knew we were getting close to the dark patch I had seen.

"Let them get close. When we get to the edge of the pit, cut hard to the right!" I shouted. Tim nodded.

The Cadillac came into view behind us, following the path of broken stalks, bouncing over the red dirt, closing the gap to seventy-five yards, then fifty. Coming on strong. Buckshot smashed into the tailgate and fender of the pick-up.

Tim plowed ahead, holding the angle. The Eldo was rapidly gaining ground, its big V-8 howling. I turned around. All I could see was a chrome grille surmounted by a ruby-and-gold Cadillac medallion. When I looked ahead, I saw dark objects lying at the base of the onrushing stalks. Old timbers used to brace the walls of the pit.

"Now!" I shouted. Tim cut the wheel hard. The Dodge heeled over, then righted itself, one row of stalks between it and the lip of the pit. Then its rear wheels dug in and the truck lurched away from the pit.

I turned in time to see the rear end of the Cadillac fishtail and crash through the last line of cornstalks. There was a loud thump as the rear wheels slid over the lip, causing the under-belly to slam the soft ground. The big V-8 screamed, a futile shriek of rage, the death spasm of a great animal, as the drive wheel spun in the air.

Then slowly, majestically, the grille of the Eldo began to rise. The front wheels lifted off the ground. The angle opened at a stately pace, exposing the chassis. For a moment, the two and a half tons of metal were suspended, in perfect equipoise with the sky and earth then suddenly they were gone. With a muffled crash, the Cadillac became an artifact.

CHAPTER 23

Tim and I stood at the edge looking at the wreck twenty feet below. The right rear wheel wobbled as it spun slowly. The quarter panels, bent in half when the roof crushed in, flared like little wings just behind a head and shoulders partially buried in the mud.

I called an ambulance from the pay phone at the rest stop. I made the dispatcher repeat the directions I gave him.

"Now what, Ken-dog?" Tim asked when I returned to the truck.

"Back to Lassington."

"Where you taking us?" Tim asked.

"You'll know when we get there. Drive."

I told Tim to turn right onto Willow Road. When we reached the Ocean Pines development, I told him to pull into the lot and park beside the Alfa. Then he knew.

"Oh, Jesus, man. Why Mulkerrin?"

"My turn to do you a favor."

"What kind of favor?"

"I'm going to let you turn yourself in to Mulkerrin and cut a deal."

"Mulkerrin can't cut cheese."

Tim slapped the dashboard and laughed. Then he turned to me, serious now.

"C'mon, buddy. Let's do it right. Get this behind us. *All* of it, man. You know what I'm saying?" He looked at me expectantly, waiting.

"Let's go see Bobby," Tim continued in a low, calm voice. "I owe you one."

"You gonna be my lawyer?"

"That's it, man," Tim replied, a hopeful smile lighting up his face. "I'm gonna make it go away. My turn, man."

I told Tim to shut up and get out of the truck. When he started to turn around, I pushed him toward the door of Mulkerrin's townhouse. I rapped on the door. After a minute, I knocked again, this time with the butt of the shotgun. Mulkerrin answered the door in a white terry-cloth bathrobe.

"Hell's this?" she asked. She looked at Tim. Then she saw my shotgun and took a step back, startled.

"Christmas present for Uncle," I replied, shoving Tim into the townhouse.

Tim turned to me, mouth gaping. Mulkerrin put her hands on her hips and gave me a freezing look.

"That's right, Tim," I said. "She's federal. You tell her— and I mean everything—or I will. But you don't get credit from Uncle for what I tell the lady

"What you planning to tell Mulkerrin?" Tim asked, looking from Mulkerrin to me.

"Whatever you don't," I replied, lying. "And then I'll tell Jamie Higgins."

They both stared at me.

"You all have fun now, hear?" I said. Then I shut the door softly.

Three days later I received a call from someone who said he was Agent Shavers. He asked me to meet him at the Statler J.A.G. unit.

The guard directed me to a low cinderblock building. A sign said "Judge Advocate General." Shavers led me down a battleship-gray hall, past a half dozen offices with unintelligible acronyms painted on frosted-glass door panels, to a day room, lined with wire mesh lockers, at the end of the hall.

Mulkerrin was there alone, standing by the radiator. She turned when she heard me come in. She was wearing blue jeans and the veteran cop look of worldweary irony. There was an FBI shield dangling from the breast pocket of her red leather jacket.

She didn't say hello. She didn't smile. She was drinking coffee from a little polystyrene cup. She didn't offer me any.

"The only option you left us was to cut a deal with Dugan which means you walk," she said, stirring her coffee with a pencil. "Smart. Real smart. But your turn will come. Uncle's got a long memory."

"You're way ahead of me."

She gave me the cut-the-crap expression cops practice in front of a mirror. Arched eyebrows. Flat, cold stare. Lips twisted down, beginning a sneer.

"Spare me the moon face. You want to paint by numbers? One, we've either got to cut a deal with Dugan or indict him. You with me so far?"

"Go on."

"Dugan's nothing. We drop a dime on him, what have we got? Maybe Renny, Gamper, and a few head boat crews. Strictly chickenshit. We indict Dugan, we blow our shot at nailing Vecchio and his protection racket buddies in Richleigh. So we got to do a deal with Dugan. That means you walk this time."

"You skipped a few numbers," I said.

"Dugan's your buddy, right?"

"Was."

"You didn't let him drown, did you? You think he forgot that?"

"Keep going."

"You let him cut a deal didn't you?"

"So?" I asked.

"So Dugan's got nothing to lose by insisting on the moon, stars, and the kitchen sink."

"Meaning?"

"Meaning Dugan made us grant him immunity for planting a half-key of flake in your truck." She paused before adding, "Whether he did it or not."

"Oh," I replied, stunned.

"Oh," Mulkerrin said, mocking my accent, stringing "oh" into two syllables. "Oh, my ass." Then she laughed, but it was a softer laugh.

"Lot of work to set this thing up," Mulkerrin said, removing her hair clip, gathering some errant strands, and replacing it. "Get the Fordham people to cooperate. Get Vecchio to hire me as an assistant DA." She shook her head.

"Not to mention putting up for six months with his 'c'mon baby' crap. Slimeball would sneak up on me, slip his arm around me, give my back a little rub, try to work a finger under my bra strap, snap it, then say 'c'mon baby.'

"I'd say 'c'mon baby, what?' He'd give me his soul of passion look, then whisper something like, 'You know, just us,' thinking he's letting his eyes do the talking. All I could do to keep from laughing."

"Tim can give you Vecchio. His testimony—"

"His *uncorroborated* testimony," Mulkerrin interrupted. "From a guy with two misdemeanor priors. You think Mikey Ryan's going to indict Vecchio on Dugan's testimony alone? Ryan wouldn't touch it with a stick with a condom on the end of it.

"So the only shot you left us was to keep Dugan on the street. See if he comes up with something hard on Vecchio. Might take six months, a year, maybe more, maybe never. But you'd figured that out. You knew Dugan could name his price and that it wouldn't be copping a plea to a lesser included. Not for putting his ass on the line for Uncle. You knew it would be total immunity."

She held up her cup in a toast. "You win," she said. "In a manner of speaking."

"It doesn't feel like winning," I replied. "Beating a frame with perjured testimony."

"Frankly, my dear, I don't give a damn," Mulkerrin replied, imitating a treacly southern accent. But there seemed to be a little warmth in her gun-metal blue eyes. Maybe it was the reflection from the fluorescent tubes overhead.

"We're going to make Ryan federalize your case whether he

wants to or not," she continued. "Ryan will give Vecchio some political bullshit about why he had to preempt. Vecchio knows McAllister's been on the horn to SBI about how you and Vecchio are buddies. So Vecchio won't be surprised."

"How long?"

"How long what?"

"How long are you going to keep me in limbo?"

"Long as it takes, love," she replied. "Can't have good ol' Timmy testifying about how he planted dope in your pickup until after we finish working him. First things first." She played with her silver bracelet, spinning it around her wrist.

"So for the next year, maybe longer, everyone's going to think I'm a dope dealer with political clout."

"You dealt the cards. You gotta play the hand." Then she added, in a gentler tone, "No way around it."

"Got any idea what that's going to do to my reputation, not to mention my law practice? What's left of it."

"Might help it. Especially the part about political clout. Besides, when Dugan testifies . . ."

"Besides, when Dugan testifies," I said, finishing her sentence. "Everyone will know the feds gave him blanket immunity. So everyone will think Dugan lied about planting the dope. They'll think good ol' Timmy lied to save his buddy's ass."

"Something else," Mulkerrin said. "Want to guess?"

"If you turn into the feds' star witness, Rennie and the guys are going to remember who introduced you to them and come looking for me," I replied.

She leaned toward me, put her arms around my waist, and kissed me. "Bonjour tristesse," she whispered. "Was it worth it?"

By April it was as over as it was ever going to be. At least for me. The guy with the shotgun, Huskins, had been DOA and Richard Shelby Samson was connected to the world through a clear plastic nosetube. Sometimes, decades later, a patient will snap out of a coma. So there's a chance Ricky will be prosecuted. About one in a million, according to the neurologist Jamie quoted in her story.

My law practice went to hell and stayed there. I had to dip into the principal of my trust to pay rent and Anita's salary.

I kept the pledge I made to Shavers, who was assigned as my contact. I kept silent. I avoided any contact, except when professional duties required it, with Mulkerrin. I stayed away from Dugan, except when I ran into him by accident. Shavers said that was okay. Have a beer with him when you run into him at a bar. But make it quick. Don't hang around.

Dean called me once, late at night, in mid-June.

Dean chatted about the campaign, not wanting to bring up the subject. Finally, Dean began improvising broad hints, speaking in a code of sorts.

"The matter regarding the ECC," Dean said. "Has there been any reconciliation of perspectives?"

"I had a frank and full exchange of views with Ms. Cubertson, if that is what you mean," I replied. Dean didn't say anything, waiting for me to continue in his silly code.

"I am pleased to report she fully appreciated your position and acknowledged the central point I communicated." I let the entailment dangle, forcing Dean to ask.

"That being?" he finally asked.

"That being if the ECC document you signed ever sees the light of day, I'm going to make sure Petit finds out who ratted on him about the trust in '85."

And the other matter? Dean asked after a long pause. I said no progress has been made on that front. Dean asked if I was continuing with the work.

"I'm of a mind to believe maybe the subject matter never existed," I said. "Maybe it was made up to make you think it existed."

"I hope that's the case," Dean said. "But I'd prefer you to continue with the project anyway. No harm in keeping on."

No harm in keeping on, I repeated to myself, finding myself capable of savoring the irony. Sure, Dean, no harm in keeping on. Then I routed the conversation back to the campaign. Up in the polls by fifteen points, Dean said. But summer polls are as fickle as summer squalls. He made me promise to keep in touch.

I saw Martha whenever I could. In between her tennis lessons, riding lessons, ballet lessons, piano lessons, junior cotillion, and visits to the campuses of potential prep schools. I know you want the best for her and understand, Renee said. Again and again.

I spent a lot of time at the camp. I read books I had bought years before and put aside, good intentions suffocated by routine. I jogged a lot. I lost ten pounds I didn't need to lose. Maybe it was due to the jogging. I started keeping a journal. Writing entries helped me get back to sleep.

Some nights I would wake in the dark, listen to my pulse, and imagine the next beat of my heart would be the last if I had the courage just to will it so. Sometimes in the middle of the night I would find myself standing before the stone fireplace tracing the bloodstain with my fingertips. Father's blood had been scoured from the stones but not from my memory. In the morning, I wake in a sweat and tell myself it had been a dream. But there would be grit under my nails and the tips of my fingers would be abraded.

Some days I pretended to fish. Fishing is socially acceptable cover for thinking, even for brooding, if you manage to cast once in a while. I took to cruising up the Pascamany to the cliffs below Holly Hill Farm. I would anchor and fish for a couple of hours. Occasionally, I would see Jamie riding. She would see me and wave. But we never spoke.

Then I would reel in the anchor and let the skiff float downstream. I kept a line in, pretending to be trolling. But everyone knows the current is too fast.

I let the current carry me past tall pines and old memories. Past the home Roger and Peyton had built and lost, past the channel that led to Aimes Point Marina, and, finally, past Courthouse Square. Once in a while an old man resting on one of the benches the Jaycees years ago—when downtown Lassington had a Jaycee chapter—had placed beside the brick walkway on the riverbank would wave.

CHAPTER 24

I knew I had to leave, an awareness I kept to myself. But I was still holding out, holding on to memories.

Peyton never flinched. She dragged me to cocktail parties and shielded me, as best as she could, from forced banter and conspicuous politeness that chilled me. She confronted every whisper with a fury that left me ashamed. Not of Peyton, but of myself. Of what I was going to do despite myself. Or maybe to spite myself.

One morning in September I awoke with a sense of certainty so implacable it frightened me. I placed a call that morning to Tom Ashburn, a classmate at Yale I'd been close to—we had both been St. A's—and kept in touch with over the years. Ashburn was head of litigation at Barlett & Reisner in Manhattan. He was delighted to hear from me and said he'd see what he could come up with. About time you woke up and smelled the money, he added, chuckling.

Ashburn, to my dismay, was good to his word. I traveled to New York one weekend when Peyton was visiting her mother, who'd been admitted to a hospice. I stayed with Tom Ashburn and his second wife, twenty years his junior, in their apartment on Park Avenue. Tom and Eloise hosted a dinner with his partners. At least the ones who mattered, Ashburn said. One of them, a wiry tax lawyer with a Bronx accent, told me having

someone around with a southern accent might be good for relations with a difficult client of his. Big paper mill in eastern
Tennessee, he said. He mentioned the name, but I hadn't heard
of it.

It's not the same kind of accent, I told him. That's hill country. I'm tidewater. Close enough, he had said dismissively.

In late October, Ashburn, ebullient, called me at the camp. I
was watching the sunset glaze the bay, watching the shadows
deepen, when he called. Congratulate me, he said. Okay, I said,
feeling dread and damned. For getting the management committee to authorize me to offer you a position as "of counsel" to
the firm, he continued. I forced myself to be pleased and worked
even harder to make my voice sound like I was. But I felt
clammy and turned my back to the bay, thinking about what I
would tell Peyton.

I decided to tell her after dinner on election night. A time of
changes, of winners and losers. I wondered which I would be
and guessed the latter, but I couldn't stop it.

I brought two bottles of a good fumé blanc and flounder I
had caught. As Peyton stuffed the flounder and tossed a spinach
salad, we watched the election coverage on the little TV in the
kitchen. Her kids were spending the night with Roger's mother
upriver at Regent's Glebe. I picked at my food, eating little.

The Richleigh returns came in with the smoked salmon appe-
tizer, shortly after seven. Dean had a narrow lead. The returns
from the rural counties started coming in at eight, with the
flounder. Just after nine o'clock, as we moved onto bourbon,
the bright young man with the permanent wave announced that
the ninety-two percent of the returns tabulated, Dean had been
projected as the winner. Beside Dean's name on the screen a
little checkmark in red was flashing. Underneath, it said,
"Channel 8 Projected Winner." Then he told us that Channel
8 was going to Lesley somebody to bring us live coverage from
the Elliot Dean for Governor headquarters.

Dean's smiling face suddenly filled the screen. He looked
good, somehow sort of glowing. Big hair with every lock in
place, except for the designated stray strands needed for the

youth look. Big moist eyes. The Anointed, grateful to his faith-
ful flock.

Dean spoke very slowly, very deliberately, radiating sincerity.
He kept eye contact with the viewer, somehow managing not
to look down at the bouquet of jostling microphones and tape
recorders shoved just below his chin by a writhing cluster of
anonymous hands. Dean kept ponderously thanking the people
of this great state for the opportunity which had been entrusted
to him by the people for the people.

He kept working with prepositions, linking different ones to
"people," which seemed to be every third word. By the people.
For the people. With the people. To the people. On the people.
A pavan of prepositions, hypnotic cadences. I walked to the
counter and clicked off the TV.

"Peyton," I said, refilling my glass with bourbon. "We need
to talk."

"Oh, Lord," she replied. "Here it comes. Might as well
get it out, whatever it is that's gone and ruined a dinner I
fixed specially."

She walked to the refrigerator, took a pack of cigarettes from
the carton on top, shook out one and lit it. Then she turned to
face me. "Get on with it."

"I've been asked to do some trial work for a law firm in
Manhattan," I said.

She didn't reply. I picked up the dishes from the table and
put them in the sink. When I looked at her again, I saw tears
streaming down her cheeks.

"Manhattan," Peyton said, with a laugh of disgust.
"Manhattan."

"It's just temporary," I replied after the silence became op-
pressive. "I didn't commit to anything."

"That's certainly a surprise," Peyton said. She tried to follow
up with a laugh but it caught in her throat.

"I would have told you about it before. But there wasn't
anything to tell. Nothing definite."

"Jesus, you're ready for this, aren't you?" Peyton asked.
This time she managed to laugh. "You're so primed you don't
even notice when I'm being sarcastic. Why don't you just go

ahead and run through the kiss-off routine you've got all ready? Get your sorry act over with instead of dribbling it out.''

"Peyton," I said softly. I wanted to be comforted by her even as I felt pierced by her words. "It's over for me here. You know that." I took a step toward her.

"Stay where you are," she said, in a tone that let me know she meant it.

"Manhattan," Peyton continued, spitting out the hard consonants, turning each into a chop, making the word a curse. "A cute little one-bedroom apartment with all your precious prints on the walls and your fancy-ass books arranged just so."

"I haven't even looked yet."

"Won't that be nice for you?" Peyton continued. "Do they still call it a bachelor pad?" Peyton tossed back her hair and smoothed it out.

"So nice for you. A little love nest where you can entertain all those high-browed, artsy-fartsy young fluffs who know all about the finer things. Maybe you and Suzy Q can write poetry together after an evening at the opera. Won't that be fine and dandy?"

"Look . . ."

"Look," Peyton interrupted, mocking me. "Well, 'course you'll look. Look all around, won't you? Like a weevil in a corn crib."

"Look," I said. "Come with me." I blurted out the words and held my breath.

"Come with me, he says," Peyton said. "'You hear that, Roger, wherever you are? The man's done gone and proposed, in a manner of speaking."

"I mean it," I said. Maybe I did.

"Bullshit," Peyton snapped, her voice tight and dry. "What you mean is you want your walking papers and a clean conscience." She inhaled, then blew out smoke with a hiss.

"'If you wanted me, you'd have told me long before this. We could have moved to Atlanta, Charlotte, Jacksonville. You've got buddies in law firms in all those towns and don't tell me no different. I'm not as stupid as you and your goddamned mother seem to think.'' She took a step toward me. Her eyes were on fire behind her tears.

'' 'Course, those towns won't do for you,'' she said, her voice quiet, composed. ''Those are the kinds of towns where you can raise a family, have a home, live a life with a mother with two children who's maybe seen her better days, who's maybe got more dimples and ripples than she used to, but who loves you more than you ever deserved.''

I started to say something, but Peyton held up her palm.

''Don't say a word,'' she continued. ''You don't want to dirty your conscience by lying. You chose New York because you hoped I'd say no when you finally worked up nerve enough to ask me. I ought to call your bluff and say 'yes,' but I've got some pride left, too little to waste.''

She tossed her cigarette into the sink and took a step closer to me.

''Sweetie, I'm going to give you your walking papers,'' Peyton whispered. ''But you're going to have to clean your conscience all by yourself.'' She turned and left the room.

I stared into the sink. I heard Peyton in the den. I waited a few minutes. Then I walked into the hall. I saw blue light flickering in the den. But there was no noise.

''Peyton?'' I walked into the den.

Then I saw it. He was on the TV screen, the coarse, shifting lines making the picture snowy. But it was Dean and some guy all right. Going at it.

I tried to pull myself away but couldn't. I don't know for how long I stared, transfixed. Maybe fifteen seconds, maybe a minute.

I walked to the VCR and punched the ''eject'' button. The tape slithered from the slot.

On the top of the VCR was a black plastic case. I picked it up and turned it over. On the cover was a gaudy photograph of Fred Astaire and Ginger Rogers. *The Gay Divorcee,* the legend read.

Then suddenly I understood. There would have been Fred Astaire, natty, tap dancing in a tux. He would have been chirping smart repartee at Ginger, being Mr. Debonair, while Roger was being pistol-whipped in the motel room.

What's this bullshit movie? Whap. Where's the tape of Dean, you motherfucker? You think I came out here to watch some twit dance? Whap. You think you can pull this kind of crap with me? Whap. Where's the tape of Dean, goddamn you? You think you can doublecross us, you fuck? Whap.

I turned and saw Peyton in the doorframe, holding the remote.

"You set Roger up," I said, turning the cassette case over and over in my hands. "You switched the tapes before he left, didn't you?"

Peyton sucked in her lower lip and nodded.

"Rog was unconscious when you got there?" I asked softly.

"I did it for us," Peyton said. "But there never was."

"Was," I repeated, letting the word hang.

"Was any us," she whispered.